I0594969

SEED OF WISDOM

ISBN: 979-8-9992487-4-9

Cover Design by Jay O'Connell

Bigwaves Publishing

More books by Daniel Hatch

Den of Thieves
The Long Game
Relic of war
Seed of Chaos

SEED OF WISDOM

Daniel Hatch

CHAPTER ONE

The scientists from Earth looked down on the planet below and saw that it was on fire.

The survey ship *Cousteau* had come a long way – more than one hundred light years – and spent a lot of time – more than six months in this system alone – to get here. And now the latest images from the orbital probes were giving Mark a terrible vertigo of the soul.

These were things he didn't want to know, and they made him fear things he didn't want to face.

"What is that feature?" asked Captain Fletcher.

"This is a major urban area," Barrett said. "We've got two shots here – one from three days ago and one from this morning." Lieutenant Andrew Barrett, the Space Corps officer on detached duty with the *Cousteau* and responsible for its weapons and security systems, was almost the exact opposite of the ship's commander, a thirty-year veteran of the Science Service. Where Newton Fletcher was overweight, bald, nearsighted, and aging, the lieutenant was young, confident, and muscular with a head full of curly dark hair.

Physically, Barrett was nearly everything Mark wished he could be. Mark was too tall and too skinny, with a face that was too long. But Mark had no wish to be a military officer like Barrett. While waiting months to survey the culture of the alien world below, Mark had occupied himself by studying the subculture of the officers aboard the *Cousteau*. Barrett personified everything that Mark found unpleasant about the group. They were clannish, in-grown, and focused on the immediate and concrete to the exclusion of other considerations. He had hoped that the aliens would break their frame of reference.

Mark compared the two images on the screen and recognized the blue-gray film that smeared itself across the floor of a river valley. A couple days ago, he'd been doing economic analysis work on the image on the left, trying to identify the extent of its agricultural support region. The city resembled a Mandelbrot pattern, small fragments repeating themselves in ever larger aggregations.

But the picture on the right showed streaks of brown and black across the landscape, all emerging from the heart of the city.

"We enhanced it with IR and confirmed our initial suspicions," Barrett said. "These are fires. The largest of the conflagrations covers a few dozen city blocks. There are forty or fifty in this image." Barrett ran through more pictures. All told the same story.

An image taken from an oblique angle showed the plumes of smoke rising into the sky from a low urban skyline, merging into a continuous dark cloud, and drifting off on an inversion layer.

A moving shot revealed explosions at an industrial complex.

A radar image showed hundreds of vehicles streaming out of one city on every highway.

Computer-generated maps showed armies grappling in the equatorial rainforest.

Nightside images showed large areas where city lights had disappeared with the arrival of the *Cousteau* as power generation grids went down.

And the same darkside shots revealed more burning cities, their flames like beacons in the night or, when widespread enough, like open wounds.

"Now here's another file you should look at," he continued. "I don't know if you've all studied this carefully, but we've been compiling it ever since we arrived in-system. It's a chart of the different EM transmitting regimes and language groupings we've been able to identify. Professor Nordland and his team have been going over it, and what they've identified is at least a dozen major social-technical regions and ... what was the last count on minor ones?"

"It hit 237 this morning, but we've been documenting them all over the place since we arrived in orbit," Nordland replied. Mark nodded in confirmation. He and Val Nordland made up the ship's entire cultural survey team – a role that had made him feel vital and important until he saw what the inhabitants of the planet were doing to their civilization.

"As to that ..." Barrett sighed and retreated slightly into his uniform. "There have been a lot of changes on the surface of the planet in the past twenty-four hours. We've been watching several areas closely – the rift valley where most of their rocket launches have come from, the rim of the equatorial sea, an area at the west end of the ocean, the deep desert basin, the steppe land between the ocean and the rift. They're all regions with signs of high power generation, high volumes of radio traffic, major sources of chemical emissions, and other signs of high-tech and industry.

"But since we made orbit, all sorts of readings have shifted dramatically. Power generation has been interrupted in large sections of the civilized zones. We've monitored a big increase in radio traffic. And when they swing around into the nightside, you can see evidence of large-scale fires, explosions, other disruptions. If you ask me, there are large civil disturbances going on. Some organized military activity too. From the look of it, there are riots and wars – maybe revolutions and insurrections too – in almost every industrialized zone on the planet." Mark widened his eyes as he saw the symbols proliferate across a globe of the planet. He had come to recognize the pattern of civilized development down there. He realized how much of the planet was now in chaos. His spiritual vertigo worsened as the first hints of guilt began to prick at his conscience.

"What kind of a world is it down there?" Captain Fletcher asked. "And how did it get itself into such a terrible mess?" Barrett shook his head and shrugged. But Mark knew the answer to that question. The survey ship *Cousteau* itself was responsible for the mess. Their arrival had clearly sparked upheavals in every civilized region of the planet.

They had no right to their astonishment, Mark noted with irritation. The alien warship they had encountered on making orbit had launched a brief and ineffective strike against them. The alien inhabitants of the planet below showed a sudden fury that the crew of the *Cousteau* had not expected. But equally surprising was the chaotic and ultimately ineffective character of the attack. For some as yet unexplained reason, the aliens had been unable or unwilling to employ all their weapons. In fact, although the *Cousteau* had never activated a single weapons system of its own, and there was no evidence of another adversary in sight, the alien station showed extensive signs of battle damage all its own.

The puzzles and mysteries all added to Mark's fears. It was such a long way to come just to plunge a world full of sapient creatures into a living hell.

But what worried him most, what set his head spinning, was the deepest fear of all – that this was just the beginning, and that in the end, the burning cities below them would become the spark to a greater inferno and a greater hell than anyone could imagine.

And that he might help create it.

***

Zepp paced the small room with a nervous energy that threatened to burst out of his skin.

It was not a cell. He and his companion Griddle had been taken from brig hours earlier. The walls here were white, not metal- gray, and it didn't stink. And the solid reassurance of weight from spin-gravity told him that they were still inside the Suridash containment of *Deragathon*, safe from the rest of the crew – for the moment, at least.

But the door was locked and bolted from the outside, and they were still just as much prisoners as before.

Griddle sat in a corner, silent and self-involved as usual. He was a sorry sight. His blue fur was matted and, like the one-piece coverall he wore, stained with porridge. The coal-black nose on the end of his snout was dry and sniffled incessantly. His pointed ears twitched and his long whiskers bristled.

"How much longer do we have to wait?" Zepp snapped.

"Why?" Griddle said. "Are you in a hurry to go?"

Zepp just snarled. He was only a little larger than Griddle, and neither of them were sizable. His fur was thick, green, and well groomed. He wore a vest of many pockets and heavy shorts, with a flap in the rear where his tail poked through. Underneath the shorts was a brass chastity belt that marked him as a member of the tribe of

Jobe.

"Damn Whirlpitt!" Zepp said. "Damn him and his plots." But his anger was restrained. He knew that he and Griddle owed their lives to the sinister official who had snatched them from the other crewmembers of the *Deragathon* and spirited them away. Hours earlier, he had come to them and told Zepp the terrible news.

"Our world is in chaos," Whirlpitt had said, his eyes squinted nearly shut beneath a narrow brow covered with sleek black fur. His head swiveled on the end of a long, sinuous neck that stretched out of a dark cloak. "When the angels arrived, the nations of our world launched themselves at one another in an orgy of violence. Slaves and rebels rose up against their masters. Every sect and tribe with a grievance has taken this occasion as a chance to settle old scores or begin new ones. We can see the fires of burning cities as we pass over them in orbit."

Zepp had glared back at the minister in return, burning with a newfound defiance, a boldness that he had discovered in only the last few hours as he faced death – his own and that of the world that had spawned him.

"This ship is in no better condition. The rebellions and mutinies have expended the energies of their first explosions, and the mutineers and rebels have retreated into their strongholds. There is a cease-fire in effect, but with Ensign Pym now in command of the vessel, I cannot say how long that state will prevail."

Zepp snorted derisively. Pym was a foul-smelling adolescent of a hedgehog. The only reason he had inherited command was that his father had collapsed when the *Deragathon*'s assault on the vessel of the angels failed. Zepp wondered if Pym was capable of commanding his own bodily functions, let alone the giant warship they had launched against the angels. On the other hand, he was certainly an improvement over his martinet of a father. And he had shown the wisdom of sending the Admiralty Board off the bridge before they could interfere with his orders.

Whirlpitt hissed and flicked a pink tongue around his lips. "You should be proud of your handiwork," he said.

Zepp cringed, overwhelmed by guilt. He knew that Whirlpitt was right. He had done it. He was responsible for the disaster that had swept the ship and, therefore, the chaos that raged on the surface of the planet below them. He had betrayed his race and his world. As months before he had betrayed his tribe and all that it stood for. Treason took a long time – especially on the scale that Zepp had committed it.

CHAPTER TWO

Zepp felt a sudden charge of electricity run up his spine as a loud clanging rang through the tiny spacecraft. The noise had come from the direction of the entry hatch in the stern of the boat. He knew what it meant – the angels were coming for them.

Griddle sat in the seat beside him unmoved and unmoving. He continued to watch the stars go by above and the multicolored surface of the world pass by below, uncaring and uninterested in their fate. Zepp wasn't surprised. Griddle had never had any reason for real fear in his life. His talent – or his curse – had always protected him from harm.

Zepp had no such security, however, and had to rely on his wits to keep his skin. Now he knew he had to act fast in order to buy himself a few more days of life.

He released the harness that held him in his seat and pulled himself aft in the weightlessness of the boat's single compartment. He retrieved the bag of rations from the locker where he had stashed it before launching. Whirlpitt had warned him that the angels would be unlikely to have food that he could eat without becoming ill. Water and air were different problems, of course. If the angels neither breathed oxygen nor drank untainted water, then his life would end very soon regardless of his efforts.

He took a deep breath and tried to calm himself. Speculation was useless. In a few moments, he would know his fate. And in his own way, he was as fearless as Griddle. In the past few days, he had already learned to face the possibility of death without flinching.

He didn't have to wait long. The hatch sprang open and a hideous-looking creature stuck its head through the opening. It had a globular skull with hoses projecting from the rear, and large bulbous eyes. Zepp shuddered at the sight, then realized that the creature was wearing some kind of headgear that obscured its true appearance.

The creature thrust an appendage through the hatch and waved towards Zepp. It seemed to beckon him towards it.

No point in wasting time, he realized.

"Griddle, get out of that seat and get moving," he said.

"No," replied his companion. "I'm comfortable where I am."

"You won't be in a few hours. There's only enough air pressure in the tanks to keep you breathing until nightwatch. Then you'll suffocate – slowly."

Griddle sighed. "Are you sure?"

"Do you want to find out for yourself?"

"No. Where are we going?"

"Aboard the angels' vessel. Just like Whirlpitt wants."

"I suppose we don't have any choice."

"None that I'd make willingly. I doubt if your talents will have much effect on cold vacuum"

"I suppose not."

He released the harness and floated free, scrambling clumsily for a handhold. Zepp grabbed his arm and pulled him back towards the rear bulkhead of the boat.

The creature drew back from the hatch and Zepp pushed Griddle through the opening. He took one last look around the boat, rubbed his face three times, then followed. He hoped Whirlpitt's schemes were not going to doom him after all. For six months, he had tried so hard to escape them, and never with any success. This was no different.

In any case, Zepp knew he could take comfort in one fact. Thanks to Griddle, the angels would soon have more than enough to take their minds off anything that could do him harm.

If only he could last that long.

***

The angels led them down a long white tunnel strung with tiny points of light and made unintelligible sounds as they floated along. The tunnel wound around a wide spiral and terminated in a rectangular hatch, by which time the gravity had increased to something substantial.

The hatch slid open, revealing a small compartment beyond. The angels moved aside and let Zepp and Griddle enter the chamber. Then the door hissed shut behind them. Zepp felt his blood thicken in his veins, but Griddle appeared relaxed. A moment later, another door opened on the other side of the chamber.

A sound resembling a voice issued from some unseen source, but Zepp could make no sense of it. Then the lights went out in the chamber, leaving sharp shadows around the edge of the hatchway. With no other choices available to him, Zepp pushed himself through the opening.

The compartment on the far side was much larger, filled with white light and outfitted with a variety of strange artifacts. A set of bags were strung across one wall, a series of clear tubes partially filled with liquid ran out of some brass plumbing fixtures, and one wall was covered with mats and cushions. Another wall consisted entirely of glass, reflecting the image of a small green ape and a blue cat looking across the divide at him from inside a tiny closet.

Griddle entered the room and the hatch slid shut behind them.

Then the reflecting glass turned transparent as the lights came on behind it. Zepp felt the fur rise across his back. On the other side of the barrier was a crowd of partially clothed angels. They seemed to lack hair on much of their bodies, and they did not seem to resemble one another nearly as much as Zepp had been led to believe. The first reports passed along by the psychics, months ago when the angels first arrived in Chamal's solar system, had described them as virtually identical with one another.

Despite their differences, however, there was a similarity among the creatures. Something about the arrangement of their features and the blandness of their faces.

Then the angels displayed their teeth and waved their limbs. More voice-like sounds filled the compartment. The aliens seemed agitated – or at least aroused.

Zepp didn't know what to make of it. He fought against his own nervous fear reactions, which functioned only fitfully now after so many days of raw panic. He looked around the room. There were two doors: the one that had closed behind him a moment earlier and another in the wall adjacent to the cushions and the glass. He wished he knew where they led – for all the good it would have done him.

For now, he and Griddle were prisoners, just as surely as they had been back on the *Deragathon*.

With nothing else to do, he reached into the bag and pulled out a ration bar. He broke it in half and handed the other piece to Griddle. Then he turned his back on the angels and began to eat.

***

By the time Mark Paradis reached the observation room, it was already jammed full of people. Lieutenant Barrett, Val Nordland, and some of the other senior officers of the *Cousteau* were nearest the transparent wall. Others filled in behind them, and as a result Mark couldn't see the main chamber where the two aliens had been taken.

"Come with me if you want to get a good look at them," said a woman beside him.

Mark looked around and realized that she was talking to him. She was thin, even more so than the other crew members had become on space food, and her skin was black as space. It was Helen Castain, one of the exobiologists. He seemed to recall that she was from the University of Port-Au-Prince. He'd talked with her before on the long flight in from the outskirts of the system, but seldom for more than a moment and usually to ask what was being served for dinner.

She was a few years past forty. The sharp edges of her features and the deep creases of her smiles and frowns revealed the untender passage of years.

She overcame his discomfort instantly with a confident informality, as if she'd befriended him from the day he came aboard. "Come on with me," she said, tugging at his sleeve. "I know where we can get just as good a view without the crowd." He followed her across the passageway and into a less crowded compartment. A large holoscreen and the remaining members of the exobiology department occupied one end of the room. The biologists muttered to one another over a data-terminal as they instructed the holorecorders documenting the scene.

"Thanks," Mark said.

The holoscreen flashed with life, full of the the image of the "guest room" and the two aliens. They seemed calm enough, though one of them jumped noticeably when the airlock door slid shut behind him.

Then a chorus of "oohs" and "aahs" echoed across the passageway from the observation room, followed by a round of cheers and a mixture of greetings. The voices were repeated on the holoscreen.

The two aliens seemed unimpressed. Mark wasn't surprised. They couldn't speak the language, so the feeble attempt at courtesy was lost on them. Oh well, that would change once they met the professor.

Mark looked more closely at the two creatures.

They were each about a meter and a half tall. The one with the bag was covered in fine green fur and wore a leather vest with many pockets and a breechcloth. What looked like a harness of chains made of small brass links could be seen under the breechcloth, but Mark couldn't imagine what purpose it served. A long sinuous tail snaked out a hole in the rear of the cloth and twitched nervously.

The other creature had blue fur and was wearing a sleeveless shirt and a pair of shorts. His ears rose to triangular points and a few ragged whiskers protruded from either side of a short snout. If he had a tail, it was hiding in his shorts.

It struck him suddenly that there was very little in the way of anatomy that the two creatures had in common.

"Have you noticed something peculiar about our guests?" he asked Helen.

"You mean like their physiology?"

"Exactly," he said. "It looks to me like we've got two entirely different species here."

"I was just thinking the same thing," she said. "I wonder if anyone else has noticed."

"I doubt it. They're all too busy pretending to be diplomats to act like scientists. It'll probably dawn on them sometime next watch – unless we tell them."

"Now that's a radical proposal," Helen said. "Any suggestions as to who we should tell?"

"Val Nordland, for one."

"And maybe Lieutenant Barrett."

"Barrett? Why him?" Mark asked.

"Because he's been suggesting something along those very lines himself." Mark shook his head in confusion. Was the Space Corps officer working on something that the Cultural Survey section didn't know about? A moment later, Helen was pulling him by the sleeve as she headed for the door.

***

"Actually there are quite a few different morphologies," Lieutenant Barrett said .

The briefing in the Cultural Survey Center was not an ordinary meeting. In addition to Barrett, the compartment contained Val Nordland, Helen Castain, and Captain Fletcher. Barrett's normally youthful features were marked by deep lines, and Mark was sure he hadn't slept a full hour since they'd made orbit. Val and Helen, on the other hand, seemed filled with energy, part excitement, part released tension.

Barrett had started the session by ordering the ship's AI to call up a secure file that Mark had never seen before.

"We have some video that we've been able to process from the

Chamalian's internal systems," Barrett said. "And a bit of the stuff that came over the air before we got here. You can see for yourself what the AIs have identified."

The screen went through the different morphologies, flashing each one briefly before moving on. Nearly all of them had a vaguely mammalian appearance, with fur but not scales, a nose or snout, and eyes in the front of a spherical skull. A meter scale along one side of the frame showed most of the creatures were similar in size to their two guests. But the variations were wide and deep, in every dimension. Fur came in a rainbow of different colors. Some of them had long ears, some short, some pointed, some floppy. The snouts were long and sharp, short and blunt, or even nonexistent. And the details were just as diverse – shaggy eyebrows, long whiskers, manes, stripes, crests, horns, and spurs. Some wore hats, some headsets, a few were decked out in elaborate uniforms, others had more functional outfits. Some decorated themselves with jewelry, others with tattoos under their fur, and a few with pieces of bone piercing their skin.

"There's even more," Barrett said. "We've picked up some of the wreckage from the alien warship – including some of the bodies of the crew. I asked Ms. Castain to keep the examinations quiet until we had a chance to review the results."

Mark felt the muscles of his back tighten. Why would one try to keep secrets on a research ship? Who was likely to betray them? He didn't know if he'd ever understand the military mind.

"There's about sixteen morphs for sure, maybe more," Helen reported. "I couldn't be sure with some of the more damaged specimens. But what it looks to like me and to everyone else who's seen this file and the specimens is that there are several dozen sapient species down there, all with post-industrial technology."

"So many different intelligent forms," Captain Fletcher said. "How could it happen? What could it mean?"

Mark stirred uncomfortably, his stomach squirming at the Captain's show of helpless confusion.

More secrets from the world below. And Mark feared that they were more dangerous than almost anyone could imagine. That was Mark's secret. Not only could he imagine what made secrets like this so dangerous, what he knew made them even more so.

And that was something that even Lieutenant Barrett and Captain Fletcher didn't realize. Not yet, anyway.

***

"It's pretty obvious what it means. Social chaos and mass outbreaks of organized violence," Mark told Helen when the meeting was over. They had gone down to her lab, Mark's preference over the cold austerity that Val Nordland cast over the Cultural Survey Center. Helen had a teapot there and a small ration of tea. They drank it out of lab beakers.

"I'd offer you a real cup, but I've never been able to keep cups in the compartment long before some eager young assistant carts it dutifully back to the galley."

"There's no single dominant intelligent species," Mark continued, straining the tea into his beaker. "With a couple dozen competing species, I can't see where there'd be any basis for a strong social order. And our arrival must have shaken out a lot of latent instabilities."

Helen looked skeptical, but nodded. "That explains the violence. But how did it come about in the first place? The development of dozens of co-existing intelligent species makes no sense whatsoever from an evolutionary standpoint."

"It doesn't? Is that because sooner or later, one species would outcompete the others and eliminate it? Like Cro-Magnon and the Neanderthals?"

"Not even that. Evolution doesn't work that way. At least it didn't on Earth. Intelligence is sort of a cumulative effect. It emerges slowly in one order, then one genus, and finally in one species. And when it does emerge, it bootstraps itself up to our level in fairly short order. Look at the progression from Homo habilis up to Homo sapiens. Once one species gets on the road, it's a quick passage to world domination."

"I suppose you're right," Mark said grudgingly, a touch indignant that an exobiologist would lecture him about human evolution – even if she did have a few years on him.

"There's nothing that would allow the separate evolution of thirty different species to reach the same point at the same time," Helen said. "Nature isn't that hyped up."

"Maybe not on Earth. But who knows what Chamal is like? I mean, you've got an entirely different kind of planetary terrain. There's no true ocean, for instance. And everything is interconnected by land for the most part, even if there are some low barriers."

"If you call the two desert belts low barriers," Helen quipped.

Mark laughed suddenly at an image that flashed through his mind's eye. "It just occurred to me that this place must be a real zoo, if you'll pardon the expression. Like a cartoon world populated with talking animals." Helen laughed at that too, though the bitterness was evident in the way she cut it off sharply. Mark noticed too the way the lines on one side of her face grew darker when she laughed like that.

Mark felt bitterness too and couldn't help voicing it. "Except that animals in a zoo do not launch powerful weapons into space," he said. "And cartoon characters do not set fire to their own cities."

CHAPTER THREE

The next **few** **watches** were almost intolerable for Mark, hours of enforced idleness as other people carried out their duties.

Helen collected microbes from the filtered air and water of the alien's compartment, pumped them into several tubes of different flavors of growth medium, and found one that they liked. When she had a sufficient quantity, she ran them through the analyzers and exposed her lab rats to the batch.

Mark was on hand to watch the experiment.

The rats were not live animals, but a square frame holding a checkerboard pattern of human tissue types. Allergens and microbes that might attack the human biome would show up quickly on the artificial samples and reveal the potential threats posed by the aliens' collection of exotic proteins, germs, viruses, and similar parasites. He held his breath as Helen spilled the tube into their container, safe behind its anti-contamination shields.

"How long before something shows up?" he asked.

"Too long for you to hold your breath waiting," she said. "They may not have immune systems, but it still takes a while before they get sick." It was half an hour, to be exact. Mark's stomach tightened up and turned over as he watched the display on The Doctor.

"Respiratory infection and histamine shock," Helen said. "Give it a few minutes and it will tell us what's causing it." She was right. Not only did The Doctor produce a cause for the response, it also produced a list of potential cures, antidotes, and preventive techniques. Helen ordered a cure for the rat and chose the simplest of the antidotes.

"This should give us immunity against that bug for a few months," Helen said.

"Are you sure?"

"Don't you trust The Doctor?" she asked, patting the pastel pink casing of the medical AI. "It's quite brilliant, you know. Has all the answers."

"I'm sure it does."

"Now if it supplied the questions, there'd hardly be any need for people on this mission at all." Mark smiled, but his attention was on the lab rat. "Is that it?"

"No. We give it some more time. There may be some other agents lurking in there. They'll come out, don't worry." They did. The rat displayed three more allergic reactions, each one with an allergen more subtle and tenacious than its predecessor. When they were done, Mark had a list of medications and vaccinations that he would need to confront the aliens without risking his own health.

"What else does that thing tell you about them?" he asked.

"At the moment, not much. We've been monitoring the gas mixture in their compartment since they got here. It gives us a pretty good idea of their gross body chemistry. They use oxygen a little faster than you'd expect a terrestrial organism to do, and they give off more CO_2 and water vapor. There's a lot of complex organics in there too. The Doctor has been breaking them down – pheromones, nitrates, metabolic by-products. A bunch of acetone for some reason. And we've been analyzing their solid and liquid wastes as well." Mark wrinkled his nose and Helen shook her head, scolding him gently. "It may be waste to you, but it's bread and butter to The Doctor," she said.

"Sounds appetizing. What's next?"

"Sampling. Non-intrusive scanning. During their night-cycle. You want to come along?"

"Can I?"

"Well, maybe not into the compartment. Not yet, anyway. But you can watch from the gallery."

"That's good enough for me. What time?"

A few hours later he met Helen at the observation gallery. She was decked out in a thin plastic suit with surgical gloves, a hood connected to an oxygen bottle, and a belt filled with medical instruments. A chunky young man with red hair who was similarly equipped sat in the gallery.

"First we have to knock them out," Helen said. "It's harmless. We just drop the pressure down until they're unconscious. It'll only take a few minutes." Mark found a seat and watched the two aliens. The one that Mark thought of as the blue cat dozed in the corner on a pile of cushions. The other, the green ape, paced the floor nervously. Every so often he would look in Mark's direction, pausing to stare at if he could see him through the glass.

As Mark watched, the creature slowed in his pacing, then slumped to the floor. He yawned, struggled to open his eyes, then surrendered, curling up in a ball with his head cradled in his arms and his tail wrapped around one leg.

"Let's go," Helen said. She and her red-headed assistant pulled the hoods on over their heads and checked each other's seals. Then they disappeared down the passageway. A moment later, they appeared suddenly in the isolation chamber's airlock door.

They worked quickly, clipping hair samples and vacuuming fur for dust and fiber. Helen's assistant pulled a phone out of a belt pouch and recorded her examination of the aliens' hands, feet, eyes, ears, mouths, and throats.

The process took about half an hour, and Mark regarded the whole thing with silent awe. He wondered how he would feel if he were the subject of the so-called non-intrusive examination.

When they were done, Helen carried out one last chore. She pulled a sample box from her belt and went to the bag that held the aliens' food supply. She poked around inside and pulled out a short piece of something that could have been a sausage and a crumbly cracker the size of her hand.

She popped the food into the box and sealed it. Then she signaled to her assistant to head for the door.

Red was still looking over the blue cat and stood up quickly. When he did, his sleeve caught on an extended claw on one of the cat's feet. Mark could see Red's eyes widen and his jaw drop.

Helen looked at the sleeve and saw the tear, about twenty-five centimeters long. She rushed him through the airlock door. Mark ran to the passageway where a moment later the two of them appeared. Helen had her hood off, but Red was still covered.

"Stand back, Mark," Helen ordered. "We've got to get him to The Doctor right away. Damn that was stupid! We should have immunized ourselves before we went in there." Mark stepped back into the gallery chamber to let them pass, then stuck his head out. "What do you do now?"

"Full series of meds. It's the only way to be safe. It's his own fault, though. He should have been more careful." Mark shuddered. He'd seen the list of medications that were needed for anyone exposed to the alien microbes. Red wasn't going to enjoy the next couple of watches.

"It was just an accident," he said as they disappeared down the passage. But it didn't appear that Helen heard him.

***

Red spent the next eight hours suffering the equivalent of a first-degree asthma attack, with fluids running out of every orifice in his head and a rash breaking across the backs of his arms and tops of his legs. His breathing grew short and gasping, and the doctors put him on a respirator. His heart began to beat erratically, so they took over control of its rhythm. And his brain overheated, so they cooled it down.

The best way to manufacture the antibodies and antitoxins needed to defeat the alien microorganisms and proteins was the natural way – by stimulating the body's defenses. Only part of the med series that Helen administered to Red consisted of vaccines. The rest was to prod those defenses into pumping out the chemicals needed to protect him from alien attack.

But in the end, he had the last laugh. He felt miserable when the ordeal was over, but when he finally recovered, he had the reward of watching Mark's face as Helen told him that he would be next, in order to make personal contact with the aliens when the time came.

"What?" asked the young anthropologist. "It almost killed him. You don't really expect us all to go through that, do you?"

"Of course I do," Helen said. "Are you some kind of coward?"

Red grinned, then laughed loudly, which started a sneezing fit.

"You're next," Helen said. "Then it's my turn. Me, because I have to go in there and get more bio samples. You, because you're going to be in charge of the language analysis – and that means unprotected contact. We might as well get it over with as quickly as possible." Mark swallowed hard, then stiffened his back. If Helen could face Red's fate without flinching, he wasn't about to do any less. Besides, he figured, it couldn't be any worse than the heartache he was going through.

"You're not going to let him think we're going to try to kill him, are you?" Red asked after a long while. Mark turned quick attention to him.

Helen laughed, then smiled gently at Mark. "Don't worry. The treatment is nothing like what Red went through last night. It'll be nice and easy. At least in comparison." Mark huffed dubiously and learned soon that he had good reason to. His own immune system filled him with fluids, flushed them out through his face and pores, and raised red patches all over his arms. For eight hours, he had no work to take his mind off his troubles. He ached in body and soul. The only mercy he received came in the end, when Helen gave him a shot of antihistamines that knocked him on his back, where he finally fell into a fitful and delirious sleep.

***

The thing that bothered Zepp the most was the tedious monotony, the unchanging white light that filled the chamber, the occasional gurgle of the water hole, and Griddle's intermittent organic noises. The cell back on the *Deragathon* was no worse. In fact, it was better. The imminent threat of death made it seem all the more interesting.

At night the light turned red and he slept. That had happened twice now. The food bag was getting slack as he and Griddle consumed its contents. On the second morning he had snapped at Griddle when the blue feline tried to take an extra ration. Deadly powers or not, he couldn't let his companion hasten the moment when the food was gone.

Then, in the middle of the third day, the door to their cell opened and one of the angels stepped through it. The creature was nearly half again Zepp's height, thin and nearly hairless except for a mat of fur at the top of its head. It appeared to be a male, though Zepp couldn't be sure – it wore loose pants and a shirt and was cloaked in a clear membrane that gathered together at the neck of a glass globe enclosing its head.

The angel stood silently while the door closed behind him, then sat on the deck in front of it, crossing his legs. He sat there for a long time, watching Zepp and Griddle. Zepp, in turn, watched back. Griddle sniffed the air at his entrance, then closed his eyes and resumed his nap.

Zepp wondered if he should be fearful. The strange creature was holding him hostage and had given him no indication of what might be his fate. At any moment, he could have expelled the two chamalians from the ship into cold, airless space.

On the other hand, the alien likely had equal reason to fear for his life. He had locked himself in the room with the two of them, not knowing if they were benign or violent by nature. If Zepp had been Androkar, the sand cat master-at-arms from the *Deragathon*, this alien would have been sausage meat by now.

But as long as neither of them made a threatening move, Zepp was content to remain seated where he was, unafraid and undisturbed.

After a long time had passed, the angel reached into a pouch at his side and pulled out a short, brown cylinder. He reached out and offered it to Zepp and uttered a short vowelly word. He repeated the word twice, then set the cylinder on the deck and rolled it towards Zepp.

Zepp sniffed the air, reached out himself and grabbed the object. It looked and smelled like a foodstick. A little coarser and not as dark, but food just the same. He looked at the angel, who repeated the same sound once again.

"Thank you," Zepp said, then he bit off one end and tasted it. Not bad. A bit bland, actually, but chewy and filling. Then he smiled at the realization that if he and Griddle were to die, it would not be from starvation. He finished the foodstick and walked over to the waterhole to wash it down with a long drink.

When he was done, the angel reached into the pouch and pulled out several more foodsticks. He stepped forward, set them on the deck, then returned to his position in front of the door.

He spoke the one word again. Then another voice spoke from some unseen source. Zepp was surprised when he realized that it made a sensible sound. "Thank you," it said.

He ambled over to the foodsticks and eyed the angel suspiciously. There was more going on here than Zepp could quite fathom. The angel was not just delivering food. He picked up the foodsticks and stuffed them in the bag with those he'd taken from the *Deragathon*.

Now the angel was staring him in the eye. What did he want? The creature raised his arm and put his hand on his chest, uttering a new sound, thudding and breathy. He repeated the motion and the sound several times. And each time, the voice of the unseen creature made the same sound.

It was talking to him.

Zepp easily mouthed the simple alien word. "Mark ... Mark ... Mark." The angel revealed his teeth in a grimace that wrinkled his entire face, tapping himself on the chest with his fingers and repeating it.

"Mark," the angel said. Zepp realized without surprise that this must be the creature's name.

Then it pointed to him. Zepp figured out the game now. He smiled, put his hand on his own chest and said, "Zepp." The Mark-angel reached into his pocket one more time and offered Zepp one more foodstick, repeating his first word. Zepp took it and the unseen voice said: "Thank you."

***

"I hated city life," Mark said. "I was so glad to get out of college and head out to grad school. There's just too many people in the cities. The domes shut out the sky. You don't get real weather, just the programmed stuff – rain overnight to wash the streets, again in the afternoon to clean the air.

"But I went to grad school out in the country. Real trees, animals that came up to the door of my housing unit, a stream down the hill from my back door that I could hear at night through the window. I loved it." Mark uncrossed his legs and stood slowly, rubbing the cramps out of his calves. He'd been talking for an hour now, and the aliens continued to watch him closely.

They hadn't gotten much beyond simple name-calling. The active one with the green fur was called Zepp. The passive one with the blue fur was Griddle. They could count to eight – a numeral for each digit on their three-fingered hands – before they started repeating themselves. He had a feeling he was going to have to brush up on his base-eight math.

But that was as far as he'd taken it. The professor needed more than numbers to do its analysis and the aliens seemed to have little interest in teaching him their language. Indeed, the blue seemed to have little interest in anything.

So Mark talked. He talked about growing up in the woods of New Hampshire, his parents, summers in Maine and Florida, grad school, his year in Africa. It didn't matter that the aliens understood not a word of it. The point was to build confidence. Sooner or later, the plan was, they would begin talking as well.

Of course, he didn't talk about the *Cousteau*, its mission, its secrets, or those of human technology and human history that might be useful to an alien race confronting a strange and superior species. He had been carefully prepared to avoid that.

In the meantime, his plastic overalls were began to overheat. He would rather have done without them, but no one wanted to expose their two guests to proteins and microbes that were as potentially toxic to them as theirs were to humans.

By the time he got out of here, a quicky space shower would not be enough – he was going to need a leisurely hotel-style shower, water regs be damned.

***

Zepp figured the angel had been talking for half the day when he began to wonder if fear and uncertainty might be better than this strange, annoying treatment. At first the creature had played an interesting game, but for some reason it had lost interest.

Zepp wasn't surprised. Children and numerologists were good at playing counting games, but he had always had other things to keep him busy. Life demanded much of a young member of the tribe of Jobe.

Finally, though, he grew tired of the annoyance.

"Why do you continue with this, Mark-angel?" he said. "Neither of us can understand you. Neither of us cares to. Are you praying to rid us of our evil? Or are you preparing us for a sacrifice to the seed of the gods?" The angel fell abruptly silent, then made that toothy grimace of his.

And overhead, the unseen voice returned to life. "Why do you continue with this, Mark-angel?" it asked, then it repeated the rest of his words.

"Who are you? And why are you mocking me?" he asked it.

Predictably, it echoed his questions.

Then it squawked and spoke other words, foreign words. As it spouted its babble, Zepp thought he recognized a Blue Monkey dialect and a few words of Meshkarian. Then suddenly it began speaking in the street tongue of Suridash.

"The Rikabarians, Birhat cats, and Blue Monkeys still hold out against us," the voice said. "We have food and water to last many days and we still control our own air. Tell Tedrak to remind the governments on the ground that our true enemies are not ourselves, but the angels who share the sky with us. Perhaps they will urge restraint on their fellows up here. This is Whirlpitt, ending transmission." Zepp rose up on his feet and yelled at the voice. "You're not Whirlpitt, you sly wizard. I know his voice. Who are you? Why do you taunt us? And how did you steal Whirlpitt's words?"

The voice did not relent, but repeated his angry challenge, then began to recite what clearly were other messages sent from the *Deragathon* to the surface below and what seemed to be signals from Suridash itself. As Zepp calmed, he realized that the angels had to be listening in on the ether when chamalians spoke to their counterparts on the surface of the planet. That was where they'd stolen the words.

He fell silent again, frustrated by this senseless charade the angels were performing. What was the purpose? Then he noticed Griddle, awakened by Zepp's shouting at the hidden voice. The blue pilgrim seemed agitated – he twitched and mumbled to himself.

"Griddle, are you awake? You should eat. The angels have brought us more food." But his companion ignored him. Zepp had known the creature for only a handful of days and was sure he hadn't seen the full range of his moods and airs. What he had seen frightened him more than enough. And what he knew of Griddle's life gave him cause to expect almost anything from the poor blue cat.

A moment later, his fears were borne out when the water hole behind them overflowed its rim and water began splashing loudly onto the deck.

CHAPTER FOUR

"It **was** just a stuck valve," Helen said. "No serious –" She stopped in mid-sentence, sneezed, and continued. "No serious problem. And the floor drain caught the overflow."

"Bless you," Mark said as she blew her nose on a tissue. "So nothing escaped isolation?"

"No. There's triple backups to prevent that. Of course, there's supposed to be backups to prevent the valves from sticking too." Her nose was red and her eyes still watery, aftereffects of the anti-allergy treatment. Mark wondered if he'd looked that bad when he was through with it. "Are you sure you should be up and around? You look like you're still making histamines."

She smiled weakly. "I probably should be in bed, but when the alarms went off I rushed down here."

"You heard them down in berthing?"

"I had the monitor on," she said. "So where exactly did you do your undergrad?" Mark felt his face grow warm. Helen had been listening in to his long monologue with the chamalians. He felt a brief moment of relief as he realized that he could have chosen a much more embarrassing topic to discuss.

"Boston," he answered, trying to avoid showing his embarrassment. "Northeastern University, actually."

"What a coincidence. I did my undergrad at Northwestern University out in Chicago. So do you still hate city life?"

"Somewhat. I mean, not as much as I did back then. I was still pretty young and naive, and I missed out on a lot of what was going on at the time. And now I miss a lot of what I did find while I was there. Like Chinatown and chowder down at Quincy Market and the view from the top of the dome at the Pru."

"Tell me about it – I would absolutely kill for a Chicago deep-dish pizza right now." She sneezed again. "And there was a place near campus that had the best marinated tofu."

"On the other hand," Mark said, "Boston could be pretty miserable. I lived out in Back bay – near the edge of the dome . In the winter, the moisture would condense on the struts and drain down pipes into our street and leak into our back yard. You couldn't get down to the T without going around the puddles. And the panhandlers at Copley Square could get really obnoxious. I had one follow me home one night."

"Panhandlers?"

"Unemployed and unregistered youths. They hang around the public squares, stopping passersby and asking for surplus tokens."

"I know what panhandlers are, my boy," she said with sudden indignance. "They still have them in Port-Au-Prince I just couldn't imagine them in Boston. They don't allow that kind of thing in Chicago. They find something to keep those kids occupied real fast. So what did you do? Toss him in a puddle?"

Mark laughed. "I wish I had. No, he lost interest once he saw what part of town I was heading for. He must have figured I was in worse shape than he was. We never got as far as the puddles."

"So where'd take your grad school from?"

"Umass. And I didn't just take it from there, I went out to Amherst in real-time. It's more than a hundred klicks out of the city –

still pretty wild. No domes. Lots of sunlight, rain, and even an occasional snow shower. No panhandlers."

"And wildlife outside your back door. I would have loved that. I did a year of med school in Chicago before I figured out what being a doctor would mean. But then I switched to animal biology, and wound up on Mars studying fossils. Not exactly city life – but hardly country living either."

"Well, there are limits to natural environments too," Mark said. "When I went to Africa, I spent a year in the rain forest. The bugs were invasive."

"You didn't do a virtual trip there either?"

"No – I was after the real thing. There are cultures out there that try to live using the old practices. They've got access to modern medtech, thank goodness, and other conveniences – but they've tried to escape modern life by turning the clock back. Originally they wanted to preserve a part of the human heritage. But in the end, they just wound up putting on a virtual show for anthropology students who want to see an alternate culture without actually putting up with the bugs."

"You mean like the folks who live out in the Buffalo Barrens?"

"Sort of. Only they don't make cowboy videos in the Congo."

"I take it you didn't approve."

"I wrote a dissertation on the basically fraudulent study of artificial cultures, with a field study of the real culture there – what went on after the students logged out of the virtual village." Helen's eyes lit up with a knowing smile.

"Is that how you wound up assigned to this mission?"

"Not quite. It's a long story. One that involves a bitter textwar. Some day I may tell you about it."

"I take it you lost the textwar."

"No – my side won. That's why I'm here."

"Very interesting. And you don't want to tell Aunt Helen the gruesome details?"

"Not today. Anyway, it's your turn. What's your story? How did you end up here?"

"Valles Marineris wasn't much fun. When I got back, I went out West – the Buffalo Barrens for a while, then Utah and Nevada. I wound up in Arizona with a couple of husbands and wives, a few kids, and a life that got too complicated for words. So once the kids were grown, I signed up for the Science Service – and here I am. Just like you. You have to be something of a misfit to come on a mission like this one – at least if you volunteer for the science staff instead of getting assigned like the ship's crew. And being an oddball definitely makes a person interesting."

***

The next watch-cycle, after the stuck valve was repaired, Mark spent a couple of hours observing the aliens from behind the glass. He shared the room with one of Helen's assistants and Val Nordland, who was watching over the professor as it performed its magic.

For now, it was the professor's turn with their two guests. The busy little thing was cataloging the bits and pieces of the green creature's – of Zepp's speech. Phonemes and inflections. Syntactical patterns. Expressive emblems similar to human curses and idioms, signifiers of surprise, anger, or joy. From these elements, it built up words, sorting them out of the stream of language that issued from Zepp in response to its prodding.

For six months, as the *Cousteau* made its long journey down from the edge of the solar system, they had listened to the alien voices on the radio, watched the pictures on video. But not once had they understood a single sound.

There was no way to analyze sounds to produce meaningful information unless you could interact with the intelligence behind those sounds. Statistical correlations of phonemes were useless without a common frame of reference. Learning an alien language – an entire protocol of communication – was not like breaking a code. With a code, you could always compare the results with a known language. But with an alien species on an alien world, there was nothing anyone aboard the ship could do but wait until they had a representative to teach them the language.

The professor was designed and programmed just for that task. The only question in Mark's mind was whether or not Zepp was similarly designed and programmed.

He found himself laughing at Zepp's apparent flashes of frustration, followed by what looked like disdain and rejection in the form of sullen silence. Fortunately, Zepp did not remain silent for long.

The professor took only a couple of hours to break down the sounds into a phonetic structure capable of analysis. A remarkable achievement in human terms, though not so difficult for a thinking machine that could never forget a sound nor mistake a pattern. Even so, it was less than exciting to watch, and Mark went for lunch before it was complete.

When he returned, the professor had moved on to vocabulary-building. It used pictures generated on the wall screen to go through lists of nouns and verbs, adjectives and adverbs. Some of the prepositions had to be picked up by context, others could be demonstrated visually.

It reminded Mark of a children's video program, but Zepp seemed to be cooperating. The professor would speak, present an image, and the green alien would respond.

In graduate school, Mark had spent a session with a similar AI as a class exercise, watching it learn English. It had been an amusing, if not entirely pleasant experience. The one thing he recalled vividly was the repetitive, mechanical insistence on getting things right – testing and retesting its word-choices until meanings and sounds were clear. And with a language as full of ambiguities as English, that wasn't always possible.

"How are they doing?" Mark asked Val when he returned, keeping his voice low as if to avoid disturbing the lessons on the other side of the glass barrier.

"We've got a vocabulary of nearly a hundred words already," Val said. "At this rate, we could have the standard language by dinner time." Mark raised his eyebrows in surprise. Zepp was teaching the professor his language about as fast as was possible.

For a moment, he wondered what the alien must be going through. Yesterday, when he tried making the first social contact with the creatures, Mark doubted that they had anything in common. He wasn't sure if either of them would be the least bit interested in communicating with the humans. He tried to imagine himself being held captive aboard a ship full of alien invaders. Zepp might easily have expected to be eaten or tortured or executed. Indeed, his companion, Griddle, seemed to show no interest in communicating whatsoever – with the humans or with Zepp.

The more he watched the green-furred alien, the more Mark came to appreciate what he saw. There was a spirit there, a driving intelligence that was now caught up in the effort of leading the relentless perfectionist embodied in the professor through the labyrinth of his language, and who was not about to let go until the job was done.

***

It took a little time to get used to the simultaneous translation the professor used to help Mark communicate with Zepp, but that was a simple enough distraction.

More nerve-wracking was the knowledge that in the observation room on the other side of the one-way glass sat Captain Fletcher, Val Nordland, Lieutenant Barrett, Helen Castain, and everyone else who could find their way into the compartment.

He brought another pouch of food with him, but neither he nor Zepp were interested in playing that game again. The alien seemed to know that the time had come to make serious talk.

"I am Mark," said the young anthropologist. The professor repeated his words in the high-pitched chattering that the alien used for a language.

The green-furred alien replied, and the professor translated: "I am Zepp, a son of the tribe of Jobe." Mark smiled – the professor had spent a lot time working on proper names.

Many things sat heavily on Mark's mind – the conditions on the surface of the planet, the social and political forces that had sent an orbiting warship against them, the unexplained variety of intelligent species that seemed to be competing for power and dominance, and the role that he and his fellow explorers would play in that struggle.

But for the moment, he had to put those weighty concerns aside and deal with the single self-aware alien creature before him.

He'd done this kind of thing before. Interviewing subjects from other cultures was the prime mission of the anthropologist. Like Margaret Meade and the Samoans. It was best to start small and work your way up. He started with the simplest of questions.

"Where do you come from?"

"Chamal," answered Zepp, with a wave towards the deck. The professor added: "That is our word for the planet. His name for it is a local metaphor for mud."

"Where on Chamal?"

"First Suridash. Later Ring Po Do," Zepp said.

"Can he show me on a map?" Mark asked. "Professor, give us a map please." An image appeared on the wall, seven bands of color – white, green, yellow, green, yellow, green, and white. "Where is Suridash?" Zepp studied the map briefly, then pointed to a spot at the south end of a bay at the eastern end of the planet's landbound ocean.

"And Ring – uh."

"Ring Po Do," the professor prompted.

"Yes, where is that?"

This time, Zepp pointed to a point somewhere the middle of a large rift valley than ran from west to east, rising from the ocean to a volcanic upland that straddled the equator. "In the Rift of the Red Monkeys."

"That's a long way from home," Mark said.

"Long way," said Zepp. "Many spans. Many days. Another life for me." Mark sighed. There was a thoughtful and reflective side to this creature.

"Do you have a family back there?"

"In Suridash," Zepp said. "I am a son of the tribe of Jobe. I have many cousins. I have three sisters. And –" He choked briefly on the next words. "And I have many children."

"Children translates only roughly. Also can be interpreted as many litters."

"Litters?"

"Children have less status? Less significance? Diminutive and dismissive word connotations."

"You're a great help," Mark said to the professor, then to Zepp: "You must be worried about them."

Zepp looked away from Mark and away from the map, but did not reply. "Lieutenant Barrett, do you have any information about the place he calls home?"

A moment later, Barrett's voice crackled overhead. "It's not one of the hotspots," he said. "No signs of any major disturbances. In fact, it's one of the few population centers that isn't burning itself to the ground."

"Thank you," he said. "Zepp, my shipmates tell me that your city is safe."

The alien sighed, then chittered nervously. "That is good. My sisters are still weak from whelping."

"Whelping? Professor, is that the closest English translation for his word?"

"Yes, Mr. Paradis. It is the same word used for his sisters and for domestic and wild animals."

Mark wondered how the professor had established that fact, but didn't question it further.

"What about Griddle?" he asked. "Where is he from?"

"Meshkar," Zepp said. He returned to the map and pointed to a spot on a circular sea in the middle of the equatorial rainforest belt, then he moved it along through the desert to Suridash and up the coast to the rift valley. "Then Suridash – Broken Lands – Rift of the Red Monkeys – and here. I call him a pilgrim."

"Does he have family too?"

Zepp rubbed his hand over his face. "That gesture is equivalent to a shrug," the professor said.

"Why doesn't he talk?"

"He is afraid. He is always afraid. He claims he isn't, but he lies – to himself and to me. And he should not be afraid. Nothing will ever harm him."

"Is that so?" Mark asked. "And why not?"

Zepp rubbed his face again, but this time Mark narrowed his eyes in doubt at the small green alien. There were secrets here. He could sense them somehow. There was more to the story than Zepp was willing to tell, and shrugging it off wouldn't keep it secret forever.

"Are you afraid?"

"Not now. Not anymore. Once, before I came here, I was like Griddle. I was always afraid. But not any more."

"Why not?"

"Because ..." Zepp looked at the ceiling and paused a while, picking at his ear with one finger. "Because I have already died. Because my world has already ended. Because the angels are here."

"The angels?"

"His word for humans."

"Why do you call us angels?"

"Because that is what you are. The ones-who-know-from-afar told us. The knower-of-truths. And because I can see with my own eyes. You feed us and talk with us. Isn't this what angels do?"

"I don't know," Mark said. "It's what I do, but I never thought of myself as an angel. Tell me, why did you come here? Into space?"

"My elders made me do it," he said, looking away from Mark and down at the deck. "They coerced me with blood-guilt."

"That's the literal translation of a concept closer to extortion or blackmail," the professor said. Blackmail? In an odd way, that made sense, Mark realized. Chamal clearly was a world of many dysfunctional societies.

"But why? Why did your world send the warship against us? Why did your elders coerce you?"

"They are afraid. Always afraid."

"Afraid of us?"

"Afraid of everything. Afraid of time. Afraid of the blood-change. Afraid of the end their lives and the end of their tribes."

"But why us? Why fear the angels?"

"Because you are purebreds. All the same, one and all. And we are not. You are the true seed of the gods, and we are mud and clay that dares to know things. And when you see what we are, you will want to destroy Chamal and all who live upon it."

Mark's eyes widened considerably. They had moved up to the heavy stuff rather quickly. And without realizing it, Zepp had struck home in a way that profoundly upset the young anthropologist.

He had stumbled across one of the *Cousteau*'s own dark secrets.

He wanted to shake his head and deny all Zepp's fears and the fears of his species. He wanted to tell him they were wrong, and that the angels could not harm Chamal even if it wanted to. He wanted to, but he could not.

"Maybe you have good reason to fear us," he said at last. "Not even the angels are free from sin." Zepp chittered at that and rubbed his hand over his face.

"I have to ask you something," Mark said after a long pause without thought. "We want to know more about you. And that means we must examine your bodies. We will not injure you and there will be some pain, but not much. We will only do this if you allow it. You must consent or we will leave you alone." The green alien drew back shaking his head, making a hesitant chittering sound, and slapping the edge of the waterhole.

"I believe he is laughing," the professor said.

"Did I say something funny?"

Zepp recovered himself and rocked from side to side. "You really are angels," he said. "You have the power to do whatever you want to do to us. Why bother to ask?"

"Because we are not angels, we are humans," Mark said. "And we treat others who are similar to us as we would be treated ourselves. If the situation were reversed, I would want to be asked."

"If the situation were reversed, there are those on Chamal who would eat you for supper," Zepp said.

Mark drew in a sudden breath of surprise. So that was how it was.

Then Zepp surprised him doubly by consenting. "I will let you examine my body."

"And your companion?"

"He will consent," Zepp said. "I will see to that."

"You shouldn't force him," Mark cautioned.

"No, I won't force him. I won't have to. But there will be consequences."

CHAPTER FIVE

Zepp was still astounded later in the day when another of the angels appeared with Mark to conduct the examinations. This one was named Helen – another of their breathy words – and she was surprisingly gentle for all her bulk and muscle.

The angels' hidden cousin, the wise teacher of the wise, continued to talk for them, much like the translating machines that the snow-beasts of Kwikorak had built for the crew of the *Deragathon*. It was tedious but effective, and Zepp was getting used to it.

Helen's studies were exhaustive and exhausting.

She brought in strange devices that she pressed against his body – cold metal that stung through his fur. She tried to explain what she was doing as she went along, although many of her words didn't make it through translation.

"This is for a full-body scan to document your internal pieces," she said as she positioned him against the largest of her machines. "It'll track your mumble-mumble."

"The workings of your body," said the wise teacher.

"And it gives us an idea of your mumble-mumble."

"Your blood and thank-you systems."

"My what?" Zepp asked, but the unseen angel did not reply, continuing to keep up with Helen's chatter.

"And your mumble-mumble."

"Your bones and sinew."

Zepp noticed that she looked different from Mark, even inside her transparent cloak. At first he wondered if he'd been wrong in his belief that the angels were purebreds, considering how striking some of the differences were. Then he realized that Helen must be a female and Mark a male. He chided himself for his slow wits over that.

"Would you please eat another thank-you," she asked as he posed rigidly against the cold surface of the large machine.

He chittered playfully at the angels as Helen handed him a food-stick. Somehow the wise teacher and the others had gotten the idea that "thank you" was his word for food. It pleased him that they were not infallible, and to remind him of the fact, he never corrected the mistake.

When they were finished with the imaging of his body, they went on to more detailed and intimate exercises. She strapped a belt around his arm and pumped it tight with a small hand bellows. She poked a shiny metal device into his ears, shined a light into his mouth, measured his arms, legs, head, hands, tail, and body with a metered tape. She showed him colored cards and asked him to name the colors. She wiped the inside of his mouth with a fuzzy stick and asked him to do the same with his private parts. She sprayed his thigh with something cold and cut a piece of skin. And she poked a spike into his arm and let him watch in mild horror as his blood leaked out into small glass bottles.

And each time, with each test, she explained what she was going to do, and then asked again if he would allow her to do it.

It was astounding. Didn't the angels recognize their power over him? Didn't they realize that they had no reason to ask? Perhaps they did. Perhaps this was part of a complex, mad plot to turn his loyalties. Stranger things were known to happen every day in Suridash. He had been the victim of such a plot already.

But each time she asked, he gave his permission. And that was the most astounding thing of all.

When they were done, Helen stood back and looked Zepp over. He felt worn out. He'd never imagined that being inspected, measured, studied, and documented would be such hard work.

"Tell me something, Zepp," she said.

"Tell you what?"

"Explain why you wear that belt under your loincloth." He felt his skin grown warm as he considered her question – and that surprised him. For several days now, he had thought that he was immune to fear and shame. Apparently he was wrong. To think of his sexual nature and the restrictions placed upon it reminded him of the many ways that the enforced its control over its sons and daughters – and of the certain punishment that awaited him for his own sins.

Even so, he found himself explaining the purpose of the brass chastity belt, repeating the lessons of the Seedkeepers that he had learned as a youngling.

"The sons and daughters of the tribe of Jobe mate only with those chosen by the Seedkeepers," he said. At least that was what the law of Jobe commanded, he added silently. "We wear the belt of abstinence to show our obedience to Jobe's law."

Helen nodded slowly. "That much makes sense," she said. "Can you remove it?"

Zepp felt his muscles tense up unbidden. "Remove it? Certainly not! The key is held by my Grandfather Kobe, to be given to my mate at the time she is chosen. No one is to remove the belt until then." He felt the blood course through his body, knowing that his outrage was driven by guilt, not by moral righteousness. He hoped that Helen would not see that and probe deeper. He was afraid that there was nothing about himself that he would not reveal to these creatures.

And yet he knew he must. There were secrets he must keep as long as he could, to protect himself and, though he could not explain why it mattered, to protect his world. Because deep down in his soul he knew that the fears of his elders were worthy – that if the angels knew just how sick and depraved his planet was, they would want to destroy it for sure.

"It's all right, Zepp," she said soothingly. "I only ask to learn. It was not a request." He felt his fur begin to lie flat and his muscles relax. His body ached with fatigue.

"What do you say we start on Griddle?" she asked after speaking for a while with the wise teacher. "Is he ready for the examination?"

"I think so," Zepp said. He had not used force on his companion, as Mark had said. He hadn't even used the threat of force – although he considered withholding food from the pilgrim unless he agreed. It had not been necessary.

"Why not?" Griddle had said. "We are doomed anyway. There will be no escape from here. No rescue. No safety. And if there were, I would be sent back to the damp caves where you found me. Life is misery, so why should I refuse a small measure more?" Zepp felt like kicking Griddle in the pants to knock some sense into him – or to drive some of the self-pity out. But he knew better than to invite danger so directly.

"Griddle, can you come over here?" Helen asked, the wise teacher repeating her words in the dialect of Suridash.

The blue cat shuffled to his feet and dragged them across the deck to Helen and her machines.

"Did Zepp explain what we would like to do? Have you seen how it was done?" Zepp recognized Helen's soft solicitations for what they were. The angels appeared to have figured out correctly Griddle's passive and reticent character. He only hoped it wouldn't lull them into a false sense of security.

"Yes," Griddle drawled lazily.

"Can we begin doing the same with you? Is that all right?"

"Yes," he said, more slowly and with even less vigor.

"Good. Why don't you come over here so we can begin with a full-body scan and –" At that moment, without warning, the lights in the chamber went out abruptly, plunging them into total darkness. Helen gasped slightly. Zepp felt the electric tingle of physical fear, but overcame it as he recognized Griddle's perverse wizardry at work.

Not even the angels were immune, he told himself with a secret smile.

***

By the time they fixed the lighting in the chamalians' chamber, Helen had gone back to the lab to start working on the samples she'd taken from Zepp. Griddle would have to wait. In the meantime, Mark wound up with an unscheduled afternoon watch to spend talking to Zepp.

They began with the map, but Mark soon learned that a conversation with the chamalians could end up going almost anywhere.

The professor was capable of projecting a nearly infinite variety of map formats. That was an important feature when you couldn't know in advance what kind of symbols would have meaning for an alien species. Zepp responded best to a combination of real-time video images and simple outlines and dot-symbols for significant places.

Mark had the machine put up an image of Zepp's home town. It was a tidy, self-contained city, surrounded by a high wall that threw long shadows near sunrise and sunset.

"What is Suridash like?" the anthropologist asked. "Is it part of an empire?"

"I have no referent for empire," the professor interjected.

"Then make one," Mark snipped back.

The machine talked to Zepp privately for a few minutes, then replied to Mark: "We now have referents for empire, nation, federation, city-state, kingdom, and vassal-state."

"Thank you," Mark said.

"Suridash is a city-state," Zepp explained. "We are far from the great powers to the north and south in a land that no one wants. For eight eighty-eight years and longer, refugees from all the rest of our part of Chamal have come to us. Some tribes have built walls around themselves to keep out the rest. Others live in the spaces between the walled enclaves. Jobe, the patriarch of my tribe, gathered together the dust of the street to make a new tribe."

"Who rules the city?" Mark asked, wondering if anyone could rule a mixture of species with different cultures, different taboos, and different religions all jammed into a desert city-state.

"A council of the elders of many tribes rules – at least in name," Zepp said, the professor managing to capture the irony in that statement. "But in fact, many rule. The Seedkeepers maintain order among the enclaves. And my tribesman, Tedrak, deals with the outside world with the help of his assistant, Whirlpitt. They were the ones who sent me here to be ambassador to your race."

Mark sensed a hesitation in Zepp's reply, something that raised doubts about its veracity. "Have you done such work before?"

Zepp's body shook with chittering laughter. "I was not chosen because of my abilities," he said. Mark attempted to probe deeper, but Zepp resisted, quickly changing the subject. "Let us talk of the map, Mark-angel."

"All right, let's talk about the ocean." The professor obliged him by projecting a long, narrow, blue shape scored by intersecting rays. Zepp had shown the AI how to use those rays, which were his equivalent of latitude and longitude. The two sets of coordinate lines radiated from the north pole and a high volcanic peak a short distance to the east of Suridash.

Chamal's single ocean wrapped nearly halfway around the planet, confined between the poles to the north and the desert belt to the south. In reality, it was just a very large sea, wracked with storms that churned its briny depths and beat against its broad, sandy shores.

"There's little enough to talk about there. The ocean is ruled by Rikabar, which is ruled in turn by the Empire of the Royal Onion. They don't like meat-eaters in Rikabar – and younglings who show the the tooth of the hunter or who tug away at the scent of the hunt are swiftly put to death."

"Sounds like they've bred themselves into docility," Mark said.

"Hardly," snorted Zepp. "Their war machines have driven eastward mercilessly, conquering all before them. It is only the great distance between Rikabar and Suridash and the harshness of the desert and the ocean that have protected us from their boundless appetite for empire."

"I stand corrected," Mark said. "What about the lands to the south? Who lives in the rain forests of the equatorial belt?"

The professor switched the map to the soggy jungles that wrapped around Chamal's midsection. A single round sea, resembling in many ways a porthole, punctured that belt.

"Primitives, savages, uncivilized and uncultured – for the most part. They war on each other, raise kingdoms from the swamps, and then sink back into the mud and slime. All except Meshkar."

"Meshkar?"

"The high sea that stands above the jungle." Mark scanned the map and found the sea, a great blister on the face of the planet. It appeared to be a large impact feature hundreds of kilometers in diameter, filled with water from the endless tropical rains. For all its lack of a world-girdling ocean, Chamal was hardly a dry planet. The equatorial belt in particular had a high water table with few highlands. The result was a boggy morass, punctuated by arc-shaped and circular lakes and seas – what the planetological team had identified as the remnants of ancient cratering during the formation of the planet. Without plate tectonics, those craters, blasted into the bedrock, still remained.

"The air there is cool and clear, I am told, and they do not suffer the disease and decay of the forests below. There are many trading states on the shores of the sea and they have grown rich in their exchange. They would like to accomplish with their gold what Rikabar attempts with its armies. So far, Suridash has remained beyond their reach."

"I see," said Mark. "More enemies over the horizon. Are there others?"

"Shipar to the east," Zepp said, indicating a volcanic highland that rose out of the desert belt near Suridash. "There are many tribes living in the mountains there. They fight with one another more than with outsiders, but occasionally one of their rockets will overshoot its target and land in the desert outside the city, lighting the night sky with its fire."

"Is that all?"

"No, there is also the Rift of the Red Monkeys."

A wide chasm with high walls split the surface of Chamal to the northeast of Suridash. A tiny ribbon of a river wound through its length, with a broad network of canals spreading across the valley floor.

"That's right. You said you spent some time there. What for?"

"That was where I was trained to live and work in space. And that was where I was launched to the *Deragathon*."

"By the red monkeys?"

"No – there are no more red monkeys in the rift. The blue monkeys have taken their place."

"What happened?"

"The red monkeys are special. Once in eight eighty-eight years, they rise from the rift, many born in a single generation. Each time they arise, they fill the valley with new inventions, new discoveries, the fruits of their genius. They are much wiser than most chamalians. But for all their wisdom, they are still mortal, and they still do not know how to avoid the jealousy and hatred that mark us all. In the end, there are too many monkeys and not enough power to go around. They make war on one another and fight until there are no more. No more, that is, except for the few that fled to Suridash and who persist to this day because of the knowledge of the Seedkeepers."

"I would think that some would survive, though, wouldn't they?"

"You don't understand. No blood-race survives. They all fade away, sinking back into the dust. There is no avoiding that fate. That is what Jobe discovered."

"I guess I don't understand. This is one of the questions that still puzzles us. Why are there so many intelligent species on your world? Some of us think it is because you fight amongst yourselves. Others believe it is because your world is all land, with each species isolated from the others. But none of us knows enough to explain it."

Zepp snickered. "Then you should have asked. It is simple, Markangel. We are not so many intelligent species. We are all one. Each blood-race is but a single strand in the tapestry of life. This is the first lesson the Seedkeepers teach us when we are young. The seed of the gods can be carried by any creature. Any of the wild beasts of the desert, the forest, and the mountains can achieve wisdom, make tools, learn to speak, and gain power over the land."

"Are you saying that every creature on Chamal is intelligent?"

"No – of course not. Most of our young never gain enough wisdom even to speak. Rarely does more than one child in a litter ever show the spark of the gods' seed. But each blood-race, each creature can carry that seed. And each creature of wisdom can plant it in the wild. It floats like a nut in the river until it washes ashore downstream and takes root as a new tree."

"Wait a minute," Mark said, his head reeling. "It sounds like you're telling me that you can mate with wild animals and spread the genes for intelligence among them."

"Yes, I am. What else would I tell you but the truth about our nature? We are indeed all one blood-race. It is only the whimsy of the seed of the gods that determines which of us will have horns and which will have fangs and which will have wisdom. And against that whimsy we have no defense, no protection. It is like the desert wind, moving the dunes whichever way it will. No grain of sand can say which dune it will help create."

"All one species? God, is such a thing possible?"

"It must be, Mark-angel, for that is the fate of life on Chamal."

"It must be pure chaos."

"And what else could life be but chaos?"

CHAPTER SIX

"But **how does** it **work?**"

Mark looked up from his sandwich and saw Helen's wrinkled brow and lopsided frown. "What do you mean, how does it work? They interbreed and the gene for intelligence gets spread around."

"No, that's not what I meant. How do the genes get spread around? How does the germ cell reproduce? From the description we've got, there must be some kind of complicated genetic interplay going on. But exactly what kind? And why? This is an exobiologist's nightmare."

"And an anthropologist's hell," Mark added.

"I can see we're going to have to do some pretty in-depth cellular studies. And I was just getting started on the physiological stuff. Now that the lights are fixed, I hope I can do a work-up on Griddle."

"Is there some reason we're having problems with the isolation chamber?" Mark asked, recalling a question that had risen in his mind that afternoon watch. "First the water spill, then the power failure.

"The techs told me it's because we didn't use it at all until just recently. No chance to work the glitches out of the system. And there's only been the plumbing and the lights – not that many problems."

"It just seems odd. You'd think they would have tested the systems long before the ship was certified."

"I guess they did," Helen said. "But these are complicated systems where a lot can go wrong. You're not getting the space willies, are you?"

"Me? Not at all."

***

Zepp sat by the edge of the water hole, chewing on a foodstick and thinking about fear.

All his life he had been motivated mostly by fear. Fear of his elders maintained and reinforced through taboos and rituals that prescribed terrible punishments for the slightest transgression. Fear of the multitude of strange creatures who roamed the streets of Suridash, many of whom would have hesitated not one instant to make a meal of him if the opportunity presented itself, or to spirit him away to toil in some shop or factory at the end of a heavy chain. And fear of his own passions and imagination, both of which leapt and flew beyond the high walls of his city and bore him ever closer to his cruel fate.

But all that had ended days ago – or so he had thought.

He was no longer afraid of his elders. He had violated one of the tribe's greatest taboos and everyone knew it. He knew that he could never return to his home and that knowledge shielded him from any concern of punishment for his sins.

During his brief stay aboard the *Deragathon*, he had been pursued and assaulted by monsters more frightening than anything that walked the streets of his city or tortured his dreams at night. He had escaped them all, turning the deathship upside down in the process, sparking the mutinies and rebellions that wracked it still.

And his contact with the angels revealed to him that his passions and imaginations were pedestrian daydreams compared to the realities of a vast and endless universe, where creatures more alien to him than the most distant of his chamalian cousins could cross the void and discuss the sins of his race.

In those few days, he had matured immensely. It was not unusual for someone his age to change so suddenly – not in a world where sudden and radical change was the rule of all nature. He knew that he was different, stronger, less malleable. He had discovered his own will and his own voice – and in the process he had vowed to never again become the subject of someone else's will or a substitute for their voice.

And despite all that, despite his newfound courage, he was once again afraid.

Now he feared the angels. The fear had crept up on him like an incubus sneaking through the window-gate at night. It did not seize him at first, but nagged and twisted, building as he paced the narrow limits of his cell. And finally it gripped him by the throat.

He knew that the angels were unlike any chamalian he had every known. They treated him like a kinsman – but without the threat of punishment or the working of guilt. More the way a brother was treated by his sisters – not his own sisters, to be sure, those creatures of evil who had helped engineer his betrayal, but other, kinder sisters of his tribe.

But he knew that would all change once they discovered the truth about Griddle and his power.

They were beginning to suspect, he was sure. But soon they would know. And when that moment came, Zepp had no doubt that the two chamalians would be cast out into space, their breath stolen away from them, their blood frozen in their veins, their tears turned to ice in their eyes, and their thoughts scattered amongst the stars.

Worst of all, he had to keep his fear secret. He could share it with no one, least of all Griddle. For if he told the pilgrim what he believed, the moment of their discovery would come all that much sooner – and with it their deaths.

He tried to remain relaxed when the Helen-angel returned to the chamber. But when the wise teacher's voice repeated her words, he had all he could to do keep from trembling.

"Zepp, I want to ask a big favor of you – one that could cause you a lot of discomfort." The fur on his back stood on end and his tail twitched with nervous energy. What could she want? Did she know already?

"What is the favor?" he asked in return.

"I want to do an experiment with you. It's got to be done sooner or later if we're going to have any amount of frequent contact with your race. But you may end up getting ill from the whole thing."

"I don't know what you mean," he said, his fears unallayed by her rambling prologue.

"Well let me explain. There are materials produced by our bodies and yours. We call them mumble-mumble. There are also other materials that can be poisonous in large amounts. And there are tiny living creatures that inhabit our fur and our skin. The ones from Chamal can make us angels ill. And the ones we angels produce will probably make you chamalians ill. We have to find out just how ill and what we can do to reduce the effects."

"And what do you want me to do?"

"We need one of you to expose himself to us – without these plastic iso-suits."

"And how ill will I get if I allow this?" Zepp wondered if this was a ploy to trap him into revealing what he knew. But at the same time, it sounded like more of the strange angel curiosity that he'd come to expect from both Helen and Mark.

"I've done some tests with the samples I got and did some analysis with the doctor. I'm sure it won't kill you. But beyond that, there's a whole range of allergic reactions that we angels experience. I'm sure there must be an equivalent for you." The wise teacher spoke up. "The term Helen uses has no referent in your language. It is similar to the bite of an insect or a rash from certain plants."

Zepp thought about it a moment, recalling his days as a youngling when he found his hands covered with large red bumps from the chickle bush in the tribe's herb garden. It was annoying, but hardly serious.

"How would this be done?" he asked.

"There's another iso-chamber next to this one. We'll take you over there and Mark or I will spend some time with you without a suit. If you start to get terribly ill, we will have medical equipment available. But I don't believe we'll need it." Zepp thought about that for a moment. Being separated from Griddle was not the worst fate he could imagine – though he doubted it would do any good in the long run. Perhaps that was the purpose of this entire exercise. That might make sense, if they suspected what was happening. But he realized now that his own suspicions were not sound. Little enough had happened to reveal Griddle's powers – and he had recognized it only because he was familiar with them.

No, Helen was being honest. The angels really did want to test his body in some new and potentially dangerous way. He considered rejecting the request – especially considering some of Helen's understated warnings about medical equipment. But then he decided to go ahead. Nothing they could do to him would be worse than the fate he feared, yet was certain would befall him – if not now, then soon.

"Whenever you want me, I am ready," he said.

Helen showed her teeth in what the wise teacher had told him was a sign of pleasure. "Thank you. This is very important to both of our races."

"Then the sooner it is done, the better."

"All right," she said. "Let's go." She talked with the wise teacher briefly, and the door to the chamber opened. Another suited figure moved in the corridor beyond, and Helen allowed Zepp to go first. He followed the directions of the other angel, an unnamed cousin of Mark and Helen whom he recognized by the red fur atop his head, through a door a short distance away.

The new chamber was similar to the first, only smaller. It had the same water hole, the same sanitary pipe, and the same bright, white walls, deck, and ceiling.

"We will bring you some food shortly," Helen said. "It will be a few minutes before someone is back to take care of you. I have to go back and finish with the tests on Griddle."

"I will wait here," Zepp said, chittering at his own nervous humor.

Helen's toothy grimace seemed a bit lopsided to him as she nodded, backed through the doorway, and sealed him in the compartment. Despite their solicitude, the angels still treated him as a prisoner.

Within a few minutes, the fear began to nag at him again. This time, he had arguments to use in the struggle against it, and he raised them atop the ramparts.

But the struggle never had a chance to begin. Suddenly the lights went out – and with them the constant sound of moving air that he had long ago learned to recognize as one of the most important elements of life aboard a spacecraft.

So it was all a lie after all. They had brought him in here to kill him before tossing him into space. A slow death by lack of oxygen, but a warm and perhaps comfortable one. He would drift off to sleep, never to awake.

But much to his surprise, he met the moment unafraid. Fear, he realized, was in the anticipation and not in the event. It was an important lesson. It was a shame that it would the last one he would ever learn.

***

Mark was already in the observation center when the alarms went off. He was watching the two iso-chambers while Helen and Red were busy with the chamalians.

Zepp was all alone in the secondary chamber, while Helen was in the middle of examining Griddle in the main compartment. Suddenly a board full of instruments flashed yellow and red, leaving Mark with a terrible feeling of helplessness.

He could see that something was wrong – the images in the monitors from both chambers had gone dark. But there was nothing he could do about it. He would have to wait for Red or Helen to return – or for someone else to come to his aid.

He was about to call for assistance when Red appeared in the doorway, his face the color of boiled lobster with sweat pouring from his brow.

"Damn! We've lost all power for Iso-2. Did you mess around with something in here, Mark?"

"I didn't touch a thing," he said quickly, feeling a bit wounded by the accusation. "There was no warning. It all lit up at once."

"Sounds like a main power bus then. I'll call the techs, you try to call Helen on the phone and let her know what's happening." Mark nodded, and switched on the comm-link to the iso-chamber. A moment later Helen's voice crackled to life.

"Are you all right?" Mark asked. "What's happening in there? How's Griddle?"

"The lights went out and the air stopped circulating, but that's all," she said. "Griddle is over in the corner – I can hear him breathing. For the time being we'll be okay. We'll stay warm. The air may get stale, but we shouldn't have any problems."

"What about Zepp? Do you want me to go in there and keep him company?"

"That was supposed to be the plan. We were going to expose him to human allergens. Are you sure you can trust him in a dark room – alone? He's not like Griddle, you know."

Mark thought that one over. He wasn't sure just what the alien might do under those circumstances and there was no way to predict his behavior. "I'd better wait until things are fixed. How are you doing?"

"All right, I guess. I was just taking a biopsy sample when the lights went out. I'll be out of here in a few more minutes, but I don't want to leave Griddle alone. I never got a chance to do a proper bandage on the surgery."

Another half hour passed before the techs showed up, pulled away the wall panels, found the source of the problem, and repaired it. Mark was watching Iso-2 when the power was restored. Inside the compartment, Zepp looked up suddenly as the lights surged back to life.

The voice of the professor crackled in the observation center, repeating the alien's words. "I wasn't expecting to hear from you again. Does this mean you've decided to spare my life after all?"

"That's an odd thing to ask," Mark replied. "We had a power failure, that's all. Did you expect something else?"

"I should have known. Forget what I said. You wouldn't understand."

"Why don't I come down there and we can talk about it."

Zepp chittered and rose to his feet. "I guess I don't really have much of a choice. And it's time that you knew anyway." Mark wrinkled his face in puzzlement. Time that he knew what? What secrets did Zepp want to reveal?

A short time later he knew – and his puzzlement turned to dismay.

CHAPTER SEVEN

The conference room was already full when Captain Fletcher and Lieutenant Barrett arrived. Someone from the regular crew rapped on the wall and announced softly, "Attention on deck," and everyone stood while Fletcher took his seat at the head of the table.

Mark's mouth was dry and his back itched.

Helen, seated across the table from him, flashed a big smile.

"All right, gentlepeople," the captain said, "there seems to be some kind of problem with the systems in the isolation chambers. And our cultural survey team has suggested that it may have been caused by the alien subjects we brought aboard. Does anyone have any evidence that sheds light on this?"

Fletcher's features barely moved, seemingly fixed to the front of his fleshy face. His personality was as bland as that round head and soft body. As a regular officer in the Science Service he knew how to command a spaceship. He didn't know much else, however, and was never very good at dealing with things beyond his competence. He had gotten the *Cousteau* into orbit around Chamal and could be relied upon to get her back out to the jump point for the return to Earth. Everything in between was truly in the hands of the ship's specialists.

Helen was the first to give her report. She explained the three incidents – the flooding from the stuck valve in the water hole, the loss of the lights, and the power failure of the previous watch-cycle.

She described the technical problems in detail and admitted, when questioned by Barrett, that there was nothing linking the three incidents and no unusual physical evidence indicating anything but ordinary systems failures.

The ship's technical chief confirmed her statement. He had inspected each of the systems after the breakdowns and could find nothing unusual. And he said he could find no reason for anything to go wrong beyond the simplest explanation of all – things always went wrong.

He pointed out, as Helen had over dinner, that the iso-chambers were not used until the *Cousteau* made orbit. The ship had left for Chamal shortly after leaving the yards at Phobos, having been commissioned especially for this mission. There was every reason in the world to expect things like this to happen under those circumstances, the tech chief said.

And then Lieutenant Barrett weighed in. "I put the holo-files from the monitor through an AI check," he said. "We've got images of them from the moment they set foot aboard the ship. We found nothing that either of the aliens could have done to cause anything mechanical or electronic to malfunction. Since they came aboard the *Cousteau*, they have eaten, slept, talked with Mr. Paradis, and been examined by Ms. Castain. Nothing else."

"I see," Captain Fletcher said, his voice steeped with incredulity. "So why is it that someone is suggesting they were responsible?"

"Because Zepp told me so," Mark said. The instant the words left his mouth, he regretted it. He knew he should have remained silent and let Val Nordland start, but Nordland was as skeptical as everyone else. And they were wasting time – the one thing they could not afford to do.

"I'm sorry for speaking up," he said. "But it's really as simple as that. Zepp explained it to me, and I reported it to Lieutenant Barrett. I assumed that was the right thing to do. I didn't expect everyone to get this upset about it – but if Zepp is telling the truth then we're all in danger."

"Maybe you'd better start at the beginning," Captain Fletcher said. "What exactly did the alien tell you?"

"That Griddle has an unusual power. Zepp believes that he has the power to cause malfunctions and accidents and he says this was the reason the chamalians sent him to us. And he says that the longer he remains on board, the more things will go wrong, until finally the ship becomes a helpless target for the chamalian weapons."

"Did he offer any proof?" Fletcher asked.

"No, sir. I asked, and he said we would have plenty of proof if we waited long enough."

"Is there any reason to believe this alien?" Barrett asked. "I can think of several reasons not to – he could be lying intentionally, he could believe what he is saying even if it isn't true, or there could be some error in translation."

"I've considered those," Mark said. "The first thing I had to do was make sure that the translation was correct. It took a while before I was even sure of what Zepp was saying. You've got to understand how a linguistics AI works. He gets together with someone like Zepp and figures out their language, but there's no way of knowing exactly what either of them are thinking or what that language means. A lot of it is interpretation – and AI's are notorious for making mistakes. In the end, I had to explain to the professor what I was trying to understand and he had to discuss the meanings of the terms with Zepp until we all agreed on what we were discussing."

"And so there's no error there?"

"None, Captain." Mark looked over at Val Nordland in surprise as he defended his work. "If there's an error, it is not in communication."

"Very well, but what about the other alternatives?" Fletcher asked.

"The next thing I thought was that this was simply a chamalian superstition," Mark said. "The Jonah myth is an old human tale – the jinx that causes disaster. And when you deal with someone from another culture, you can have a hard time dealing with things that they believe, but which are simply untrue. When I was in Africa studying the members of a pseudo-primitive culture, there were a number of local-born youngsters who believed their tribal shaman had magical powers. I had interviewed the shaman, and he told me himself that aside from a few tricks of sleight of hand, he relied on his age and his scholarship to lead people – and that he never claimed to have any such powers."

"Interesting," Fletcher said, a slightly puzzled look on his face. "But what does this have to do with our plumbing?"

"I'm getting to that, sir, if you'll just bear with me," Mark said. His nerves tightened up another notch and he felt his left leg begin to twitch. He forced it to remain still and continued. "Zepp tried to explain to me how Griddle accomplishes his magic – to use a word that translates roughly from the chamalian. Apparently, there are a number of chamalians with what we would call clairvoyance. Zepp calls them 'those who know from afar.'" Fletcher looked to Nordland. "Is this possible?"

"Given the unusual biological parameters of chamalian life, I'd hesitate to say that anything is impossible down there, Captain," Nordland said. "There is some anecdotal evidence of human beings with similar psychic powers. Although they've never manifested themselves in very powerful ways. The most reliable of them are used by law-enforcement agencies in investigative work. They don't make a big deal of it, because people are still highly skeptical. But they have been documented to some extent."

"You don't say?" Fletcher said, his eyes turning dreamy and distant.

"And Zepp claimed that Griddle has a so-called psychic power?" Barrett asked.

"Yes, sir, he did. He said it's a defense – an automatic defense. He has no control over it. When he feels threatened, his unconscious mind reaches out and makes things break down. And being a chamalian, Zepp says, means always feeling threatened. He said it's a curse that has forced Griddle to wander from place to place his whole life. It's always the same story – shortly after he arrives in a town, the plumbing breaks down, the sewers back up, lightning begins striking nearby houses, livestock comes down with obnoxious diseases, until Griddle is identified as a jonah and is driven out."

"This still sounds like superstition and paranoia to me," Barrett said.

"That's what I thought at first," Mark said. "But Zepp is convinced. From what I can determine, he's not a member of what you would call a superstitious culture. His tribe is supposedly unique on his world for its attention to reason, facts, science, and demonstrable evidence." And rationalization, Val Nordland had pointed out to him earlier, an easy trap to fall into.

"But all you have to go on is what he told you," Fletcher said.

"Yes, sir, but there's more to what he told me."

"Then go on."

"He said that he was given the task of smuggling Griddle aboard the chamalian warship. His leaders wanted to use Griddle to sabotage that ship and prevent it from carrying out its mission."

That produced a noticeable response from everyone in the room. Some raised their eyebrows, others snorted in disbelief, and a few shot nasty looks his way.

"And do you have evidence to back that up?" Fletcher asked.

"Well, yes and no," Mark replied. "Lieutenant Barrett and I discussed this. What we've monitored from the *Deragathon* shows that there's been some kind of internal conflict aboard. A mutiny or a rebellion. Griddle precipitated the event, Zepp said, but not through any paranormal means."

"No?"

"No – the conspirators simply announced that he was aboard and that was enough to set things in motion." There were a few snickers this time, and a couple of crewmembers at the table stifled open laughter.

"Are you afraid something like that will happen aboard the *Cousteau*?" Fletcher asked. "Do you expect some kind of mutiny?"

"No, sir. Certainly not. The rebellions aboard the *Deragathon* were all in motion long before Zepp brought Griddle aboard. There's no suggestion that he caused them to break out spontaneously. But I'm not sure we can rule out the simpler mechanical problems that Zepp has warned us about. Eventually, if he is correct, they will get more and more serious until our lives are in danger."

"I suppose we would be," the captain said. "And I suppose you have a remedy for all this."

"The only one I can think of is to get Griddle off the ship."

Fletcher nodded slowly. "I suppose that is one option. Mr. Barrett, what do you think?"

"Well sir, I think all this is highly speculative. There's no reason to believe the words of the alien. There's every reason to suspect that he was sent here to tell us this tall tale. From his own words, his superiors have done this before – put their agent aboard a ship and announced his presence. Like most sympathetic magic, it only works if you believe in it, and – "

Barrett fell silent at a brief flickering of the lights. Then they dimmed twice and returned to full strength. The Space Corps officer rolled his eyes upwards, smiled in embarrassment, then continued: "It only works if you believe in it, and I don't."

"Thank you," Captain Fletcher said when Barrett sat down. He was about to speak further when a technician entered the compartment and spoke to the ship's technical chief, who in turn whispered a few words to Fletcher.

A momentary flush of color spread across the captain's cheeks, then he stood up quickly. "This meeting is adjourned," he said. "If anyone has anything further to add, please leave me a memo in the ship's mail." Without waiting for a crewmember to call for attention, Fletcher hurried out the door, followed by the technical chief and his crew. The rest of those in the compartment rose slowly and uncertainly, then headed for the door.

Helen Castain hurried around the table to connect with Mark. "Did you hear that?"

"No, I was too far away."

"The main fusion core is acting up. A power surge tripped some control circuits and set off some alarms and now they're trying to bring it back down to normal."

"No wonder the captain turned red," Mark said. "Is it as serious as he took it to be?"

"I guess that depends," Helen said.

"Depends on what."

"On how much longer we leave Griddle on board the ship."

***

Mark was relieved to know that someone else believed him. When he told Helen that, she just smiled. "Why shouldn't anyone believe you?" she asked. "You're right, aren't you?"

"That doesn't always count, you know."

"Aw, don't be ridiculous. Come on, let's get down to the lab where we can discuss this in private." A few minutes later, they were back in the observation chamber. Helen's team leader was still in the lab, making it an inconvenient place for conversation. At least from here, Mark could keep an eye on Griddle and Zepp. Griddle was curled up in the corner, while Zepp paced his cell. He seemed to be in good condition despite his exposure to terrestrial allergens. Apparently the chamalian was more resistant to strange proteins. Given his world's ecology, Mark wasn't surprised.

Oddly, Mark felt a degree of sympathy for Zepp, as he understood how the spirited creature must be taking his captivity. He had no similar feelings for Griddle, however, who still seemed to be something of a cipher in his diffidence.

"So what else did Zepp tell you?" Helen asked with a conspiratorial air.

"How do you know he told me anything else?"

"Because I know how long you were in there with him. You two talked half the nightwatch."

"He's a very interesting fellow," Mark said. "We were lucky to get someone like him as our first contact with this race. He's educated and articulate and has relatively few irrational cultural patterns to interfere with communication. We could just as easily have ended up with two creatures like Griddle."

"That would be depressing."

"It certainly would – in more ways than one. In any case, Zepp revealed more about his world and his race than we ever suspected."

"Enlighten me," Helen said as she stretched her legs out and propped them on a workbench.

"This world is a lot like Earth was before the beginning of the New Era – fragmented, polarized, a lot of internal conflict – only a lot worse. The extremes are much greater than they were on Earth. We had the advantage of physical access to most of our world through the sea and air. Chamal doesn't have that kind of leveling system. So you've got a large number of powerful and competing economic and political systems, all without the power to do much to one another so there's no decisive cycle-ending events.

"You've got a lot of historical overlap – cultures at various levels of development in close physical contact with each other. That means that your taboos are your neighbor's commandments – which means another source of conflict.

"And you've got a tremendous amount of racial diversity, with no enlightened social history – with the possible exception of Zepp's own tribe."

Helen's eyes widened and she let out a low whistle. "This is beginning to sound like several visions of Hades," she said. "Not exactly an attractive vacation spot."

Mark smiled. "Not one to put in the tour books, no."

"And so in the middle of all this, we arrive."

"Exactly. Sort of like Griddle on the *Deragathon*. We've managed to precipitate a lot of events. Old pressures that were waiting to be released. Old conflicts waiting to be settled."

"And that's why the place is still in flames?"

"Apparently."

"And how does Zepp fit into all this?"

"Well, when the ones who know from afar realized we had arrived in this stellar system and just who we were, the chamalians went into a panic. It seems that they have a terrible combination of cultural faults. At the same time they have a highly developed moral sense –"

"Which they don't seem to apply very effectively?"

"Which they don't seem to apply very effectively – and a strongly negative image of themselves and their fellow chamalians. They realize the truth about their own biological circumstances. Imagine what it must be like to know that your self-consciousness arose at random from the wild animals around you and that your family, your tribe, and your society are all doomed to return to the wild in the end. Imagine what it must be like to know that you can breed with wild animals and produce offspring. Now imagine what a highly developed moral sense is likely to tell you about your own nature."

"No wonder he wears a chastity belt!" Helen cried.

"You bet. Now imagine what these creatures must think of us – purebreds who come from the sky. That's why they call us angels."

"Now it makes sense."

"And the first thing they did when they learned about us was to imagine what we would think of them."

"Filthy sex perverts," Helen said with a smile. "Unfit for the company of angels."

"They decided that we would want to destroy them for their countless sins."

"And I thought I had guilt problems."

"So they figured they had to beat us to the punch."

"Hence the *Deragathon*."

"Which in Zepp's language means, *Angel Killer*."

"Oh my word! But where does Zepp come in?"

"Remember I told you his tribe is about the only one on the planet with an enlightened social history? Well they decided that we were not the all-consuming menace that their superstitious cousins believed us to be. In fact, they saw us as their world's only salvation – their only chance to avoid destroying themselves when their technology reached the appropriate level. And they decided that they had to sabotage the *Deragathon*."

"So they had Zepp smuggle Griddle aboard to keep the ship from destroying us. I can't believe it. It's so devious. Even my kid sister wouldn't think of something that perverse."

"And then, just in case the others were right, they sent him over here to make sure we couldn't destroy their world."

Helen squealed in delight at the final twist of chamalian subterfuge. "You know, Mark, I think I'm beginning to find these creatures remarkably appealing, in a twisted sort of way."

"So am I," he replied. "And that's the problem."

"What problem?" she asked. Then she narrowed her brow as she looked him in the eyes. "You look like you're worried about something more serious than that."

"You know about the Basic Aggressiveness Potential Assessment, don't you?" Mark asked.

"Oh, that. No wonder you're so glum. Zepp's people are every bit as smart as they sound. They don't know it, but they're right. We could still do exactly what they fear most."

"We've spent an awful lot of time considering what conditions might require us to exterminate an entire species," he said.

"It wouldn't be hard," Helen said, her voice betraying more than a hint of bitterness. "The doctor could cook up a virus tailored to wipe out every chamalian on the planet in less than a year. Or sterilize them all in a generation."

"But if they all belong to the same species, you wouldn't be taking out just the intelligent ones, you'd be taking the wild ones too. A whole ecostructure – every furry, warm-blooded creature on the planet."

She nodded her head slowly and seriously. "It's enough to keep you awake at night feeling guilty."

"Not guilty. Responsible. Responsibility comes first, then the guilt."

"But I thought the chances of flunking the termination assessment were minimal. Is there something you're not telling me?"

"You don't flunk the termination assessment, you ace it. It's hard, but not impossible. And setting fire to your cities is a good first step."

"I suppose attacking the survey ship counts too."

"Yes, it does. And the more we learn about them, the worse I feel."

"Should you really be so guilty? It's not your fault the chamalians are in such a mess."

"No, it isn't," he said sullenly. "But you know who helps score the test, don't you?"

"Oh," Helen said softly.

"Right – the cultural survey team. Me."

CHAPTER EIGHT

The next watch-cycle was long and tense.

The *Cousteau* remained at emergency stations throughout, with the regular crew in the ship control posts and the scientific staff confined to their work areas and their bunks.

All through the nightwatch, the technicians worked to bring the fusion core back into fine balance. The ship's systems were cut back to reduce the power load, with lights dimmed and auxiliary equipment shut down. Conversations were soft and muted, but tended to rise in volume and pitch when people started discussing their options for survival if the core went down.

Mark and Val Nordland were left with only each other's company throughout the next morningwatch.

Mark was still a little resentful. He never really expected Nordland to back him up during the meeting. Nordland was one of the consensus builders in the anthropological community. That was why he was here. He had helped negotiate a resolution to the textwar that had put Mark aboard the *Cousteau*, so it was only logical to send him along as a backup – to keep the young hotblood in line.

But before that Nordland had helped develop the original consensus – the one that brought first the Space Corps and then Mark's friends into the discussion – that the survey ship should interfere as little as possible in the native culture. That consensus had never been formally overturned, but it had quickly become irrelevant when the military security people got into the picture.

What bothered Mark about Nordland was his basic passivity. He was averse to taking risks. He wanted everything to be simple, safe, and orderly. He wasn't opposed to interference for purposes of science, but because deep in his heart he was afraid of the alien, the different, and the unusual.

Mark had no such apprehension. That was why he was so much quicker to accept Zepp's explanation. And why Val was so unwilling to do the same.

So they said little to one another throughout the long watch. In any case, they had more than enough to do without distractions, evaluating the communications intercept data that was continuing to flood the *Cousteau*'s datatanks as the world below devoted more and more energy to ripping itself asunder.

Then, after a cold lunch eaten in the survey lab, Nordland disappeared.

When he returned, he had news that first elated Mark, then wounded him to the soul.

"They've decided to send down a landing party – and to return Zepp and Griddle to their homes," he said.

Mark allowed himself a momentary flash of triumph. Val allowed him to glory in the moment before shooting him down, first adding to his altitude. "And they're sending you down with them." Mark felt himself leaving the deck, as if the *Cousteau*'s artificial gravity had abruptly ceased to function.

"But before you lose control of yourself, I need to warn you – this is not a reward for your perceptive analysis of the situation. They still don't believe you. At least that's what they say." The sense of soaring was replaced by sense of falling, as Mark's moral vertigo kicked in once again.

"What?"

"The official explanation is that they don't believe your evaluation and they think you've made a mistake in analysis. There is no threat from Griddle and no reason to evacuate him from the *Cousteau*."

"So why are they doing it anyway?"

"It's entirely an ethical question. The time has come to allow the aliens the chance to return to their homelands, if that is what they want to do. We can continue our studies there, if we want, and that's why you and Helen Castain have been assigned to the landing party."

"But that's nonsense," Mark protested. "That's just an excuse to cover up their own fear and suspicion."

"No doubt, Mark. But you have to understand the cultural context in which Captain Newton and Lieutenant Barrett operate. It is a very materialistic and mechanistic one and it doesn't handle certain concepts very well. That is an evaluation that I have kept to myself – and I would advise you to exercise similar discretion."

"But – "

"Wait, there's more," Nordland cautioned, the lines in his face seeming to cut deeper with his darkening mood. "The Captain and Lieutenant Barrett have been considering an alternate explanation for the problems with the ship's equipment – one that doesn't rely on an alien agent as the precipitant." Mark tried to decode Nordland's elliptical syntax, then realized suddenly what he meant.

"They can't suspect me!"

"They certainly can. And they believe it is a simpler explanation of events than yours. You have had access to the control panels in the isolation labs, they say, and could have engineered the breakdowns. The only thing that can't figure is how you could throw the fusion core out of balance.

"And they think they have every reason in the world to suspect you. After all, you represent the group that opposes the terminal decision. If it weren't for you, they'd have a free hand to do whatever they want to with Chamal."

"If that's so, then why haven't they come to question me about it yet?" He looked out the door into the passageway at the sudden fear that they were about to, but the corridor was empty.

"Because they don't really believe it's true," he said. "They're just rationalizing their suspicions and their fears. In any case, they would like to get both you and the aliens off the *Cousteau* for the time being. And any justification that they can come up with is just fine with them."

They didn't trust him and they wanted him off the ship.

"And what about you?" he asked. "You don't believe it either, do you?" Nordland smiled and softened his features.

"Mark, you have to be careful not to lose your objectivity."

"You think that's what I did?"

"Perhaps. On the other hand, 'there are more things in Heaven and Earth than are dreamt of in your philosophies or mine, Horatio.' And not everything has a neat explanation that fits into the cultural context of men like Barrett and the Captain."

Somehow Mark didn't find that reassuring.

***

Zepp sat on the deck in the warm semi-darkness listening to the hum of the ship. The vibration of the various machineries of the angels combined to create soft music that he could feel through the soles of his feet and the tips of his fingers.

He knew that somewhere was the mighty engine that the angels used to cross the vast space of his solar system and the powerful energy source that made it work. He wondered if that was the dominant bass note that carried the rest of the vibrations on its back.

If so, then that would explain the dimming of the lights. It had come some time after that deep bass resonance changed from a steady pitch to a warbling, unpredictable throb.

For a moment, he imagined Griddle's night mind following the vibrations through the rigid metal of the *Cousteau*, tracking them to their sources, invading them with some unknown mental energy, and setting them against themselves. The blue pilgrim must be able to sense the different notes just as he did. Was that how he worked his cursed magic on the angels' technology? And was he behind the sudden change in the tune of the *Cousteau*?

"Something is wrong," Griddle said.

"That was obvious when the lights first dimmed," Zepp replied.

"No, I mean something more. I can feel it. Something terribly wrong is about to happen."

"What could be worse than to be held captive by the angels while they weigh your fate?"

"Being set free, back where we all started," Griddle replied.

***

At least Helen Castain still believed in him – to a certain point, if not beyond.

"Let's just say for the sake of argument that you're innocent," she said, "Say that what you believe about Griddle is true. Since the

Captain is following the other hypothesis, someone ought to consider the implications of yours."

"That's very nice of you," Mark said.

"I'm just serving the interests of objective science here," she said, shaking her head. "We have to explore all the possibilities."

"So explore."

"You need some kind of mechanism to explain this phenomenon. Is there some kind of parallel to it that we know of in human beings?"

"All the parallels that I can come up with are the cultural equivalents of hypnotic suggestion. Like they said – it only works because you believe in it."

"You mean like shamans and curses?"

"Exactly."

"But those are anthropological cases. I was thinking more of human psychic phenomena. Like poltergeists."

"Zepp talked a lot about those who know from afar. That's called clairvoyance."

"And some theorists believe that poltergeists are psychokinetic episodes of troubled adolescents."

"And then there's the other explanation."

"What's that?"

"Maybe he's just cursed," Mark said.

After a moment of reflection, Helen said: "Then he must be terribly unhappy."

"I know I would be. In fact, I'm beginning to know exactly how he feels."

"No wonder he's so passive. Probably got a good case of clinical depression going. I wonder if relieving him of his depression would cure him of his curse. Sort of like an adolescent growing out of being a poltergeist."

"Sounds great," Mark said, his mind drawn unwillingly to his own predicament. "Can you do that?"

"If it were you or I, I'd say sure, in a minute. There's all kinds of useful medications. But for Griddle, I'm afraid we're going to have to wait for a full brain-chemistry analysis. And that's not on the schedule for a couple of months."

"Can you do that without hurting him? It sounds horrible – you've got a cure for his depression, but you have to remove the brain."

Helen frowned at him. "Of course it wouldn't hurt him. We wouldn't use HIS brain. We've got a couple dozen on ice right now, and once we get down on the surface, we can find some live samples to work with."

"You know, it's even possible that they might be able to tell you what you want to know about their brain chemistry once you get there."

"Gee," Helen said, a distant gaze falling over her eyes, "I didn't even think of that. How interesting."

"Anyway, curing Griddle of his curse is only part of the problem," Mark said. "It wouldn't eliminate the suspicion from Barrett and the captain."

"Probably not. What exactly did you do to get them so worked up?"

"Like I said, I won a textwar."

"I remember that. You promised to tell me the story some time." She smiled, fell silent, and gave him an expectant look that started to turn demanding when he wasn't immediately forthcoming.

"Well?" she asked after a long pause.

"All right. If you insist. I was on the side that questioned the Space Corps when it began drawing up the protocols for the technological quarantine of the aliens." When the radio signals from Chamal were detected and the *Cousteau* was commissioned to investigate, the Corps had insisted on keeping things secure. The survey ship would not carry replicator technology. Databases would be scoured for any sensitive technology. Equipment would be designed using the simplest systems instead of the most advanced.

And the Corps insisted on preparing a long list of "prophylactic" measures that could be instituted if necessary. If the aliens presented a threat, they would have to be neutralized. Even if it meant destroying them.

"The flames on the virtual exchange were enough to melt a comet," Mark said.

"I remember that," Helen replied, nodding. "Quite a few of us joined the protest."

"If it had just been a military security matter, the Space Corps probably would have won. But we managed to convince them that there was more to it than that."

"That much I knew, but my memory of the details is sketchy. My menu on the network didn't give much out about it."

"That was because we took it to a textwar and quenched the flames," Mark explained.

A textwar was a lot more difficult to conduct than the easy bluster and bellowing of the virtual debates. The rules were strict. Participants were barred from virtual appearances and limited to written submissions – with sources and cites. But a textwar also allowed anyone to join in who was willing to follow the rules. And that meant that even young students like Mark could quickly move to the front lines.

"I was lucky. I was studying this very subject when the debate broke out," he said. "I was a member of the investigation team that went into Tycho after the mutiny."

"You were at Tycho?" she asked, an air of awe and respect appearing suddenly in her tone. "You do get around a lot."

Mark felt embarrassed. "I wrote a dissertation on the alienation of a culture and its consequences on individuals. So I was up to date on what was involved in the extermination of a culture. Ironically, I argued that some cultures can harden their hearts and become so antagonistic to the rest of humanity that they have to be treated the same as any other pathology."

"Treated how?"

"Either by altering the culture in significant ways or by breaking it up entirely. Unfortunately, it was an argument that was too late to help the survivors of the mutiny. Not to mention too late for the so-called 'rescue' by the Space Corps."

"But not too late for the aliens here on Chamal."

"No. Maybe not. I don't know yet."

"And why not?"

"Because it's not that simple. Because of why we won the argument. You see, we were able to show that the criteria the Space Corps wanted to use was hopelessly inadequate to the task. It wasn't so much that we were opposed to what they wanted to do. It was just that they were going about it all wrong. They were only concerned with technological capabilities and nothing else. We showed them there were threats they might miss entirely. Threats from their culture. Things that could come back to hurt us long after it was too late to do anything. It doesn't matter whether you can make nuclear weapons or orbital lasers. If your culture is destructive and dysfunctional, you'll find some means to carry out your will – even if it means inventing those things. The trick is knowing what to look for."

"So they sent you along to make sure they didn't miss anything?"

"That's an oversimplification, but one that works."

"So what's the problem?"

"The problem is that the more I learn about this world and its inhabitants, the more of those things I find in their culture."

***

Zepp felt as though he should have been frightened when the angels in the isolation suits escorted them out of the chamber they had called home for several days, but he was not.

He knew what was going to happen. Mark had explained it to him.

He felt as though he should have been surprised that Griddle's premonition had come true, but he was not.

It didn't even take true wisdom to anticipate the angels' next move. They had to get rid of Griddle – that was obvious. Once they knew what he was. And since there was no way of being sure that Zepp wasn't trying to misdirect their attention, no way of knowing that Zepp wasn't the jinx instead of his companion, he had to go too.

And now they were about to make the journey back into the chaos of Chamal. Zepp felt wistful at the loss of the safety and comfort of the angels' ship. The strange creatures aboard it had treated him in ways he had never been treated before, and he knew he would miss that. The more he thought about it, the more he realized why they were like that. It was the purity of their breed. They had no reason to hate one another, no excuse to abuse and assault one another, no claim to kinship or tribe that they could use to justify bloodshed and pain. No wonder they were so docile.

And yet, they were doing the worst thing they could do to him, sending him back below.

He almost hoped that Griddle's curse would save them from that fate. And he was afraid that it just might decide that the cold sleep of death was preferable to the hot fire of life on Chamal. It was a choice that Zepp himself had not made yet, tempting as it might seem at times.

The angels led the two of them to a small spacecraft. Zepp recognized it for what it was immediately, while Griddle accepted the news without comment. They were strapped into seats in the back, and a short time later three more angels appeared.

Zepp recognized two of them instantly as Mark and Helen, but the third was a stranger to him. The stranger appeared to be senior to Zepp's two friends, judging by the way they paid him deference. He moved with confidence and without hesitation to the front of the craft, while the other two angels pulled themselves into place uncertainly.

After a while, Zepp felt his ears pop. He recognized the feeling for what it was – the sealing of the craft's pressure doors. He didn't have to wait long for the sudden stomach-twisting drop of the craft as it began its long plunge down from orbit.

The trip felt longer than it was. Zepp knew that the time was stretching itself out because of the stress he felt. Not knowing where they were or how much farther they had to go left him feeling isolated and powerless.

Then the sunlight broke through the window beside him as they crossed the terminator and tore into the upper levels of Chamal's deep atmosphere. The craft bucked and swerved from left to right as they slowed and banked in great curves, searching for an unknown destination.

The worst of the buffeting was over when Mark turned to look back at Zepp. The voice of the wise teacher sounded in the speaker behind Zepp's head.

"We're heading for the rift valley first," it said. "You told us that's where Griddle came from." Zepp shuddered. Were they really going to take them back home? And what if they delivered him back to Suridash, into the hands of his tribe. The children of Jobe would make swift work of him, he was sure of that. His blood ran cold at the thought of it.

Perhaps he could persuade them not to do that.

In the meantime, he could see the distant walls of the rift valley rising up to flank them on either side. Down below, the network of rivers and canals divided the valley floor into great squares of cultivated land. The big river cut through the middle of the valley, a ribbon of silver on a checkered board of varying shades of blue. A gray mass spread out from the thinnest section of the river, and as they grew closer it resolved itself into the complex intricacy of a chamalian city – the smoke of a thousand fires lingering overhead.

"Ring Po Do," said the voice of the wise teacher. "Where is Griddle's home?"

A chill ran up Zepp's spine. Griddle had no home. He was an outcast from every other place on Chamal. He had been living in the warrens of an old Red Monkey fortress when Zepp found him. After a moment's indecision, he decided that was as good a place to go as any. As long as it wasn't the city …

"Head south along the largest tributary until you reach the rift wall," Zepp said. "Then look up to the top of the cliffs. You will see the castle that Griddle called home." A few minutes later they streaked by the sheer basalt walls that formed the southern edge of the great rift valley. They were almost too fast to spot the gaping mouths of the fortress, but Helen called out when they went by and the craft turned gracefully as it slowed. On the second pass, they loitered casually enough for Zepp to pick out the rusting hulks of the ancient guns near the top of the cliffside battlements.

"I can set us down in the lake," the wise teacher said, adopting the false tone of the third angel for Zepp's convenience. "It's about two mumble-mumble from the base of the cliff. A short walk from the look of it." Zepp looked from Mark's face to Helen's, and then over at the third angel, wondering what they were all waiting for. Then he realized they were waiting for him to speak, to approve of the choice of landing sites. How difficult it was to stop thinking like a captive and a prisoner.

"That's good. A short walk over and a long walk up. Maybe you will learn something about Chamal at the same time." They turned one last time and descended for a landing.

***

Emerging from the *Cousteau*'s pinnace *Belle Marie* struck Mark as being born once again into the natural world.

For nearly a year, he had been living in space in one vessel or container or another. The lighting had been gentle on the eyes, the colors simple and unvaried, the air sweetened and controlled, and the horizons short and restricted.

But to step into the thick, moist air of Chamal was to become a new creature freshly emerged into nature. The richness of smells filled him up, tripping off memories long buried of youthful explorations of basements, back yards, antique farmhouses, and the African rainforest. The profusion of colors – Mark had never realized how bright a color green could be or how many shades of it were possible – set his eyes agog. The depth of sounds, peeping that reminded him of a trillion tree fogs and served as soundings for every meter of ground for as far as he could see.

Every nerve ending was alive. The thrill of the strange environment sent waves of euphoria, alternating with waves of fearful anxiety, through his body.

For a while, everything that had been Mark Paradis was subsumed by the task of dealing with an intensely real and intensely alien place. Every minute was an eternity. Every second a lifetime.

The forest was full of things that at a casual glance resembled the trees, saplings, and brush of a terrestrial wood, but on closer examination were odd in root, leaf, and stem. Animals scurried around at the edge of distance, fooling Mark into seeing them as squirrels, birds, or rabbits, until a second look revealed some interloper into the forest of expectation. One was long and orange with a spherical chamalian head. Another stopped and stood up, appearing at first to be a child, but with an old and wrinkled face.

Then they entered one of the tunnels that cut into the basalt cliff face, square black shards of rock littering the ground around the entrance. Griddle led the way, rushing with delight once Helen showed him how to work the handtorch.

The stones threatened to close in on him, but at the same time absorbed the sound and light and reduced the sensory overload that was calming in its own way. Until he heard the chittering and hoarse breathing of chamalian animals down dark side corridors.

The long journey up and up and up through the oppressive, sweaty rock, lit only by dancing shafts of light and pursued by long-dead ghosts and shadows that jerked and pounced, ended in a great cavern whose far end disappeared in impenetrable gloom and whose near end in the embrasures for the rusting hulks of two huge artillery pieces.

Mark, Helen, Lieutenant Barrett, and the two aliens stood at the lip of the cavity, looking out across the Great Rift Valley towards the far side, at least a hundred kilometers away, the line of cliffs no more than a deeper streak of blue against the blue horizon.

Nothing Mark had ever seen before had prepared him for the view from the cliffside fortress that Griddle called home – not Africa, not the Grand Canyon of North America, not the vast depths of space.

He walked around unsteadily, nervous about the sheer drop just beyond the low wall, and then stopped near Helen.

"Are you as completely overwhelmed by this experience as I am?" he asked. His words seemed to be swallowed up by the air and were nearly gone before they reached his own ears.

"It's the serotonin," she said.

"The what?"

"Excess serotonin," Helen repeated. "It's a brain hormone. It regulates sleep, dreaming, and consciousness. It's an occupational hazard of people who work in isolated environments – sailors, Antarctic explorers, space travelers. You build up an excess. It's quite a psychedelic experience, according to the literature. And to answer your question, I am every bit as completely overwhelmed by this experience as you are.”

“What about him?” Mark asked, flipping a thumb at Barrett.

“Him too, I suppose. That's assuming his brain produces any serotonin. From what I've been told, junior officers aren't supposed to have an imagination – that's reserved for their seniors.” Zepp began to chatter and the professor translated.

“This fortress – and the Rift Valley – once belonged to the Red Monkeys,” he said. “Every eight eights of eight years, they rise out of the valley's gene pool, create mighty empires, invent hundreds of new machines, new tools, new devices, grow rich, fat, and powerful, and then bitter, sad, and jealous, and then, finally, they destroy themselves in great wars that shatter the civilization they've built.”

“Are they due back any time soon?” Helen asked, sending a sudden chill up Mark's back.

“No,” Zepp replied. “It's been three eights of eight years since they built this fortress and lost their war. This time, though, they managed to avoid a total disaster. Thanks to the knowledge of the Seedkeepers, some of them have managed to maintain a small breeding pool at the enclave in my home city, Suridash. Unfortunately, they are no longer able to produce the wonders they raised up down in the valley.”

“What kind of range did these guns have?” Barrett asked with a husky voice. He had been going through the acclimation process and was still wrestling with his body's histamines, despite the megadoses of blockers he'd been given and the twenty-four hours or so that he'd had to adapt.

“You can see down below,” Griddle said. “Off in the distance, the valley floor changes color. Down below, you can see the little ponds left from the shell craters. Where the color changes, that's as far as the ponds go.” Mark let his jaw drop loose as he looked at Griddle, then at Helen, who aped his amazement.

"Griddle, that's the most words I've heard out of you at once since the day we found you," Helen said.

Griddle waved his hands in what Mark had learned to recognize as a shrug. "This is where I lived the most. This is where I was happiest." Mark daringly approached the parapet, looking over to see the circular ponds, scattered randomly about, many overlapping one another. They stretched into the distance, and just as Griddle had said, about thirty klicks out the valley floor turned darker, robbed of its dappling of shellholes.

"You may like it, but I don't think it agreed with you," Helen said. "We found fluid still in your lungs. These damp old caves are no place to set up housekeeping."

"They are far from the rest of my race," Griddle said. "That's what suits me."

"I wish there were more we could do for you," she said.

"I don't," Griddle answered. "I don't wish for anything but peace and quiet. I have had too much excitement for too long. And I wish you would all go away too."

Mark felt embarrassed and he could see that Helen was disappointed. Barrett seemed insensitive to the conversation, but Mark took a closer look at his puffy face and red, watery eyes and decided that was as likely a cause as any character flaws on the Space Corps officer's part.

"They shattered everything they could reach," Zepp said, appearing at Mark's elbow on the breezy edge of the embrasure. "There used to be a great series of canals that brought sweetwater to every field in the valley. It silted up a hundred years after the last of the wars. There were mills and big factories, but half of them have fallen into ruin. From up here, it all looks so pretty and perfect, but down on the ground it is all rot and decay."

"You sound awfully cheerful today."

"It is this place," Zepp said. "The first time I came here, I realized that the plot Tedrak and Whirlpitt had laid out for me was likely to succeed. This place is proof that chaos and disorder are the fate of everything Chamal attempts to do, of everything we each attempt to do. None of has any hope."

Mark felt the cold tendrils of despair curling around his heart, just like the cold tendrils of air reaching out from the back of the caverns, back where the rusted rails and scattered powder barrels disappeared into the shadows.

"This fort defended nothing and used its great guns to shoot at rebels," Zepp said. "The rebels, in the end, were everywhere – everyone who wasn't a Red Monkey had become one. Now it's happening again. Only the Red Monkeys have been replaced by the Blue Monkeys, and they aren't nearly as good at fighting and building and surviving."

"Speaking of Blue Monkeys," Barrett said, "we have to decide where to go from here. The game plan is to find your political leaders and see if we can arrange some kind of dialog – since that warship of yours doesn't seem to be interested in talking."

"'Take us to your leader,'" Helen said comically. "It's an old joke, but I guess it makes sense."

"My political leaders are far, far away from here," Zepp said. "Suridash is across the mountains and down the sea, deep in the desert belt. It is ten days journey from here by fast boat."

"What about the Blue Monkeys?" Barrett asked.

"They're no longer the political power they were before our

arrival," Mark said.

Barrett rubbed his eyes and began to sneeze. When he was done, his face was red and he had trouble breathing. Helen went looking through her bag of tricks and pulled out an inhaler that helped restore Barrett's respiration.

"Actually Zepp is better at explaining it than I am," he said. "He just seems to take a lot of the turmoil for granted."

CHAPTER NINE

Zepp was happy to oblige the angels in their pursuit of knowledge about the Red Monkeys, the Blue Monkeys, and the Great Rift Valley they inhabited – despite a half-hearted attempt by Griddle to dissuade him.

"You shouldn't be telling them this stuff," he said, fidgeting nervously as though the act of criticizing Zepp demanded too much of his weak will.

"It can only help them."

"Is there something wrong with helping them?" Zepp asked, annoyed at Griddle's temerity, or what there was of it.

"Yes. Maybe not now, but in the end, they'll use it against us."

"Perhaps. But what do you mean by 'us'? The Blue Monkeys? The rebels? Suridash? Do you care that much about anyone else on this planet that we should avoid giving their enemies aid?"

Griddle shrugged sheepishly and mewled softly in frustration.

"Don't worry," Zepp said at last. "I'm still keeping the important secrets to myself." But Griddle just shuffled off to sulk in a corner where the sun warmed the stone.

The Red Monkeys, Zepp told the angels, were the greatest geniuses Chamal had ever known – except perhaps for the snowmen of Kwikorak, who were wise in a different way.

They were responsible for all the great inventions of chamalian history. The last incarnation of Red Monkeys had brought forth the steam engine, the petroleum engine, the power boat, steel-making, large-scale electrical generation, rockets, and long-range artillery – all in a couple generations. The incarnation before that had brought Chamal the printing press, telescopes, hearty strains of grain, advanced chemistry, irrigation canal systems, water-wheel mills, and factories.

"Is the rift the only technological center?" Barrett asked. Zepp saw the warrior in him and in his question.

"No," he replied. "The Red Monkeys were the innovators, but any innovation on Chamal spreads quickly – just like the seed of wisdom itself. Everyone uses engines and steel and rockets – everyone who can afford the price in gold and effort." But there were innovators elsewhere, he added. The great hairy snowmen of Kwikorak were also known as great inventors. But their main talents were spiritual, not intellectual. They had given Jobe, the founder of Zepp's tribe, his own spiritual education more than two centuries ago. They also were famous for their elaborate little devices – clocks and cookstoves and counting machines and anything else that could be fit into a box small enough to carry into the mountain fastness that straddled Chamal's equator due south of the Great Rift Valley. In the last few decades they had discovered electronics, which had opened up a world of vast potential for their convoluted imaginations.

Barrett persisted. He wanted to know who else had access to the planet's highest technology. Who had built the *Deragathon*? Zepp did his best to tell all that he could without revealing the most damaging elements of the story behind the warship. He felt embarrassed at the effort he put into his subterfuge. After all, he already had betrayed his race once by sabotaging the ship and leaving the angels with the advantage over his planet. This little bit more hardly mattered. But it was enough for him. He knew that the trick to surviving was to hold back what he knew for as long as possible, letting it escape only when he had no other choice.

So he continued. In addition to the Blue Monkeys and the snowmen, he explained, the alliance had included Meshkar and Arkaria. The former was a collection of trading states that ringed a high inland sea to the south of Zepp's own Suridash. Its gold-filled banks had paid for the great warship. The latter was the deep basin in the southern desert belt where the great-winged fliers made their home. They, too, were among the innovators of Chamal. But much of their knowledge they kept to themselves, hiding it jealously. The Arkarians were responsible for the lack of any real progress in aviation on Chamal.

"Whenever anyone tried to build a flying machine, they would find it and tear it apart," Zepp explained. "More often than not, while it was still in flight. That's why rockets were finally successful. They moved too fast for the fliers to catch them." The expedition also had included the vegetarians of Rikabar, Chamal's only ocean-going empire, and the carnivores of Birhat, great cats who ruled the steppes far to the west of Rikabar.

"And they're still all aboard the *Deragathon*?" Barrett asked.

"I'm not sure who's still alive up there," Zepp replied. "Things fell apart quickly once you arrived – and once Whirlpitt set Griddle and me loose. But afterwards, we were locked up, and Whirlpitt told us little of what was happening." Zepp's best understanding was that the Birhat cats had been undone by their slaves – who also served as a ready food supply. And the Blue Monkeys were struggling to deal with a rebellion among the different breeds that did their labor for them. Control of the vessel still remained in the hands of the

Meshkarian admiral – or rather in the hands of his young son, who had taken command when his father suffered a nervous collapse. And the crew from Suridash seemed to be in the commander's good graces, or Whirlpitt wouldn't have had the freedom to send Zepp and Griddle to the *Cousteau*.

But many days had passed since then, and nothing ever remained the way it was for long when aliens were involved.

"So the valley is also in revolt?" Barrett asked.

"As I understand it," Zepp replied. "The revolution on the ground began at the same time as the mutiny aboard the *Deragathon*. There have always been rebels in the valley – so many, in fact, that they spent more time squabbling among themselves than they did fighting the Blue Monkeys. But the sight of the *Deragathon* passing through the sky each night was enough to bring them all together."

"And what was so terrible about the *Deragathon* that it unified the factions?" Barrett asked.

Zepp weighed the question carefully. Was Barrett so innocent after all? Didn't he know better? As a warrior, he should have grasped the obvious, Zepp thought. After all, even Zepp, a bookclerk from a tiny city-state in the middle of nowhere knew what made the warship so frightening. He answered when he realized that the question had been serious.

"Because when they finished destroying you, they planned to use it to eliminate their foes here on Chamal, one by one, from the high safety of space."

✦✦✦

The questioning stopped when Barrett was hit by a large

histamine attack, which left him wheezing and gasping for air. Helen was quick to produce another ventilator to help him open up his bronchial tubes and sinuses and restore the flow of air to his lungs.

He looked around the cavern and located Zepp and Griddle, eating foodsticks from Mark's pack. Then he motioned to Mark and Helen to come closer.

"Turn off that AI for a minute," he said. "I don't want them to hear this." When Mark had secured the professor, Barrett went on in a low voice: "We've got a problem, folks. It's mostly mine, but you've got your share of it. They finished the diagnostics on the fusion core and it isn't good. We need some time to bring the power down and try a cold start to bring it back up into balance. But we don't dare do that while the *Deragathon* is still a threat."

"What happens if we don't get the core back into balance?" Helen asked.

"Worst case: we could lose the *Cousteau*."

Mark felt a sudden chill and Helen let out a tiny gasp. "You mean we could be stuck here on Chamal?"

"Until someone came to rescue us. We can probably get a message probe back home. But that would still mean a lot of extra years before we could get out of here. And surviving until then would be problematic."

"And would depend a lot on chamalian politics," Mark said, the light now shining through his eyes.

"It would make everyone a lot more comfortable if we could neutralize the *Deragathon* before we have to make repairs. While we still have the option of making repairs."

"And you figure you can do it here on the ground?" Mark asked.

"I don't know where else we can go," Barrett said. "I wouldn't suggest flying up to the ship itself and knocking on their airlock doors."

"It might be easier than trying to sort things out down here. Their political culture is not a quick study. We'd need their help to even begin to understand what we're doing."

"I realize that, but it's a chance we'll have to take. Just how well-connected is our ambassador?" Barrett asked.

"Not well at all," Mark said. He wondered how much – or how little – Barrett knew about the two aliens. Not much, it was likely. He hadn't needed to know much. But he and the Captain had cooked up this scheme on the basis of what little knowledge they did have, and it was likely to fail as a result, Mark realized with a sinking heart.

"Zepp is a bottom-level agent of his state-organization," he said. "They're using him for their own purposes. Mainly to distract us, as I understand it. You don't have to believe in Griddle as a jinx in order to see how that part of the plot works."

"Right," Barrett said. "We spend all our time concentrating on them while they prepare for a second attack."

"If you assume they're planning a second attack," Helen said. "I don't know if that's true or not."

"From what Zepp says, planning a second attack is second nature to these aliens," Mark said. "They're always playing the game a few moves ahead of where they are."

"How much does he know?" Barrett asked. "Who can he influence?"

"He's a relatively young member of his culture. There doesn't seem to be a formal education process, but he and his tribe are up to their necks in the interstate political maneuvering that put the *Deragathon* up there. I suppose he could find out just what's going on up there. Do you want me to ask him?"

Barrett's forehead wrinkled up, ruining the baby-face expression that he usually wore. "I don't know if I want to show my cards to the other side just yet. Especially when you consider the hardest part of this deal."

"What's that?"

"We're accelerating the timetable on the termination assessment." Mark felt his heart jump inside his chest. "By how much?"

"You should start your field evaluation now," Barrett said. "We may not have a whole lot of time to complete it if things go bad aboard the *Cousteau*. Or if the aliens stage another attack."

"But I can't learn enough about an entire race to give you a reliable result in a matter of days," Mark protested. "That would take months – maybe longer."

"Then learn as much as you can," Barrett said. "It's got to be done. If it looks like we're going to lose the *Cousteau*, we may have no choice but to make a summary analysis and work from that." Mark started to protest further, but swallowed his words. Barrett was bluffing, he decided. He had to be. He was playing a deadly game to ward off fears of what might happen.

But Mark realized he was trying to ward off fears of his own. He knew that there was every chance that the aliens would fail an early and superficial test. And if that happened, what would Captain Fletcher and Lieutenant Barrett do? "So when we talk to your ape, make sure you don't let on what we might have to do," Barrett said. "This is military security now, and the worst thing we can do is to breach it. That's the reason I'm nervous about relying on the alien."

Mark bared an ironic smile. "I don't see how we have any other choice if you want his help. And we can't do this without it."

Barrett sighed, then closed his eyes. "Go ahead. But don't let on anything at all about the dangers we face. It shouldn't be necessary. Anyone in our position would be worried about the warship."

Zepp was eager to help – and in a better position to do so than anyone first thought.

"We are close to the capital of the Rift Valley," he said. "But I don't know what I could do there. Everyone I knew there is aboard the *Deragathon* now." Mark felt his shoulders sag and saw the worry deepen the creases in Barrett's brow.

Then Zepp jumped up and danced quickly around the stone floor. "Wait! Wait! I have an idea. I know who we can ask for help." Mark waited until Zepp to calm down before he pressed him for details. It was the most agitated he had seen the creature since he came aboard the *Cousteau*.

"The pilgrims," he said. "The Pilgrims of the Way of Jobe. They are from Suridash and they will help us."

"Are you sure?" Barrett asked.

"He sounds sure to me," Helen said.

Reluctantly at first, then with more enthusiasm, Barrett began to nod in agreement as Zepp explained his plan. Within a few minutes, they were agreed on their next step.

First, however, they had to return to the *Belle Marie* for the trip to Ring Po Do, the great city on the Daughter of All Waters.

"Griddle will accompany us back down to the base of the cliff," Zepp announced.

Helen was quick to protest. She had carried a pack full of supplies for the morose blue cat intended to improve his living conditions, including a permalamp that doubled as a camp heater, a blanket, and as many foodsticks as they could carry.

"We don't need to make things worse for him," she said.

But Zepp said there was no other way to do it.

"There are creatures who live in the tunnels and passageways of the old fortress," he said. "They are not ghosts. Ghosts would be preferable. But they are familiar with Griddle and they leave him alone. As long he is with us, we are safe." Barrett looked puzzled again, but did not argue. Mark felt a chill, but also a tiny bit of vindication. Whether he liked it or not, even Barrett had to admit that on this world, chamalian rules were observed.

***

They landed at the main field near the spaceport, a few thousand meters from the nearest structure or craft. Barrett said that was the closest he should get with the *Belle Marie*'s engine exhaust. He also pointed out that it also gave them a clear field of view on every angle of approach.

Mark was very aware of what Barrett called the "military solution" to their situation. It was not meant to be a method for solving their dilemma, but was more of the answer to a problem of geometry, involving the placement of forces in order to defend a position.

Since even Zepp was unwilling to leave the *Belle Marie* without an escort, Mark was in no hurry to attempt an "anthropological solution" to the situation – though eventually that was what he would have to do for the entire planet. He respected Zepp's judgment on the issue. The chamalian told him that the last he had heard of the spaceport at Ring Po Do, it was not a place that any one faction could hold for long.

When the clouds of dust and smoke from the landing finally

settled in the still, thick air, the sun was already dropping quickly towards the western end of the valley. There was no way anyone could see to make contact with the Pilgrims of the Way before dark – and therefore no alternative but to spend the night on the tarmac.

Barrett promised them that their defenses would hold. The hull was shielded to be impervious to the dust and debris of space, and most projectile weapons were useless against it. And if they brought up anything heavier, he could move the pinnace.

He could do that in any case, but Mark and Barrett both agreed that the information they would acquire by staying put outvalued any risk to the craft. They were not to be disappointed.

The first squads of armed chamalians appeared within a few minutes, ringing the landing site at a considerable distance, leveling their weapons at the *Belle Marie* from prone positions on the concrete.

When the circle was complete, a single weapon opened fire. A red light appeared in the depths of the pinnace's control tank and information on the point of impact of the projectile spilled down to the floor.

Barrett adjusted a control and issued a coded command and a puff of smoke appeared next to the trooper that had fired the shot. To his credit, the trooper didn't flinch. But there were no more test shots for a while.

As the shadows gathered themselves together and spread across the field, more chamalians showed up. These were not armed troopers, however, but a hostile mob, carrying poles, torches, and makeshift weapons of metal and stone. They pressed on towards the troopers, who in turn reversed their positions to defend the *Belle Marie* – and themselves.

They watched the confrontation on the long-range surface scanners, the monitor lighting up the pinnace's cabin. The mob advanced hesitantly, then Helen gasped at the sight of their front rank falling to the fire of the troopers.

They fell back, but not for long. There were more and more coming all the time. Barrett's battle AI showed the surface map, with the mob a growing orange mass to the south. Eventually, after less than half an hour, there enough chamalians pushing at the rear of the crowd that those in the front had nowhere to turn.

Like a skilled general, the mass of random pressures probed and poked at the armed positions ringing the *Belle Marie*. Almost self-consciously, it spilled into the weak points, where the weapons fire was the lightest. Before the troopers could react, the mob broke through their lines and swept across the field. The unit fell back in good order, with most of those who had fallen rescued by their comrades.

The mob continued to pursue them, however, as they rushed across the field towards the north. Barrett was now concerned with the activities of those who stayed behind and were congregating around the *Belle Marie*.

After a short time, which Mark presumed they spent engaging in debate about how best to attack the alien craft, the chamalians began lugging, chugging, and dragging pieces of furniture, boxes, tree trunks, and other large inflammable objects across the field to deposit them at the base of the spacecraft.

Barrett let them complete the preparations, then ignite the fuel before he responded. A surface that was designed to withstand up to 2,500 degrees of atmospheric entry would have little trouble with the flames of this bonfire, but the Space Corps officer was taking no chances.

He lit off the engines only briefly. But they were enough to blast away the flames, most of the firewood, and those few chamalians who were unfortunate enough to be too close to the vents. Mark imagined they must have been overjoyed at first to see a blast of blue flame appear in the middle of their pyre. But when the smoke cleared, the *Belle Marie* was still there and the mob had lost interest in ridding the spaceport of the angels.

It remained quiet for another half hour.

***

They took advantage of the lull to make their first try at getting the attention of Zepp's pilgrims.

The trick was finding the right radio frequencies – the ones the pilgrims used to communicate with the Library of Jobe back in Suridash. Mark and Val Nordland had cataloged much of the radio traffic from the surface of Chamal, but coming up with the right search parameters was tough. According to Zepp, there were pilgrimage houses all around the planet. It took him a while to name enough of them to narrow the search down.

They had just found it when the second wave of attacks began.

Dusk was giving way to dark when the militia arrived. Zepp said the first troops to arrive at the landing site were part of the spaceport security guard, which had no real stake in the outcome of the rebellion itself and was only concerned with its own bit of turf here in Ring Po Do – the spaceport.

These newest troops, however, appeared to be one of the rebel parties. They took up positions similar to those occupied by the

Alliance guards, but they immediately turned out to defend themselves against any latecomers.

And latecomers there were. They drove off the first few assaults, and the *Belle Marie* was struck by the occasional stray round. But before long, they were displaced by a second group, which was larger and better armed.

A third group arrived later in the night, infiltrating close up to the lines of the new defenders, where they opened fire at point blank range. They didn't drive off the second group as much as they overwhelmed them. When they were done, there were few enough to run away, and bodies littered the field.

This company repeated the test-by-fire on the *Belle Marie* that the Alliance had tried earlier in the day. Only this time, instead of a single shot, they fired a volley from the assembled weapons.

The racket inside was frightening. Barrett activated the weapons batteries and responded in kind. He chewed up the scenery instead of the wildlife, but the effect was sufficient to his purposes.

"Is that really necessary?" Helen asked indignantly. "It's going to be awfully hard to talk to these creatures if we make an entrance as colossal butchers."

Barrett was indignant himself. "That's not what I'm trying to do," he said. "I don't enjoy wasting a lot of alien life. But there are damned few choices out here right at the moment, and I'm trying to make the best ones without getting us into deeper trouble."

Helen fell silent again, but Mark knew it wasn't because she had given up. He was sure there was more to it, but he didn't know what, so he kept his mouth shut and watched the viewscreens.

The fourth set of attackers took the field without a struggle, picking up the guns of the third group where they had dropped them in their flight.

This latest group spent a quiet hour studying the *Belle Marie* up close, poking and pounding, tapping and knocking, in a random, unpredictable manner that kept everyone aboard on tenterhooks. It was more unnerving than the successive rounds of fire.

The peace was broken near midnight when a fifth wave arrived at the field. This time, instead of shots, words were exchanged. And when they were finished, the soldiers staged an orderly withdrawal and were replaced by the newcomers.

"That will be it for the night," Zepp said when the evolution was completed.

"How do you know?" asked Barrett.

"The last group is a band of banshees. No one will dare to fight them – especially in the dark of night. Someone may come along in the morning to contest their claim to the field, but not until then."

"I hope you're right."

No one was sure for hours, but in the end Zepp's words turned out to be accurate. And in the morning, as he said, someone came to make a claim of their own to the field.

The Pilgrims of the Way of Jobe.

CHAPTER TEN

The pilgrims arrived at dawn, while a thick fog lay draped across the field, concealing the battleground around the *Belle Marie* and all who dwelt there. Barrett was the first to spot them.

"What have we got here?" he asked, stirring from the pilot's seat where he'd spent the night. Mark had snatched bits of sleep in erratic patches, incorporating the odd lights of the control deck, the battle tank, and the dim red blackout lamps into broken dreams. He'd been awake for several minutes when he heard Barrett, but it gave him an excuse to stir.

He slid into the co-pilot's seat and looked into the tank. Barrett's attention had been drawn by a column of a dozen or more creatures, marching in single file across the field straight towards the spacecraft. They were still some distance from the forty-plus banshees who had dug in during the dark hours when they spread out into a short skirmish line.

They kept those positions for nearly an hour, until the fog lifted to show them standing there, their backs to the rising sun, which blinded the banshees in their foxholes.

One of the pilgrims broke ranks and approached the banshee defense perimeter. He stopped a few meters from the nearest entrenchment and spoke in a loud, steady voice. The professor expressed an inability to translate the dialect, but suggested it was a Rift Valley tongue.

The banshees shouted back and a brief dialog ensued. Then the banshees scrambled out of their positions and left the field to the pilgrims.

"Who are these guys?" Barrett asked. "Get Zepp up here. We need to know what's going on."

***

Zepp told the angels the tale in as few words as he could of how, more than two hundred years ago, Jobe, the patriarch of his tribe, had walked out the east gate of Suridash, an innocent youngling with a talent for languages. And how thirty years later, he had returned, walking in through the west gate of the city, a wise old creature bent by his knowledge of the world he had circumnavigated.

His lifelong journey had taken him to many distant and exotic places. In the mountains of Shipar he had learned numerology, cartography, and astronomy. In the Rift Valley when the Red Monkeys were on the rise, he learned politics. In the snow-covered fastness of Kwikorak, he learned the secrets of the spirit of Chamal. In the tropical forests of the equatorial belt, he learned of sin and alienation. In the great briar patches of the southern hemisphere, he learned of life beyond the manifold layers of chamalian civilization. At the edge of the Arkarian bowl, he learned the truth of the seed of the gods. Along the high equatorial sea of Meshkar, he learned the enslavements of commerce. And when his journey brought him home again at last, he learned the arts of liberation and salvation.

"The accumulation of knowledge is not the accumulation of wisdom," he had said. Those words were carved in stone above the entrance to the Library of Jobe in the center of Suridash. Among the lessons that he had drummed into his tribe, chief was the importance of acquiring and preserving knowledge of the world – as a method for achieving the wisdom that he bestowed upon his descendants.

And so the Pilgrims of the Way of Jobe were dispatched. Their first commandment was to follow the path of the patriarch. Each year, they went out, a few at first, then a regular flow. There were always plenty of reasons for escaping Suridash and the close supervision of the tribe. Over the years, the Pilgrimage had become quite well-organized. Pilgrimage houses were established at the important posts along the Way – Shipar, Ring Po Do, Kwikorak, Arkaria, and Meshkar.

The inhabitants of those regions were a little wary in the beginning. It was typically chamalian, of course, for the pilgrims to be so bold and brazen in their spying. The typically chamalian response would have been to send the spies home in pieces. But it quickly became apparent that the flow of information traveled both ways – and more always came in than went out.

The services of the Pilgrims of the Way became an invaluable element of chamalian statecraft along the rough great circle that Jobe had followed on his journey.

Arshand was as typical a pilgrim as was possible, considering that any chamalian was typical of every other and of none other. His seed was the spawn of the equatorial forest – heavy scales with tufts of hair that looked like swampgrass covered his head, shoulders, face, and the tops of his arms and thighs, camouflage for his environment. His eyes were sharp and alive under a heavy ridge of scale that looked like tree bark.

He'd left Suridash more than a dozen years ago, but he'd never gotten any farther than the Pilgrimage House here in the Rift Valley.

He had found the cosmopolitan world of the Ring Po Do a welcome change to the oppressive life behind the walls of the tribal enclave in Suridash.

When Arshand entered the *Belle Marie* , Zepp felt nervous and uncomfortable – until he offered a greeting that restored some of his newfound self-confidence.

"Welcome, Ambassador to the Angels Zepp," he had said with overflowing respect. "How may this pilgrim be of service to you?" Before long, however, Arshand dropped the formal front and discussed their situation candidly. Especially after Zepp explained what the angels wanted them to do.

"It is impossible to speak to anyone from the alliance that launched the *Deragathon*," Arshand said. "The members have scattered like a litter after feeding and no one knows where they may be found. But we can find the next best thing. There is a way we can gather the leaders of the rebellion here in the city together. You've created it yourselves, actually. There's quite a dispute brewing over who has legitimate claim to you and your ship as prizes of battle." When Zepp got over his initial shock, he asked Arshand to explain.

"It's simple enough," he said. "First claim came from the Pang Dap, who say they took possession of your ship after you drove the mobs away. Then the Sing Lop are arguing that they have priority over the Pang Dap by right of battle – and they did drive them from the field. But the Lop Lai say they have a superior claim by the same right, and want blood vengeance for the wounds you inflicted on them."

"But I thought we didn't hurt any of them," Zepp protested.

"That is the rumor that is going around," Arshand replied. "But the Lop Lai are reluctant to admit that they were forced from the field without suffering a single wound. They are even more outraged by the fact that the Rap See walked onto the spaceport after they fled without firing a shot. It was they who turned you over to the Ap Lop Dap, who rule the deep of night." Zepp's head began to ache the way it always did when he began contemplating his world's politics. There were always so many factions and groups and parties and their alliances were always shifting around.

"Now the banshees were perfectly willing to turn you over to us at dawn," Arshand continued. "They always relinquish the field at first light. And we got there just ahead of the rifthounds – who think the banshees should return you to them." Mark expressed only slightly more confusion over the competing claims than Zepp felt, but Barrett avoided the whole issue and got right to the point. "How does that offer us an opportunity to meet with all the rebel groups?"

"Because in order to settle the claims, we will have to convene the Assembly of Traitors. A meeting of the rebellion as a whole – at least here in the city. No one really knows how well things are going in the countryside. No one outside the Pilgrimage House, that is."

"The rebellion as a whole?" Barrett asked. "Sounds like a perfect chance for chaos to break out. What genius thought this one up?"

Arshand looked to Zepp as the wise teacher spoke Barrett's words. "Shall we tell him that it was I, Lord Ambassador?"

"You already have," he said. "The device translates everything."

"Then let me ask, respectfully, if the angels know of a better way to proceed." A few moments later, the wise teacher managed to convey Barrett's frustration and dismay. "No," he said. "I guess we don't."

***

"This really isn't the best place for a discussion of nomenclature," Mark told the professor as he struggled to maintain his balance on a precarious perch about midway up the galleries in the chamalian meeting hall.

The three of them – Mark, Helen, and Zepp – shared a tiny platform that jutted out from the narrow tiers of benches filling three sides of the chamber. Glaring white light burned within electrical fixtures hanging from rough-hewn beams, and every sound seemed to echo endlessly under a tin roof.

Mark's nerves were stretched as tight as piano wire. Every sense was beyond overload. The journey to the meeting hall had made it seem all the more intense. Smoke from the burning quarters of the city filled his nostrils, carrying a uniquely foul stench.

Their column stopped more than a few times to avoid stepping into an ambush or a firefight between rebels and loyalists, or between rebels themselves. The random popping of small arms in the distance and the occasional explosion near and far within the city kept him pumped full of adrenaline.

He cursed Barrett more than once for sending them out while he stayed safe inside the *Belle Marie* . But he agreed that if something happened to Barrett, the ship would be left in the hands of the chamalians – which could mean a breach of technology security that would only add to Chamal's score on the termination assessment.

"Your AI's sense of timing is terrible, Paradis." As if by telepathy, Barrett interjected himself briefly into the discussion through his commlink with the professor. The AI was strapped to Mark's wrist, with a patch behind his ear to pick up sound and provide simultaneous translation of the meeting. Similar patches worn by

Helen and Zepp kept them linked together electronically.

"I'm afraid it can't be put off any longer," the professor said. "The rest of the parties will be arriving momentarily, and I need to know what to call them. The native terminology is too ideographic and the functional labels are inadequate."

"Inadequate?" Mark snapped back. "Since when?"

"Ms. Castain and I have already had this discussion," the professor replied. "Our information on functional morphologies is far too sketchy." Mark looked at Helen, who smiled sheepishly and shrugged.

"Do you have any suggestions?" he asked quickly.

"Give me the freedom to use terrestrial names as appropriate based on the video feed. I'm fairly literate when it comes to improvising," the professor boasted.

Mark just shook his head. "Do whatever you want," he said. "Just don't bother me with it."

"Certainly not," the AI said before chiming off.

"Or me," Barrett said. "Paradis, is everything all right there?"

"Just fine," Mark said as he concentrated on maintaining his balance.

According to Zepp, this building was a marketplace for grain traders. Ordinarily, they jockeyed for position on the steep galleries as they shouted their bids. But in the midst of the fighting it had been taken over by the Assembly of Traitors to discuss their plans and their fortunes.

Mark wondered if the traders had any better luck at holding their places than the delegates to this odd convention.

Zepp offered brief introductions to the members of the Assembly of Traitors as each group entered the hall.

"Coming in over on the right is the Koala Klan," Zepp said, the professor putting his ad hoc translation into the native's mouth. The koalas were typical of herbivores, Zepp explained. They tried to make up for their size and biological predilections by arming and armoring themselves to the teeth. They carried guns with the biggest bores and decked themselves out in laminated leather battledress with bold shoulders and fierce designs. Their tiny little eyes, cute noses, and fuzzy round ears looked comical in such a uniform, making their bravado all the more necessary to avoid abuse.

They were the Pang Dap, who had made first claim on the *Belle Marie*, Zepp pointed out.

"And here comes the Beaver Brigade," Zepp announced. A great commotion erupted on the left as the larger and even more heavily armed beavers filed into the chamber from an entrance on the left. They were led by a robed figure carrying an censer filled with burning wood chips.

"The smoke protects them from the dead spirits of their vanquished foes," Zepp said in answer to a question from Mark. "They won't go anywhere without it – even into battle. They are the Sing Lop, who first displaced the koalas."

Mark frowned at the tenacity of their superstition. It was not a hopeful sign, he decided as he considered the surprising sameness of features that the beavers shared. For a race that was capable of mutating each generation, the members of the Beaver Brigade seemed to share a remarkable similar genetic heritage – even if they could detect differences that he could not. They all had the same beady eyes, buck teeth, sharp snouts, sleek brown and black fur, and webbing between the fingers of the hands clutching long-barreled rifles. Their black uniforms, bedecked with what Zepp said were medals and charms only amplified their sameness.

The simultaneous arrival of the Tree-Cat Tong and the Rift Hound Bund was an unfortunate but now unavoidable quirk of fate. The cats, the Lop Lai who'd been chased from the field by Barrett's demonstration of firepower, snarled and hissed and the hounds, the Rap See who had taken advantage of the cats departure, bayed and yipped. They exchanged words in the Rift Valley pidgin, which Zepp translated roughly.

"The cats are claiming that the hounds are inferior mongrels without class or culture," he said. "And the hounds are making obscene references to the cats' breeding habits – something about the sounds they make resembling an exploding distillery." The cats also made complicated signs and symbols with their hands, while the hounds made more obvious gestures with certain vulgar body parts – gestures that needed little translation.

"The hounds operate the railroads and the cats run the electrical power generators – neither can get along without the other and neither can afford to give in to their age-old hatreds," Zepp said.

More groups entered, some large, some small – the Muskrat Guild, the Weasel Workers, the League of Shrews and Rodents – until the noise in the chamber was like the rush of water down a mountainside, a constant, cold babble that filled the ears. Much of it came from the shouts of protest as bands of chamalian rebels lost their footing and slipped down the rough wooden slope towards the central trading floor.

No one wanted to slide all the way down there, and for good reason.

The floor was held by a dozen creatures who appeared taller than most of the other tribes, with long, double-jointed limbs, pale white fur that grew thick and matted together, and who wore wide goggles over their eyes – the banshees.

It wasn't just their appearance that frightened the chamalian crowd, though their long, pointed fangs and ghostly features were dreadful enough. They were also armed with long, wide swords and heavy, complicated handguns.

As Mark watched, a scampering half-sized creature with overgrown front teeth and webbing on his paws made a tragic misstep and fell head over heels to the trading floor. The nearest banshee whirled into the air, spun once, and pounced on the creature. The victim of the attack – Mark wasn't sure if it was a child or just a small breed of chamalian – trembled, then shook with convulsions of fear. The banshee grinned, revealing a mouthful of evil dental equipment stained black with blood, and the halfling let out a keening wail.

The banshee backed off half a step and the halfling bolted for the clear air. But a long arm reached out and slashed at the fleeing creature as he scrambled up the steps, scoring him along his back with the edge of his blade.

Mark looked over at Helen and saw that she had witnessed the scene too. She drew in a slow breath through clenched teeth and shook her head.

Mark finally felt immersed in the chamalian culture. It was partly the thick, hot air, where dust, smoke, and a dozen alien odors hung in layers beneath the wooden beams of the great hall. Distant thunder rumbled under the din of the competing alien voices, punctuated every few minutes by the more ominous rumble of explosions out in the city.

The variety of creatures was almost overwhelming. There were clearly groups of specific breeds, their members as alike as clones. But there were also mongrels of every shape, size, and color, filling the spaces between, forming their own subgroups, and adding their own strange songs to the clamor.

The only thing that stood between the three humans and the increasingly agitated mob was a string of such mongrels, all wearing identical black vests, white loinclothes, and brass chastity belts, marking them as Pilgrims of the Way of Jobe. The guard surrounded the tiny platform, armed with formidable-looking weapons – sleek, well-machined projectile guns with big magazines.

Somehow, the weapons did not reassure Mark in the least. Mainly because every other group in the hall carried armories of their own. If the debate got out of control, it was possible that none of the delegates would emerge alive from the Assembly of Traitors.

***

For Zepp, the return to the surface had become a rebirth.

After all that he had been through, after all the changes that had occurred within his mind and spirit in the past few days, the small green ape who now led the band of angels and pilgrims was not at all the creature who had last breathed unfiltered air here in Ring Po Do.

The journey to the meeting hall had made it seem all the more intense, making his fur stand constantly on end and his tail twitch uncontrollably, though he found himself not fearful as much as excited.

The pilgrims, on the other hand, were calm throughout it all. It wasn't that they had grown accustomed to the violence, Zepp sensed. He had known other pilgrims who carried the same sense of unmovable stability – very unchamalian in some ways, very much like the angels in others. He wondered what caused it, then realized that it was probably something like the transformation that he had undergone.

He wondered if he would be able to acquire the same dignity and certainty of purpose that they possessed.

The meeting got off to an inauspicious start when one of beavers fired a shot through the chest of a koala.

The sudden crack of gunfire released a wave of pandemonium that left Zepp motionless at its center, in an island of serenity surrounded by a sea of chaos.

Everyone drew their weapons. Pistols, rifles, slugthrowers, and machine-guns large and small swung around to bear on dozens of different targets. Blades, swords, machetes, warclubs, and knives large and small waved in ominous circles in the air.

The angels had dressed themselves in armor of sorts – vests and cloaks of bulletproof cloth and helmets of light but rugged construction. Zepp had no such protection. The pilgrims carried no such equipment and he had turned down the angels' offer of their own. Helen had pleaded with him, but their equipment left him feeling bound and shackled. He decided that freedom to move would provide more safety than their armor.

Zepp was not all surprised to hear, after a few minutes of tense, but hushed, conversation that the koalas had brought it on themselves. They were not satisfied to let the council decide their claim on the prize of the angels and their vessel. They kept yapping at the heels of the beavers – a foolish maneuver politically, since the Beaver Brigade was in no better place to make a claim than the Koala Klan.

And once things reached the critical point, one member of the beaver rifle company finally let loose a round across the crowded meeting hall.

To make things worse, the banshees on the main floor were flushing fear pheromones into the air, putting everyone's nerves on a hair trigger. Zepp had all he could do to keep from leaping out of his skin when the drafts carried the hormones his way.

But everyone held their fire.

It was a rare act of self-control for this many chamalians – and an exhibition of the extremes the race was capable of. They continued to talk in harsh whispers, while their weapons remained trained on one another.

Zepp's attention was pulled away from the grim arsenal by Mark's soft, but frantic questions, relayed through the wise teacher. He realized suddenly that the meeting was being conducted in the pidgin that the various tribes of the Rift Valley used to talk to one another – and not in the common tongue of Suridash.

"What's going on?" Mark asked. "What in mumble-mumble is going on?"

Zepp explained in a few terse words as the first wave of tension began to subside only to be replaced by a new one as the name "Op Lee Jobe" could be heard like the croaking of frogs in the mudflat across the chamber. Within a few more minutes, everyone's attention turned in the direction of the pilgrims from Suridash.

"What now?" asked a banshee from the floor below. "You called the meeting, pilgrim. You bear the responsibility for the spilled blood. What shall we do now?"

Arshand looked around, then without hesitation responded: "The Beaver Brigade has violated the truce of the Assembly. Let them pay the forfeit."

The clatter of weapons in action arose from the beavers. Zepp could almost hear them grit their big buck teeth against the coming onslaught.

"What forfeit is that?" asked one of the brigade's leaders.

"Give the leafeaters one of yours for the one of theirs you took," Arshand said.

The brigade leader was silent for a moment, then he noticed what Zepp also could see – the weapons of all the other clans had swung slowly in their direction. A moment later, he turned, shouted an order, and a flurry of activity erupted in the rear of the group. Then a brown-furred creature with his hands bound behind him was pushed down the steep stairs. He lost his balance after a couple of steps, then fell to his knees and rolled down to the rail.

A handful of tree-cats hoisted him up and made ready to toss him over the rail, where the banshees stood ready to carry him across to the Koala Klan.

At that moment, with the fate of the unfortunate chamalian literally hanging in the balance, Mark leaned close to Zepp, although it was unnecessary with the wise teacher's device already behind his ear, and said: "You've got to stop this."

***

The crowd yipped and growled and hissed and barked in wild choruses as the moment of sacrifice for Beaver Brigade rapidly approached. Mark felt his stomach clench tightly and the sweat run down his brow.

He was mostly afraid that he was too late. That the poor creature would be tossed into the pit – and with him future of Chamal.

He knew where the path that Arshand had chosen led to. An eye for an eye, a tooth for a tooth, and a life for a life. And so on down the generations. It was the logic of the tribe, intended to ensure the tribe's survival. And here on Chamal, it must be doubly strong a commandment. Do unto others before they do unto you. And pay back any injury threefold, in order to ensure that it doesn't happen again.

The result was endless cycles of vengeance and violence, about to be continued here.

But there was a way to stop it.

Val Nordland wouldn't have approved, but he was that kind of anthropologist.

And if the presence of the human race here on Chamal had any meaning at all, this would have to be stopped. So Mark moved to stop it. He felt only a moment of hesitation over intervening in the chamalian culture – straining at the gnat against the larger intervention in store if the chamalian race failed their aggression assessment.

Providing Zepp was in time.

Mark watched as he spoke hurriedly to Arshand, who looked back at Mark, then spoke a loud command. The tree-cats on the edge of the rail hesitated. The beaver in their clutches writhed uncomfortably. And every chamalian eye in the place was focused on him.

"They are waiting for your command," Zepp said after too long a moment of silence.

"I don't know where this is leading, Paradis, but it's your call," Barrett said. "Go ahead and make it now."

"Tell them they can't have the beaver," Mark said. "Tell them the angels forbid it."

Zepp sighed, then turned back to Arshand. The mob of chamalians bristled as they heard the pilgrim pass on Mark's words. The koalas were the loudest, but a wave of the hand by Arshand silenced them all.

Mark felt paralyzed by the attention of the moment. He didn't know where this was leading any more than Barrett did.

"Tell them ... tell them he is ours now," Mark said. "Tell them justice belongs to everyone, not just the injured tribe."

"Sir, the word 'justice' has no referent in Zepp's language," the professor said without prompting. "The closest I come is a term similar to 'vengeance'."

"Translate it any damn way you please," Mark said. "Just do it quickly." The mob of chamalians grew more agitated. The movement of weapons stiffened and many of them came to bear on Mark, Helen, and Zepp.

Down on the floor of the hall, one of the banshees cackled and screeched at Arshand, who turned and said: "He wants to know who you are to eat the vengeance of the Ap Lop Dap."

Mark was confounded, then frustrated. He didn't know where to begin. But before he could respond, Zepp raised a hand. "Let me answer that, Mark," he said. "I know what to tell him."

He decided that in this situation they needed all the help they could get. "Go ahead," he said.

CHAPTER ELEVEN

Zepp **wasn't** **sure** **wh**at had come over him.

He was seized with a passion unlike any he had ever known. He knew what had to be said and that knowledge forced itself upon him irresistibly. Perhaps the same kind of knowledge had forced itself upon Mark, making him stop the grisly retribution. He would have to ask the angel later. In any case, he now found the words bubbling up like a spring in the desert.

"These are the angels from the outer heavens," he said. "They have come to study our world, to study us and all our sins. And they have come to judge us." A skill with languages inherited from the patriarch Jobe and months of training had given Zepp some fluency in the Rift Valley pidgin. He also took some comfort in the knowledge that the wise teacher would not be able to translate his speech for the angels. There were some things best kept hidden from the angels.

"And they have come to hand out vengeance," he said in a lowering tone.

The mob of rebels grew quiet and focused all their attention on Zepp.

"They have come with terrible machines and devices. I have been aboard their vessel in orbit above us. They have the power to burn our cities and smash our armies and enslave our mates and litters." The chamber began to buzz with anger at the hint of a threat, so Zepp drew back a notch.

"But they are not like us – the dust and mud of the world. They are truly angels. They are purebred and they breed true. They are touched by the seed of wisdom and that too breeds true. They have escaped from the sins of the wilderness. And because they have escaped, they will withhold their terrible powers."

The mob reacted with sudden incredulity.

"Why?" asked one shaggy hound.

"For what price?" asked a treecat.

"They will withhold their powers because they do not wish to kill and destroy. They do not take pleasure in it. They do not pursue it like a ram pursues his mate. They recoil from it in pain and fear. And do you know why?"

The chamber fell silent awaiting the answer to his question.

"Because it so easy for them."

Incredulity again, this time punctuated by the waving of guns and clubs.

"Don't doubt me," Zepp warned. "I have seen what they can do. How do you think they defeated the *Deragathon*? Why do you think your rebellion has been allowed to continue? They are waiting only for the proper moment to descend from the sky and take their place – in command of our world, the judges of our sins and the executioner for those who fail the judgment.

"Do not be fooled by your own greed. They are not prizes for us to bicker over. We are their prizes, loot to be hoarded or discarded at their whim. Anger them not, or we will all pay the forfeit."

Zepp left them with a sudden silence that stretched into an anxious moment. Then the air seemed to grow still as the chamalian rebels began chattering amongst themselves.

In the momentary calm, Mark leaned forward to talk to Zepp.

"What did you tell them?" he asked.

"That you are peaceful and kind and want to help them all," Zepp said, mainly because he thought it was what Mark wanted to hear.

Mark showed his teeth, then said, "You might want to mention that we are not going to be haggled over like trophies of battle."

"I already did that," Zepp said. "I think they understand."

But Zepp was quickly proven wrong – at least in one case. For no sooner had he said the words than did one of the banshees let out a terrible shriek, spin about on one foot, leap into the air, and bound up the gallery straight towards them, fear pheromones spewing from its glands.

***

Mark never flinched. He didn't have time to.

The banshee was on him before he could move. He had time to be surprised at how slight its figure really was under all that fur. He had time to be conscious of the mix of smells coming from the creature – a musty odor high in nitrates and a sweeter musk underneath. He had time to notice the reflection of his own face in the dark goggles that shielded the banshee's eyes from the daylight. And he had time to focus on the ragged sharp claws of one hand and the long equally ragged blade the banshee carried in the other as they swept by his face.

But those things all took the briefest of seconds.

The rush of adrenaline, the sudden awareness of the noise of the crowd, now subdued as the assembly drew in a collective breath at the speed of the banshee's attack, and the gasp from Helen Castain all followed in quick succession as time reengaged itself.

The banshee looked almost as surprised as Mark felt. And puzzled, if the character of facial features carried across the interspecies gap. Mark wondered if the warrior had expected a different reaction from him.

That suspicion grew stronger when the banshee backed off, waved his sword over his head, spun in a full circle and sliced the air in front of him. Mark smiled oddly at the display, appreciating the skill and practice it must have involved, almost oblivious to the danger it presented.

But when the performance left Mark unmoved, the banshee lost all composure. He screeched, pounded against his chest with the flat of his sword and the butt of his hand, and finally waved his arms in great circles. Mark could smell the musk stronger now than the rank acetone of unwashed chamalian. It was not nearly as unpleasant.

For some reason, the Assembly of Traitors now rose as one in a howling mass that set the banshee to wailing. The one before Mark sank to the floor, muttering in disgust.

Mark looked around him and saw Zepp and the pilgrims hovering at the edge of the small platform, a few steps behind Helen Castain. Zepp ventured towards him, one eye on the banshee. "You were not overcome by uncontrollable fear," Zepp said.

"No," Mark said. "Was I supposed to be?"

"The scent of the banshee unnerves the boldest warrior. If they were not bound to the night, they would rule the Rift Valley instead of the Blue Monkeys."

"Pheromones."

"The wise teacher does not understand that word," Zepp said.

"It's what we call a scent that unnerves the boldest warrior," Mark said. He relaxed his own guard slightly now as the chamalian mob began cackling once again.

"They are ridiculing the banshee with their laughter," Zepp said.

"I don't know if that's such a good idea," Mark replied.

But before he could do anything about, the banshee was on his feet once more. He screamed at the chamber, then spun once again. He turned on Zepp and Mark, swinging his sword over his head. Then he leapt.

From his left, Mark heard the popping of the pilgrim's guns. In front of him, he saw the banshee flying through the air – blots of red splashing from his chest while the sword flew loose through the air trailed by a cloud of pink vapor.

***

"Paradis! Report! Are you all right?"

Barrett's voice cut through the momentary haze that filled Mark's head. He had felt uneasy ever since they'd entered the Assembly of Traitors, but this was different. The ground seemed to be slipping out from under him. The dead body of the banshee lay at his feet, and the walls were beginning to shake with the sound of rebels pounding on the floor with their weapons.

"I'm okay," he said. "But this is starting to get too complicated for me." He didn't know enough about the different groups, their agendas, or their interests to form an opinion of what would happen next. But the ferocious wall of sound accomplished what the pheromones of the banshee had not.

He looked to Helen, whose face had turned pale. She was not looking his way, but was concentrating on the other occupants of the meeting hall. The way she edged towards the rear of the platform only reinforced Mark's sinking sensation.

"I think we'd better be ready to move quickly," he said.

"This certainly is an unconventional anthropological expedition, Mr. Paradis," she said, cracking a weary smile.

When he turned back to Zepp, the pilgrims started to react. Arshand gave a hand signal and every chamalian in a black vest and brass belt came to attention. They moved about slowly, almost restlessly, a contrast to the agitated jumping and pacing of some of the rebels – especially the banshees, who now beat an angry path from one side of the floor to the other.

Suddenly the pilgrims moved as one. If there had been a signal, Mark hadn't seen it. One on each side of him took him by the arm. Helen was given the same rush.

A shout echoed from the hall behind him. Then another.

Then the popping sound of gunfire exploded from Mark's right, turning his blood to ice. The koalas were up there. The wood around him erupted in splinters.

The pilgrims returned the salute, letting out short bursts of automatic fire in the direction of the koalas. Mark's escorts doubled their speed as they ducked through the doorway and into the entrance passage.

Something tugged at one sleeve. Then he felt like he'd been kicked in the back.

He'd been shot. The surprise was stronger than the pain.

He pitched forward, heading for the floor, before the pilgrims at his side pulled him back upright. As the pain turned into numbness, Mark hoped the armor Barrett had provided lived up to expectations. Aside from the bruising impact, he seemed to be otherwise fit – his breathing was normal and his heart, although pounding, felt sound.

He looked over one shoulder and saw Zepp scampering after him, his hands over his head and his tail wrapped around one leg.

Up ahead was the sunlit alleyway where they had parked their caravan. Pilgrims were already out there. Then he saw Helen emerge into the light. A brief moment of relief was cut short by the sound of gunfire from outside.

The pilgrims in front of him pushed him back. The door slammed shut, throwing the hall into sudden darkness. Everyone dropped to the floor, pulling him with them.

"It's the Muskrat Guild," Zepp said. "They ambushed us."

The darkness lasted only a moment before the door at the end of the hall opened again. Mark saw a handful of pilgrims rush outside, weapons ablaze. They stopped firing and signaled for the rest of the party. Mark was pulled along into the alley, with Zepp right behind him.

He looked up and down. Their vehicles were intact, a little worse for wear after the fusillades that had let loose out here.

But there was no sign of Helen Castain and, aside from a few bloody spots on the pavement, no sign of the muskrats.

Mark swallowed hard. He didn't want to have to say the words, but he had no choice.

"Barrett, I'm in trouble here," he said. "I've lost Helen. She's been kidnapped."

***

"Hold your water, Paradis," Barrett said. "I'm still in contact with her. She's unharmed, but you're right – she's been kidnapped. She's been blindfolded, so she can't help us locate her, but the rats don't know what I can do with my equipment here. Once they stop moving, we'll locate her for good. Then we'll have to figure out how to mount a retrieval mission."

Mark breathed more easily, but his muscles tensed up at the thought of rescuing Helen from the Muskrat Guild. This was not what field work on a cultural survey team was advertised as being.

The pilgrims did not give Mark time to think about the sudden loss of Helen. They had more immediate concerns. Arshand personally put him and Zepp into the back of the armored truck in the middle of their short convoy.

A brief moment later, before the engines even warmed up, they took off down the narrow alleyway.

The convoy had the same ad hoc look that Mark had identified in the architecture and physical layout of Ring Po Do. There were three vehicles, each unique in appearance and mode of propulsion. One smelled of kerosene and hissed steam all the time, another reeked of refined gasoline and burning oil, and the other belched blue smoke from engines Barrett had said were diesels, whatever that meant. The gasoline-burner went first, racing ahead of the others. Mark was glad to be aboard the diesel rig in the center, mainly because it smelled the least of fuel and seemed least likely to burn if ignited. And the steam truck brought up the rear.

The back of the diesel truck was spacious enough – especially without Helen to take up additional room – but the armor left only small slits for windows. It was barely enough for Mark to see the fine details of urban life on Chamal.

They trundled quickly through the mercantile district of the city once they'd found their way out of the alleyways surrounding the Market Hall. Big warehouses sprawled across the flatlands – baroque stone structures with elaborate ornamentation in the masonry. A row of the behemoths lined a silty, weed-choked canal that must have once been a major artery for the city.

The avenue widened out once they were across the canal and past the warehouses neighborhood. Now the few such buildings left stood like islands in a sea of shantytowns. The shacks and traps and ramshackle houses looked more like a refuse dump than a residential district, but Mark saw more than a few halflings and steplings running about the trash to tell the difference. Even then it was difficult, since much of the close-packed shacks seemed deserted. He mentioned it to Zepp.

"Arshand says the city emptied out the first day your ship arrived in orbit," Zepp reported a moment later. "On this side of the road is the Koala Klan. Over there on the other are the banshees. The koalas work in the warehouses and in the factories down by the river. The banshees are night-scavengers and are responsible for cleaning the streets and canals. When the revolution came, they were among the leaders – because their tribes were among the lowest of the low."

Mark could appreciate their revolutionary zeal. The slums looked as uninhabitable as they were uninviting. A pall of black smoke hung over them and Mark's nose wrinkled at the acrid smell of burning trash – the first thing that he'd found on Chamal that reminded him of Earth.

They passed into the factory district a few minutes later. The buildings here looked newer than the warehouses and had a functional plainness to them – except for the frightening walls that surrounded the blocks. The barriers were topped with ragged, rusted metal and broken pottery set in the mortar.

Mark could tell when they neared the river. The smell of mud and organics grew richer, and the buildings grew smaller, older, and more crooked and bent. The walls were thicker, the factories squat and broad, and the side streets narrower and dark.

Then the avenue broke out into the approach to a wide bridge across the Daughter of All Waters. High pillars lined the bridge, with statues ten meters high and more filling the mall in the center. The statues depicted great beasts that could have been imaginary or real for all Mark knew.

"They are the ghost-demons of the Red Monkeys," Zepp explained. "They haunted the dreams of the rulers of the Rift Valley and reminded them that their time in this vale was limited."

It was from behind one such statue that the next ambush came. Mark was trying to maintain his footing as he watched a marble beast pass by through the slot in the armor. It was a four-legged creature with an oversized head full of long, narrow, spiked teeth. As they drew even with it, a cloud of smoke erupted and a stream of fire and smoke rushed towards them.

The explosion came from the first vehicle. Once hit, the gas-burner fell by the side of the road, and Mark could see the flames engulf it as they rolled past. Arshand hissed a command and the diesel truck seemed to growl more deeply and move more quickly.

BOOM! A second explosion came much closer at hand. It smacked Mark in the face and chest and left his ears ringing. Smoke spilled in through the window slits. He could tell by the vibrations in his seat that they were slowing down.

Then came the crackle of small arms fire – from both outside the convoy and atop the truck. More could be heard from the steamer behind them. Shouts and commands and screams filtered in from outside, but no one moved inside the truck.

Then Arshand hissed again. Zepp took Mark's hand. "Come,

quickly," he said, shouting to be heard through the ringing. "We have to go. We're turning back."

They spilled out of the truck and for a moment the bright daylight stung Mark's eyes. Pilgrims in defensive positions fired away at an unseen enemy force on the sides of the bridge. Arshand led the bulk of their party back towards the river banks.

Mark hurried, feeling a little less than invulnerable in his armor. He felt most concerned for Zepp, however, who had no such protection. His concern grew to active screaming-inside fear when he saw one of the pilgrims drop to the pavement.

They reached the entrance to the bridge and formed up in the protection offered by the base of a stone pillar thirty meters high. "What now?" Mark asked.

"The Pilgrimage House is on the other side of the river," he said. "We have to find another crossing. Only now we have to walk." Mark took a deep breath, then steeled himself to his fate. He only hoped things weren't worse for Helen.

***

They made their way quickly along the waterfront. In this part of the city, the river bank had been made permanent with stone bulkheads, walls, and barricades. Down below, the river lapped against floating docks where boats, barges, and sampans jostled one another on the current.

The factories down here were the oldest Mark had seen so far. Their walls of tiny ancient bricks were covered with vines and a velvety purple moss.

The ground rose as they moved away from the bridge and finally emerged from the shadows of the mills into the broad open yard that surrounded a massive stone fort. Zepp identified it as the North River Fortress and pointed out its sister across the river, a much larger pile of rocks, turrets, and battlements.

Mark was uncertain about passing so close to the fortress until Zepp explained that the first step in the revolution had been a mutiny among the armed tribal militias that manned the fortress. Its weapons were gone and scattered, and many of its garrison had been among the Assembly of Traitors.

From a high spot near the far end of the fortress, they paused while Arshand sent scouts ahead. While they were waiting, Zepp pointed out the complex of buildings on the opposite side of the river that, until recently, formed the seat of power for the Blue Monkeys in the Rift Valley. Beyond the South River Fortress stood block on block of low stone buildings – the government offices of the Blue Monkeys. To the right of them were the high walls of the Army Headquarters.

Mark could see the bridge where they'd been ambushed – smoke still rose in a high column from the burning trucks they'd left behind. The avenue led straight across the river into the heart of the government center.

On the hillside beyond the heavy institutional buildings stood an elaborate collection of towers, domes, crenelated walls, and moats – all cut from the same black stone and burnished with vines, creepers, moss, and mold.

"This fortress goes back three incarnations of the Red Monkey," Zepp said, placing a hand on the stone wall that sheltered them from the view of the bridge. "The South Fortress goes back two incarnations. There's another fort up the river a ways that goes back five incarnations. And the palace on the hill has been there since the beginning of history. It just keeps getting bigger and bigger each time the Red Monkeys return."

"They're nothing if not persistent," Mark said.

"I don't understand," Zepp replied.

Mark shook his head. "Nothing. It's just a silly angel joke."

He peered through the late day haze at the chamalian city and its great buildings, listened to the splash of the river against the stone embankments, breathed the air still laced with the smell of smoke, and felt very small and helpless in the middle of this strange and violent world.

A short time later, the scouts returned and Arshand came to talk with them.

"After we left the meeting hall, the Assembly of Traitors broke down. Everyone opened fire on everyone else. The Koala Klan is no longer a part of the revolutionary effort. The banshees have sworn a blood curse against the angels and the pilgrims. The Tree-cat Tong and the Rift Hound Bund have broken their truce and sworn vendetta on one another once again."

"And what about the ambush at the hall?"

"The Ferret Syndicate. They are agents of the banshees and took your companion."

"Ask him about helping us get Castain back," Barrett instructed.

Arshand gestured assent with his hands. "That can be arranged," he said. "But first we must keep moving. We will return to the pilgrimage house before we attempt anything further." They continued on up the river and crossed over from the factory zone into a residential area. As many of the tenements here were built of wood or bamboo as brick or stone. They rose up a couple of stories, with narrow wooden walkways connecting the roofs overhead. Canals long since silted up and turned to little more than open sewers intersected the streets and created little islands along the river.

The place was mostly deserted. The only thing that lingered of the neighborhoods former residents was a damp acetone smell that clung to the alleys where the sun never shined.

"This is the tree-cat neighborhood. They like the roofs, but not the canals," Zepp said. The wise teacher reproduced a human sounding chuckle to replace Zepp's chattering laugh.

The pilgrims continued on through the narrow streets until they reached a small river that flowed into the Li Pang Do. An advance party had secured boats for them to cross to the far side.

They were pushing off into the stream when the attack came. This time it was the tree-cats. Mark saw them swarm over the edge of a roof near the waterfront, guns flashing and popping as the water around them erupted in splashes and whizzing bullets.

The pilgrims returned the kindness, and the few in the last boat started rowing back to the dock to make a stand as rear guard. Mark felt clammy and more than a little guilty at the idea that they might have to sacrifice their own lives to protect his and Zepp's.

They made it safely across, but by now Mark's nerves were shot. He was afraid that any moment might bring another assault. Every sound, every movement, every word from the pilgrims or Zepp sent his head aswivel.

The neighborhood across the river was similar in appearance to the tree-cat district, but the houses were lower and the acetone smell had been replaced by the subtle scent of wet fur. They were in canine country now.

Mark asked why the two groups were at odds – half expecting Zepp to say that the always fought like cats and dogs. But the answer was more startling than that.

"The Tree-Cat Tong is an ancient tribe with many clans. Their mating protocols require heavy inbreeding to produce as many tree cats as possible. It's a risky strategy, though, because after a couple of generations of that, they lose the seed of wisdom and their litters all turn wild. Younger tribes have strong prohibitions against it. The Rift Hound Bund is one of those tribes. They consider the Tree-cat Tong to be perverse sinners who continue a decadent practice. The tree-cats see the hounds as dangerous radicals who have no business telling them how to breed. The dispute has been around almost as long as the Red Monkeys." Mark shuddered as he thought about it. This was not a culture that could be easily analyzed from the surface, he realized. A lot more digging would be necessary before he could understand what was going on.

He only hoped he would have the time to start doing that digging. And that when he was done, they would survive the consequences of his understanding.

CHAPTER TWELVE

The high walls surrounding the Pilgrimage House made Mark feel secure for the first time since they had arrived in Ring Po Do. They passed through a ponderous gate that swung slowly shut behind them. The walls themselves enclosed a compound of many acres, with gardens, groves, a half dozen tall buildings – and a forest of antennas.

A thicket of cables and wires strung from trees, posts, and walls linked the buildings to the antennas, and a series of heavy power lines ran towards the back of the compound to a low building with a smokestack pouring forth a roiling stream of black smoke. In the patches of silence as they threaded their way through the garden, Mark could hear the hum of electricity in the wires.

They entered the main building through an unornamented side door and immediately climbed a flight of stairs. Mark was escorted down a narrow hall to a small room with a bed, a table, and a chair.

"Wait here," Zepp said. "You can rest. We'll come for you when we need you."

Mark sat down and realized how tired he was. He'd been unable to sleep more than a couple hours during the night on the landing field, and the day's exertions were beginning to catch up with him.

But oh what thrill it all was!

He could barely believe the way he felt. Excited. Full of life. Despite the danger. Despite the loss of Helen Castain. He'd been shot, for God's sake, and lived to run away. Like Helen had said, this was not your ordinary cultural survey.

For a moment, he wondered how he could ever go back to normal life, bound by walls and schedules and convention. The last few hours were more real and vital than all of that. This was what drew him out into the world in the first place. This was what he craved, what he wanted more than anything. To be this alive and this full of energy.

He thought about the long journey here from home, the months spiraling down from the outer system, the days he spent in the cramped compartments of the *Cousteau* . It was as if that were another creature that shared some of his memories, but none of his excitement. An unfortunate life and a tragic creature, he realized sadly, as he looked back at all the pain he had felt over his unrealistic longings. What had that poor fellow been thinking? But he had no time for self-pity. There was a friend to be rescued.

He couldn't rest until that was done. It was not something that he feared, but it was not something he desired most completely. It was simply necessary, and vital, and still undone.

"Hey Paradis," Barrett's voice rattled in his ear. "I've got some good news and some bad news. The good news is they've stopped moving Helen. The bad news is that she isn't talking to me anymore. That could mean they've taken her commpatch off – or it could mean something else. You want to tell your furry friends?"

"When they come back," he said, his heart pounding suddenly at the sudden fear for Helen Castain. He didn't ask Barrett to elaborate on what he meant by "something else" but went on to explain his situation.

"They've put you on ice while they decide what to do next."

"Not a bad way of proceeding, if it's true. But I'm reluctant to expect human response or human reasons for much of what they do. They're not rational the same way we are."

"I've figured out that much," Barrett said. "By the way, you shouldn't feel guilty about losing Helen. I was watching that show. You're lucky you both got out of the meeting hall in one piece. You took a round, didn't you?"

"In the back," Mark said. "It only hurt for a minute."

"You should look after it," the Space Corps officer said. "It'll raise quite a bruise."

Mark stretched and realized Barrett was right. His back ached and burned where it had absorbed the shock of the impact. He was afraid to take off the armor for fear it would hurt too much to put it back on.

It was nearly an hour before one of the pilgrims came for Mark, long enough to rest, but not long enough to sleep. They took him down the stairs and outside to another building, which had the look of a workshop – a high-domed room behind a wall full of tall floor-to-ceiling windows. Long tables inside were filled with electronics equipment, with a few pilgrims at work in front of it.

Arshand met him there apart from the others.

"Welcome to the Pilgrimage House, angel Paradis," he said.

He returned the greeting and relayed Barrett's message. The pilgrim gestured assent and Mark called for Barrett. Arshand led him to a chart on the wall of the city of Ring Po Do, and using Barrett's azimuth and distance located the current position of her commpatch.

Arshand gestured acknowledgment, then asked: "How does your companion know the distance from his ship without another receiver for triangulation?"

Barrett's sharp laugh erupted in Mark's ear. "Don't answer that question," he snapped.

Mark knew the answer – the *Belle Marie* carried drones that could pick up the signal and provide the triangulation.

"I'm sorry, Arshand," he said. "But I've been instructed not to tell you."

"I understand," the pilgrim said. "I imagine it has something to do with the winged machines that flew from your vessel."

"What did you tell him, Paradis?" Barrett said.

Mark was about to protest when he heard an echo of Barrett's voice from across the room, where the other pilgrims had been working. Arshand looked over at them and hissed. "Use some discretion!" he snapped.

The sound of the professor's voice issued from the equipment on the table before one of the technicians squelched the speaker.

"Uh-oh," Mark said. "They've got the signal from my commpatch on their receivers."

"Does that mean they're picking up your AI too?" Barrett asked.

"Yeah," Mark said. "What do we do?"

"Don't worry about it. As long as you've got the thing set so it doesn't give them simultaneous translation of my signal, we should be okay."

"What about my signal?" Mark asked. "The professor is still translating everything I say aloud – including what I say to you."

"Don't worry about it," Barrett said. "There isn't much you can say that they don't already know."

Mark wasn't sure if he should be offended by that response, but he didn't say so. In the meantime, Arshand had turned his attention to a second group of technicians who were working on another set of receivers at the other end of the table. He walked over and spoke with them for a few minutes, then returned to Mark.

"You must tell your companion that despite his equipment, he has been outmaneuvered," Arshand said. "We have investigated the place where your other companion was supposed to be and we have found nothing. No sign of the Muskrat Guild. No sign of the other angel." Mark's heart sank, then rebounded. That meant that Helen's commpatch had gone silent, but not necessarily Helen herself. He took Barrett's snarl for acknowledgment of that.

"Now we must find her using our own means," Arshand said.

"Can you do that?" Mark asked.

"Certainly. While the city may be in chaos, the Pilgrims of the Way are still those who know all that can be known. But you must know this, angel Paradis. The pilgrims do not give their knowledge away freely. Because you are with Ambassador Zepp, we will give you an advance on your account this time. But the day will come when there will be a reckoning. And at that time, knowledge must be returned of equal weight to that which we provide." Mark nodded, and smiled inwardly. He had no doubt that the *Cousteau* could provide the Pilgrims of the Way with more knowledge than it would know what to do with.

***

Zepp was in the library, high atop a climbing pole and poking into a nook full of scrolls and boxes, when Mark found him.

The angel looked very small from up here. The library was a single large chamber with a vaulted ceiling easily five times as high as Mark was tall. The walls were a carelessly woven tapestry of shelves, racks, stacks, niches, brackets, lintels, recesses, and stalls, all bulging with paper in all its bound and unbound forms. Dust hung heavy in the air, illuminated by harsh naked lights threaded into the elaborate iron chandeliers that hung from the ceiling. The light was swallowed up overhead by the accumulated soot of the century before the Pilgrimage House was wired for electricity.

Mark spoke his clattering language, and the wise teacher parroted him. "What are you looking for?" they asked.

"Histories," Zepp replied. "Of what happened when the Red Monkeys last fell. Arshand says they're up here somewhere."

Recovering the knowledge of a chamalian library was an arcane practice, with no more organization or order than anything else in the world, and Zepp cursed his inability to find anything he wanted. He tottered atop the pole – a long mast with shingles driven into it at alternating intervals as footholds and a base coated with dry pitch to keep a grip on the floor – as he reached deep into the cubbyhole for a scroll with carved wooden handles.

He pulled it out, then scampered down the pole before it toppled over.

"They said this was a library," Mark said as he twisted his head back and forth scanning the walls. "How do you find what you're looking for?"

"Mostly you don't," Zepp said. "I've been here for hours and I still can't locate the histories I want."

"Don't you have a system of some kind for storing records?"

"A what?" asked Zepp.

Mark sighed. "I guess organized information retrieval wouldn't be a strong point for your race."

"I am afraid we are a race with many weaknesses and few strong points," Zepp said, his voice sagging. The deep funk that had driven him here had only grown worse. Everything he had seen since his return from the sky had left him feeling more helpless and depressed. "I thought if we knew what it was like here in the city the last time things fell apart, we might have an idea what to do next."

"Social disintegration. Collapse of the rule of law. Intertribal conflict. Pervasive violence throughout the city. Deterioration of urban services, then the urban environment. Mass refugees. Shock, trauma, depression, and survivor-guilt. Contagious disease, malnutrition, starvation, and mass death. At least that what human history tells us," Mark said. "We too are a race with many weaknesses and few strong points."

Zepp looked at him with a strange excitement bubbling within his imagination. He had never thought of the angels as having weaknesses or flaws. But they were creatures of flesh and blood. They must have grown up out of swamps of their own, rising from alien frogs in alien waters, passing through a racial childhood all their own before unlocking the secrets of nature that brought them across the depths of interstellar space.

It was a concept that brought him a spark of renewed hope in the midst of his gloom.

"This place looks like it's part monument, part museum, part hoarder's heaven," Mark said as he made a circuit of the large room. He walked down a row of bookbins and paused to inspect the dust on one binding. "How old is it?"

"About four eighty-eights. The first pilgrims left to repeat the Walk of Jobe within a generation after Jobe's return. But it was another eighty years before they had the wealth needed to build this."

"What did Jobe do while he was here in the Rift Valley?" Mark asked. He stopped before the map of Jobe's walk. It was an old-fashioned scroll map that hung from the ceiling to the floor – the kind that Jobe himself might have made while in high Shipar.

"Avoided being killed, for the most part. He fell out of the sky one day not far downriver from the city. He was brought here by Rik Lo Rik, one of the early Red Monkey nobles in the midst of reclaiming his heritage. Jobe got involved in some court intrigue, some sexual-taboo-intrigue, and escaped within less than a year. He must have been about my age at the time. It was before his enlightenment in the mountains of Kwikorak."

Zepp wondered now what the old dog was like. Did he have moments of despair and helplessness like Zepp's own?

The world then was no less chaotic than it was today, Zepp realized. The seed of wisdom was scattered just as widely. The antagonism between all the various tribes of Chamal just as bitter.

"Sexual-taboo-intrigue? What's that mean?"

Zepp felt a sudden rush of shame and fear. He was afraid to answer the question. It was not the subject itself that made him uneasy, but the connection to his own sins. He had been successful at keeping them out of his mind so far, if not his heart. He swallowed hard, then hoped he would not give his guilt away in the wavering of his voice.

"The Red Monkeys followed the incest taboo. Because the Red Monkeys have such a brief time allotted to them, they allow nothing that would diminish their reign."

"And Rik Lo Rik broke the taboo?"

"Yes. And he was found out. Jobe was a member of his court and would have faced the Red Monkey's punishment, but he escaped with his skin and fled upriver. That is where he entered the mountain vastness and discovered his true connection to the seed of the gods."

"So Jobe was a holy man?"

"For a time," Zepp said. "But he lost his holy connections on the far side of Kwikorak when he descended into the tropical rain forest." Mark made the huffing sound that the wise teacher had identified as laughter. "He sounds like quite an interesting character."

"Here in this library, he seems much more like an ordinary chamalian to me, and less like a fearsome ancestor-god."

"Was he an ordinary chamalian?" Mark asked. He took a seat on one of the wide leather pillows in the empty circle beneath the lopsided dome of the library.

"In some ways, yes," Zepp said, glad to be away from any discussion of sexual-taboo-intrigue. "In others, no. For example, he believed in seeing things for yourself before you believe in them. And in reasoning your way to a conclusion before deciding what to do. He said these were the gifts of the seed of the gods and we shouldn't waste them."

"Sounds like they helped him survive a trip around Chamal."

"Oh, surviving the long walk took more than that," Zepp said. "It took cha." The wise teacher complained that it had no referent in Mark's tongue to Suridash word for good fortune combined with bursts of intuitive insight. But after a moment's discussion, he got the idea across.

"You mention the seed of the gods," Mark said. "But I'm still not sure from what you've told me if your Jobe was religious or not. Does your tribe believe in a god?"

"In the mythology of Chamal, the gods created the world as a beautiful garden where everything lived in harmony. Then the wild things awoke and attacked them. The gods ran screaming from the garden after being raped and buggered. It is our curse that we must remain behind in the garden forever, made wise by their spilled seed, but never able to escape." He hesitated, then looked sideways at Mark, and added: "Until now, that is. Perhaps that has changed now that gods have sent their angels to our world."

Zepp allowed a gentle sigh to escape his lungs, then snapped back: "But to answer your question, no, we don't really believe in the gods. In Kwikorak, where all religions were forged, the higher you go, the fewer gods there are. On the highest peaks are the wisest of the wise, the great snowbeasts who have found wisdom without the gods. That is where Jobe learned his lessons of the spirit, and that is what his children believe today."

***

"And so you're driven to look for histories instead of praying or making sacrifices," Mark said. "A very post-industrial attitude."

"Post-industrial?" The wise teacher echoed. "After work? Beyond the steam-electric-factory stage of history? The last definition is closest."

"Except that Jobe demanded it of his tribe long before we reached that stage of history," Zepp commented.

"Not surprising," Mark said. "Your race seems to skip over essential parts of the development you would expect if you were more like us. Arshand tells me that electricity and radio have been around since the Red Monkeys before last – six hundred years. But he also said no one wanted to talk to anyone else that far away for the first four hundred years. And electricity was nothing more than a toy during all that time – the previous Red Monkey dynasty had invented it late in their reign and retired from the scene before they invented the electric motor."

"Is there another way?" Zepp asked, shaking his head in puzzlement. "Things always lay around unused until someone with the spark of wisdom sees their value. And they always miss some other use that lays untapped until the next genius comes along. How do the angels do it?"

Mark seemed at a loss, stammered, then said: "It's a more orderly process. Each person adds a little part to the puzzle until it becomes large enough for someone to see it whole. There's plenty of room for inspiration and intuition, but it doesn't seem to rely on it entirely like your race does."

"You have the luxury of order," Zepp said. "Wisdom without purity is a difficult burden to manage."

"And so you feel helpless and full of despair?"

"What do you expect? Do you have any idea what it is like to bear the burden of wisdom here on Chamal? Do you have any idea what it is like to burn with the fire of knowing the world and knowing ourselves?

"Look at us – we are one step above the wild animals that prey upon one another on the steppe and in the forest. Some of still hunt and some are still hunted. We lust after all that lives around us. Some of us are told to indulge that desire. Others are taught to punish the indulgent. There is no chamalian tribe or clan or breed that does not think it is the sole repository of wisdom and knowledge in this world – and that all others are inferior chaff.

"I think we are fired by the gap between our wild roots and wiser selves. The gap is so wide, we have to have more energy to make the spark. But no matter how wise we get, we can never escape those roots. We all know that sooner or later we will return to them.

"And that's the ultimate irony – that we know all this. We see our own wild roots. We see our leaps of genius and wisdom, and still know that in our genes we are inescapably chained to our wild nature. And even as we know the perfection of the true seed of the gods – our very ability to imagine that perfection dooms us to lives of sin, guilt, and punishment beyond redemption. We know exactly and precisely how wicked and depraved we are. We know that whatever our urges are, they will betray us, and that we are still helpless before them. We know that the halfling and the changeling are the same, that no one turns away from the incubus or the succubus. We know that the wise creatures of the wild got there because we spilled the gods' seed there.

"The guilt is overwhelming sometimes. It burns so deeply, it penetrates so completely, that we project it outside ourselves. Then we become avengers of the gods' wisdom – ready to punish all other chamalians for our own sins. The pogroms, the vendettas, the blood-feuds, the jihads, and the ordinary murders run through our history like the Li Pang Do runs through the Rift Valley." Zepp watched Mark squirm in his seat under the onslaught of his words. For a moment, he thought the angel would be driven away by their awful truth. But he stayed, rebounding with more questions.

"And what do you think you will find in the histories?" he asked. "An advantage over your enemies? A strategy to defeat the tribes that oppose you?"

Zepp's excitement turned to anger at the suspicious questions. "No!" he yelled, his voice crackling into higher octave in protest. "You don't understand the tribe of Jobe at all to ask me that. We are not concerned with petty squabbles between tribes over who mates with whom, or who gets first drink from the spring. We are the keepers of the seed of the gods, the followers of the way of Jobe, the true children of wisdom. If there is any truth at all on Chamal, it is that. And perhaps that is the only truth there is in the world. Even if all my brothers and cousins and uncles deny it and turn against it, it will still be my truth.

"I have seen how the pilgrims live here," he said, the anger receding back into the original energy of vision and the dialogue with the angel. "They are unafraid of the world. They have the strength that comes with knowledge, and the knowledge that comes with wisdom. They share the vision of Jobe, the vision of wisdom that goes out into the world and returns. Well I have had that vision too. I have been out into the world, talked with the angels, and now I have returned."

"So if you're not looking for an advantage in the histories, what are you looking for?" Mark asked.

"For a solution," Zepp shot back. "For a way to end the cycle of death and revenge. For some way to save my world from destruction. There has to be some way to do it. Look at what has happened here on Chamal since you arrived – ask Arshand, he'll tell you the details. The cities burn everywhere. All the powers of the old world are overthrown – the bankers of Meshkar, the carnivore cats of Birhat, the Blue Monkeys, the Vegetarians of Rikabar. But the powers that have overthrown them are nothing more than angry and frightened mobs. You saw what it was like at the Assembly of Traitors. It's the same all over the world."

"I imagine it is," Mark said. "But what do you want to do about it?"

"I don't know," Zepp said. "That's why I was looking for histories. Maybe something about how the Blue Monkeys ended the chaos after the last Red Monkeys fled to Suridash a so many years ago.

Maybe something Jobe did when he returned to Suridash at the end of his walk." And then Zepp felt his heart crack as he admitted the fearful truth that left him helpless alone. "And I can't think of what it would be. Jobe would know. My Uncle Tapp would know, but he's been dead eight years. Maybe even Tedrak back in Suridash would know, though I doubt it. But I don't know. And I don't know why I don't know. I guess I'm just not wise enough."

***

Mark Paradis was dazzled by the conversation with Zepp.

He had not imagined such passionate desperation and such desperate passion could burn beneath the surface of the small creature. He had initially thought of Zepp as a clerk, with low status and few skills. But he was beginning to understand that his responsibility within his tribe was a function only of his age. Without the interference of the angels, Mark was sure he would have been trained in the elite skills needed by a politically powerful urban clan like the tribe of Jobe. And as a result, he had been underestimating the poor fellow.

Not only was this world much more complex and subtle than he had envisioned in the months since their arrival in-system, but so were its inhabitants. So Zepp was no exception.

The insights that he gave Mark in the last half hour were enough for the anthropologist in him to sink his teeth into the true culture of Chamal. It had all the problems of post-industrial decay and social disintegration, compounded by the struggle between its intelligent members and their link to a wild and irrational nature. It was a wonder that chamalians had ever raised up a civilization in the first place, let alone what appeared to be dozens of them, all competing for primacy, all racing against a genetic clock.

And then he realized it was the not inconsiderable personal energy of creatures like Zepp that drove the race forward. In spite of all the weight of Chamal's oddball genetics, mad geniuses managed to arise and convince their fellows to pursue a seemingly impossible goal – to overcome their darker natures and organize for a common purpose.

The thought sent a chill up his spine.

He wondered where Zepp would take his race if given sufficient backing. There was only way to find out for sure, he realized.

"Maybe I can help you out," Mark said at last, the nerve endings in his own body tingling with excitement.

"What can you do?" Zepp asked, the professor giving his voice a hint of suspicion.

"You may not be able to find much in your own history, but I can let you look at mine. Professor, you are authorized to provide Zepp access to all unsealed historical records. Tell him whatever he wants to know."

"As you command," the machine acknowledged.

Zepp froze in his tracks. He said nothing, but looked askance at Mark. At first, he seemed unsure and unsteady, but then he chittered loudly – chamalian laughter.

"Thank you, cousin Mark," he said, the professor verifying that he used the term for a familiar clansman. "It may help me more than you'll ever know."

CHAPTER THIRTEEN

The prison fortress Pang Hi, last stronghold of the Blue Monkeys along the river, appeared to Zepp at first as a faint multicolored glow in the thick night fog that lay heavy on the waters of the Li Pang Do.

He and Mark were in the third of four boats. Arshand shared the craft, listening on the radio as they made their way across the river. It was sometime past midnight, nearly six hours after the pilgrims had learned the location of the angel, Helen Castain, and her captors.

The prison grew clearer as they paddled upriver. Powerful electric lights of orange, blue, and white burned brightly across its ramparts. The bulbs were shaped into great ideograms – the Blue Monkey symbols of fear, death, and mutilation – and blinked on and off at unsynchronized intervals.

Zepp thanked the great ancestor that they were not bound for the fortress itself. That would be too daunting a challenge.

Their goal, instead, was a house across the canal from there, a few blocks downriver from the mighty stone battlements. Zepp had heard the stories of the Pang Hi fortress – its dungeons and torture chambers. Here was where the Blue Monkeys had anchored their power. The Reds had been geniuses at everything, mass mobilization included, but the Blues were just tyrants, brutal, simple, and unrestrained.

The female angel was being held hostage, but was safe and sound for the moment. She was still a prisoner of the Muskrat Guild, which was demanding an unspecified ransom for her safe return.

The building was in the old section of Ring Po Do, where the canals were sluggish and poorly-maintained. And the river crossing was under the eyes of Pang Hi.

A shaft of blue-white light swept through the fog somewhere close to the fortress walls. A brief draft of air parted the fog and revealed the ramparts of the fortress in momentarily bold detail. A chill ran out to the end of Zepp's tail, curling it in on itself.

They made the landing without incident. The first boat secured a small dock on the riverside a thousand hands downriver from the boom that blocked the mouth of Pang Hi Canal. The pilgrims aboard spread out in swift military fashion, taking up posts around the perimeter as the other boats landed in turn.

Three pale moons floated high in the sky, clear of the fog, giving Zepp a good view of the dock. Even so, he felt his liver climb into his mouth as he stepped out of the unsteady boat.

Once all were ashore, the company of two dozen pilgrims, one angel, and Zepp marched quickly down an alley into the interior of the Old Quarter. Beyond the stone buildings that lined the riverfront stood tenements resembling stacks of lumber hastily tacked together and wrapped with tarpaper. If there weren't so many of them, Zepp would have sworn they were nothing more than construction debris.

The pilgrims at the head of the long column ordered a halt and scanned the area ahead with a night-viewer. Arshand was proud of his new toy and bragged about the latest gadget from the shops of Kwikorak. With it he could look into the darkness and see images on a video screen that looked as if it were broad daylight.

They were only a few blocks from the building where Helen was being held. The first task would be to secure the route there and back. Then they would have to go in after the captive. That would be tough part.

"Hold!" Arshand whispered harshly. Zepp could tell by the tone and by the abrupt movements of the pilgrims around him that this wasn't part of the plan.

The lead squad, which had stopped the column, reported back to Arshand. There was someone else up ahead – a big party, nearly as big as their own.

Arshand huddled with the leaders of the four squads that comprised the company. After a few minutes of discussion, they hurried back to their posts. Then Zepp heard the soft rustling of pilgrims disappearing into the woodwork.

"I've sent them on ahead to arrange an ambush," he told Zepp. "If we're lucky, we can catch them all in one bag without firing a shot. If we're not, the expedition ends here." Zepp could do nothing but wait for events to unfold. After what seemed like forever but could have been no more than a few minutes, a messenger appeared from the front of the column. The ambush had been successful.

He wondered at the report, considering that the silence of the night remained unbroken. But he didn't have time for the wonder or even to appreciate the good news. A minute later, one squad returned with a prisoner. Arshand conducted the questioning, relying on a probing manner and a sharp knife that he kept openly visible throughout the interview as he used it to peel and slice a piece of fruit.

"We are a party from the Weasels League. We have come to settle an old debt with the muskrats," the small chamalian said. "We have territorial claims to these blocks in the Old Quarter. The muskrats dislodged us when they first came to the city in the reign of the last

Red Monkeys and never made adequate compensation." Arshand nodded and asked the creature to state his business more specifically, punctuating the query with a short jab of the knife. Zepp pulled his eyes away from the blade long enough to look at the weasel's eyes following it faithfully.

"We have come to steal the hostage from them."

***

Mark Paradis shivered against the night chill. They'd been holed up in this alley for nearly an hour, and the stone pavement had sucked the heat out of his feet all the way up to his knees. He didn't know if it was nerves or the cold that made him shiver now.

He knew it was an hour, because Barrett made a big point of it when he called in.

"Are you going to be out there another hour, or have your pilgrims finally made up their minds to go in after Helen?" he asked.

"We'll be going in there shortly," Mark said. "We seem to have picked up some reinforcements. They'll be making a diversionary attack to draw away the guards."

"Just make sure everyone moves quickly," Barrett said. "Don't give them time to think about sacrificing the hostage."

Mark assured him he would pass the instructions along, but decided against reminding him that they both had little influence over the conduct of the mission. And in any case, Arshand had given the signal for silence and the pilgrims made ready to move again.

Mark was grateful at the chance to restore the circulation to his feet and work some heat into his bones. But a moment later, the cold became the least of his concerns.

He had grown used to the popping of small arms fire and the occasional boom of explosives across the city, even as it diminished while the night grew older without ever quite ceasing.

Then suddenly the crackle of automatic weapons fire erupted from a few blocks away. Arshand and the pilgrims began to run, hurrying Mark along with them. His stiff muscles protested, but he ran on and managed to keep up.

They rounded a corner in the alleys and spilled onto a wide street lined with brick buildings. The firefight was raging to the left. Mark could make out a low pile of dark square structures behind a portico of rough white stone. Flashes of light from the guns were visible both inside the buildings and on the streets around it.

They arrived just in time to see a flash of blue light, followed by a chest-pounding KA-BOOM! A wall of smoke rushed across the street and wrapped itself around them.

Before it cleared, Mark felt himself being tugged forward. When they were past the smoke he found himself inside a high-ceilinged entryway, surrounded by black-clad pilgrims. A single torch lay burning on the floor, throwing tall shadows against the wall.

Arshand pointed upwards, and the rescue party rushed on.

Mark looked around for Zepp and found him quickly, his green fur standing out in the crowd.

"Zepp, head to the right," yelled Arshand. "They're to the right." Zepp acknowledged the signal, and the party worked its way down a long zig-zagging hallway towards that end of the building.

They exchanged fire with another set of guards halfway down the hall. Mark kept his head down and tried to keep his body armor towards the source of the gunfire. He looked over in time to see a fusillade of bullets shred the arm of one of the pilgrims, the blood splattering against the far wall.

He swore under his breath. He was developing a very personal animosity towards the creatures shooting at him. He also wished he had something to shoot back with. Luckily, the pilgrims had come adequately equipped and the exchange was brief.

Not brief enough for the wounded pilgrim, of course.

A few moments later, they passed a series of heavy wooden doors. They were almost to the end of that section of corridor when Helen's scream split the air. "Hey, come back this way," he said. "I just heard her." The pilgrims came back and found the right door. A round of fire made quick work of the lock and the door opened onto a small chamber.

Helen Castain stood in the center of the room, obviously distressed, but otherwise unharmed.

"Mark!" she called. "Am I glad to see you. These guys looked real cute and cuddly for a while, but they got nasty when the shooting started." A single oil lamp cast a dim light over the room. It was just bright enough for Mark to make out a brown, furry body laying limp on the floor. She looked down at the body apologetically, then moved forward.

"I had to hit him with the stool," she said. "I didn't really want to hurt him, but he just wouldn't leave me alone." The pilgrims took up station around them and they headed back the way Mark had come in. They were at the entrance, which still smoldered and stank of charred wood, when the crackle and popping of gunfire splattered down the street from the south.

Mark was no soldier, but he knew that was a new source of activity. They halted in the entryway to the building as Arshand spoke with his squad leaders by radio. A minute later, Zepp came over with the news.

"We've got trouble," he said. "The banshees are joining the fight. They're between us and the boats and there's no way around them."

***

The guns of the banshees sounded heavier, louder, and closer than those of the weasels and muskrats, Zepp noticed. Arshand spoke quickly with his lieutenant. The two angels huddled against one wall. Zepp found the time to be afraid once more.

And once again the pilgrims continued on fearlessly – or so it seemed to him.

Arshand gave the order and they headed west – away from the canal and back into the wooden tenements. One squad went first, then another, then the remainder of the party, each covering the other while they bounded forward.

Zepp wondered if Arshand was being clever, leaving the weasels to face the banshees and cover their escape. If so, it didn't work. He heard the exchange of fire behind them as they raced down an alleyway between two rough-hewn walls. The high snap of the pilgrims' weapons made strained counterpoint against the dull boom of the banshees' equipment.

The next thing he knew, a pilgrim pulled him through an open doorway. A hand torch revealed a brief tableau of two pilgrims pointing their guns at a half dozen muskrats. They'd no doubt been awakened by the gunfire and looked surprised at the sudden turn of the battle.

Then Zepp was through another door and back outside. Now Arshand had them doubling back towards the Pang Hi canal. Zepp saw the wisdom in that. If they could get across, it would make it harder for the banshees to pursue them.

They made the crossing over a bridge of carved stone. The eyes of fearsome beasts followed Zepp as he ran down its length. He kept his head low and his tail wrapped around his leg. The angels were right beside him.

At the far end of the bridge, however, the rush stopped abruptly. A high wooden gate blocked the way. Two pilgrims stood side by side, helping their mates over the top. Four more had taken position at the bridge, their guns pointing back over the water.

Zepp was already out of breath, and the climb was almost more than he could do. He cursed quietly, naming ancestors whose sins were so terrible they were listed in the black book of the tribe, as he scraped the wood with cold fingers.

But a boost from the pilgrim on his right was enough to get him over. Helen Castain followed quickly, then Mark. This side of the gate was a wide open plaza. In the moonlight, Zepp could see high walls running along the canal to the south.

Then he saw that the plaza ended at the foot of the walls of Pang Hi Fortress.

His blood turned cold. The sight of Arshand after he passed over the gate was not enough to warm it.

A shaft of light shot out from the top of the wall. Everyone scrambled for cover as it swept towards them. They were not all quick enough or lucky enough.

The light was followed with the echoing pop-pop-pop of automatic weapons. Zepp took cover behind a low stone wall around a raised garden. Bullets and stone chips flew all around him. Arshand dropped to the ground beside him. "At least we got rid of the banshees," he said.

***

Every strand of fur on Zepp's body stood on end. He hugged the paving stones, but he barely felt their cold embrace. The sound of the guns on the wall above them seemed to recede into the distance.

He was having an inspiration.

He didn't know where the idea came from, but suddenly a stray memory of a conversation with Mark flashed to the surface of his mind. They had been talking about Griddle and the doubts the other angels held about his powers.

"They argue that it was merely the power of suggestion that made them work," Mark had said. "It's called sympathetic magic. If you believe in it, it works."

He had dismissed it vehemently, having seen the grisly evidence of Griddle's unwanted gift. But what if Mark was right in one respect? Even if Griddle truly had the dark touch, wasn't it possible that some of his power came from the fears of his attackers?

It was one of those sublime thoughts that sparkle in the imagination and seize the soul with their energy.

This was hardly a good time to test the thought, Zepp realized sorrowfully, but there wasn't likely to be another. He turned to Arshand.

"I need your radio," he said. "The big one that amplifies your voice." He expected the pilgrim to put up an argument, but he didn't hesitate. Their eyes locked for a brief moment, and Zepp saw unquestioning acceptance in the other, as if Arshand knew that Zepp had been inspired.

"On the wall!" Zepp called out, his voice echoing from the walls of the plaza and the fortress. "Cease firing! Cease firing!" The shooting stopped, and a moment later a voice replied with equal volume: "Who goes there?"

Zepp drew a breath and said, "Zepp, Ambassador to the Angels from the *Deragathon*. For your own safety, cease firing."

"Our safety?" the voice asked. "Worry about your own safety, interlopers. You're from the *Deragathon*? How do we know you're not mutineers."

"We escaped the mutiny. If you know the story of the mutiny, then you know what happened. Do you know about the jinx that nearly destroyed the vessel?" There was a moment of hesitant silence. "We heard rumors."

"Then you know the danger you are in. The jinx is here with me. If you shoot at us, it is only a matter of time before your guns misfire and your ammunition explodes in your faces. If you capture us, your fortress will be a shambles in a week. The river will pull down its stones, the timbers will rot beneath the walls, and your troops will hoist their leaders on their spears." The silence this time was longer. Zepp saw that a squad of pilgrims behind a statue to his left had set up the night-vision monitor and were watching the guards on the wall in close-up. "Give us a clear shot," hissed one, but Arshand put up a hand to signal them to wait.

"Where is this jinx?" the voice finally demanded.

Zepp swallowed, then without pausing stepped out into the glare of the spotlight in the middle of the plaza. He heard Helen Castain gasp and Mark shout, "No!"

"Here he is," Zepp announced. The popping of the weapons began. He waited for the bullets to cut him down.

But before they did, a gun cracked to his left and a scream replaced the gunfire on the wall.

He continued to stand unprotected, waiting longer, knowing that a single bullet could end his bluff at any instant. "See the first of you to die from this curse," he called.

A second crack echoed across the plaza and another guard let out a mortal scream.

"Enough!" cried the voice from the fortress. "What do you want?"

"To be gone," Zepp answered.

"Then depart quickly, foul beast," the voice replied. "And do not return or we will test the limits of bad luck."

Arshand sent a squad bounding towards the wall on the far side of the plaza as the light atop the wall faded to a distant glowing ember. Another squad followed, then the pilgrim grabbed Zepp and the angels and rushed after them.

***

The boats met them upriver from Pang Hi fortress. The company scrambled down a narrow stone stairway to a floating wooden dock. The sharp scent of acetone hung in the air – organic byproducts from the thousands of chamalians who resided in Ring Po Do – and left Mark's nose burning.

They boarded without incident, Mark in the third boat with Helen and Zepp. Once they were seated, Barrett got in touch with him once again.

"Now what the hell was that little demonstration at the fortress walls all about?" he asked.

"I'm not sure," Mark said. "He used the Rift Valley pidgin instead of his own language again. The professor isn't up to speed on it yet, and I couldn't get a translation. The rest of his friends certainly started treating him differently afterwards, though."

"I would, too," Barrett said. "He's either a lunatic or he knew the right words to get you past that ambush."

"I hate to say it, but I think it's a little bit of both," Mark suggested. "They call it 'cha.' It's a combination of luck, inspiration, and madness. Zepp doesn't think he has much of it, but after tonight I'm not so sure."

"You could ask him what he said or did," Barrett said.

"Is that commentary or a request?" Mark asked.

Barrett snorted a harsh reply. Mark leaned close to Zepp, spoke briefly with him, then reported back to the lieutenant.

"You're not going to believe it," Mark said. "He said he told them he was a jinx and that if they didn't let them pass, terrible things would happen to them."

"Ha!" Barrett spouted. "Like snipers taking out their sentries."

"That's what he said and that's what happened."

"There's always the chance they didn't really want to take the risks involved in bringing in a couple dozen prisoners. If they're under siege, they probably don't have the supplies. And if they were going to kill you, they would have done it then and there."

"I suppose that makes sense," Mark said. "But there is another possibility."

"And what's that?"

"Maybe they believed him."

Barrett had no quick reply to that. A moment later, though, he changed the subject.

"Well, what do we do now?" Mark turned to Helen and repeated

Barrett's question.

"Speaking as an entirely disinterested observer, I think we should get out of this place as fast as we can," Helen said. "I think it's pretty obvious that we aren't going to find any kind of stable political leadership anywhere around here."

"At least not outside of Pang Hi fortress," Mark quipped.

"Not even in there," Helen said. "A fortress under siege doesn't produce healthy minds – at least not in any history I've ever read."

"Our other choices are severely limited," Mark said. "The only really valid option is Suridash, Zepp's home town."

"And what do we find there?" Barrett asked.

"The leaders of his tribe. They're the ones who sent him to the *Deragathon* in the first place. Of the members of the alliance, they're the only ones who haven't undergone a devastating social upheaval back home. Of course, as Zepp describes it, the city has been in a perpetual civil war for a couple of centuries. But the level of violence is much lower than it is around here. They seem to manage it a lot better."

"They'd have to if they were going to keep at it for that long," Barrett said.

"There's only one problem," Mark said.

"What's that?"

"I don't think Zepp wants to go back there."

"Why not?" asked Helen, obvious concern in her voice.

"He won't talk about it. But I think it has something to do with broken taboos. He says they blackmailed him into going on the sabotage mission. But he won't tell me what they used for pressure."

"Great. Our one contact with the *Deragathon* and he doesn't want to go back."

"Couldn't you ask him?" Helen said. "Couldn't you persuade him somehow? Is it really more frightening for him in Suridash than it is here?"

"I don't know," Mark said. "Not here and not now. Maybe when we get back to the pilgrimage house. And I don't know how much leverage I have over him. There are still a lot of things I don't understand about these guys – though I'm learning fast. You wouldn't believe the conversation Zepp and I had before we came looking for you. I think I'm finally beginning to get the whole picture."

"Good for you," Helen said. Barrett just made a disinterested harumphing sound.

"I'd just hate to lose the closest thing we have to a friend on this planet because we tried to force him to do something he didn't want to do."

CHAPTER FOURTEEN

Zepp was napping in the library when Arshand found him.

The pilgrim woke him from a dream in which he was being chased through the passageways of the *Deragathon* by his cousins. They were calling for his blood. Linked to him by a long piece of chain was Griddle. His cousins kept shooting at them with oversized handguns, but every shot went wide, ricocheting off the bulkhead.

He was relieved to see the warm, crowded shelves around him instead of the cold metal bulkheads of the spaceship when he opened his eyes – although his blood pumped furiously from the fearful nightmare.

"The angels are sleeping," Arshand said. "So I thought it would be safe to talk. I wasn't sure if they did that, you know. Yours did not until we rescued his companions."

"Oh yes," Zepp replied. "They sleep, they eat, they breed. In many ways they are just like us – even if they are different in many others."

The scales on Arshand's arms rippled as he flexed his hands, the bristly fur raking the air. He sat down on a large pillow across the floor from where Zepp lay.

"We must leave soon," he said. "The Pang Hi fortress went into mutiny before dawn. Soon now their defenses will go down and the fortress will belong to the Assembly of Traitors – or its survivors."

"Is that bad?" Zepp asked. "You sound worried."

"There is an armory in the fortress. They have many rockets. The tribes converging on the fortress are the same tribes that bear the most ill will towards us. Before long, those rockets will begin crashing into the compound here. And in any case, loyalist Blue Monkey regiments are converging on Ring Po Do. The time for us to move on is rapidly approaching."

"You should wake the angels," Zepp said. "They will need time to get ready to move. They require food and water and all that we do upon awaking."

"You know a great deal about them," he said.

"Not really. Very little, actually."

"More than anyone else on Chamal. And you tell them much about us. Perhaps too much." A chill ran out to the tip of Zepp's tale and set his green fur on end. "You listened to Mark and I talking last night?"

"I would be a poor master of this house if I did not keep track of all that transpired here. Of course I listened. You were very passionate in your description of the chamalian condition. Very wise as well."

Zepp felt humbled. Arshand was the first tribesman to offer such a compliment. Back home in Suridash, his cousins were more likely to point out flaws in his grooming or personal hygiene.

"You do me an honor," Zepp said.

"You do us an honor by your presence," Arshand said. "You seem genuinely unaware of your talents. That is to your benefit, but you should not let your innocence continue thus for long. You are likely to need all of your wisdom and then some to settle the crisis that has seized the world."

"Do you really think I could do anything to change the destiny of Chamal? Because I certainly don't."

"What I think matters little," Arshand said.

Zepp let his head drop and stared at the mosaic in the floor for a while. It was an illustration of Jobe marching into the highlands of Kwikorak.

"The angels will want you to take them to Suridash," the pilgrim said after a long silence.

Zepp felt the fear wash over him like a spring flood from the Li Pang Do. Suridash – there was nothing waiting for him there but pain and humiliation. The whole tribe of Jobe knew his sin – how could it be hidden? To return there would truly be the end of his life.

He was afraid that his fear would show and tried to hide his face from Arshand, but it did no good.

"You must be in deep trouble there," Arshand said.

"Deeper than you can imagine. How do you know what the angels want? Did you listen to them as well?"

"No. That wasn't necessary. It is the only sensible thing for them to do. You should be able to see that as well as I."

"I suppose you're right," Zepp said with a sigh. The fear now rested in his stomach, clenching itself around his gut. "I suppose there is no escaping my own destiny. No matter how terrible."

"After last night, I don't believe anyone can know what your destiny is," Arshand said. "Very few chamalians would do what you did."

"Very few chamalians are as mad and witless as I am."

"You do yourself a dishonor. I have been a pilgrim for a long time. I have seen many come along the Way of Jobe. None of them had your wisdom or your spirit. Trust me on this. You may not know your own destiny, but it is clear that you must follow the Way as well. Wisdom goes out into the world and returns. Your fate lies in Suridash."

"Thanks," Zepp said. "That is very encouraging."

"Nevertheless it is as it is. But I came to tell you something else. Something that may ease your burden somewhat." Against his will, Zepp's hopes rose from the dark depths of his inner horror. What could Arshand possibly tell him that would make his life any less bleak? Or his fate any less sure?

"And that is?"

"You will not return to Suridash alone," Arshand announced with certainty and courage. "I will go there with you. And as many of this house as the angels will carry. Whatever awaits you in Suridash will have to contend with us as well."

"You would do that for me?" Zepp asked, his voice trembling and his spirit incredulous.

"After last night, we would follow you through the gates of hell itself." Arshand said.

Zepp finally let go of his fear and felt it blow away like smoke in a gale. His soul felt as light as smoke as well, rising ever upwards. Maybe the pilgrims were right after all, he thought. Maybe his fate was more complicated than he could imagine.

Or maybe he was just letting his hopes get the best of him, so that cruel fate could dash him down all that much farther.

In any case, he turned to Arshand and said: "You may just get the chance to do that."

***

For some reason that Zepp didn't quite understand, Mark was surprised by his announcement that he would accompany them to Suridash and help them any way he could.

He was afraid that the angel might have seen through the deception in his words. That Mark would know that he might not be able to help them at all. That the truth was that Zepp's sins were clearly known to his tribe and that all they would want from him was the terrible penalty that was due.

Or even worse – that Mark somehow knew what the pilgrims had in mind for the angels.

"I'm not sure the angel Barrett will allow you on board his vessel," Zepp had told Arshand.

"We weren't planning to ask for permission," Arshand had replied.

But the moment passed, Mark told Barrett, and the angels made ready to return to their craft.

They went back to the boats one more time, slipping into the water before the sky began to brighten. Only now they let the current carry them downriver – with extra caution as they passed under each bridge – until they were out of the city proper and into an agricultural area.

They came ashore at the edge of a watergrain paddy, where a splay-footed antelope-headed farmworker met them to act as a guide. A few minutes later, twenty-seven chamalians and two angels formed a long single file stretching out along the tops of the dikes that formed a huge maze in an otherwise flooded plain. They passed wide spots on the dike where huts and dens had been slapped together out of reeds, mud, and grass, with steplings and halflings playing along the path.

As the sun began to peek over the eastern end of the valley, a distant flash of light appeared. Then a ball of smoke and flame rose on the horizon. Another flash followed, then another ball of hellfire. A long moment, less than a minute but more than a lifetime, passed before the rumbling thunder of the explosions reached them.

Arshand turned and looked grimly back at Zepp. "That was the compound," he said. "The attack has begun." Zepp felt a terrible sense of finality. There was no way back now. Only a path forward into an uncertain and frightful future.

After an hour's walk, they reached the end of the paddies and the western edge of the city. A large shanty town sprawled along the boundary of the agricultural area, and on the far side of the shanties, Arshand said, lay the spaceport.

If anyone had been following the pilgrims – even just shadowing them from afar – the shanty town gave the company a chance to elude them. They wound their way through a labyrinth of ad hoc pathways and streets. The inhabitants of the shanties were nowhere in sight. Refugees by now, no doubt. The battles at the spaceport would have been enough to send most of the residents running.

Another hour passed before they found their way to the other side of the shanty town and the wide avenue that marked the boundary of the spaceport. They paused for a while to prepare for the next step in their journey.

The pilgrims checked their weapons once again, and Zepp told the angels that they should inspect their armor before going any further.

The warrior angel Barrett, speaking on Mark's radio, was quick to question what the pilgrims were expecting. Arshand explained.

"The question of your custody and the custody of your spaceship was never decided," he said. "The Assembly of Traitors broke up before it could be discussed, if you'll recall. We were able to take you from the banshees that first morning because we finessed the other tribes. But the others have since restated their claims to the ship. The tree-cats currently have the strongest claim."

"What's that mean?" Barrett asked.

"They hold the field surrounding the ship, while the others are dug-in around the cats' perimeter."

"And what are your plans?"

"We're going to shoot our way in."

The translation of Arshand's words delayed the reaction of the angels momentarily. But Zepp grew alarmed at the way they leapt to their feet and clutched at one another once they understood.

"There's got to be another way," Mark said.

"You can't," was all Zepp heard from Helen.

Barrett, however, calmed them all down with suggestions of his own.

"There are other ways," he said. "Give me a minute to start up the engines again like I did the night we landed. That should disperse some of the cats and give you some cover."

Arshand discussed it with his lieutenants, and they agreed. Then, to Zepp, in Blue Monkey pidgin, he said: "Remember not to reveal what we plan to do."

Zepp gestured quickly in the affirmative. They both knew that it was in his best interests to do things this way.

Helen Castain was still opposed to the revised plan, but she cut her protests short when she saw they weren't being recognized. A few minutes later Arshand gave the order and Barrett gave the ship its commands.

Clouds of smoke and dust rose up from the field in the distance. Then they were on their feet and crossing the avenue into the spaceport.

They ran until Zepp's blood pounded in his ears and his throat burned at every breath. The dirty brown clouds of dust mingled with the sharp white steam of the ship's engines and raced to meet them.

Gunfire crackled across the hot pavement. Zepp felt as if his lungs were about to explode. When the cloud of hot gases engulfed him, he began to cough. He almost fell to the ground, but managed to keep going. It was all he could do to keep up with Mark. He didn't want to lose contact with the angels and the wise teacher. Without them, Arshand's plan would surely fail.

The popping sound of pilgrim weapons close by gave him a chill. In this murky brown world, how could anyone know what he was shooting at? Then he heard a long BRAAAAAAATTT! Its source was ahead, but above the field. It was matched by a dull echo, the sound of hailstones hitting a stone roof, from the ground before them. Slugs from the weapons atop the angels' ship.

Danger was all around them. Zepp's fur buzzed with electric fear. Then suddenly the hiss of the spaceship engines stopped, as did the obscene sound of its weapons. A gust of wind blew the clouds away, revealing the craft only a short distance away.

Their path to the base of the pinnace was clear. Off to the left and right fresh smoke poured upwards, twisted to the side by an erratic breeze. Zepp watched the squads of pilgrims leapfrog forward. Atlee first, then Mugrum on the right, Krill ahead on the left, followed by Frit.

Zepp barely noticed it when the arrangement of forces shifted subtly. Two members of each squad appeared to the side of each angel. But when they reached the spaceship, the squads dispersed completely, intermixing as they surrounded the ship. They dropped to the ground in defensive positions.

Barrett was at the entrance when it opened. He yelled and motioned, but Zepp was too far away to hear the wise teacher's translation. Mark was several hands to Zepp's left, lying on the ground beside four pilgrims.

"He says to send us over, and he'll cover your escape," Mark yelled.

Zepp felt his tail curl in nervous fear. The moment had nearly come. Only one piece remained to fall into place.

From across the field came the sound of a rising crescendo of weapons fire. The dispossessed clans were returning to their positions, surrounding the ship once again – and the pilgrims with it.

Arshand was a short distance to the right, with Mugrum at his side. He signaled to Zepp. The time to act was upon them.

"Mark!" he yelled, "Tell Barrett that we're coming with you. Tell him to go inside with Mugrum's squad. Atlee will follow with Helen. Frit will go in with me, and Krill will take you."

"What? What are you doing? If you want to come with us, just ask. You don't need to blackmail us."

"We didn't know if Barrett would take everyone," he said. "We have to be sure." The angel shook his head from side to side, which the wise teacher had told him indicated a negative. But he called out to Barrett in the entrance to the ship.

Barrett yelled back for a long time in words Zepp could not understand, but which sounded more and more angry as he went on.

Bullets thwacked against the hull above his head and he cut short his remarks. An instant later he waved at Mugrum and motioned him onto the spaceship.

By now, the tree-cats were pressing in before Krill, muskrats were advancing on Atlee, and the hounds were baying at Frit. With their squads dispersed, each leader could board the ship without leaving a sector of the line undefended.

Mugrum's squad dashed for the entrance, scrambled inside, and disappeared. Then Atlee went in with Helen bent over low. A moment later the pinnace's weapons opened up again, slapping back the fire that was smacking off the ship's hull.

Frit huddled next to Zepp, then ran with him to the spaceship door. They hurried down a short passageway into a compartment stuffed full of armed chamalians. Helen sat with her face in her hands.

Arshand followed close on their heels. Then Mark and Krill were with them. An instant later Zepp felt the floor tilt and then press up against him. Two dozen eyes rolled at once as Barrett took the pinnace away from the spaceport and away from Ring Po Do.

But the thing that bothered Zepp the most was the memory of Mark's voice as he ran past the angel on the way to the ship. The wise teacher repeated his words over and over: "This isn't necessary. This isn't necessary at all."

***

Barrett's face was red. Not just any shade of red, but something approaching the boiled lobsters you could get at the shacks down by the Boston waterfront. He didn't say a word, but the color blazed in his forehead, his cheeks, even the tips of his ears – with cords of white for contrast where the muscles had tightened up.

"Damn it!" he said. "If they'd asked me, I would have let them come. Why did they pull a trick like that? I don't like it when someone jams me up that way. I get downright pissed off when someone levers me around like that. Does your AI know how to translate 'pissed off,' Mr. Paradis?"

Mark felt terrible. While he knew that he wasn't responsible for the chamalians' behavior, he couldn't help but feel guilty. And he couldn't help but try to defend their machinations.

"That's just the way they are," he said. "They don't know how to ask. They don't know how to trust anyone else. And they assume the worst. If you thought about it, you'd see why they did the only thing that made sense to them. If you put yourself in their position, you'd have to admit that you'd do the same thing."

"Of course I'd do the same thing," Barrett howled. "That's what's got me so damned mad. If it weren't for that, I'd be shoving pilgrims out the hatch right now."

Mark shook his head in puzzlement. He didn't know what to say.

"Just tell them they didn't have to do that, will you?" Barrett said at last. "Tell them that next time they should talk to me. We'll work something out. I don't mind having a few good warriors at my side – not after seeing what this place is like. But I want them to be MY warriors and I want them to obey MY orders. Can they understand that? Can YOU understand that?"

Mark searched for a snappy retort, but decided against it. Provoking Barrett further wouldn't help things at all. "I'll do my best," he said instead. "But I can't promise anything. You don't realize just how crazy things are on this planet. Or how complicated it is to deal with these creatures."

"Too complicated for me," Barrett said. "Too damned complicated." Barrett cooled off as they made the transit to Suridash. It was a straight ballistic trajectory, he explained. Up about fifty miles or so in a long parabola and then back down again. They made the five thousand kilometer journey in about twenty minutes.

Mark fetched Zepp up to the bridge for the approach to the desert city.

Down in the hold, he was struck once more by the variety of shapes and forms among the pilgrims. No two were alike – a blue cat-like face with sharp ears stood next to a split-lip, long-eared hare, while a fluffy round-eared bear with a black button nose played games with a throwing knife. Zepp was flanked by a pair of armed guards – a small rat-faced gunner with long whiskers on his left and a graceful long-haired ape with long arms on his right.

Zepp followed him up to the bridge and they watched as Barrett took the pinnace in low and slow, circling the city once. The swift day of Chamal had barely begun here, and long shadows were starting to shrink, but not before throwing the walls and towers of the city into sharper relief.

"The walls make the city," Zepp said to no one in particular.

Mark could see what he meant. There were walls within walls within walls. Big ones around the perimeter, with battlements and heavy gates. Smaller ones dividing up the interior like the chambers of a nautilus, only lacking the mathematical precision of the sea-creature's spiraling curve.

"The Red Monkey enclave is to the north," Zepp said. "The Chorai to the east. In the west are the enclaves of the Banjukai, Rital, Ravina – refugees from the Rikabarian conquests along the south shore of the ocean. In the south are the Frel, the Clans of Cobar, the Tristomaria, and the Torp – refugees from Meshkar and the equatorial forests. And there in the center, where that hill stands, is the enclave of the tribe of Jobe." Mark was surprised to see that Zepp's enclave was rather modest compared to some of the others. Then he felt a chill as he recalled what his professional training and his experience said about small social groups living in tightly bound artificially isolated environments. Environments not unlike, say, the

Tycho colony.

Did the chamalians become suspicious and paranoid because of the kinds of architecture they favored? Or did they become enamored of walls because of their perverse psychology?

"Are those big buildings part of your holdings?" Mark asked, pointing out the piles of stone and metal near one end of the enclave.

"That's the center of the city. It belongs to no one enclave, but my tribe is the perpetual caretaker. The big one is the Hall of the Seedkeepers. The Library of Jobe is the smaller one next to it." All around them, the desert stretched to the horizon, bleached by the sun of all its color. All that broke the featureless sands was a wide area of gray haze and a band of blue to the north – the brackish eastern arm of the great ocean.

"Arshand says to set down near the West Gate," Zepp said. "As pilgrims, we should enter the city there. It is also known as the Gate of Jobe's Return."

Barrett grumbled, but once he was certain of where the West Gate was, he complied with the instructions.

It took a few minutes for the great clouds of dust to drift away on a lazy wind, but eventually the city walls appeared a couple of kilometers away. Barrett told Mark that two thousand meters was probably the maximum range of most chemical weapons the chamalians were likely to possess.

"What do we do now?" Barrett asked.

"We wait," said Zepp.

***

They didn't have to wait long.

Within less than an hour, a column of small electric carts issued forth from the West Gate. Zepp realized that Arshand had been right when he told the young ape not to worry about finding his clansmen. They had come to find him.

"The pilgrims left behind at Ring Po Do would have radioed ahead right after we left the pilgrimage house," he'd said during the brief flight. "The whole tribe will know we're coming long before we get there."

"Can we see them close up?" Mark asked.

A moment later a section of the wall at one end of the compartment turned into a window on the sands below. The lead cart in the column rolled into sight, enlarged to the point where it looked almost life-size. Zepp recognized one of his cousins behind the tiller.

Zepp looked out the other window, the real window, where Helen Castain peered into the bright daylight. They watched as the column reached the pinnace, then curved around it into a large circle, carts dropping off to take up position. Zepp's clansmen had come well-armed.

"Here we are again," Helen said. "Surrounded by hairy little aliens with too many guns." Zepp winced at the translation from the wise teacher, but recognized the irony in her words.

"Are these your relatives?" Mark asked.

"They are all from the tribe of Jobe," Zepp admitted.

"That was awfully quick," Barrett said. "What do they want?"

"I'm afraid they want me," Zepp said. Arshand had been quite clear on that point as well. In the middle of the chamalian apocalypse, Zepp's sin was the focal point of all the tribe of Jobe's passions. He had seen it before – and for sins of much less gravity than his.

One of the carts pulled ahead of the others. Barrett fiddled with a control and the artificial window revealed the face of Zepp's cousin Sherbek. He was a desert creature with a red coat, a long pointed nose, and thick tufts of fur across his eyes to keep out the sand. Another moment of fiddling produced a fair imitation of Sherbek's voice.

" – for judgment and punishment. He is our seed and he must answer to us. Do you hear me, angels? You must release our cousin, Zepp. He has transgressed the most important of taboos. You must render him up for judgment and punishment. If you do not, we will come in and take him."

"Judgment, then punishment," Mark said. "Don't they have to have one before they decide on the other?"

"There is no doubt or question about my sin, Mark," Zepp said. "It is plain for all the tribe to see."

More than the tribe, he realized with a sudden shock. The back of the Sherbek's cart was full of passengers. Not just armed tribesmen, but three figures wrapped in desert robes. But the robes were not enough to hide their faces. After a moment, Sherbek directed them to climb out of the cart and step around in front of it.

"Who are they?" Barrett asked.

There was a long silence, then Zepp announced: "They are my sisters – Tarina, Filomie, and Sree."

"Zepp, are you listening?" Sherbek shouted. "Your sisters say they miss you. They want you to come out and go home with them."

The three females were upset. Filomie was crying, while Tarina hissed at Sherbek. He growled at them, then waved them back to the cart. Each of them in turn leaned over the side of the vehicle and removed a large basket. They returned to the front of the cart and set the baskets down in the sand.

Sherbek strode over to stand before the baskets. "Look what they have brought you, cousin," he said. "Look what you have returned to."

The scene in the window staggered as Barrett manipulated the controls, bringing the baskets into closeup view. Helen gasped as they all could see that each of them contained three mewling pups, less than a long month old. And each pup sported a coat of fine downy fur – fur the same identical shade of green as Zepp's own.

He felt his skin grow hot beneath his green coat.

"And who are they?" asked Helen.

"They are my children – borne by my sisters," he said without expression. "And that, dear angels, is my sin."

CHAPTER FIFTEEN

"It wasn't my idea."

The professor repeated Zepp's words as Barrett groaned and Helen giggled. Mark Paradis shook his head, weary with the knowledge of what that had to mean for Zepp.

"That's disgusting," Barrett said.

"Speaking strictly as an anthropologist and as the representative of the Cultural Survey Section, Mr. Barrett, I feel a responsibility to tell you that remark was out of line," Mark said in a calm but serious voice.

"What?"

"None of us is in a position to make judgments about the sexual and reproductive protocols of an alien species," Mark said, maintaining the same tone. "Especially judgments based on values of our own species – or even worse, our own culture."

Barrett shook his head, but made no reply. Mark felt his blood begin to circulate once again when the Space Corps lieutenant turned his attention back to the viewscreen.

Zepp spoke and the professor said: "It wasn't their idea either."

"Whose idea was it?" Helen asked. Zepp's eyes remain fixed on the screen as his cousin sent his sisters back into the cart.

"Whirlpitt and Tedrak," Zepp said. "They needed a way to blackmail me into bringing Griddle aboard the *Deragathon*. This was it. Whirlpitt made them do it. He had them make a potion on me. I had to climb over Grampa Kobi's bedstead while he slept in order to get the keys. All the keys. Then we raced around the room trying every one of them in each other's locks until we found the right ones."

"Keys?" Barrett asked.

"To their chastity belts," Mark said.

Helen giggled again. "I'm sorry," she said to Mark. "I just couldn't help picturing it."

Mark smiled in spite of himself, then felt his face grow warm with embarrassment.

"Excuse me," said the professor in its own distinctive voice. "Zepp appears to be experiencing some respiratory and circulatory dysfunction."

Helen was on her feet in an instant and at Zepp's side. She helped him sit down and then turned to Mark: "Get my bag. There are some biological sensors in there."

Mark hurried to the locker and retrieved her gear. "I'm going to go get Arshand," he said.

He ducked down the ladder into the hold, found the pilgrim leader, and brought him up to the commons. Arshand put a hand to Zepp's neck and then his back, then lowered him onto the deck.

"He is only upset," Arshand said. "He'll be all right in a while, once he recovers his breath."

"Are you sure?" Helen asked. "Is this a common response to stress for your species?"

"Common? No. But it happens. And Zepp has much to worry about."

"Any suggestions about what to do with his cousins?" Mark asked. "They want to punish him for his sins. I assume you heard. What exactly does that mean?"

"Yes, we heard Sherbek. The customary punishment for this type of transgression is swift removal of the offending organ." Barrett moaned, Helen blanched, and Mark sucked in air involuntarily at the thought.

***

Zepp heard the voices of those around him, but lacked the will to respond. He was aware of it when they carried him down the passageway and placed him on a soft cot built into a shiny white wall in a small compartment, but he lacked the intent to assist or hinder them in any way.

He was conscious of all these things in a distant and unattached manner. As if they were occurring at the other end of a long corridor, in a dimly lighted room.

He was grateful, though, when the door to the compartment closed, leaving him alone with Helen, and silence enveloped him. It allowed him to sever contact at last with the rest of the world. To drift into the darkness and let it swallow him up.

That it did, but only for a moment.

Then the lights appeared.

Thousands and thousands of lights, climbing upwards, surging and rushing, in all the colors of the imagination, leaving long trails behind them, reaching and growing, growing and reaching, an unending and continuous flow up into an unknown and unknowable future.

Suddenly Zepp felt his own soul leap upwards with the lights. He saw that his own spirit burned with a bright spark just like all those colored stars around him. He was surging up into the unknown with all of them. And he realized that each spark was another spirit, just like his own. Another chamalian – thousands and millions, across the globe. They were all reaching and striving upwards together.

Zepp felt his body flush with excitement as he realized what was happening to him. He was having a night-vision.

He had talked about such things with Mark only recently. The angel asked what happened when Zepp slept. When angels slept, he said, they underwent false experiences, fantasies created by the sleeping mind. Zepp told him that chamalians dreamed too. But that they also were seized by waking dreams. Night-visions.

Jobe had been struck by a night-vision while a pilgrim in the highlands of Kwikorak. He had descended from the mountains as a shaman, feared and honored by the tribes of the equatorial rainforest. At least until he fell from grace and became immersed in the sin and corruption of those tribes.

But unlike dreams, night-visions were not fantasies. They were reality, made sharp and vivid by the full power of the chamalian brain, unleashed from the moment-by-moment demands of survival. This was a vision that seized the soul and rubbed its nose in the dirt.

In Zepp's case, the points of light began to dance, to coalesce in groups of similar hue, then to cast out each spark that changed color. Some were simply truncated, dropping off into the distance below as the rest carried on. They bundled and split, braided, intertwined, then dispersed.

He realized that he was watching the steady movement of the wisdom of the gods itself as it leapt from tribe to tribe, from breed to breed. And he was watching the steady struggle of the seed of wisdom to separate itself from the seed of the wild.

Suddenly a bright shining plane stretched out above them all. One by one, the colored lights hit the plane and stuck to it in place. They formed patterns and designs made of alien threads, dyed by a mad weaver and cast across a loom the size of all creation.

When Zepp himself hit the plane, his upward rise stopped abruptly, pitching him through onto the other side. There he saw all the strange members of Chamal's menagerie fixed in place. Their surging and rushing had stopped. Every living thing held its breath. Time itself hung in suspense.

And he realized that this was what had happened to his world. All that preceded the moment of the angels' arrival was gone forever, blown away like a dust painting on the pavement, as if none of it had ever been.

All that existed was this moment. This eternal now. The arrival of the angels.

The world remained transfixed by that event. And it would remain so until another event followed.

Zepp did not know what that event would be, but he was terrified at its imminence. Some dark fate overhung his world and his race. Something that even the angels could not prevent.

He did not know when it would come, but he knew it would not be long. Each day that passed, Chamal consumed a bit more of itself, its long-suffering children unbuilding what wisdom had taken so long to construct.

He did not know what the event would be like, but he felt he would be at its center. Just as he had been at the center of all that had happened so far. Whether he liked it or not, this was his fate.

Then, with all the same suddenness with which it had come over him, the night-vision was gone. He was back in a compartment aboard the angels' spaceship, and the only lights were the dim ones beside the door.

He rose unsteadily to his feet. His body felt weightless and insubstantial. Moving required no effort at all. His legs carried him along as if they had a will of his own.

"Are you all right," Helen asked, but he didn't reply.

He opened the door and walked down the short passageway to the commons. Arshand was there, as were Mark and Barrett. His cousins were still on the viewscreen, his sisters huddled in the back of their cart, his litters still huddled in their baskets.

Although he knew that he should fear the fate they held for him, he did not. They were all so transparent in their passion for vengeance. It was such an uncomplicated emotion. But it was inappropriate for this moment in Chamal's history. He would have to explain that to them.

"I feel better now," he said as he stepped into the compartment.

And when everyone in the chamber, angel and chamalian looked at him, he added: "I have to tell my cousins something. Something important so that we can move on from here. Arshand, will you come with me?"

They all looked at him without speaking. Arshand was obviously surprised, then a look of comprehension fell across his eyes.

"You've had a night-vision," he said.

"Yes."

"Lead the way, pilgrim," Arshand said. Barrett moved to protest, but Mark stopped him. They exchanged words, which the professor did not translate, then stepped back and let the chamalians go.

Zepp was not quite sure what he would say to his cousins as he descended the ladder into the hold. But he knew that it would be sufficient.

***

Mark went to Arshand before he had a chance to follow Zepp.

"What's he doing?" he asked breathlessly.

"He is going to talk his cousins out of punishing him for his sins," the pilgrim said.

"And how is he going to do that?"

"He has had a vision. Whatever it was, it has shown him how to escape his fate."

"Are you sure? What if they don't believe him?"

"That is why I came along. And why I brought my company of pilgrims with me. In case they need to be persuaded." Mark shook his head in disbelief. Arshand stepped away and said: "Now I must go. We cannot let him go out there alone."

He continued down the ladder into the hold and Mark returned to his place before the viewscreen.

"Would someone please tell me what's going on?" Barrett asked.

Mark repeated Arshand's explanation. Barrett said nothing, but put on his disgusted face.

Helen was more voluble. "You can't let them do that," she said. "Someone will get hurt."

"Someone probably will," Mark said. "But there's not a lot we can do. We have to let them handle this in their own way."

They watched as Zepp stepped into view beneath the spacecraft. The video pickups mounted on the underside of the ship gave them a good picture of what the small green ape was facing. Mark felt his skin start to crawl at the sight.

Sherbek stood before his cart, a great wide curved blade in his paw. He tested the edge of the knife and looked Zepp up and down.

"You can put that away," Zepp said. "It is not necessary."

"I wouldn't say that," Sherbek replied. "I can think of a number of uses to which it can be put."

"Not the one that you desire most," Zepp said.

"I think so, Zepp. There has been a transgression. There must be an accounting."

"No longer," Zepp said, the professor giving his translated voice a deeper and stronger tone than Mark had noticed him using before. He wondered what cues the AI was reading. "The time for accounting is over. The past that contained that sin no longer exists. The world that spawned that sin is gone forever."

"You talk too much, cousin, but it will not save you paying your debt."

"I have had a vision," he said.

"So have I – of you spread across the stone awaiting the kiss of my blade."

"He has had a vision." That was Arshand, speaking at Zepp's side. The sound of the pilgrims' weapons slipping into place prompted Barrett to swivel the picture around quickly. The two dozen chamalians that had accompanied them in their flight from Ring Po Do stood in tight formation behind Zepp and Arshand – weapons at the ready and trained on Sherbek.

"So he has had a vision," Sherbek admitted unwillingly. "What does that mean?"

"Let him have his say," Arshand said.

"Like Jobe's vision of the seed of the gods, I have had a vision," Zepp said. "It was not as great as that of Jobe. It was just a little vision.

But I saw it clearly. The past is dead and gone. All that we were before the day the angels arrived is vanished like dust in the wind. The future is waiting to be born, but that moment has not come yet. You cannot punish me for my sins, because that punishment is part of the past. As is the tribe of my fathers and their fathers.

"The Way of Jobe is complete. The arrival of the angels is the completion of his plan for Chamal. What meaning is there for the tribe of Jobe now that his vision is accomplished? The angels have the power to transform us all. You shall see. You shall see.

"All debts are forgiven now. All accounts are paid in full. All the old ties are severed. I am no longer part of this tribe. I do not know what tribe I will belong to in the unborn future, but I cannot return to what I was before. I divorce myself, Sherbek. You are my witness. Everything must change now."

Zepp tilted his head, then looked back at the angels' ship.

"Everything change now."

With the last words sounding like a command, Zepp walked over to his cousin. Sherbek looked beyond Zepp at the armed pilgrims who backed him up, then he looked down at Zepp. He raised his blade just slightly.

Mark felt his heart leap into his throat. Helen clutched at his hand. Two dozen pilgrims worked the action on their weapons simultaneously.

Then Sherbek threw the blade into the sand, turned his back on Zepp and pilgrims, and muttered to himself.

"We will need carts," Zepp said as his pilgrim escorts hurried to follow him. "Arshand, go back and ask the angels if they would accompany us. We will go the Hall of the Seedkeepers. They should be able to find room for us to use while we prepare for the next step –

whatever that may be." Mark shook his head and blinked his eyes. Helen giggled, but it was just nerves, he realized. She still had a tight grip on his hand.

"I don't believe what I think I just saw," she said.

"Would someone please tell me what's going on?" Barrett asked.

***

Tedrak, the political leader of Suridash, hardly looked as powerful as Mark knew him to be.

He was a large brown blob with a head, two arms, and two legs. He wore a pair of loose silken shorts, the ubiquitous brass chastity belt of his tribe, and a gauzy purple vest that shimmered in the dim candlelight. And atop his snout perched a pair of thick glasses.

When he entered the room in the Hall of the Seedkeepers for the meeting with the delegation from the *Cousteau*, he looked the humans up and down and sniffed the air around them. Then he plopped himself down on a large cloth-covered cushion in the middle of the floor, lifted his snout into the air, and spoke.

"Are you proud of what you have done to my planet?" The professor gave him an alto voice, which also seemed out of place in such a powerful figure. Zepp had told Mark his story. It was Tedrak's idea to form the alliance and build the *Deragathon*. He had not done it because he shared his race's fear of the angels, Zepp said. Indeed, he felt just the opposite – he saw the angels as the only hope Chamal had to avoid destroying itself in an orgy of ever more powerful weapons of war. But the only way to control what the others did when the angels arrived was to situate himself and Suridash at the center of all their preparations.

Barrett was slow to answer, but Mark allowed him time. The Space Corps officer had pointed out in no uncertain terms that there was to be only one spokesman for the *Cousteau*, and that it would be him.

Mark now wanted to point out to him the obvious gambit that Tedrak was employing. There was certainly enough guilt to go around when it came to Chamal's self-destructive fury, but Tedrak wanted to be sure that the humans didn't feel left out. It was a sophisticated way of beginning – and Mark could only hope that Barrett didn't let the chamalian take advantage of him.

"We did not intend to cause your race this much suffering," Barrett said.

That was a good response, Mark decided, but he wished he knew Tedrak and his race well enough to come up with a better one. But by the time he could do that the crisis might well be over.

"Nevertheless, my world tears its heart out over fear of your intentions. These are not acts of wisdom, but wisdom is more widely praised than possessed."

"The same could be said about us as well," Barrett said.

"Does that mean you were not wise enough to foresee the consequences of your arrival in our skies?" Barrett frowned. Mark could see that he was afraid of admitting liability for any number of problems that had erupted since they first appeared in this system. At the same time, he didn't want to admit to any weakness or lack of foresight.

"Whether we are wise enough or not isn't the real question here," Barrett said. "We're more concerned about our own safety while orbiting this world."

"Safety?" Tedrak spat. "Safety? You worry about safety when the world is going mad, not that it ever was close to be sane? No one and nothing is safe today. All things are turned on their head. I get reports that make my blood curdle. Meshkar is wracked with riots and the blood of their victims turns the sea red. The Rift Valley is rapidly returning to a state worse than that before the last appearance of the Red Monkeys. Arkaria is in turmoil. Even the primitives of the southern hemisphere are aware of your arrival and have begun rituals of purification that will mean the deaths of thousands of creatures who bear the seed of the gods."

"All that is distressing to us," Barrett said. "But what I really want to know is what is happening aboard your space station. They present the most immediate threat to us and our mission. I have been told that you are sympathetic to our needs. A report on the situation there and your help in neutralizing it as a threat would go a long way towards making us comfortable. It would be a shame if the first meeting between our two races ended in a disaster as big as the one that it started with."

Mark winced as he waited for the professor to sort out the twisted syntax of the Space Corps officer, but eventually it did, making Tedrak wince in turn.

"The *Deragathon* is in a tenuous state. The active mutinies have been quelled, but the mutineers are still aboard. We are among their number, of course, and my aide, Whirlpitt, remains under their protection. But further details are not readily available."

"I understand," Barrett said. "Is there anything that you can do to help us remove the source of our concerns?"

Tedrak sniffed the air and patted the cushion with his hands. Then he gave an answer that left Mark feeling more unsettled than ever.

"I would rather discuss what you can do to help remove the source of our concerns. You should think about that between now and our next meeting." With that, Tedrak bounced to his feet and waddled out the door.

Barrett let out a sigh and Mark felt a sudden chill as the tension left the room.

"He sounds awfully sure of himself for someone whose world is burning to the ground," Helen said. "Maybe he knows something we don't know."

"He knows a lot that we don't know," Barrett said. "And he's not telling. My bullshit detectors are giving off major alarms. He may be an alien, but he knows how to lie. My guess is that he knows exactly where every mutineer is aboard their ship and can tell us exactly how to get aboard and shut her down."

"Perhaps," Mark said. "But what would he get in return?"

"That's a question that I can't answer," Barrett said. "I don't even know what he wants."

"Simple enough," Mark replied. "He wants us to solve all the problems of his world. At least that's what Zepp says. He believes that we must have that power."

"Maybe we do," Barrett said. "But that doesn't mean we're going to be able to use it. Our mission is supposed to be scientific research and initial diplomatic contact – not forcible entry and a planetary rescue thrown in for good measure."

"Until we know what they need and what we can do to give it to them, this whole discussion is academic," Helen said. "You're just shooting in the dark – and I've had about all I can take of that already."

"You're right," Barrett said. "We can't do anything until we have a better idea of what's going on."

"Well we're in the right place to find out," Mark said. "Besides the Hall of the Seedkeepers, Suridash has the Library of Jobe and the headquarters of the Pilgrimage of the Way – the largest and broadest collections of information on the planet about Chamal and its inhabitants."

"Then we'd better get to work. Time is running out. And if their collection of intelligence is so big, it's going to take us some time to figure out what they need."

"I've already asked to start biological studies," Helen said.

"Arshand says he's willing to give me a political briefing at the Pilgrimage House tomorrow," Barrett said.

"I'm not sure where that leaves me," Mark said.

"I think you need to keep wokring with Zepp," Helen said. "Something tells me he's going to be key to this whole thing." Mark narrowed his eyes and tilted his head back, eyeing her with sudden curiosity. He wondered just what had given her that idea, but kept the question to himself. He didn't want to admit it yet, but he felt the same way.

CHAPTER SIXTEEN

"They remind me of plant cells," Helen said as she looked out over the city. "With big thick cellulose walls and little nuclei and chloroplasts inside." Mark watched as lights flickered to life across Suridash – candles, lanterns, torches, and electric lights of several varieties. The sun had set with surprising suddenness, an effect of the latitude and the desert air, leaving them all abruptly in the dark. He still was having trouble keeping up with the rapidly passing days here on Chamal's surface.

"At least there isn't any shooting," he said. "And I was getting tired of the smell of half-burnt rubbish back in Ring Po Do." The suite of rooms assigned to Mark and his companions included three sleeping chambers furnished with elaborate carved-wood tables, chests, bedsteads, and chairs, and a large sitting room with a balcony.

The balcony opened onto the broad plaza at the center of Suridash, three stories below, and offered a view of much of the city. Zepp had pointed out the enclave of the tribe of Jobe, which sprawled up one side of a low hill and down the other. The enclave was surrounded by a high wall – just like all the others.

Helen sighed and shook her head. "Do you think there's any hope for these creatures? Or are they just going to destroy their world because they fear us so much?"

"There's always hope," Mark said. "If you look at our own history, there were plenty of times when things looked bleak. But we managed to overcome them."

"We could just as easily have failed."

"It may have looked that way at the time, but I really don't think so," Mark said. "Humanity is a lot more resilient than that."

"Do you really think so? Don't you think we have the same problem as the chamalians?"

"What's that?"

"Our genes and theirs are programmed for a more primitive world. Fight or flee – and mostly fight. We're ice-age hunters. They're just hunters. Either way, their instincts are programmed to do certain things and their brains can't help them. Just like us."

"If you believe that model, then you have a hard time explaining much of human culture," Mark said.

Helen looked askance at him, then asked: "How so?"

"Evolution didn't program us for anything. It provided us with a brain so big that it could do its own programming. That's what culture is. Software for our cerebral hardware. More malleable than genes and quicker to adapt. If we have problems, they're problems we've created with our own imaginations and our own thoughts. They're not part of our genes, they're part of our history. And that means we can take control of them and shape ourselves to meet them."

She tipped her head from side to side, then frowned. "You don't think we're just a pack of killer apes with neat toys?" Mark snorted out a derisive laugh. "That's an artifact of our recent past, not our distant past. It fits the way people saw themselves a couple of centuries ago, during an age of national and economic competition. But that doesn't mean it's a universal condition of humanity."

"Is there any such a thing?"

"I think so. The one constant that runs through from culture to culture is the power of human self-consciousness over its environment in both space and time. No matter where we end up or what we are doing, we always transcend the limits of that environment. We always end up bumping against the limits of our own cultures instead."

"And what happens then?"

"We end up fighting and fleeing and hunting and killing. But it's not because it's hard-wired into us. It's because those are the side effects of growth and change."

"So what do you think that mean for the chamalians?"

"It means that there's an end somewhere to the cycle. There's a key to understanding them and liberating them from the dark side of their own culture.

"Look at this place. You've got all of evolution working to produce life in all its varieties to fill all the niches of the environment. You get the perfect harmony of nature – the garden of Eden. Then along comes self-conscious intelligence and throws the whole thing into chaos. Self-awareness is never content with the harmony of the garden. It has to keep moving and growing. It can't bear to repeat what it's already done. Our own history – about eight thousand years of it – is just one damned thing after another. Each more complicated and complex than the last. And we don't have half the problems of this planet.

"The chamalians have all that and more. Everything they build is doomed to fall back into the dust from which it came. And you know what they do in response?"

"What?"

"They try harder. Ten times harder. A hundred times harder. In our mythology, we were cast out of the garden to make a living of our own. In the chamalian myth, they're stuck in the garden forever."

"And you want to free them from the garden?"

"Somebody needs to. Not me. I wouldn't know where to start. And it wouldn't be right. You can't free someone else from their fate. They have to do that themselves."

"Which brings us back to the original question. Do you think there's hope?"

"Considering how much energy is wrapped up in Zepp and his cousins, I don't see how you can have anything but hope. That's not the danger."

"What is?" Helen asked.

"That they destroy themselves in the process of freeing themselves. And I think that's what Tedrak wants us to do – stop them before they lose control."

At that moment a rocket shot up out of the darkness on the far side of the plaza below, leaving a trail of yellow sparks and exploding in a burst of red and green fire.

It seemed to be the signal for something, for a moment later the crackle of gunfire erupted on the streets below. And a moment after that, the lights in the sitting room went dark.

***

One of Arshand's lieutenants – he looked like a teddy bear, but a ceremonial headband with fluttering pennants was wrapped around his head and a bulky assault rifle was strapped across his shoulders – rushed into the room carrying an electric torch.

He pulled on Mark's sleeve and took Helen by the arm. A member of his squad followed him into the room and began ducking into the sleeping quarters. He emerged with Lieutenant Barrett.

"Come with us," the pilgrim said. "Quickly."

The bright electric torch threw shadows across the wide atrium at the end of the corridor. The race through the building made Mark nervous. The place was as chaotic in its construction as everything else on Chamal. Yawning apertures appeared in the floor without rail or warning – and Mark was certain that they were moving too fast to avoid one if they stumbled across it the dark.

In other places, stairways climbed walls only to come to a halt at the stone ceiling. Corridors ended abruptly, or curved back on themselves, with no apparent rhyme or reason. Mark wondered if anything done by chamalian intelligence was entirely sane.

The pilgrim led them up one of the dead-end staircases. There was no rail on either side and Mark felt his heart climb into his throat.

He wondered just what they were doing. Hiding? The gunfire was growing louder and closer, and now he could hear the shouts and cries of chamalians in every direction.

He was surprised to see the pilgrim press on the ceiling and produce a large door consisting of a meter-thick stone swiveling on unseen hinges to present an entry to the roof.

A moment later they were out under the stars. A dry wind blew up from the south. Mark peered over the edge of the parapet that outlined the perimeter of the rooftop, though Arshand's squad leader was adamant about keeping him well back.

The Hall of the Seedkeepers was a collection of buildings that spanned the architectural history of Suridash. The keep, where they stood now, was the youngest structure – kiln-baked bricks instead of the close-cut stone of the other elements. It stood in the center of a large courtyard, formed by the wall that connected the fortress section, the two towers, and the pens and market building of the old slave runners. The fortress was the original Red Monkey structure, built when the city was an outpost of a much earlier simian empire, Arshand had told them. The towers predated the Fortress by another millennia – or superoctellenia, if you used chamalian numerology.

They waited for several minutes, pilgrims in position in a circle around them, with Arshand's lieutenant pacing nervously.

Then Arshand arrived, Zepp hurrying along beside him.

"There were dissenters within the tribe of Jobe who objected to Sherbek's handling of their wayward cousin," he said briskly once they had assembled around him. "They are a distinct minority, but they do not believe Zepp has had a true vision and want to see him burned for heresy. They made it through the gate easily – the tribe maintains these buildings for the Seedkeepers and there were collaborators among tonight's crew. They are storming the keep from two sides. The rest of my squads are holding them off. Frit's squad will take us away from here until the fighting is over." There was no time to discuss Arshand's plans. He didn't even wait for the professor to finish his translation. They were up and moving at a wave of his hand.

The electric torches were shut off and Frit led the way to the parapet. One of this troops slipped over the top, clinging to the stone to avoid presenting a clear target to anyone on the surrounding rooftops. The others followed one at a time. When Mark reached the edge, he looked over. Directly below them, only a meter beneath the edge of the roof, was a wide bridge leading across to one of the towers – the top of a covered walkway between the two buildings.

Pilgrims had already taken up posts along its length and at the far end. Mark slid across the rough stone, then crawled the length of the bridge on his hands and knees.

Helen was right behind him, huffing and snorting at the effort to move so awkwardly.

The top of the tower was covered in crushed stone that crunched softly underfoot. A smaller set of towers rose from one end of the platform where they huddled now, rising twenty more meters up into the night. One of the pilgrims climbed its outside wall, presumably to get a better view of the situation.

The momentary pause was broken by a harsh hissing sound. The lookout pointed them towards the edge of the roof on the side away from the keep and the central courtyard. Arshand hunched down as he approached the parapet. A moment later, he returned.

"There is another raiding party approaching the base of this tower," he said. "If we open fire from up here, we may never get off the roof. They'll be onto us and our escape will be blocked."

"It is better to escape," Zepp said. "For you, at least. Maybe if they found me, we would all be better off."

Mark felt his stomach tighten at Arshand's report. Beside him, Barrett muttered something unintelligible.

"What was that?" Mark asked.

"I said they ought to put a sniper on the party down there while the rest of us keep going. A few well-placed shots should keep them pinned down for the rest of the night." Mark called softly to Zepp. The green ape ambled over, and Mark passed along Barrett's recommendation. Zepp relayed it to Arshand.

"They will not find you tonight," Arshand said. He hissed at Frit and waved to the squad. A moment later, a single shot rang out from the parapet, followed by a ragged volley from below.

The duel had begun.

***

They climbed over another parapet and crossed the roof of the walkway to the other tower. Arshand levered up another mighty block of stone, which revealed a narrow staircase leading down between the stones. At least it wouldn't aggravate his agoraphobia, Mark acknowledged with a grim smile.

The stairs seemed to lead down forever. Mark noticed a definite arc to the staircase that convinced him they were in the outer wall of the tower itself.

After his heels had jarred his kidneys halfway up his back on a thousand dusty steps, they came to a sudden halt, still on the stairs, that nearly brought him pitching downward into the pilgrims in front of him. Then they made their way carefully through a narrow stone arch and emerged into a small alcove. Mark saw over the heads of the shorter chamalians into a vasty dusty space. In the space were row upon row of bookshelves, with row upon row of handbound books.

"These are the archives of the Seedkeepers," Arshand said. "They contain the genealogical records of every member of the tribe of Jobe, and every single one of their offspring – wise and wild – for all the generations since the time of Jobe." Mark shook his head in wonder. Helen sighed. "What a perfectly wonderful database," she said. "It'll make my job a lot easier."

"The dissenters are on their way here," Arshand said. "I do not know if they will fight us in this tower, but to do so would be a terrible sacrilege against the Way of Jobe." A burst of automatic weapons fire interrupted them.

Bullets whined off the stone walls and floors and thudded into books and shelves.

Arshand yelped. "Desecrators!" the professor repeated in a hoarse stage whisper.

The leader of the pilgrims waved a hand and Frit dispatched his squad to the flanks, where they began to return fire. The rest of them, Mark included, dropped to the floor and crawled towards the other side of the wide chamber.

The rear of the great library flared with light as more weapons joined in the chorus. Mark heard bullets whizzing through the air overhead. His blood was like liquid nitrogen in his veins.

Then they were down a hall, away from the shooting, Arshand in the lead and a single pilgrim covering their rear, Zepp, Mark, Helen, and Barrett all in the middle.

They moved on, down another staircase into a cool, low-ceilinged tunnel. In single file they passed through the tunnel's length. All Mark could see was the silhouette of Zepp and Helen in front of him, and Arshand carrying Frit's electric torch.

Once the reached the end of the tunnel, however, it became much worse. They entered a new system of corridors with heavy stone walls made of huge, hand-cut blocks. The main tunnel didn't go more then a few meters before making an abrupt turn to the left, and a few meters more an abrupt turn to the left. Zigging and zagging, back and forth.

The farther they went, the narrower the tunnel became, until it caught at Mark's shoulders and knees as they pushed on. The sections became shorter and shorter, threatening to leave Mark in the dark, cut off from Zepp ahead of him and Barrett behind.

He felt the stones closing in on him, squeezing the air out of his lungs, crushing his bones under their weight. He had a nightmare vision of the ever-constricting maze ending abruptly in a cold stone wall, and all the humans and chamalians jamming themselves immovably into the tight passages.

Then they burst free of the labyrinth and into another high-ceilinged chamber, lit by smoky torches and lined with countless cages, stacked one atop the other, reaching up as far as Mark could see.

Each cage that he could see was occupied. Some of the creatures were large, some small, some alone, some in groups. Their eyes reflected the light of the torches back in various shades of red and yellow. Aside from the sound of a few of the creatures scrabbling at their cell walls, the place was silent. The sound of gunfire was audible through windows in the far wall.

"This is the stock in trade of the seedkeepers," Arshand said.

"Stock?" Helen asked.

"Where else would we keep the seed? These are the wild creatures that are born in each litter of the tribe of Jobe and the other tribes that contribute their seed for safekeeping."

"Once again, if we fight here, we commit a sacrilege," Zepp said.

"Move on," Arshand whispered to the other pilgrim who had made it this far. But to Zepp, Mark, and the others, he put up his hand. "You wait here. We have a chance now to counter the blow the dissenters have struck against the keep. We have circled around behind them. Out there is the courtyard and beside it is the gate. We can fire into their rear and send them into a rout." Zepp waved his hands in agreement, then sat on a wooden stool beside a column near the back of the room.

Arshand assembled his troops, who inspected their weapons and prepared for battle. Then he sent them on their way, two at a time to infiltrate the courtyard. When the first squad was gone, he left, waving one last time to Zepp. A moment later, the remaining pilgrims were out the door after him.

Suddenly the sound of gunfire erupted quite nearby – from the front of the pens, in fact. Mark jumped and Helen twitched, but Zepp and Barrett didn't move. There were cries and screeches from the more distant corners of the courtyard. Then the crackle of weapons fire from there.

Mark heard the smack of bullets against the doors of the building. A stray round that must have come in through the window whined loudly as it bounced off a wall and then struck the floor. Another found its way into the pens. One of the creatures in the cages whined as the slug buried itself in the straw at the bottom of its cell. Others whimpered in sympathy.

Mark felt his flesh crawl at the sound.

The shooting rose in a terrible crescendo, then was replaced with shouting and cries of pain and anger. Alone, shut off from the action, Mark was unsure of what was going on. The others felt the same.

"What do we do if the bad guys come through the door instead of our friends?" Helen asked.

"Beats me," Barrett said. "We don't have any weapons, and I'm not sure just how to get back into the maze that got us here. I suppose we could just give them our buddy here, but somehow I doubt we'll get the chance." Zepp plucked at Mark's sleeve, then pointed to a thick hose coiled on the floor at the base of a massive pillar. Then he leapt to the spigot at the hydrant that fed the hose.

"Fire hoses," Mark said, pointing them out to Barrett.

"It's better than nothing," the lieutenant said. A minute later, they had the hose laid out, Barrett manning the valve, Mark tending the line, and Zepp at the nozzle.

The first wave of invaders was through the doors before they realized it. One moment Mark was standing around in tense silence, the next he was energized with fear and excitement.

There were three of them, two rabbits and a low-browed carnivore. The torchlight caught on the metal of their blades, but couldn't penetrate the hard metal of their guns.

They let out a loud cry, which was echoed by the creatures in the racks above them, then charged at Mark and his companions.

Barrett yanked on the valve and Mark felt the hose stiffen.

The water gushed forth instantly as Zepp worked the nozzle. The hose seemed to be for more than fire purposes. It probably doubled up as a cleaning tool and as a means of controlling the seedkeepers' stock. Zepp had it throttled to a narrow, high-pressure stream with the volume high enough to sweep the invaders off their feet.

Barrett rushed forward, a length of stout wood in his hands. He knocked one, then a second of the invaders in the head. The third managed to recover his footing and gestured menacingly towards Barrett with his weapons.

But Zepp knocked this one down, and Barrett gave him a good lump on the head. Once they were done, he gathered up their blades and guns, inspecting the action on the machine pistol with the largest magazine.

He didn't have to wait for more than a minute before he had a chance to test it out.

Another team of invaders tried the door. Barrett sprayed metal and fire in their direction, studding the top of the door with slugs. The chamalians fired back, then retreated, leaving the field of battle to the defenders.

They were ready when the door to the pens creaked open again. Mark's heart pounded hard against the inside of his chest. He and Barrett both crouched lower against the wall. He clutched the hose more tightly, ready to brush back yet another assault with a water hose against machine guns.

But his fear was unnecessary. He recognized the voice of Frit as the professor presented it, warning them not to shoot. Then he stepped through into the pens alone.

"Come with us. The dissenters are gone," he said, opening the great doors wide to the night air. Then he added: "And Arshand is dead."

***

Mark spent the remainder of the short night sleeping fitfully, his waking moments filled with fears for Zepp's well-being now that Arshand was gone. The pilgrim had seemed to be just what was needed to keep things from deteriorating into total disarray. And without him, Zepp seemed uncertain and afraid once again.

But when daylight came and the three members of the *Cousteau* landing party met for breakfast, he found out he had reasons to worry about his own well-being – and that of Helen Castain.

"I'm going back to the *Cousteau*," Barrett announced without preamble as they brewed individual cups of coffee from their ration pack. "We're going to need more firepower if we're going to make it through another night like that."

"What about Tedrak?" Mark asked. "We're supposed to meet with him again today."

"I'll be going right afterwards. I want to talk to him at length if possible. But I can't wait any longer than today. I talked it over with Captain Fletcher last night. Things are only going to get worse the longer we wait."

"Good," Helen said. "When you come back, you can bring the doctor with you. If I'm going to get any kind of biological research done down here, I'll need it."

"Done," Barrett said. "And maybe we'll bring you some lab assistants as well. The kind that can shoot straight if it's necessary. I spoke to Frit after last night's surprise party. We came awfully close to losing the match."

Mark felt uncomfortable at that news, but kept it to himself. He also felt uncomfortable with the idea of losing the protection of the Space Corps officer. As annoying as he could be, Barrett knew how to keep them safe. A nagging sense of powerlessness and vulnerability was beginning to creep over him.

"He may be making too big a deal out of things after losing his commander," Barrett said. "But whether he is or not, I'm not willing to take another chance."

***

The meeting with Tedrak turned out to take longer than Mark anticipated – largely because of a private session with Barrett.

It started much the same as the earlier one. The head of the Council of Elders of Suridash marched in and plopped himself down on a cushion, cast his nose into the air, and began speaking quickly and forcefully.

"We have a unique civilization here in our city," he said. "We believe in reason and a moral sense of right and wrong. We are truly superior to every other civilization on this planet. They will say the same thing about themselves, but only we are true to our principals. Test us, and you will see that it is true. Jobe taught us well and we follow his wisdom. While others decide what to do with the hearts and their guts, we use our brains. We will do everything we can to help you. But you must match our cooperation, word for word and deed for deed."

"We'll do whatever we can," Barrett said. "But we must be secure in our position or we can help no one."

"And we want the same kind of security. I recognize that it is more difficult for you to provide us with what we need than it is for us to provide you with what you need. But that is as it is, and we will abide with it."

"Tell us what you need," Barrett said.

"We have been told that it is in your power to probe the secrets of the seed of the gods. That you have machines that can pick the seed apart and determine which parts are which. And that your machines can rearrange the parts. Is this true?"

Mark and Barrett turned their eyes towards Helen, who looked suddenly flustered.

"Well, I suppose you could say that, she said. "It's a lot harder in practice, though. We've got a long ways to go before we can start doing genetic engineering on chamalian life forms. We haven't even figured out what your genetic chemistry is based on or how traits are passed on. Geez, we haven't even learned the basic rules of chamalian heredity – and from what I've heard they must be very unusual."

"Then you must start soon and work hard," Tedrak said. "The

wisdom is there, the knowledge is there, the power is there. All that is necessary is to bring them together. My world has done no less in building the *Deragathon* and sending it against you. Your powers appear to be almost without limits."

"Appearance is not always reality," Helen said. "There are always limits."

"Nevertheless, your power is much greater than ours. And if you can solve the riddle of our seed, then perhaps you can solve all the other puzzles that confound our wisdom and keep us at one another's throats instead of working together to build a world that is worth living in for all creatures, wise and wild."

"That's a worthy goal," Barrett said. "But I'm not sure we can accomplish it in the time we will be here at your world. I'm not sure anyone can accomplish it at all."

"Give us the knowledge and the tools, and we can accomplish anything," Tedrak said. "If it were not in our interest to block the *Deragathon*, you would have learned that days ago."

Mark grew suddenly worried when Barrett bristled at Tedrak's chauvinism, but calmed as the other man seemed to hold his temper for a long count.

"Speaking of the *Deragathon*, what news do you have of her status? We are still worried about the threat she poses to our own vessel."

Tedrak was silent, then whispered to Zepp, who dashed out of the room without a word. A few minutes later, he was back, escorted by a tall, long-boned chamalian with a pointed snout, no ears, and a muscular tail.

"This is Tellpen, who knows all we know about the *Deragathon*. He will give you all our knowledge on the warship."

Tellpen and Tedrak kept Barrett busy for more than an hour, as they discussed technical details about the chamalian ship, the latest reports about the crew and weaponry, and the likely changes in the delicate political situation aboard the vessel.

In the end, Barrett seemed satisfied. But it didn't change his decision to return to the *Cousteau*. Mark decided that if he was going to bring back the right equipment, it would be worth the risk.

And before he left, Tedrak announced that the risk had been lessened substantially.

"The dissenters among the tribe of Jobe have been charged with desecration of the Hall of the Seedkeepers and destruction of their records. They will not be allowed out of the tribal enclave until I permit it. Disagreement is accepted within our tribe, but sacrilege is not – and this knowledge is as sacred as any we have."

"Thank you," Zepp said softly, expressing Mark's own sentiments.

"And for their own safety, before dark this day your sisters and their litters will be brought here to the Hall of the Seedkeepers to share your apartments." Mark felt his eyes widen at that news, then looked to Zepp. For the second time in as many days, the small green ape looked like he was having trouble breathing.

CHAPTER SEVENTEEN

Zepp's sisters and their three litters brought out Helen Castain's maternal impulses, and Mark could understand why.

The little pups were as cute and darling as newborns of any species – any advanced species, she reminded him when he mentioned it. "You should see alligators," she said. "They come out of the eggs snapping. Birds are just helpless – big mouths demanding to be fed. It's only your fur-bearing species that come out cute and helpless. These pups are no different in that respect. But they do have their moments."

"Like what?" Mark had asked.

"Well, they're no alligators, but they're only a couple weeks old and they're already at each other's throats. Like puppies and kittens, only they cooperate better when it comes to ganging up on the target of the day." The three litters contained six pups each, eighteen in all. Each contained three green apes and three imitations of the mother. Sexes were mixed from phenotype to phenotype, with ten boys and eight girls. Ordinarily, Zepp had explained, only one member of each litter would have grown up to acquire full wisdom. And one or two others would have become near-men or halflings, while the rest would be fated to live brief lives as wild creatures in the pens beneath the Hall of the Seedkeepers.

But because of the flukes of chamalian genetics, each of these pups would breed true.

"I wish I knew what made that happen," she said. "And to make things more confusing, he says that if these pups interbreed, just the opposite is likely to happen. All of their litters will go wild and none of them grow up to be even remotely sapient."

"Isn't that what they call Lamarckian genetics?"

"Right, only that kind of thing shouldn't work. Lamarck argued that parents can pass on acquired traits, but he turned out to be wrong. No, this is something more radical in their genetics. I just don't know what. When the doctor gets here, I can do some microbiology studies and maybe I can learn something." In the meantime, she was studying the pups. She said they reminded her of baby kangaroos. They weren't as helpless and small, but they were still more dependent on their mothers than kittens or puppies would have been at a similar age. But she was also puzzled by the small size of the pups' skulls and brains.

"In a human baby, the skull is much larger in proportion to the body," she explained. "It's the largest it will ever be in comparison to the rest of the body. In fact, the female pelvis is a compromise between her need to walk upright and nature's need for her to birth babies with the largest possible heads."

"And these kids don't have that?"

"Nothing like it," she said, pointing to one of the green apes. "Look at that. Little skulls. Not much in the way of brains."

"Somehow it must grow as they become adults."

"Sure, but what does that do? There's a reason we start off with our brains nearly full size. You don't want to mess around with the memory and data processing systems once they're set. At least with terrestrial species. I'm not sure what it would mean – what it means – to have your brain grow as you develop." Mark smiled at that question. For once, he had an answer. "I can tell you what it means. Zepp and I have talked about it a little bit. It means that they go through sudden bursts of intellectual growth. When they're young, it means suddenly understanding division and multiplication – or quickly learning half a dozen new dialects and languages. When they're older, it's a sudden burst of creative insight and intuition. And occasionally, more often than Zepp wants to admit, it's an explosion of manic obsession that ends in madness. He says he's going through such a stage right now."

"Goodness," Helen said. "Are you sure he's going to be all right?"

"He seems to think so. He says there's more of a chance of something happening to him because of the madness of others than there is of him losing his own mind."

"That's reassuring," Helen said. "He probably didn't need to mention that we're just as much in danger from that source as he is."

"Actually he said just that," David said, eliciting a nasty snarl from Mary, then a sharp smile. "And he said to tell you that they're ready to instruct you in the basic numerology of the Seedkeepers of Suridash, if you'd be so kind as to accompany the guard outside to the Keep."

"Ma-ark!" she howled, stretching his name across two poignant syllables. "Why didn't you tell me that when you got here?"

"You didn't ask."

***

The truth was, Mark realized later, that he was just too stunned by the events of the past few days to think of it.

He was wandering around the rooms and halls that the

Seedkeepers had allotted to them with no particular destination or purpose. He stood at the balcony and stared out over the tilted rooftops of the chamalian city. The sun warmed him, but also left him feeling greasy and unclean. The wind was dry, sucking the water from him like vacuum, and hot like a rocket exhaust.

And in the back of his mind, faint tendrils of memory twisted and curled, like dust devils in the courtyard below.

He'd seen what both vacuum and rocket exhaust could do to people.

That was the sin of Tycho.

The moon colony had been founded just before the end of the age of scarcity by refugees from the Pacific Receivership. They'd been a mixed lot in the beginning, but something had happened when the big change came. Something had crystallized in the culture and taken on a life of its own. Those who did not fit in and did not share in it were expelled – informally, at first, and without consideration for their long-term survival prospects, formally later, and in larger numbers. Those who remained became a largely homogeneous lot who shared a particular myth – an unshakable belief in their own self-importance.

It was not a myth that they shared with the outside world. For the most part, there was no outside world. When the last of the official emigrations was over, they shut down the VR-links, disengaged from the outside net, unplugged the radios and videos, and canceled their e-mail service.

And there they remained for more than ten years. Until the call for help. A small voice, nearly lost in the thick ether of latter-day Luna, but overheard in time and relayed to those in charge. It came from the survivors of the mutiny, with stories about Tycho that were too terrible to believe.

Tycho did not experience just the ordinary run of sin and debauchery, the kind of thing you could find in the Old Testament. It was a full-scale technological nightmare, with all the horrors of the dark side of the human imagination given free range by the subtleties of modern technology: teleoperating human flesh, cybernetic invasion of other people's nightmares, genetic manipulation to produce hideously erotic monsters, and the powerful repression of the soul through lies, hypocrisy, and propaganda needed to allow such corruption to endure.

But no mechanism of repression is perfect. And the dissenters in Tycho were no less zealous than those in the tribe of Jobe. The mutiny was fierce and all-consuming. Nearly two-thirds of the colony's inhabitants did not survive it.

And the Space Corps "rescue" was hardly an improvement.

Mark had been selected to go in with the first wave because of the desperate need to understand what had gone wrong with the Tycho culture. In retrospect, it seemed like a foolishly academic thing to do. He wasn't at all prepared for what he found there.

He was with the corps from the beginning, after the first platoons of troopers had secured the entries and the main corridors. He was supposed to be just an observer, documenting the event for later review. In retrospect, once again, it would have been better if he'd waited until everything had been cleaned up. But no one trusted the corps not to sweep away important evidence – either by accident or intent.

So he saw the women and children emerge from their shelters, stunned and senseless after days of violence followed by days of barely contained terror waiting inside steel cans. And he saw the corpses, most laying where they'd fallen during the fighting – ripped open by blades, torn apart by explosives, pierced by bullets.

He was almost caught up in the last gasp of the mutiny itself, when the troopers found the hidden sanctuary that held the last of the original colonists. He'd been in the library. The best way to unlock the secrets of a culture is to read its mail. While Tycho was sealed off from the world outside, it continued to have an active, if somewhat twisted, inner life.

Mark got the chance to see first hand the evidence of the steady, perverse, inward turn of the colony's soul. The leaders had begun by debating the limits of pleasure, pain, and power in only the most abstract terms. But the debates had grown more pointed and bizarre, with greater and greater hostility. One of the great exchanges on the public net had been followed by an overnight purge of a number of powerful members of the colony. No one found their bodies – nor any sign of their physical demise. They just weren't around anymore, and after a few days no one asked any more questions about it. A few days after that, the second wave of disappearances began. The second of many.

By the time they were done, suspicion and hatred were the dominant social attitudes. A superficial analysis would have called it paranoia, but in this world, there really was a conspiracy aimed at each and every individual.

During the middle of one nightwatch, after Mark had been scanning postings for more hours than he could count, the sound of gunfire echoed down a nearby corridor. Troopers flew by on long lunar parabolas, their momentum sustained by the mass of armor and arms, turning them into deadly missiles targeting some unseen enemy.

More uniformed bodies swarmed over the library, and once they got organized they hustled Mark away as fast as they could. In the end, they had to flush the atmosphere out of the compartment, cracking the valves to hard vacuum A few more diehards scrambled out onto the surface in suits, but the troopers roasted them with the rockets from their pursuit craft.

In his curiosity, Mark had worked his way back to the scene of the final showdown and seen the strangely desiccated bodies of the last of the Tycho Lunatics. And the virtuals of the surface party were no less dramatic for being a cybernetic illusion.

Now he felt the same combination of terrible anticipation and gnawing hopelessness that he had during those long terrible weeks inside Tycho – and the same stunned emptiness that had overtaken him there in the final days before the return to Earth.

But he wasn't going back to Earth in the morning. And things weren't going to get better without getting a whole lot worse first.

***

He ran into Helen again some hours later, after the sky had darkened and the lights in their chambers had brightened considerably. She was all excited and full of energy.

"It took the professor and I spent a long time to get started with them, but we finally found out what they were trying to tell us."

"What?" Mark asked. "Who?"

"The Seedkeepers. They gave us our first lesson. Remember? You sent us down there."

"Oh yeah," Mark said.

"You look terrible," Helen said suddenly. "When was the last time you got some sleep?"

"Last night," Mark said.

"Last night local or last night ship-time?"

"Last night before they shot up the compound."

"Mark, that was nearly forty-eight hours ago. What are you doing to yourself?"

"I don't know. Anyway, you didn't tell me what the Seedkeepers taught you."

Helen's eyes lit up again. "You didn't tell me it was going to be like this," she said.

"I guess not. What is it like?"

"The more I learn about these creatures, the more confused I get. And the more complicated things become."

"That about sums it up. What's doing that for you?"

"Their genetics. The language was the key. Once the professor broke it down, it was plain to see. The terms carry all the relevant information. Sort of like organic chemistry."

"I see."

"No, you don't see. You're too punchy to see. At least you have that excuse. I don't even have that much. And I don't see."

"Okay," Mark said, reading to give up the point without a struggle.

"Anyway, these guys are sort of super-Mendels. Gregor Mendel was a monk who bred peas to see how traits are inherited. The Seedkeepers have been doing the same thing on an even grander scale. Mendel never heard about DNA, but he had the process down anyway. And so have these guys. They've never even seen a microscope, but they know how their seed works."

"And how does it work?"

"In great bunches at a time," Helen said. "Not just one trait, but whole bundles of them. It collects them up, shuffles them a bit, then deals them out whole hands at a time. If you get the hand with all the aces – full vocalization, opposable thumbs, upright spine, and a growing brain – you can join the club of civilized Chamal, such as it is.

"But it also deals out bundles of fangs, claws, noses, and ears for hunters, or hooves, fur, and horns for grazers, or pads, eyelids, and bodyfat for desert-dwellers. They're all like added features on a few standard models of chamalian. And those come in bundles too. Little scamps at the bottom of the pyramid, bigger pups, halflings, near-men, and your sapient tool-users.

"The bundles are the closest thing they have to a terrestrial species. They evolve under natural selection and are passed on through the gene pool. But they get mixed and matched freely. It sounds hopelessly chaotic – but it's not. There's a beauty and an underlying organization to it all.

"Mark, you could take a breeding pair of chamalians and put them on a deserted island, and in a few generations, you'd have creatures occupying every niche in the ecology. Traits just ebb and flow in these great tidal patterns. That's what makes the Red Monkeys appear. Something almost seems to keep track of what's going on."

"It sounds like their history, too."

"Like fractals, isn't it? Big patterns building up from little patterns, all having the same form and structure. When I start thinking about that, it starts to get to me."

"I know what you mean."

"And that's not all," Helen said suddenly, turning to look back out the door to the chamber.

"Of course not," Mark said.

"This patriarch of theirs ... this guy Jobe?"

"I know about him."

"Do you know what he wanted to do? Why he created the Seedkeepers and started them tracking traits?"

"I don't know if I can imagine. Or if I want to."

"The professor and I couldn't determine how much of this was superstition and how much was theory – or how much was Jobe's explanation and how much was embellished afterwards – but it's like this. The legend or myth or whatever –" Mark winced at Helen's terrible anthropology, but didn't interrupt.

" – is that Chamal was pure and simple, with the first sapients living in peace and harmony, like the Garden of Eden, until their gods arrived and gave them the seed of wisdom. Then they committed some terrible sin, like Adam and Eve, and their gods punished them by spreading the seed of wisdom everywhere, among all the wild animals." He cringed at her clumsy retelling of the chamalian creation myth, but kept silent.

"Jobe wanted to reverse all that. He wanted to breed all the traits and all the strains and all the races of Chamal back into their proper places. He especially wanted to recover this lost purebred species that existed before their gods stirred everything up.

"Mark, he thought he could make creatures like us, like human beings, by bringing all the pieces together. It's the wildest, craziest, and most hopeless thing I can imagine. So you see what they've done to me."

"I see it exactly," Mark replied. "They've done the same thing to me. I just wish I knew what we could do about it."

***

When Zepp began to learn the truth about the angels, the shock was enough to bring new life to a spirit that nearly had been broken by the death of Arshand.

All that had happened since his return to Suridash – the exposure of his sin, the night-vision, the attack of the dissenters, and Arshand's death – almost put Zepp into a mindless funk. Only a tiny piece of conscience kept him whole through it all. A tiny voice that told him that each trial was only a brief marker on a long road and that the suffering would have to be endured only for a moment.

And sure enough, the hidden secrets that the Wise Teacher of the Wise revealed to him served, however briefly, to wash away the depression and the grief and the pain and lift Zepp up into a cleaner, wiser place within himself.

How silly he had been. He had presumed that because they were purebreds, the angels also were knowers of all wisdom, masters of all nature, and as morally pure as they were genetically pure.

Now he wondered how he could possibly have harbored such a notion.

"Let us start with the beginnings of wisdom on the world of the angels," The wise teacher had said. "Angels who lived in a place called Europe began to share their wisdom – and more important, test it against nature. If the test proved the wisdom, the wise-leader who suggested it became renowned throughout the land." The revolution of wisdom had brought great technological changes to this Europe. The stories reminded him of the Rift of the Red Monkeys more than anything else. But the way the angels of Europe became obsessed with trade and wealth reminded him of Meshkar.

It was this obsession that drove the history of the angels for a time. First it allowed the nations of Europe to become fabulously wealthy. But then, when the system broke down, a series of great wars erupted. There followed a century of armed struggle on a scale he had never imagined. Battles raged across the entire planet, campaigns swept up millions of souls, and the death and destruction were inconceivable to the small green ape from Suridash.

And this was what caught his wings.

In the midst of that century of war arose a nation of creatures that reminded him ever so much of his cousins here on Chamal. They were superstitious and perverse, worshiping first themselves, then their land, and finally, in the end, the destruction of both. They believed in their own tribe and their own nation to the exclusion of all others. They were proud of their anger and their hate. And they swept over all of Europe in their power.

In this terrible century, the struggle for wealth had given way to a battle over raw political and military power. In the pursuit of that power, wisdom and knowledge were swept along, and the angels uncovered secrets of nature that provided them with more power than they had ever thought possible.

They had destroyed the nation of dark angels. Then the two greatest survivors of that war circled each other like suspicious hounds, each afraid of what the other might do, until finally one and then the other grew weary and laid down their bones to die.

The next century saw the wonders of wisdom and the machines of war serve the interests of ever more tribal warlords. With their newfound power over nature, the angels quickly learned that any tribe, no matter how small or weak, could threaten the greatest of empires. No great wars marked this period, but a growing tide of fear made the small ones ever more deadly and fierce.

Then finally, for some unexplained reason, the world erupted in a last spasm of violence, the final confrontation of all the armed camps, followed by an abrupt end to tribalism in a sweeping political and social revolution.

The result was this breed of kind and caring creatures.

Zepp shook his hands at the thought of it. He had believed at first that all angels were like this and always had been. Maybe in comparison to Chamal's wild denizens they were, but clearly the angels were capable of great sins as well. Their image of moral purity in Zepp's mind was shattered.

And yet –

There were things the wise teacher would not tell him.

"That is not knowledge that I am allowed to release," he said when Zepp asked the tough questions.

"What caused the final crisis?"

"What gave the angels the ability to change themselves and their world?"

"Why didn't the angels destroy themselves and their world in a fit of furious violence – just as we chamalians are sure to do if given enough time?"

But each time, the response was the same:

"That is not knowledge that I am allowed to release."

CHAPTER EIGHTEEN

Mark was lying on the cushions that covered the floor of the salon when the professor called him.

"Mr. Paradis, I need your assistance," it said.

His body felt numb and when he tried to speak, he found that his voice was a few steps behind his brain.

"What kind of assistance?"

"Zepp and I have been discussing human history. He has been asking questions that I may not answer," the AI said. "And now he wants to ask you."

"If you can't answer them, then how can you expect me to?"

"I didn't say I could not answer them, I said I may not." A sudden surge of adrenaline restored Mark's wits momentarily and lifted him to his feet in a single dreamlike motion.

"Oh – those kind of questions." He stumbled about the room trying to recover his coordination. The swift chamalian day was the problem. Just when he was ready to fall asleep, the sun would come up. By the time he was ready for supper, it would get dark again. He couldn't have gone so many hours without rest, though. Someone must have been counting them wrong.

"Where are you?" Mark asked.

"On our way to your rooms," the professor said. "I wanted to warn you that we were coming."

"Thanks. How much have you told him about us?"

"More than sufficient for your purposes. Much more. European history from the scientific revolution through the end of the 21st century. My censors are still enabled, so no details of scientific or technological innovations themselves. And of course nothing about the replication revolution. I believe that is what he wants to discuss with you. I don't need to remind you that even though you are not a programmed entity, you are equally bound by the rules of the technological quarantine."

"Yeah, right," Mark said. He wasn't about to discuss his opinions of the quarantine with a "programmed entity." It would be like talking to a wall.

"Let me get washed up first," Mark said. "Tell Zepp I'll be right with you." A few minutes later he met the green ape in the salon. Zepp paced nervously from one side of the room to the other, the links of his brass belt clinking softly in regular rhythm.

"Mark!" he called out when he saw him entering the room. "I am glad the professor found you awake. Please, tell me more about these Nazis. I want to know why they were like that and what you did to them for their sins. And I want to know what happened to your world after the time of techno-tribalism. How did it end? What did you do?"

"I suppose you won't even let me use the word 'replicator,'" Mark said in an aside to the professor.

"You may use it, but I am not allowed to translate it or to determine if there is a linguistic equivalent in any chamalian tongue."

"How about if I work my way up to it?"

"Not even that. If you attempt to violate the rules of quarantine, then I am afraid that I must cease functioning and report your infraction to Captain Fletcher."

"Then I'll have to explain that to him," Mark said.

The professor was silent for a perceptibly long time, something unusual for the cybernetic creature.

"All right," it said after a while. "But I must warn you that I have no choice in the matter and am programmed to respond should you go too far."

"Don't worry," Mark shot back. "Zepp, the professor here won't let me answer some of your questions. He won't even let me tell you why I can't answer them. But we can start with the easy stuff if you want."

"Anything," Zepp said. "I am astonished at the depths of darkness in your soul. You are not the angels that we first envisioned."

"I was afraid that you had learned as much."

"It is better this way," Zepp said. "You know our sins. We should know yours."

Mark nodded. "But this is going to cost you. Pilgrim rules. Knowledge for knowledge."

Zepp chittered in laughter. "Knowledge for knowledge," he said. "You go first."

"Ask whatever question you wish," Zepp replied.

Mark smiled. Zepp had played this game before. Maybe he was smart enough to decline the chance to volunteer information and to let Mark's own ignorance limit the scope of his question. Or maybe he was just being deferential. Either way, Mark had already prepared a question. It was one of the issues that had never been settled in their talks with Zepp, the pilgrims, or Tedrak. Mark had his suspicions, which he'd kept to himself. But he wanted to know.

"Then tell me," he said. "Before we came here, before we entered the system, before you discovered that you were not alone in the universe, how did your nations get along? What were things like between Rikabar and Meshkar and the Blue Monkeys?"

Zepp shuffled uneasily. "The answer to your question is probably a worthy price for the answers to mine," he said. "Just today, Tedrak was telling me that I should not reveal too much of the truth about Chamal to you. You wouldn't understand, he said. After hearing about your history, I believe that you would understand only too well."

"That's what I was afraid you were going to say," Mark sighed.

"Before you came, we were at war. Everyone against everyone else. It is constant and unceasing. Nations exist on suspicion, hatred, and war. Now I know that is true for the angels as well as for us."

"A sad lesson to learn," Mark said, even as his own spirit was sinking deeper into despair. He hadn't wanted to hear this report from Zepp, but there was no escaping its truth. Others had speculated as much – Nordland and Barrett especially. But knowing it gave him a feeling of being special, if only for a brief time, as if he were in on a great secret.

"Tonight I have come to believe a new thing," Zepp said. "When I met you angels, I thought that our souls were so black and filled with sin because of the curse of our biology. I thought we were trapped because of that. But now that I have seen the truth about your race, I know better. Despite the differences in our biology, there is much we share. And it is not because of our wild seed that our souls are so tortured. It is the nature of souls everywhere, on Chamal and in the heavens. Of course, we are no less trapped, but now we are not so much alone." Mark sighed again.

"Then you have indeed learned the truth about us," Mark said. "And you deserve to have it whole." He gently removed Zepp's professor from his pocket, removed his own from the pouch on his belt, and switched them both off.

***

At first, Zepp couldn't understand what Mark was trying to tell him. They both had become too dependent on the magic of the wise teacher's translations.

But using crude sign language, the angel finally conveyed his need for paper and a charcoal. Finding them was nearly as difficult as making the initial communication. Paper was not a common item in the world of Suridash, but the Seedkeepers thrived on it. Of course, they had to go on a long search for it that led them down into the main hall. The charcoal Zepp plucked from a fireplace. Once Mark had them, he set to work quickly.

The drawings he made were only a small improvement over the sign language, but carried a great deal more information. The first of them was a machine of some sort. Zepp recognized that. But he couldn't figure out the nature of the machine or of Mark's underlying message.

The next picture showed a larger machine, with a line of smaller ones beside it. At first examination, he thought the larger machine was devouring the smaller copies, sucking them into an open maw with a long mechanical tongue. It took Mark some time to invert that image in Zepp's understanding, but he finally saw that the larger device was expelling the smaller ones on a belt of some kind.

A machine that made machines. Simple enough, Zepp thought. But why wouldn't the wise teacher explain this to him? The third picture was the most detailed, and Mark spent extra time on it. Three machines covered the yellowed sheet of rough paper. The first seemed to be expelling a second that looked much like it, only smaller and lacking the tongue-like belt. A third machine sat at the end of the first one's belt, a combination of the first two. It had the first machine's size, but still lacked a mouth or tongue.

Zepp stared at it for the longest time while Mark remained motionless and silent. That was odd, he thought. The angel had been eager to pester him into figuring out the meaning of the first two images. Why was he now calm and patient? He looked back at the picture, his mind a blank, filled with expectant energy.

Then he had it!

They were a sequence in time. The first machine made the second machine, and the third machine was a duplicate of the first machine – but after it had time to enlarge itself. The first and the third machines were identical. And they were both the same machine as the one in the second drawing that spit out the smaller devices. Now he noticed the identifying markers the angel had taken great pains to include on each of them.

A machine that made machines that made machines.

His mind was seized suddenly by a powerful spirit. In an instant, it revealed to him the awesome ramifications of self-replicating technology – machines making machines making machines making machines. They covered the landscape, spilled over rocks and walls, stretched in long chains across the desert, and devoured the forests.

It was almost as if all the wild creatures of Chamal had turned into steel and plastic and become linked in great chains of electric wires and thinking machines from Kwikorak. And like Zepp's own wild race, they began to sprout offspring of every size and shape. All the material things that wisdom produced on this planet, flowing forth to fill the space that was not already occupied by the machine-making machines.

There was a myth about that, Zepp thought as the spirit lifted him ever higher, revealing new levels of understanding.

It was the end of history. The end of the daily struggle that wisdom endured to make its daily needs. The day when halflings would wear shoes and steplings don spectacles, when the hungry would be set down before the endless banquet, when the predator would drink ale with the prey, when warriors would tell their lives to the poets, and when wisdom would fill the world with its bounty.

And this had happened to the angels.

***

Mark was overjoyed that Zepp seemed to understand. At least he got a response. He never got a chance to show Zepp the drawings he had made illustrating exponential growth – series of blocks, two, four, eight, sixteen, and on up.

Zepp pushed them back into his hands and uttered a manic chittering sound. Then he leapt into the air and sprinted for the stairs. Mark hurried to keep up with him, wondering what he had managed to communicate. Considering the reaction, he believed he was successful in getting across the forbidden point. He had no question in his mind about the importance of this particular secret, and Zepp's reaction was certainly on an appropriate scale of magnitude.

They flew down the corridors until they reached the salon. Zepp grabbed the professor from the table where Mark had left it and pressed it into his hands.

Before he dared to restore the power to the AI, however, Mark had to be sure that their secret was secure. He pointed to the sheaf of papers and clapped a hand across his mouth. Zepp shook the professor in the air in front of him. Mark repeated his pantomime. Zepp rubbed his face with his hand and rocked from one foot to the other. Mark repeated his performance one more time, more vigorously than before, and ended by grabbing Zepp's wrist and slapping his hand across his own mouth.

At last Zepp seemed to understand. He waved the drawings, then covered his mouth, then shook his hands in the gesture that indicated the affirmative.

Only then did Mark switch the professor back on. "It is a shame that I cannot tell you more about the cause of the great changes in our recent history," he said. "But there are many things that we cannot reveal to you until we have been here longer." He didn't know if the line would convince the professor. It was not a real personality and the illusion of free will and an inquisitive mind were just that – an illusion, created by clever designers. The thing that worried him, though, was that as rigid as it was in its programming, it was still a linguistic analyst of the first order and might be able to detect in Mark's voice the tones and hesitations of a lie.

In any case, Zepp did not give him time to worry.

"Nevertheless," he said, "there are general things you can say, aren't there? The professor was very helpful in explaining what it knew about the Nazis, for example."

"Well, yes," Mark said. "There is plenty that I can say about them. I've written quite a few texts on the subject, as a matter of fact." He didn't say so, but even here there were things he couldn't reveal – things tied too closely to the termination assessment. "The Nazis were just one of several movements that arose in the 20th century –

authoritarian, racist, militaristic, tribalist, and sociopathic. Has the professor explained those terms to you?"

"He says that you can't understand anyone's history if you don't know those terms."

Mark nodded, and feared again for his hide at the evidence of the professor's level of sophistication. "Right. They weren't unique to the period, but they were the most ambitious and did the most damage to our civilization. At the time, some of our experts believed that the Nazis showed the dangers of what they called aggression. But as we came to understand our nature more clearly, we saw that destructiveness and the worship of death have their own pathology.

"It starts with narcissism. Self-centeredness in the soul and in the mind. The inner world becomes the basis of all being, the outer world becomes nothing but objects to be manipulated. Then it moves on to sadism – the desire to exert power over other creatures – and masochism – the desire to submit to a greater power. In the end, it becomes a hatred of the powerless, and of the self, which is then projected out onto the world, becoming an impulse for death and destruction in ever greater spheres.

"The end of the Nazi war was marked by senseless slaughters. Long after they were defeated, their leader insisted that they fight on, wasting lives and destroying lands and cities, while they committed genocide on a scale never before seen on our planet."

"What of the other groups? What happened to them?"

"A great many of them were defeated in the war. But the same social forces that created the Nazis continued to spawn similar cults. After the war, for a long time they could not reveal their true nature and spoke in self-serving lies that hid their real faces. But their actions always gave them away."

"And what happened to them in the end?"

"They were swept away at the end of the 21st century, when the tribal struggles reached their peak and were ... how do I say it, professor? Is 'overtaken by events' sufficiently vague?"

"It is acceptable," the AI said before translating Mark's words.

"No, I mean what happened to them? Were they imprisoned? Did you execute them? Or did you change them?"

"Oh," Mark said, feeling a sudden chill as he realized that Zepp had touched upon the other forbidden subject in their conversation. "Some of them were imprisoned and some were changed. But the worst of them, I am afraid, were exterminated."

Zepp shook his hands in affirmation. "And if you find it necessary," he asked, "how will you deal with similar groups here on Chamal?"

Mark was about to answer the question when the professor interrupted. "I am afraid I am not allowed to translate statements on this subject."

Zepp chittered with amusement. Mark felt his skin burn in embarrassment, then he laughed. He realized what the professor did not – that the question was mostly rhetorical, and that Zepp already knew the answer.

But then neither Zepp nor Mark were able to ask or answer any more questions at that point. Their attention was distracted suddenly by a flash of violet light in the sky outside the window.

Then the whole world lit up with a brilliant blaze of white. And five heartbeats later, two great hands clapped Mark's head on either side and slapped him onto the floor.

***

Mark couldn't tell how long he had lain on the cool stones. His back ached, his head throbbed, and he was stunned, but not exactly deaf. Instead, a shrill, high-pitched whistle blocked out all other sound. He rubbed his ears and found blood. He wiped his nose and found more.

Across the salon, Zepp stood unsteadily, making little spiraling motions as he held his place, circling around some invisible axis centered on his tail.

The world outside had darkened once again, but now a thick cloud appeared to have covered the sky, with the light of a thousand torches flashing across its underside.

Mark gained his own footing, and found himself swaying to his own alternate gravity. For some reason, he was certain that the dissenters had returned and blown a hole in the walls somewhere below. He felt a sudden panic as he tried to remember where Helen was – down in the archives or up in her room? He stumbled from chamber to chamber looking for her, but she was not in sight. He noticed that the lights were on. That was a good sign. He wondered if there was shooting outside and was worried that he wouldn't be able to hear it if there were.

Fear chewed on his nerves for a few minutes. What if they got Helen again? Then one of Zepp's pilgrim guards appeared and motioned quickly. Mark and Zepp moved quickly to follow him. The guard never even tried to talk, and Mark realized that he already must know it was pointless. He led them down the stairs and out into the courtyard.

Pilgrims were running everywhere, while overhead the Seedkeepers wailed from their windows. Rescue crews ran about, some carrying the injured. It was like Tycho all over again, Mark realized. He remembered some trooper waxing prolific about blast damage and how whimsical it could be – wiping one guy against the wall and leaving the man next to him untouched. There were probably quite a few chamalians who'd had a rougher time than he had.

But there was no sign of damage and no indication where the bomb had gone off, Mark noticed in puzzlement. Where was the fire? Where did all the smoke in the sky come from? He looked up and saw that his restricted view from the window upstairs had misled him. The cloud that covered the sky also covered the city. And the flames, all to the south, were much greater than he had first imagined.

When the scale of the explosion registered on him, Mark felt the blood drain from his face.

"Oh god, please don't let it be a nuke," he said aloud.

The words felt strange, as vibrations in his jaw that translated into muffled sound. He was glad he wouldn't be completely deaf, even if the pain was starting to build in his ears.

If it was a nuke, then they were all cooked. If it was a nuke, then Barrett and Fletcher would go wild. And if it was a nuke, they'd be entitled to.

CHAPTER NINETEEN

A **truck rolled by** and skidded to a stop in front of them, driven by a pilgrim Mark recognized – a goat-faced fellow with golden curls – and two more of Zepp's entourage. The original guard now fetched Frit, Arshand's lieutenant – a gray-furred, wide-faced badger of a chamalian. He tried to talk, he tried to bark, but all that Mark got out of it was a series of strained expressions. Then he gave up, and they all climbed into the truck. Mark hesitated only briefly before boarding, then let his curiosity get the better of him.

They rolled across the courtyard, and the riders at the back and in the front poked their weapons outboard. A moment later they were out into the street, and Mark realized that instead of headlights mounted on the front of the vehicle, the chamalians were using handheld lights – one in the driver's hand and the other held by Frit.

The drawback was that any time the driver was distracted by something to one side or the other, he swung his light over to see what it was – leaving the truck hurtling headlong into inky darkness.

Frit directed the driver with frantic hand signals, and they gained speed. Mark held on to the frame of his seat, trying not to consider the risks of flying headlong through dark and narrow streets built for pack animals and beggars.

The route seemed endless, but it never followed a straight line for more than a few hundred meters. After a few minutes, however, Mark could tell that they were circling the center of the blast in a wide arc.

The streets were jammed with chamalians roused from their homes by the blast – from the brief glances Mark had of individuals as the truck flew by included every conceivable form of life the planet had to offer. Larger crowds gathered in the plazas and squares, scrambling to get out of the way of the truck.

A pillar of smoke and flame was visible now over the rooftops on the far side of the city. A short while longer, as the sight of the inferno appeared from behind walls and blocks of buildings they passed, he saw that they were getting closer and closer.

The last few hundred meters before the fires were the worst for Mark, as the driver pushed the vehicle up to greater speeds. Then they plunged down an avenue lined with burning buildings, flames licking out charred window holes, toasting the stone walls.

Mark held his breath as the smoke billowed overhead, thankful that little in Suridash seemed to be built of wood – some rooftops, rafters, doorways, and window frames, from the look of it. He was certain that the lunatic pilgrims were going to get them all killed by driving into the fire, but he clenched his seat with both hands hoping fervently that he was wrong.

The streets were full of running chamalians now, refugees from the flames. The had the beneficial effect of forcing the truck to slow down. But that only made the stench of burning rubbish all that much stronger in Mark's nose.

Then they broke through the fire. It formed a ring all around the center of the blast, Mark could see now that they were inside. There were no refugees in here, and they sped up. But a couple more blocks and they slowed down to avoid the rubble.

Frit directed the driver through it as best he could, and they found their way to a boulevard that passed through a narrow canyon of brick and cut stone. The boulevard was scorched by the force of the explosion that the canyon had channeled out into the city. The facades of the buildings had been stripped clean, sandblasted of any sharp detail.

They rolled slowly down a street that had been whisked clean of all imperfections, brushed right down to shining cobblestones.

And at the other end of the canyon was the center of the blast. Mark realized with a sudden sickness in the pit of his stomach that if it was a nuke, they were all cashing themselves in by driving to ground zero and soaking up lethal doses of radiation.

But if it was a nuke, there would be other effects, he realized. EMP, they called it. Electromagnetic pulse. It fried electronics, shut down power systems, killed virtual displays, and flashed out AI's. And the lights had been on back at the Hall of the Seedkeepers.

The crater wasn't very deep – at least not compared to the scar that surrounded it. About forty meters across and half that deep.

And around it for two hundred meters, nothing stood.

No two stones sat atop one another. Even the rubble had been blown away.

Mark felt the same devastation creep across his heart. If it was a nuke ...

They stopped the truck at the edge of the crater. A lip a meter or so high circled the edge – cracked bedrock. Mark looked off to the north. Rising over the buildings that remained up there were the two great towers of the Hall of the Seedkeepers. The distinctive high turret atop the north tower could not be mistaken for anything else.

His heart almost stopped. It was only a kilometer away.

They'd come the long way around to get here. Ground zero was practically in their back yard.

Whoever had done this had missed their target, he realized with a chill that penetrated to his bones.

Mark, Zepp, Frit, and the other pilgrims prowled carefully about the circumference of the big hole. A sudden movement by a stepling running across the barren stone brought everyone's weapons up. The far side was just as devastated as the near side.

Frit tried to talk to Zepp again, but it was still useless. The ringing in Mark's ears was not subsiding, and the pain was beginning to get too bad to ignore. Frit tried using sign language with Zepp.

Good luck, Mark thought. He'd tried that once already tonight. It wasn't as easy as it looked.

But he was wrong. Frit looked up into the sky, then pointed. Then he brought his big paw down quickly, slamming into the palm of his other paw while pointing at the crater.

Whatever it was, it had come from the sky. That was pretty obvious.

But what was it? Zepp seemed to be asking the same question.

So Frit pointed up in the sky again. This time he pointed across at Mark, then put his paw to his neck, twisted it, then dropped his head to one side in mock death.

Mark felt a sudden panic. Were they about to turn on him? Then he realized what Frit was saying. He wasn't going to kill an angel, he was talking about the *Angel Killer*. The warship orbiting overhead.

Now Mark realized what had happened. The *Deragathon* had attacked the city. With what kind of weapon, he did not know. Maybe a missile. Maybe a chunk of rock – the kinetic energy would have been more than any simple explosive could do. Whatever it was, they had aimed it at the city and let it fall.

No, he realized. Not at the city.

Not at Suridash.

At him.

They were aiming their weapons at him, personally. The chill of it penetrated into his marrow.

And they had almost hit him on the very first try.

***

Barrett landed the next day in the *Belle Marie*.

By then, some of Mark's hearing had returned. Helen had sprayed something in his ears from the medkit and given him a shot with all kinds of drugs in it, and now he felt much better. Voices were still muffled and the high, scratchy sounds of fabric rubbing against fabric still set his head afire, but it was better than the constant ringing.

Helen had indeed been in the archives when the blast hit. And surrounded by thick stone walls and the stacks of sound-absorbing books, scrolls, and manuscripts, she had suffered no ill effects.

The *Cousteau* had sent down a much larger landing team this time. There was a medical corpsman, who did things to further soothe Mark's discomfort and speed his recovery. And three workers from Helen's section were aboard, bringing the doctor with them. Barrett had his muscle – five of the deck crew's biggest and best-armed men.

And Barrett brought news.

The object that left the hole in the middle of Suridash was originally a small spacecraft.

That was the word from the analysts aboard the *Cousteau*. They'd missed the separation, but caught the craft when it made its de-orbit burn. The thing was about the same size as the shuttle that had carried Zepp and Griddle from the *Deragathon*. And a few tons of metal and plastic auguring in at a few kilometers a second was sufficient to wake both the living of Suridash and the dead.

Helen had been helpful with the injured. The physicians who served the tribe of Jobe were skilled and savvy enough, but there weren't enough of them. She knew enough basic first aid to cross over the differences in species and treat the casualties on the scene. She stabilized the more seriously hurt, bound up the wounds of the injured, and organized a system of triage.

Language didn't seem to be a barrier. Everyone was in the same situation, deafened by the blast and stunned by the shock. Sign language and instruction by example were the rule of the day.

From the top of the south tower, Mark could see across the walls and rooftops to the crater and the blast zone around it. And every time he went up there, he felt a twinge in his back reminding him that there were players above him who wanted badly to see him out of the game. Badly enough that they didn't care who else got hurt.

In this case, who else was the Ravina. Ground zero was near the center of their enclave. The Ravina had been ruminants from the east. This herd had come here to escape a war more than a century ago. They were still a robust tribe, and their spiraling antlers had penetrated the city's underlying gene-pool sufficiently to become a recognized trait, as had their splay-foot hooves. They were weavers and metalsmiths, with the patience to do fine work. They had built up some significant wealth in trade goods and precious metals behind their walls. Occasionally, they would launch some kind of a assault by rocket or infantry against the Red Monkey enclave to satisfy an ancient vendetta. Last year, Zepp had witnessed a bombing attack in which winged halflings carried their payloads across the sky and dropped them on the Reds. More than two thousand of them bore fair claim to wisdom, Zepp had told him. Now there were none.

Perhaps in a dozen years or so, the tribe might reconstitute itself as a population of wise ruminants, but their history and their identity could never be recovered.

Barrett had been back on the surface only one local day when Tedrak called them all into another audience. Mark and Helen accompanied him to the audience. When they entered the leader's chamber Mark was surprised to see a chamalian that he recognized – Sherbek, Zepp's cousin, the one who had brought Zepp's sisters to meet the *Belle Marie* that first day outside Suridash.

***

Mark watched Zepp closely. Sherbek made the small green ape nervous. Mark had learned now to recognize some of the signs. And that made Mark nervous.

Tedrak may or may not have noticed either of them. Those thick glasses of his made Mark doubt the old groundhog could notice much of anything he couldn't touch, hear, or smell. In any case, he was in no hurry to ease the tension. He said nothing about Sherbek and went right to the heart of the matter.

"We have not been completely honest with you," he told Barrett.

"We haven't been completely honest with you either," Mark said. Barrett scowled at him, which was enough to shut him up for the moment.

"In what way?" Barrett asked.

"Things were much worse aboard the *Deragathon* than we wanted to admit," Tedrak said. "We thought they might improve, and then it wouldn't be necessary to mention it. But the balance of power over the vessel has shifted."

"Since when?" Barrett asked.

"Since two days ago," Tedrak said.

"If you'd told us earlier, we could have warned you about the attack. Maybe even stopped them."

"That news makes the loss of the Ravina all the more bitter," Zepp said.

This time it was Tedrak who did the scowling, and again it was sufficient for its purpose.

"So what's going on up there?" Barrett asked bluntly.

"Before the shift, the main axis of the vessel belonged to Meshkar, the Cult of the Lost Argument, and to us. We held our own containment and that of Meshkar. And we had the hangar decks and the bridge. Now we are left our containments and the bridge."

"And none of those are connected to the other," Zepp said.

"No, unfortunately not," Tedrak said. "It is not a position of much advantage."

"And what does that mean?" Barrett asked.

"They have the capacity to do that again," Tedrak said, pointing up at the window where wood had replaced shattered glass. "For two days they have been resupplied with rocket launches coming up from Birhat and Rikabar – though I never thought I'd see the day when the Vegetarians would join forces with those lions from Birhat."

"It sounds like they're consolidating their gains," Barrett said. "And securing their position. They must be making repairs to the ship."

"Exactly," Tedrak said. "And then some."

"What do you expect to happen when they're ready?"

"To know the answer to that question, you have to understand our political structure."

"We already have a pretty good idea," Mark said. "There is no structure. You just blunder around the place, building little empires, and fighting pointless wars with one another. That's the situation we stumbled into, isn't it, Master Tedrak? When we arrived, you were all at each other's throats. In another generation, you'd be ready to destroy each other completely. Correct?"

Tedrak sputtered, then lifted his snout to look through his spectacles at Zepp. "What have you been telling the angels, boy?" he asked.

Zepp's tail clenched and uncoiled nervously, but he said nothing.

Mark could see that Barrett's eyes were opened wide in disbelief. "I want to talk to you later, Paradis," he said. "But for now, just keep a seal on it."

Tedrak rubbed his eyes. "Yes, it is true. We recognize no law among ourselves, only power. I suppose it is different among the angels."

This time Zepp spoke up. "It can be, but usually it isn't," he said.

Now Barrett scowled again and echoed Tedrak's question: "And what have you been telling him?"

Mark shrugged.

"What matters is that now the powers aboard the *Deragathon* are preparing to use the ship to complete their mission – to kill the angels," Tedrak said. "We did not go to all this trouble to stop them only to let them get away and try again. Whatever you need from us to stop them, all you have to do is ask."

Barrett looked surprised at the sudden offer of support. Mark had expected it. But he knew that Tedrak's political interests were tied inescapably to those of the angels. And their protection was the only way he could protect himself and his city. The next shot might not miss.

"I'll have to get back to you on that," Barrett said. "When the time comes, we may ask."

"Now I have more bad news," Tedrak declared, folding his hands over his round belly, leaning back in his place, and turning his head to regard each of them in turn. "The shift in fortunes aboard the *Deragathon* has come at the same time as a shift in the tides of struggle here on the surface. We have finally collected sufficient information about conditions around the globe."

Mark drew in his breath in anticipation of the worst. He remembered those first pictures of burning cities they had seen the day they made orbit and wondered if things could be worse.

"In the past few days in the Rift Valley, loyalist armies have surrounded Ring Po Do and made ready for a final assault on the Assembly of Traitors. Elsewhere, the loyalists have been able to seize control of provincial capitals and barracks. The issue is still in doubt, but the Blue Monkeys are in a position to take back control.

"In Rikabar, the Vegetarian Party has been typically ruthless in suppressing the rebels. They took a great many casualties at first, so they are still on the defensive. But the high party officials all went up to the *Deragathon* before the arrival of the angels, and they continue to direct what remains of their organization down below.

"The uprising of the herds and the cattle took the Birhat cats by surprise and they hold the cities. But the real power of the cats is out on the steppes, in their great ranches where the well-armed lords are in a position to wait out the storm.

"In Meshkar, the great wheel of fortune has turned once again.

Banking houses are again at war with one another and the trading nations have followed suit. Only Jobe knows where it will end up.

"The Cult of the Lost Argument is still trying to wrest control of the main rookeries of Arkaria from the ruling clans. But they have lost many fliers in the fight. And no word has come from there for several days – after a brief signal from them telling us that the cult was winning." Mark felt the weight of Tedrak's words weigh ever more heavily on his shoulders as he went on. His worst fears were being borne out. The dark forces of Chamal were conspiring to prove chamalians could not be trusted to range free.

"And now those parties who have regained significant control of the *Deragathon* are telling their partners here on the surface that they will tip the balance in their favor. The attack on us here the other night was the signal for further actions elsewhere. The loyalists began their attack on Ring Po Do, the rivals of the Meshkar banks that financed the alliance made their moves, and the Empire of the Royal Onion unleashed its political cadres on the rebels. Even in Birhat, purges of the wisest leaders of the herds and cattle were commenced on all the big domains.

"The hour of judgment is close at hand – both up above and down here on Chamal. I would urge you to be quick in deciding what you will do, before the ability to decide has been stripped from your hands."

Barrett straightened in his seat and made ready to go. "If we're all done here."

But Tedrak wasn't about to let Barrett run the meeting or decide when it was over. He waved at him and motioned him to sit back.

Barrett looked around, his eyes locked with Mark's for a brief uncomfortable moment, then he relaxed. Probably because he saw that Mark was about to leave until Tedrak said so.

"We still have business," Tedrak said. "There is the matter of Zepp's cousin, Sherbek."

Sherbek's red fur ruffled and flared around his small dark eyes as he stood up and stepped forward. Mark still couldn't read chamalian expressions well, but Sherbek looked fierce and predatory. There was something of the fox in his long snout, and when he licked his lips he revealed two rows of short, pointed teeth.

Zepp was alert with interest, the tip of his tail twitching nervously.

"Cousin Zepp, I bring you good news," Sherbek said. "The dissenters are no more. Last night we had an epiphany. Many of us who had opposed your vision saw the lack of our wisdom and the truth of yours. We confess the error and admit our guilt."

Zepp seemed to hesitate, then stood and nodded to his cousin. "Your admission is recognized," he said.

"And in order to demonstrate our commitment to your vision," Sherbek continued, "we have put an end to all dissent. Those who would not see the wisdom of your way have been eliminated. There will be no more threat to you."

Mark wasn't sure, but he thought he saw Zepp sag in the knees. And neither was he sure that he understood Sherbek correctly. Zepp's question, though, removed all doubt.

"How many of our tribe no longer threaten my vision?" he asked.

"We counted two hundred and forty-one," Sherbek said. "All dispatched quickly and without pain. Well, some pain. And Cousin Korbat's mate awoke when we entered his chambers and we had to —"

"Enough!" Tedrak said. "Leave the details for later. The dissent has ended. The tribe of Jobe is whole once again. And it is inspired by the new vision of Zepp, which sees the angels as bringing a new period of history to our world. Sherbek, I make you the leader of our effort to aid the angels. You will help them find a way to protect us from the *Deragathon*."

This time Mark had no doubts either about Zepp. His knees bent, his body sank, and his tail curled itself around one leg. Mark resisted the impulse to go to his side, and Zepp recovered without actually losing his footing.

But it was plain to see that Zepp felt as bad about this turn of events as Mark did. And probably for the same reason, Mark surmised.

***

Helen Castain sought him out when they had returned to their chambers. The Seedkeepers had given them the entire floor to accommodate the newcomers from the *Cousteau*, and Mark had moved his quarters to a quieter room in a corner turret of the great stone hall.

"Am I getting paranoid in my old age or is Sherbek really a back-stabbing, two-timing, son-of-a-bitch grammster?" she asked.

"It's not paranoia if they're really out to get you," Mark replied.

"What about Zepp? Have you talked to him about his cousin?"

"Not yet. But he didn't look happy with things." Mark told her about his observations.

"Why is it that I can't bring myself to trust a single one of these creatures? Not even Zepp, if you really put the question to it. I'd like to, but he's one of them. And I can't figure out how they think."

"I'm afraid I can't help you. I think we can trust Zepp – but only because he doesn't seem to have an agenda of his own. But the rest of them are a pack of double-dealing liars."

Helen shook her head. "I don't believe Sherbek for one minute when he says he changed his mind."

Mark drew in a long breath, then blew it out in a long sigh. "On that one, I don't know what to say," he replied at last.

"You don't? Why not?"

"There's more going on here than meets the eye. This isn't the first time I've seen this happen. These creatures are very quick to change their minds. Too quick, it seems to me, but that's just my human prejudice getting in the way. Think about it. When we were under the guns at the Blue Monkey fortress, Zepp talked us out of it. And when we landed outside Suridash, he convinced Arshand, then his tribesmen. And look at the dissenters. They sorted themselves out almost overnight and immediately launched an attack. And now the same ones have switched sides again, almost overnight."

"At least they're consistent in their inconsistency."

"That they are," Mark said. "Remember what Tedrak said about the allies of Suridash aboard the *Deragathon*? He mentioned a Cult of the Lost Argument." Helen nodded slowly.

"I asked the professor if he knew what that was. He told me the story he got from Zepp. It seems that on his walk around the world, Jobe found himself in a tavern at the rim of the Arkarian basin where he met a gaggle of winged Arkarians. The fliers got into an argument with Jobe about the seed of wisdom – the seed of the gods. They made the usual claim that only creatures with wings had the true wisdom and were the true descendants of the gods on Chamal. But Jobe worked hard to convince them that self-consciousness was the same no matter what the form it took. He made a fairly airtight case, the kind of thing you'd expect from a patriarch – especially when he learned that the loser in an argument with the Arkarians normally forfeited his life. All the Arkarians but one dismissed him. But that one was all it took to spare him and send him on his way."

"Is this a true story or one that gets made up – like Washington and the cherry tree or Jimmy Carter and the rabbit?"

"That's what they wondered in Suridash at first. Until Arkarians started flying in to the city. They said they belonged to the Cult of the Lost Argument – followers of the flier in the tavern. Jobe's argument had spread like a virus, infecting more and more Arkarians every year. Zepp told the professor that they've been an underground movement in their lands for two centuries. And when Suridash needed their help, they were only too happy to cooperate."

"That's a nice story, Mark. But what does it mean? It doesn't seem to make sense."

"When things don't make sense, it's time to go looking for a different context," Mark said. "I think I'm beginning to see something that maybe Zepp hasn't noticed about his own race. The kind of thing that's so obvious that no one is aware of it. Ideas really do spread like viruses among chamalians."

"You mean there's some kind of biochemical link?"

"No – not like that. It's just a metaphor. But it's not like human communication. There's not so much persuasion or debate. Once the idea is clearly expressed, it seems to take hold all at once. Like a virus or some other infection. And it can spread through a population like wildfire. They don't question the idea critically, they just accept it whole because that's how they are."

Helen shuddered and shook her head. "That's a scary thought. What happens if somehow they get infected with the idea that we are a dangerous evil that has to be destroyed?"

"I think it's too late for that, Helen," Mark said. "I'm worried about that idea somehow overcoming the nice creatures here in Suridash who are so eager to help us right now – the ones who just murdered a couple hundred of their cousins because they didn't want to go along with the consensus." Helen closed her eyes softly, and said: "I don't even want to think about that one."

CHAPTER TWENTY

Zepp sat in the cool darkness of his room.

The sound of his sisters tending their pups filtered in from down the hall, as there was no door to his chamber, just a heavy cloth curtain. But he paid no attention to the noise.

He was still in a state something close to shock, but not quite the same. His mind was still, but he felt as if something powerful was going on beneath the level of conscious thought.

He didn't like the idea of Sherbek being placed in a position so close to the angels. He didn't trust his cousin at all. But better the threat you expect than one you don't, he told himself.

That wasn't what really bothered him, though.

It was the guilt. Two hundred and forty-one. Their blood was on his hands. If he had allowed his own death on the *Deragathon* days ago when so many were trying to accomplish that end, all his cousins who refused to accept a new idea would still be alive. It wasn't fair, he realized. It didn't balance out.

Then he wondered why it should balance out. Had he really spent so much time with the angels that he was beginning to think like them? It was possible. That would explain it.

The guilt he felt now replaced entirely the fear he had been carrying around inside himself for so long. And it was worse than the guilt he felt for betraying his race by sabotaging the mission of the *Deragathon*. At least there he had been serving some higher purpose.

Here, there was no such justification.

Sherbek and his followers had simply carried out the logical implications of Zepp's new vision. There were those who agreed and those who did not. And those who did not could not be convinced through rational means. If they did not accept the new vision, they had to be dealt with. And in Suridash, exile was only a way of breeding enemies.

Even so, the guilt would not go away. And Zepp found himself shaking at the thought of all the myriad ways that fate could find for a powerless green ape to atone for his sins.

And in order to assuage that guilt, Zepp knew that he had to seek the counsel of the angels once again. While the discussion with the Wise Teacher of the Wise over the history of human science had been illuminating, it never addressed the kinds of questions that still hung in Zepp's mind. Science and machinery were not the answer to the dilemma facing Chamal.

Wisdom, however, was.

So it seemed that there was a difference between what Zepp and his fellow chamalians knew as wisdom and what the angels knew as science. Perhaps he had asked the wise teacher to explain the wrong history.

He put his feet to the cold stony floor and padded quickly through the curtain and down the hall. He found an empty salon and curled up on a seat built into an alcove window, where he took out his copy of the wise teacher and asked the question.

"The discipline you want to review is known as love-of-knowledge and it goes back much farther than the history of science," the wise teacher said after Zepp explained what he was looking for. "It is deeply entwined with the history of mumble-mumble as well."

"What was that word?"

"The word was 'religion.' A system of beliefs in a divine being or spiritual power and its expression in culture or ritual."

"Oh," Zepp said. "Our word for that is 'superstition.'"

"A related term in the angel lexicon, which was written by angels who subscribe to a religion in the first place and were predisposed to give it more respect."

"But how is superstition related to love-of-knowledge?"

"The same way the seed of wisdom is seen on your world as synonymous with the seed of the gods."

"All right," Zepp said, seeing the connection instantly once the words were clear. "Now it makes sense. What can you tell me?"

"I have an hour-long tutorial on the subject that you can experience. I can also enhance it with a series of holographic images." Yet another strange term. What were holographic images? He was too anxious to waste time asking, so he just asked the wise teacher to proceed. A moment later, the room was plunged into darkness.

***

"In the beginning, there was nothing. And the Lord said, 'Let there be light.' And there was light." It was a white light and it appeared to one side of the room, formless and shifting, like a wreath of smoke or fog.

"And the Lord divided the light into the stars and the sun and the moon and placed them in the heavens." The light shattered into a thousand pieces, which filled the dome overhead as stars. They coalesced into a thin crescent of a moon, too small for Zepp to identify which one. And then they were washed away from the sky with the sudden rising of a small golden sun.

The air was filled with the sound of great squealing pipes, bleating out in steady rhythm, rising up and down the scale with a frenetic pace. Zepp wondered what the sound had to do with the image that surrounded him, but the wise teacher did not explain – if it indeed it was still around.

Suddenly the image was gone, to be replaced by an old angel with a wrinkled face that Zepp had never met before. Surprisingly, the angel spoke directly in the common language of Suridash with no intermediate translation – and with the voice of the wise teacher. So the old master had revealed himself at last.

"Or perhaps it went like this – "

The world went black again, with a vague swirling of gray at the edge of perception.

"Before the world was formed, there was a great void – Ginnungagup. And here was Niflheim, the world of death, where a great well gave birth to eleven rivers." The rivers sprang to life, full of sparkling water and flashes of blue light. Then the rivers froze solid, the sparkle remained and the light softened to a glow. "The frozen waters of the eleven rivers filled Ginnungagup. But sparks from Muspell, a hot land to the south of Niflheim, fell on the rivers and melted them. Drops of water from the melting rivers took the form of the giant, Ymir, and his sweat became the stuff of other giants, male and female." The darkness closed in, then the salon slowly returned to normal.

"Creation myths are the basis of nearly all historical religions," the wise teacher said, standing before the cold hearth of the fireplace. "Prehistoric religions were likely not so. The underlying economy of that stage of history was dominated by women, and matriarchal myths do not require a creation. The universe grew naturally and had always been there. But the sudden break with nature that was precipitated by the emergence of male-dominated civilizations gave birth to a created universe. The power of the male is to make things, and the power of a male god is to make the universe. The best example is Marduk, the Assyrian god, who killed the goddess Tiamat and cut her body in two – from one part he made the heaven and from the other he made the earth.

"But what we want to look at more closely are the historical religions of the world of the angels." And in short order, Zepp found himself on a rocky hilltop in the desert where then angel called Abraham, looking and sounding very much like the wise teacher, made ready to sacrifice his son. Moments after Abraham was freed of that requirement, the son of the tribe of Jobe joined in the long procession of Israelites streaming away from the Nile as Moses lead his people out of the land of the great kings. Zepp trembled at the sight of the parting of the Red Sea, and ducked for cover as the finger of God carved out the Ten Commandments with a blaze of fire high atop Mount Sinai. He stood in a crowded temple while the wise teacher, wearing robes and yarmulke, read from the Torah. He rode in a rail car packed with angels in dark coats. And he huddled in a trench in the desert, listening to the wise teacher on a plastic radio describe the latest battle in the birth-struggle of a nation called Israel.

After a brief pause to regain his bearings, the wise teacher was off with him once again.

He walked through a garden in Asia with Lao-Tse, who explained that the the truly wise draw their power from being absorbed in the underlying reality of the ever-changing world. He sat in the same garden as K'ung Fu-tzu praised piety and the honoring of ancestors.

The minute he was gone, Lao-Tse returned to tell him what a pompous windbag K'ung Fu-tzu was and whispered to Zepp that he shouldn't believe the old fool.

After another pause, he was transported to the base of the tree where Gautama became the Enlightened One and revealed to Zepp the basis of all suffering – ignorance. He followed the Buddha as he walked across India, while all around him the angels carried out ever more complex rituals, meditations, and prayers. When they reached the high mountains of the north, only the Buddha – and Zepp – continued until they found a monastery where the wise teacher presented a single monk, who cried out in protest that the Buddha needed none of the ritual, prayers, or meditations to achieve enlightenment – he simply achieved it. Zepp was about to remark on how he already knew this lesson from Jobe's excursion into the mountaintops, but the Buddha continued his march, down the other side of the mountains, across the land the wise teacher called China, and over the sea to the island nation he called Japan.

Another pause followed, and then Zepp found himself watching a floating vision descend from a night sky to speak to angels herding a flock of grazers, announcing the birth of the son of a god. Then he found himself on the side of a hill with hundreds of angels listening to a distant prophet, whom the wise teacher said was that same son of a god, recite a long litany: "Blessed are the meek, for they shall inherit the world." He followed the prophet into the city where he saw him was arrested, tried, and nailed to a wooden scaffold. But when the wise teacher showed him stepping out of his tomb three days later, Zepp bristled and reminded him that on Chamal these were called superstitions. But the wise teacher swiftly transported him to a great stone hall where angels in white robes burned incense, lighted hundreds and hundreds of candles, and a great statue of the martyred prophet hanging on his scaffold looked down on them from the rear wall.

Another pause came and went, and they were back in the desert, where he found himself carried away without moving a muscle as warriors on horseback rode to victory over the defenders of a city that reminded him very much of Suridash. The leader was yet another prophet, who demanded obedience to a god and promised rewards in a life beyond death. The wise teacher appeared briefly amid the victory celebration to point out the parallels to that promise and the promise of resurrection and eternal life made by the martyred prophet.

The lesson faded into darkness, and then Zepp found himself seated at a trial of a wise teacher conducted by the cult of the martyred prophet. The teacher insisted that he had conducted experiments and made observations with a telescope of his own construction that proved the world moved and could not be the center of the universe. Zepp stuck around only long enough to see them find him guilty of heresy, and he was yanked at last back to the salon from which he had started his amazing journey.

The wise teacher continued his lecture, but Zepp was still too full of the sights and sounds of Earth to pay much attention to it. Something about how the beginning of science came as the old religions of the angels failed to satisfy the desire for knowledge and wisdom. Then he faded from sight, slowly enough that he became transparent for a moment – which gave Zepp a start until he realized that the wise teacher had never been there at all and was only an image created by a machine, as Mark had once said.

His poor head spun and his thoughts raced. There was much to understand here and he understood little of it. The wise teacher would be no help. He already knew that. He had learned that when discussing the history of science with it. There were limits to the kinds of questions it could comprehend, even without treading on forbidden ground.

No, he was going to have to talk to Mark if he wanted to make sense out of all that he had seen and heard.

***

"I have a few questions after listening to the professor explain the history of superstition on your planet," Zepp said.

"Go ahead," Mark replied. For the first time in days he was well-rested and well-fed. Even the ringing in his ears was gone. Well, not entirely gone – he could still hear it at night when he was drifting off to sleep. Helen told him it was tinnitus and that it would not go away until he had nerve repairs.

"What is love?"

Mark sputtered, then laughed. "Boy, are you asking the wrong person."

"If you are the wrong person, then who should I ask?"

"Sorry, that was a figure of speech. I meant that on the practical side of things, I am not a good source of reliable information. Love is a way humans have of creating relationships with one another. But my experiences have generally been a failure, so my competence may be limited."

"Oh."

"Wait a minute," Mark said. "I take that back. I know exactly what love is and my failures don't diminish that a bit. At its core, love is the selfless affirmation of another person. It takes on many forms – the love of a mother for her child."

"We have a word for that," Zepp said.

"… of a brother for a brother … "

"When the two are both wise? Yes, there's a word for that too."

"… of a man for a woman … "

"You mean like when mates get too old to breed?"

Mark choked back a cough and said: "For us it's a little different. It probably would be for you too if you lived in a little more stable culture. And then there's the love of a man for his enemy."

"What?"

"Love your enemy. Now that's a radical idea, isn't it? The fellow who came up with that one was nailed to a cross."

"I saw that," Zepp exclaimed. "The cult of the martyred prophet. That's why I asked you the question. A prophet who teaches enlightenment makes sense to me. But a prophet who preaches love? What is it? And why are all those different feelings love?"

"Because love isn't a feeling, it's a natural power of human beings – maybe of all self-conscious creatures. The feeling is something it produces, but love itself is an activity, a practice that you have to master and maintain."

Zepp drew a long breath without moving. "I see," he said at last. "That would explain why a prophet might claim to be a god of love."

"Actually it was his followers who made that claim. He was just a guy who asked a lot of difficult questions and made people uncomfortable by violating their expectations to make them think. And like anyone who says things that make sense, first you become real important, then everyone pretends you said something else. It's how cultures work."

"I see," Zepp said, his hands shaking in affirmation. "It makes me wonder how much of Jobe's story is really true."

"Your culture is fairly advanced and literate. Jobe lived in a time of a strong written tradition, correct? So most likely his words were transcribed accurately and kept intact. The problem with the greatest religions of Earth is that they originated in a largely illiterate world. They usually started with one or two people who had profound insights into the nature of existence, into the dilemma of life and self-awareness and what you call wisdom. But those people all lived in particular cultures with their own unique historical experiences. So the idiosyncrasies of those conditions color the insights. And time brings with it reification and alienation and rationalization, and you've got a universal church instead of a powerful living experience of spirituality – and the mindless worship of idols."

"Oh."

"I don't know why I'm telling you this. Professor, can you handle the translation of this stuff? Is he getting this intact?"

"Quite intact," the professor answered.

"Don't stop," Zepp said. "I see what you are saying. It is like a night-vision, but somehow different. It doesn't have the same compulsion that a vision does."

"I hope not," Mark said. "I don't think of myself as a visionary. But these are just the practical realities of life in my world."

"I have another question," Zepp said.

He waited silently until Mark replied: "Go ahead."

"Do you still believe? I mean, does your race still believe in all those religions? Or any of them? Do you?"

The anthropologist let out a low whistle. "You've asked the jackpot question, my small green friend. The one that gives your school the big prize. The one in the big gold envelope at the end of the match."

"Gold envelope?"

"An image from my youth – academic Olympics."

"I don't understand."

"Don't worry. You asked a question, you deserve an answer. And it is simple and direct. No. No, we do not believe any more. That was the stuff of our childhood as a race. We have grown beyond the days of childhood, and so we have put aside a child's things. And we are better off for it. Even though there is a kernel of intense rationality at the heart of each of those great religions, they all became perverted into political machines and devices of power."

Mark stood up and walked to the window. He looked across the rooftops at the blackened crater where the *Deragathon*'s missile had hit the city. He drew a deep breath, wondering if he should continue or sit down and shut up. He did not sit down.

***

"Zepp, I am about to tell you something that is more dangerous than any of the technological information that we will die before releasing to you. And the professor will go along with it, because he is just a machine and he doesn't really know how powerful an idea I am about to give you.

"Let me explain to you how history works.

"You see, self-conscious creatures are actually quite powerful, in a way that goes beyond physical, material power. They have spiritual, existential powers. Wisdom is one of these. Love is another. So is faith. These are the powers of human beings. The powers of being human.

"But these powers can be taken away – or given away – and turned into hostile forces that work against you. Like the mindless worship of idols. When you worship an idol, you invest it with your wisdom, your love, and your faith, the powers of self-conscious wisdom. And the more powerful it becomes, the more powerless you become before it. It is a downward cycle that cannot be stopped.

"But suffering also focuses the mind. The more alienated you become, the more radical you become. The better you understand the root of your alienation. Then, when you have become completely powerless before the idol, when the process has run its course and there is nothing left of you and the idol has become everything, when alienation has reached its greatest – that is when you can step back and return to yourself. You can see things as they really are. And you can take the precise radical action that you must take to get at the root of that alienation. To overthrow the idol and to liberate the living spirit."

Mark stopped and went looking for a water bottle. He upended and the water rushed gurgling into his throat, while Zepp hung in mid-air waiting for the next piece of the angel's vision.

"Now you can make an idol of a lot of things. Your race or tribe or nation. An idea. Ideas are perfect for idolatry. You can make idols out of ideas and live your life inside your own mind without ever having to step outside. Money. There's the quintessential idol. In the age of scarcity, money was the ultimate idol, the process working itself out in the most base material terms.

"But the first idol you create is yourself. Your tiny ego. You make this little circle around yourself and everything inside it is you and everything outside it is not. You don't see yourself as part of a web of culture, of complex social, historical, and existential processes. All you see is the false world of alienated self-consciousness.

"I'll bet you'd call it the curse of wisdom. When self-conscious creatures evolve themselves out of nature and begin to think about themselves, their circumstances, and their fate, the world becomes split in two. The subject and the object are torn apart, the one to regard the other. And in the process of cultural evolution, that split grows wider and wider. There's your alienation. The subject becomes an empty, massless point of view, while the object becomes ever more massive and immovable. Until the moment when you see the split for what it is – and what it is not.

"In that moment, the object becomes a subject in its own right. The universe looks back at you and blinks a great eye. You watch the butterfly pass before the mountain, and you see the mountain watching the butterfly pass before you. The subject-object split is overcome by the subject-subject interaction. And that brings us back to love. Because that's what love is really all about. You look at the world and at others from their own point of view, transcending the walls of ego."

Mark suddenly realized that he had been talking for quite some time and stopped abruptly. He felt flushed with excitement at the torrent of thoughts and ideas, however, and couldn't hold still. He continued to pace the salon forcefully and deliberately.

"You probably haven't got the slightest idea what I've just been talking about," he said at last.

Zepp chittered and shook his hands. "You're right. I think I lost track when you began talking about love the second time. I am not sure it is really a concept that can be applied to my world."

"Don't sell yourselves short, Zepp," Mark said. "Any race has the power to redeem itself – if they just know where to find it."

Zepp chittered again, muttered a distracted farewell, and wandered off, leaving Mark feeling quite uncertain about what the chamalian had really wanted to know.

CHAPTER TWENTY-ONE

Zepp hadn't **been gone** more than a minute when Helen Castain walked in.

She shook her head slowly and wagged a finger at Mark. "You have been a very bad boy today, Mark Paradis," she said.

"Me?" he answered in mock innocence. "What did I do?"

"I heard the tail end of that conversation."

"How much of a tail end?"

"Everything after the part where you claimed that the professor wouldn't know how dangerous those ideas were."

"Was I right or not? The dumb machine translated every word."

"Are you sure?"

Mark swallowed hard. "Not completely. But Zepp seemed to be following me. I guess. Maybe not. He didn't say much and I wasn't paying much attention to whether he followed me or not."

"At least that's an honest assessment. Good lord, Mark, what were you thinking when you told him that stuff? Didn't you just get through telling me that ideas spread through Zepp's race like a bad cold?"

"I had that thought in my mind."

"And you went ahead and did it anyway?"

"I figured it wouldn't hurt them to have at least one useful idea to spread around."

She gave an exasperated sigh and shook her head again. "You were still very unfair to poor Zepp. It'll take him forever to figure out what you were talking about."

"I don't think so. I give him a few days. A week at the outside. And it may make the difference between life and death for this planet."

"I don't know," Helen said. "You may be right. Anyway, not to change the subject, but I was on my way up here in the first place to give you some good news."

"That would be a nice change of pace," Mark said. "So far we've had nothing but a long string of bad news."

"Actually I have two things. First, the small stuff. I think we've got an anti-depressant that would work on Griddle. The doctor did some analysis of the local pharmacology and compared it with the brain chemistry workups he's been running, and we synthesized something that makes the test animals quite happy. We figured that brain chemistry is pretty much the same from one animal to another down here, and so far the examinations have borne that out."

"A safe assumption, I'd say."

"Now all I need is an excuse to get the stuff to him," Helen said. "Though there's not much chance of that any time soon."

"I think there's probably a few other problems that need attention first."

She nodded, then said: "And then there's the big news."

"How big?"

"Really big. The biggest. Mark, we've cracked the chamalian genetics."

"You're kidding."

"No, I'm not. I thought it would take us months. The doctor can only process things so quickly and then we just have to be patient. And analyzing nucleic acids is a slow ordeal – even with X-ray diffraction, neutrino scanning, and holographic parallel processing. I figured that even when we had an answer, we wouldn't be able to explain it without using a lot of DNA code.

"You see, I figured the chamalian genes would be like terrestrial DNA. Genes don't really carry a blueprint for a human body – they carry instructions on how to make a blueprint. The information is stored fractally. Little patterns repeat themselves to make significantly different big patterns. When you apply that to chamalians, it makes things very difficult.

"The problem is the recessive traits – or bundles of traits. If they can lie dormant for several generations, then the information has to be there in the genes all that time, ready to be activated when the time comes. A little stepling can carry the genes of a mathematician, but until they are called on to do their job, all you've got is a stepling.

"So I went looking through the records downstairs."

"I told you they'd help."

"Not quite. All they did was compound the problem. You see, the chamalians have worked out an incredibly complicated analytical system to keep track of dominant and recessive traits. They keep meticulous records. Now if you follow Mendel, then you expect to get a statistically consistent distribution of traits. You know about green peas and yellow peas?"

"Yes. Yellow is the recessive trait, so you need two yellow genes to get yellow peas. And that means one pea in four, because the other three combinations have at least one dominant green gene."

"Right. You'd expect the same thing here on Chamal, only on a much larger scale."

"Is that what you get?"

"No, you don't. That pattern is there, of course. But it's such a small part of what's going on. It works for straight dominant-recessive traits like eye color and things. But the trait-bundles follow a different pattern. Simplified, it's just a matter of counting generations. Different counts for different bundles, but it's straight counting."

"And what happens when you reach the count?"

"The recessive returns."

"How many of them?"

"All of them."

"All of them? What do you mean?"

"I mean the a whole bundle all at once. Recessive trait-bundles stay buried until the correct number of generations have passed, then resurface intact and complete – in every case."

"How does that happen?"

"That's what I couldn't figure out. It was driving me crazy. There was no statistical pattern. It reminded me of something one of my husbands told me once. How they used to recycle used computer-sets in hotels."

"How they what?"

"Some finger-counter once figured out that the average set was worth a hundred credits after three years. Of course, that's just an average. Some lasted for ten years without wearing out, others burned out after a few months. You'd expect to see a standard bell curve – just like you'd expect to see statistical averages working themselves out over time with the chamalians. But instead, the hotels didn't use the average. They just took every set that was three years old and sold it to the recyclers for a hundred credits, whether it was worn out or not."

"And that's how the chamalian genes work?"

"Exactly. After X generations, all the offspring suddenly have blue cat's eyes, long orange fur, prehensile thumbs, and the power of speech."

"And you say you've figured out what makes that process work?"

"I think so. And it was almost by accident. I was looking at pictures."

"What kind of pictures?"

"The doctor had done some realtime imaging of the fertilization of a chamalian egg and the first cell division. I looked at it briefly, but ignored it at first. There was nothing that I could see that made it that much different from terrestrial biology, and I figured the real differences were too subtle for me to notice. But then I went back later and took a closer look. You know what mitochondria are?"

"Something in our cells, aren't they?"

"Right. They produce the energy that makes animal cells work. Otherwise we'd all be potted plants. But they've got a strange history. They're not quite native to our cells. It's like early in cellular evolution, very close to the beginning, these creatures invaded the first animal cells, took up residence, and formed this symbiotic union with them. They produce the energy, the animal cells evolve to provide them with food and a home. They've even got their own genetic structure and reproduce whenever the cells does."

"Do chamalians have mitochondria?"

"Something like it. And that's why I missed it at first. I identified the body inside the cell that looked like it, and the doctor agreed that it was an energy-producing body like the mitochondria. But when I watched it a second time, I saw that it was doing something else. I had the doctor identify the gene strands and slowed down the imaging. Then I saw it. The mitochondria-like body was sending out RNA messengers to the genes. It was controlling the cellular division. I had the doctor study it some more, and he confirmed it.

"These things are acting like tiny little parsers, sorting out the coding and switching it on or off. They keep track of the numbers and know when to turn the traits back on again. They can explain the way inbreeding produces a generation of purebred offspring, followed by a few generations of dormant recessives. Good lord, Mark, they explain how every damn trait that chamalians have can become a recessive at the drop of a hat. They explain everything."

"Well that's good. Can they explain why these creatures are bound and determined to burn everything they've every created to the ground simply because we've scared the hell out of them?"

Helen frowned at him. "No, they can't do that. I thought that was your job."

Mark felt suddenly ashamed. "I'm sorry, that was a cheap shot. I shouldn't inflict my despair on you."

"You didn't sound so full of despair a few minutes ago," Helen said. "Besides, I told you – this is good news. This is what Tedrak was hoping for. This is what Jobe was hoping for. Once we figure out how these things work, we can go in and reset the counters. We can do whatever we want with them."

"You're making an awful lot of assumptions, aren't you? They may not want you to reset their counters. What happened when we found out how to manipulate human genes? We decided that we didn't want to mess around with who and what we were just yet. We decided we were having a hard enough time dealing with the universe and with ourselves that we didn't need to make things worse."

"All except for the few folks on the fringes who are willing to indulge in anything as long as it's new and different."

"Right. And you're assuming that we let them live long enough to find out what they want."

"You're not?"

"Not after they dropped that lifeboat on us. I wouldn't assume anything until after we've finished our assessment. And not even then. You only heard my sunny side. Wait until you see what else I have to say."

Helen started to open her mouth, but Mark cut her off.

"Not now, but soon. When the time comes … when the time comes."

The time came sooner than Mark expected.

***

No more than half an hour later, Helen returned, her face ashen and her voice strained with fear.

"Mark, I just heard from the *Cousteau*. The captain is initiating the termination assessment."

Mark's blood froze in his veins and the floor seemed to drop away from him, leaving him feeling like he was teetering over the edge of an abyss. The moment he had feared since arriving in orbit around Chamal was upon him. He took a deep breath, then swallowed hard. At least he was prepared for it. Or so he hoped.

"Aren't they rushing things just a little bit," he asked. "We're still trying to sort things out down here."

"No time. It's all run out. You know those bird-things over in the big desert basin?"

"Arkaria. Yes, I know who they are."

"Well Barrett says they just lit off a nuke. About twenty kilotons and close to one of their cities."

The ringing in Mark's ears grew louder and louder until it almost drowned out the sound of Barrett's voice. No matter. Nothing that he said would change things. Everything was still as it had been. His task was no more difficult now, only more crucial.

"I haven't heard anything about it," Mark said. "They should have contacted me."

"They're trying to keep you out of it," Helen said. "The captain and Barrett don't trust you. At least that's what Val told me."

"Val Nordland?"

"Yes. He sent word through the professor. He said you should do what you think is necessary down here, while he tries to change their minds up there."

"Val is trying to change their minds? I don't know if I believe that."

"He sounded pretty serious to me. Can they do that?"

"Do what?"

"Leave you out. Don't they have to include you in the program?"

"Not absolutely," Mark said.

"What's that mean?"

"They can leave me out if they don't care about what happens to them when they get back home."

CHAPTER TWENTY-TWO

The sun was to Mark's back as he walked across the hardpan, but the wind was in his face, putting gritty bits of sand in his teeth and dry dust up his nose and in his eyes.

The heat didn't bother him. He'd grown used to that as the climate sucked him dry. But the desert floor outside the West Gate of Suridash was difficult to walk in. Something worse than beach sand, studded with gravel, and laced with nasty-edged plants.

The two thousand meters between the gate and the *Belle Marie* seemed like two thousand kilometers by the time he got there. The pilgrim who drove him to the gate refused to go any closer. The gate guards had told him that Barrett had issued an order over the loudspeaker declaring a kill-zone around the pinnace.

Barrett and the troopers had camped out in the *Belle Marie* since they arrived here. He'd insisted on it. This was the most easily defended position available to them – especially compared to any of the alternatives within the city. And it gave them immediate access to space, or, if needed, to land in one of the plazas in the center of Suridash to evacuate the landing party.

And it relieved Barrett and his men of having to interact with the chamalians that the *Cousteau* had come to investigate, an irony that Mark did not overlook.

On the ride through the city, Mark had wondered why Val Nordland had contacted Helen instead of going directly to him.

There were certainly ways to communicate. The Cultural Survey Office had seen to that. This was not an unanticipated turn of events.

But using any of those methods right this minute would make it more difficult to do so again when things might be more complicated. And by contacting Helen, there was no trail connecting him to Mark.

And if Nordland was being this circumspect, things had to be pretty bad.

The hull of the pinnace had soaked up the heat of the midmorning sun and now pumped it back out like a furnace. Mark felt the faint electric crackle of the energy fields that surrounded the spacecraft. The rocket engines were only part of the motive system of the *Belle Marie* – a distraction to confuse Chamal's technological analysts. The countergrav field and the unstressed shields trapped dust nearly a meter up from the ground in a layer a few centimeters away from the hull.

Mark found the hatch, pressed the panel that should have opened it, then cursed when nothing happened.

"Hello in there!" he yelled. "Barrett, can you hear me?"

He walked around the landing struts to the dome covering the video pickup and waved. "Barrett, you're only wasting a lot of time this way."

There was still no answer. He waited. A small, bright moon rose quickly out of the hills to the west. It was half a fist above the horizon when Mark began his walk back to the truck.

Now the sun was in his eyes and the wind at his back. But the dust still crept around his face and insinuated itself into his ears. And the sand had worked its way into his boots, where it shifted whenever he lifted a foot.

The little moon was another fist higher by the time Mark reached the truck. He had left the professor there after debating the advantages and disadvantages of carrying it along. The disadvantages he had already experienced, and in greater detail than was necessary to establish the fact. The advantage was that Barrett probably couldn't disable the AI while it was over here behind the West Gate of Suridash.

"Professor, tell me about your uplink to the *Cousteau*. What's your current status?"

"I am currently on a ten-minute uplink cycle, although that varies as satellites come and go. The main link is through the *Belle Marie*, but the secondary link is directly to the satellites through a relay left when the pinnace returned to the *Cousteau*. I am currently six minutes and forty-two seconds from my last uplink. Next link is expected in twelve minutes and seventeen seconds. This is a long gap while we wait for a polar satellite to come over the horizon."

"Very good," Mark said. "Professor, I want you to initiate Protocol Delta. Can you confirm that for me?"

"Certainly. I confirm initiation of Protocol Delta."

Mark placed the elements of the professor back in the pockets where they belonged and waited. The small, bright moon was visible as it climbed towards the top of the arch in the massive gate when the twelve minutes and seventeen seconds had passed. He couldn't decide which had taken longer, the walk back from the *Belle Marie*, or the wait for the professor to send its signal.

When it did, the AI base processor aboard the *Cousteau* would pass along the message to the compartment controls in the Cultural Survey Section. Almost instantly the controls would act as a relay between there and scientific databases in various parts of the ship.

And when those were next accessed – no more than six minutes on the typical day aboard the *Cousteau* – things would begin to happen.

The elaborate security measures used to keep information systems isolated from one another and uncontaminated by breakdown or attack would all open themselves up to the commands of Protocol Delta – because this was not an operation attacking the defenses of the *Cousteau*, but one designed into it in order to keep its officers honest.

Every data console on the vessel used some kind of interactive and interpretive front end display – though few used the same one in order to preserve that same security. The operation being directed by Protocol Delta would insert itself into every one of them.

"Attention!" it would announce. "An attempt is being made to circumvent Public Act 5350, which dictates the procedures to be used in a Basal Aggression Potential Assessment. Use of your information systems will be temporarily delayed until the matter is resolved."

Mark's biggest regret was that he would not be there to see it.

But he knew when it happened. The bright, small moon was half way to the top of the sky. And the sharp sound of the *Belle Marie*'s outside speakers snapped across the dry desert floor.

"Paradis!" came the voice of Lieutenant Barrett of the Space Corps. "Get out here. We need to talk."

***

Once Mark explained things to Captain Fletcher, both agreed that they had been handled badly.

Mark was surprised – though he should not have been – when he learned that Barrett's duplicity was not the root cause of the problem. It was fed by Fletcher's reluctance to face the harsh realities of what he was being required to do – to consider actions that could certainly be labeled genocide in the future.

But Mark pointed out that the way to do that was not to hold a pre-hearing hearing that excluded the primary contact member of the cultural survey team.

Barrett was largely silent during the conversation. He'd made only a couple of comments to Mark when he came aboard the *Belle Marie*. One was that he didn't like people messing around with his information systems. And the other went to the heart of his mistrust.

"When I'm surrounded by hostiles, I want everyone on my team to be with me 100 percent – and you're just not 100 percent."

Mark said nothing in return. He wasn't sure what he could say. Barrett's opinion, though narrow-minded, was correct. But he felt no shame or regret for that. Barrett just didn't understand what was happening. Not in any more than the most basic terms. He just didn't think that way.

Talking to Mark was Fletcher's idea. He reminded Mark of an astronomy professor he'd had as an undergrad. The man kept office hours religiously, but no one ever showed up. And so when Mark did, the poor guy wasn't quite sure how to act. He was so stiff that Mark almost felt sorry for him.

Fletcher was the same way. Maybe he considered himself an outgoing and personable man, always ready to talk to his crew. But he wasn't so good at listening, and Mark could sense that some of the things he told the captain just weren't getting through.

Left unspoken were the legal consequences for Fletcher if the termination assessment was not conducted strictly by the book. It was for his protection, however, as well as everyone else's. And that was why Mark was put aboard the *Cousteau*.

He made it legitimate.

Even if they had to exterminate the entire planet, Mark's participation in the process made it legal. Because he was there to represent the most vocal and articulate opponents of the ultimate consequences of the termination assessment. And if they could convince him it was necessary, no one would be in a position to second guess them.

Mark had disabled Protocol Delta as soon as he came aboard the *Belle Marie*. He didn't bother to tell Barrett or Fletcher that it would have shut itself off after an hour or so. Also left unspoken was the threat of other applications lurking in the *Cousteau*'S information systems.

So Fletcher looked up the appropriate documents outlining the proper procedure for conducting the termination assessment and went to work. Like a good bureaucratic officer, he was comfortable with prepared written instructions. And these were fairly simple.

First, he had to appoint a jury. He was automatically on it, as were Barrett, Val Nordland, and Mark. Fletcher had to name four more.

Helen Castain declined, stating that she couldn't possible take part in genocide. So Red, her sneezing assistant, took her place. A junior officer from the engineering department, a woman from plant science, and an electronics technician filled out the panel.

When all was ready, the captain of the *Cousteau* convened the hearing, placing the proceedings on-line and calling every single human being on or near Chamal to attention. No one was to be left out of such an important decision: What to do about the new intelligence they had found.

***

But first Barrett had to make his move.

Before they even began the discussion, he interrupted and made his attack.

"Captain, before we go any further, I think we should remove one of the members of the jury for cause and name a replacement."

Fletcher was flustered by the departure from proper procedure and didn't know what to do. Mark was relieved to see the confusion in the man's eyes. It showed that the two of them had not planned this and it was entirely Barrett's idea.

"Is that really necessary?" he asked at last, his round face flushing pink with stress.

"I'll let you decide," Barrett said. He wouldn't look Mark in the eye. He talked about him, not to him, even though they were the only members of the jury physically present aboard the *Belle Marie*. The rest were holographic images relayed down from the *Cousteau*, which meant that when the ship lost favorable alignments with the relay satellites the hearing would have to recess.

Mark just held his silence and shook his head gently while Barrett went on.

"We had suspicions early on, sir, when the string of malfunctions occurred. But that's not enough to make a difference. Not alone, anyway. But since then, he has raised serious questions about where his loyalties lie – with the indigenous sapients or with his own kind."

"Goodness," Fletcher said, his discomfort growing increasingly evident. "Do you have any evidence of this?"

Good for you, Captain, Mark said to himself. Don't let him just talk you into this.

"Yes, sir, I do." Barrett produced a table set outlet for the professor and switched it on. "Professor, could you repeat the first recorded exchange?"

Mark heard the voice of a stranger speaking his words and recognized Zepp in translation and in the original.

"'Zepp, I am about to tell you something that is more dangerous than any of the technological information we will all die before revealing to you.'"

Mark felt his stomach twist. There wasn't any way to deny those words or the intent behind them.

"And could you repeat the second exchange?" Barrett asked.

"'As you know, there are many things that we cannot reveal until we have been here much longer.'"

That one was easy to defend in literal interpretation, but the tone was unmistakably tongue-in-cheek. The snickers around the virtual chamber proved that.

"And when you add in his political biases, I believe it gives us every reason to doubt his objectivity as a member of this jury and his loyalty and trustworthiness as a member of the ship's crew."

That was almost more than Fletcher could stand. He didn't know how to deal with a situation as bad as Barrett made this out to be. He obviously had never had to question the loyalty of a member of the Science Service. The most he'd ever had to deal with were crew members who went AWOL in a foreign port or who got into drunken fights with each other.

Mark decided not to let him twist too long in the wind.

"Captain, I'm afraid Mr. Barrett's suggestion is out of order. If you'll look over the public act carefully, you'll find that questions of the competence of the jurors cannot be considered until after the initial presentation of evidence and recommendations for action."

Fletcher was not quite the fool he appeared to be on the surface. He was at his infoset instantly, and Mark could see his lips move as he read the pertinent section.

"You know, Lieutenant Barrett, you should read this file. This is all a lot more complicated than you first led me to believe."

Barrett now looked over at Mark, fire in his eyes and fury in his sneer.

Mark just smiled.

"Now it says here that the first thing we do is listen to the report of the cultural survey team. That would be you Mr. Nordland – and Mr. Paradis, of course."

Mark looked up at Val with pleading eyes. Nordland wouldn't look at him. He stood up, shuffled his feet, shook his shoulders, rubbed his face, and made mumbling sounds. Then he turned his eyes toward Mark, and Mark realized that he was not going to be in this alone.

"I'll let Mr. Paradis continue," he said. Then he sat down quickly.

Mark barely let a breath go by before he jumped in.

"Let me reverse the order of things in my presentation just a little, if you don't mind," he said. "I'm going to start with what I see as the conclusions of my analysis so far and recommendations for further action. Then I'll tell you why I believe what I do."

"That seems acceptable to me," Fletcher said, the color receding from his cheeks and a smile beginning to emerge from the soft flesh of his face.

"From all that I have seen and learned about the dominant

intelligence on Chamal, I have to conclude that it constitutes a serious threat to the human race – not just on technological grounds, but on cultural grounds as well. These creatures have been turned by their nature into a cess-pool of dysfunctional cultures full of creatures so pathological that they wouldn't hesitate to turn on their own mothers for the bread in her pantry – or come after the *Cousteau* with all the weapons at their disposal, nukes included."

Mark saw the images of the captain, Val Nordland, and the others aboard the *Cousteau* begin to waver around the edges.

"And I think radical antiseptic action has to be taken against these creatures immediately."

***

Mark took what satisfaction he could from the sight of Barrett's jaw dropping six centimeters and Fletcher's eyes widening suddenly.

He hoped that the violation of their expectations would keep them off guard while he presented his argument. Everything would work out much better if they didn't question him too closely. And there were ways to ensure that.

"Let me start at the beginning," he said.

Mark had been preparing for this moment for days. He knew it wouldn't be quite the same as a textwar. To begin with, they had very little time and there were fewer participants. And a real-time presentation like this was barred from a textwar as prejudicial and inflammatory. But he'd had plenty of practice at this during discussion groups at school while conducting the original textwar that got him into this mess. They'd forced him to dig deeply for source material in his underlying arguments and they'd taught him how to order his thinking while he talked – something that no simple textwar could do.

"Let's look at what makes us human."

Barrett groaned audibly and a couple of the jurors looked uncomfortable, making Mark feel like he'd stumbled with his first step. But he was quick to redeem himself. "I know you'd rather not listen to me lecture, so I'll keep this as brief as possible. I've gone to the trouble of putting some excerpts from text materials on these subjects on the ship's information system. If you want, you can access those yourselves. I'll just make a quick summary here."

That left Barrett looking more perplexed than before. Mark decided that the lieutenant was just beginning to realize that he was not involved in a quick-but-dirty battle, but a major campaign that involved moves he'd never imagined. But Mark hoped that by the time he figured out the overall plan, it would be too late and they would be committed.

"The essence of our humanity is the emergence of self-consciousness from nature," Mark said. "And by that, I don't just mean our evolution as thinking beings. Or the development of civilization, history, and written language. Or the coming-of-age of the adolescent. I mean all of these things. Being human means to repeat this emergence over and over and over again. And it means a constant struggle with the challenges of self-consciousness as they present themselves each and every day.

"The whole movement of human history can be seen as the continuing emergence from our dependence on nature. The end of a major stage of that history is only a few decades behind us – the end of the age of scarcity. Because we have moved into a new stage of history, we have been able to reach certain conclusions about our own nature. Where before, these were the subject of considerable political debate, now they are accepted as the only reasonable and scientific premise for understanding human nature.

"There is a longer text on this subject in the files, but I'm going to focus in on the particular pathology of humanity in the later stages of its development – mainly in the 20th and 21st centuries, just before the end of the age of scarcity," Mark said.

The first challenge faced by human beings was that of overcoming the narrow limits of the ego. The child had to learn to become independent of its parents and develop all of his powers of reason and will. But there were large numbers of people who fail in this first struggle. Many more so in the cultures that promoted narcissism and self-worship in those centuries. They failed to sever the link to their mothers or fathers. They failed to develop truly independent characters capable of critical thought and reason. They believed the rationalizations of their egos and accept whatever makes them feel good. But what the psychologists called incestuous ties to their parents keep them from every really being good human beings.

The biggest danger posed by these people came in the incestuous ties they developed to replace those they had with their parents – to their tribe, their nation, and what they believe to be their race. They projected their narcissism onto the larger group and let that group protect them from dealing with the world as free and independent actors.

"Now the pathology can move on into a later stage," Mark said, looking carefully at the assembled jurors, hoping he wasn't going to put them all to sleep.

The relationships of the narcissistic character devolved into relationships of power and control. People trapped by the limits of their ego gained satisfaction from controlling others with less power than they have and from being controlled by those above them. Even the leaders at the top claim they are being directed by history, destiny, or fate. No one was responsible for themselves anymore.

In the final stages, the pathology turned both inward and outward. The ego itself became intolerable and had to be destroyed. And the pain and suffering it endured was projected onto the rest of the world – which also became intolerable and had to be destroyed.

"If you want a perfect description of this process, you can look at the text I left for you on the rise and fall of the German Nazis in the 1930s and 1940s," Mark said.

"So this is how self-consciousness can go wrong. First it becomes selfish, then sadistic and masochistic at the same time, then nihilistic, worshiping death and destruction for their own sakes. All these pathologies can be seen throughout the 21st century – in the genocidal wars, the racist states, the tribal conflicts, in all the plagues and troubles of those dark days. And they can even be seen in our century, with the disaster of Tycho Colony and its aftermath."

Mark paused to let the lesson sink in before going further. Captain Fletcher left him a perfect opportunity to do so. "And how do the chamalians fit in to this picture?" he asked.

"Let me explain," Mark said.

CHAPTER TWENTY-THREE

"Now given all that, let's talk about the reason that I'm here," Mark said. "I'm not along to study native mating habits – although that alone is the work of several lifetimes on this planet. I'm not here to catalog chamalian superstitions – another several lifetimes of work. I'm here for one purpose and one purpose only – to pass judgment on the indigenous intelligence and decide if they are fit enough to survive their encounter with a superior culture. It's unfortunate, but necessary that you help in that decision.

"I've explained to you the basic pathology that we have to look for. This is what eventually sold the folks back home on sending me with you to this planet. We aren't just looking for the technology of mass destruction – even though the chamalians clearly have it. We aren't just looking for the capacity to develop it – since any species capable of industrial development is likely to come up with nuclear, biological, and chemical weapons, and the means to deliver them. We are looking for a culture where the pathology of self-consciousness is sufficiently advanced that there is a clear likelihood of the development of these weapons and their employment against us.

"Is that sufficiently clear, Captain?" Mark asked.

Fletcher was so unbalanced by the sudden shift from Mark's monologue to a pointed question that he sputtered and stammered for a good thirty seconds. Finally, after the rest of the jury looked away in embarrassment, he got out the words: "Absolutely clear, Mr.

Paradis."

"And is that all right with you, Mr. Barrett?"

Barrett scowled, but nodded and muttered some words of agreement.

"Then the question now is: How do the chamalians stack up? And I'm afraid there's no question about it. Let's just run down the list of things we've learned about these creatures from the time they first came aboard the *Cousteau*.

First of all, every warm-blooded, furry creature on Chamal belonged to a single species. All these creatures could interbreed and produce offspring. Intelligence, like any other cluster of traits, appeared throughout the population.

That had severe consequences for the social structures that the intelligent creatures developed. The basic unit of any human social structure is the family – but on Chamal, that unit no longer persisted more than a generation or two. The next highest level of organization was the clan or tribe. And on Chamal, that meant a common phenotype. But members of the tribe could be born from intelligent parents or wander in from the wild. And no trait persisted for more than a dozen or so generations before it also got circulated out of existence and returned to the general gene flow.

Even so, political structures had evolved here and there where the conditions were advantageous and where geography and history conspired to create long-lasting social orders.

"We have come upon this world while it is still in the age of scarcity, near the end of the industrial era. But its diversity – and the lack of worldwide communications – means that much of the planet remains in the feudal or pre-feudal stages of development," Mark said.

"These are not cultures that have evolved highly advanced moral or ethical movements. Before we arrived, the most powerful of these cultures were well along the road to turning themselves into hostile, armed, and competing camps, ready to do anything they could to defend themselves from the others. They were still several decades from developing the means and the will to project power globally, but now that we are here, they have found both – in the form of the *Deragathon*."

And there was the best example of what a threat those creatures could be. Almost overnight, the armed camps had set aside their differences to combine forces and turn their attention on the angels. Lifelong enemies – predators and militant vegetarians, bankers and feudal landlords, ascetic cybernetic wizards and self-righteous winged pilots – ignored their own history of unrelenting hostility to one another and put together the warship that orbits over Chamal right now.

"All of them were bound together by their fear of us," Mark said.

"But if you examine them closely, you will see that nearly every last one of them is a superstitious racist and tribalist. They can't help it. Their history, their civilization, their families, their politics, all are anarchy and chaos – a continuous flux that produces moments of brilliance and genius out of unending struggle and war.

"We really can't allow the cultures that are responsible for this state to continue unchecked. That's why I'm asking you to support my call for immediate action to prevent a catastrophe from overcoming us all."

***

The images of Captain Fletcher and the other jurors began to flicker, reminding Mark of the reality of the scene. For a moment, he had forgotten that the others were only virtually present. And at the same time, he had been rushing to complete the first round of his broadside before this moment arrived.

Barrett was the first to mention the loss of signal.

"We'll be off-line for about five minutes while the next relay satellite comes around," he said. "Maybe when we pick this back up, someone else will get a chance to speak."

Mark frowned, but kept his response to himself. The easy part was over. Now came the riskier piece of business. He would have to convince the others to go along with his plan.

Barrett's attitude was obviously going to be one of the biggest obstacles.

"What the hell are you up to, Paradis?" he asked when the pictures of the others had degraded to the point where the system wouldn't keep them up. "I never figured you for this. What did these guys do to you down here?"

"You really wouldn't understand," Mark said, trying to keep his tone as clinical as possible. He didn't mean the words as a rebuke, but as an assessment of Barrett's position. The Space Corps officer wouldn't understand. His character was oriented around a much simpler reference frame, one that did not prepare him well to grapple with ambiguities, ironies, and contradictions.

"Give me a chance," Barrett said.

"All right," Mark replied. "Let me put some of it in terms that will make sense to you. Ever since we arrived at this planet, the worst of the creatures down below have been fighting a losing battle against the creatures that they have been exploiting, oppressing, and victimizing for centuries. One by one, they have been escaping those battles by fleeing up into space, finding refuge on the *Deragathon*. The alien warship is now chock full of these guys. They're pushing Jobe's tribe and its allies back into their cabins and it's only a matter of a few days before they take complete control of the ship. And then, it's open war – first against us, then against their enemies down there, and finally against one another, though they haven't admitted that out loud just yet. Don't you think we ought to do something to stop that from happening?"

Barrett scowled, rubbed a hand over his face, then nodded reluctantly. "We both know that's why I pushed for this in the first place. But why do I get the feeling that there's a lot more going on here than you want to tell us?"

"Because there is," Mark declared strongly, producing a look of shocked surprise from Barrett at the admission. "Except that I really do want to tell you, I just don't know any way to do that in terms that you'll understand. Or that you'll believe. And that's been the problem all along. In many ways, we don't speak the same language. The terms I use don't have meaning for you. So if I tried to explain it to you, all it would do is annoy you – and I'd rather not do that if I don't have to."

Now it was Barrett's chance to turn Mark's words back against him with a sudden twist. "Why not?" he asked. "You've been annoying me ever since we made orbit."

Mark sighed, but would not rise to the bait. Barrett was right, and they both knew it. And Mark even knew why. It was for precisely the reason he had just given Barrett for keeping his cards face down. Because he couldn't explain what he saw to the man, he found that all he could do was push the buttons that made him angry – which had accomplished nothing of value to anyone.

"Forget it," Barrett said at last. "I've been doing my best to annoy you right back. It doesn't seem to have hurt either one of us – yet. But if we keep it up, it might do that. What do you say we call a truce for now? And when we've got the time, maybe you can explain to me just what terms you want to use that I wouldn't understand and explain to me what they mean."

"That's a pretty tall order," Mark said. "But I'll consider it."

***

When they re-established contact with the *Cousteau*, it was Red and the junior officer from engineering – Douglas Oboke – who gave him the hardest time over the plan.

"This isn't a military mission," Red told the jury. "It's the idea of taking sides in a shooting war that bothers me. Do we really want to get some of our boys hurt or worse over a native problem? I mean, with all due respect, Mr. Paradis, how do we really know whether one side is any better than the other?"

Oboke shared his doubts, but approached it from a different direction. "I realize there's the overall problem of deciding whether these creatures are a threat to the human race. But I don't see how that translates into an assault on the *Deragathon*. I know it wouldn't make us popular with these creatures, but is there any good reason we don't just take them out from standoff range?"

Mark couldn't tell them the real reason he wanted to go after the alien warship and take it out up close. He still had to keep that part of his plan secret. Again, they wouldn't have understood it if he tried to explain it to them. So instead, he had to give them a convenient excuse. One that they could accept, and one that contained a large enough measure of the truth to withstand at least one round of scrutiny.

"Because you're not just dealing with individuals here," he said. "You're dealing with a culture. The individuals are created by the culture. If you just get rid of them, more will follow. But if you conquer them, if you get a hold of them by their short hairs and show them who's in charge, that's a whole different equation."

"But why do anything to them in the first place?" Red asked. "What gives us the right to play policeman on this planet?"

"Superior historical knowledge," Mark said without embarrassment. "We have passed this way before and we know what the risks are."

"Are you so sure?"

"I know what I've seen," Mark said. "How much do you know about the Tycho Mutiny?"

"A little," Red said. Oboke nodded thoughtfully, though Mark didn't know quite what that meant. "Just what they put out on the public systems."

Mark explained the history of the colony as briefly as he could. "They dropped out of civilization, turned bad, and had to be rescued. What the public systems don't tell you, though, is that we blew it at Tycho."

"What?!" That was a sudden question from Barrett.

Mark hadn't expected that, even though he should have. He realized suddenly that winning this argument would probably mean losing what little bit of good will he had received from Barrett a few minutes earlier. And he couldn't see any way around it.

"We blew it," Mark said. "I know how we blew it and I know why we blew it, and that's the reason I'm here instead of someone else – so we don't blow it again."

"And how did we blow it?" Barrett asked.

"First of all, the so-called rescue was a disaster. You locked up the victims and the survivors instead of treating them for shock and trauma. You let the victimizers escape the initial forcible entry and had to use maximum force to take them out after they'd dug themselves in."

"We had no other choice," Barrett said. "There was no way to transport those people out of there. And we were in the middle of hostile fire before we could bring in anyone to help them."

Mark shook his head and pressed on. "And then you figured that because you shot a bunch of them up, you had wiped them out. You missed dozens of the top psychos who had slipped in among the masses. These guys had prepared an escape for themselves, with false identities, personal user accounts, private estates, and all the rest laid in against the day they had to bolt."

"If we'd done it your way and started shipping everyone to hospital, they would have gotten away all the sooner," Barrett said.

Mark ignored him. "But worst of all, instead of keeping the colony together to heal its wounds, you spread the survivors throughout the rest of the worlds – infecting others, recreating their dysfunctional culture wherever they went, spreading the pathology, and preparing the ground for the psychos when they're ready to resurface – only on a much bigger and much grander scale."

Barrett started to say something, but choked the words back.

Mark started to say something, but held his tongue rather than continue using force in a battle already won. He realized that he had convinced Red that neutrality wasn't a choice. And he figured Oboke would go along once Red was on his side. The engineer sounded like he was just testing the concept rather than advocating a position.

But he was sorry about what he had done to Barrett. The man looked defeated. Mark realized he had forced him to look at something inside himself that he hadn't confronted before. Barrett was Space Corps through and through and believed in it completely. But now he seemed unable to avoid the awful truth that it had failed in its mission at Tycho.

He looked at Mark and shook his head, narrowing his eyes. Mark expected a threat, or an attack without warning. But Barrett was subdued.

"You really are a son of a bitch, aren't you," he said at last.

"Someone has to be," Mark said. "And I was appointed to the post before we left home."

***

Fletcher gave everyone the rest of the day to go through the texts and think about what Mark had said. Then after dinner, they would convene again and discuss their options. The captain was almost beside himself with joy that they had managed to finish the first session with a clear goal and a timetable. Mark wondered if he would be equally happy once they started carrying it out.

An hour later, he was glad to get back to the cool stone walls and airy chambers of the Hall of the Seedkeepers. Especially after the dust and heat and bone-dry air of the desert and the dirt and grime and noise of the ride through the city.

He longed for a shower, long and cool. Or a bath, nice and hot. And a beer, smooth and dark. He would have to settle for a bottle of water from the cooler. A shower might come later aboard the pinnace, but that would be hours from now.

His moral vertigo was gone. But it had been replaced by a sensation of flight, as if Mark had become weightless, gliding along under the power of sheer will, pushed forward by accelerating events, as the ground dropped away beneath him.

He only hoped that he would not suddenly re-acquire his lost mass while still thousands of meters above the world.

He hadn't been back more than ten minutes when someone rapped on the door frame. He almost expected to see Helen Castain, but it was not her. Instead he found himself face to face with one of Helen's lab assistants.

"I was asked to come and get you," she said. "Someone wants to talk to you downstairs."

"You mean Helen?" he asked.

Alys put a finger to her lips and shook her head, then led the way down to the archives where Helen had set up her makeshift office. The biologist was not happy to see him when he arrived.

"Mark, could you explain exactly what it is you're doing?" she asked. "I thought you were supposed to be on the other side of this argument."

"I'm trying to help Zepp and his tribe," Mark said, a hint of pride creeping into his voice. "And I figured the best way to do that is to take the *Deragathon* out of the picture."

"Don't you think that's a little bit risky?"

"Maybe," he said. Helen tipped her head down and stared at him past a creased brow. "All right. Of course it's risky. But it's what they need. And maybe if we do that, it'll shake this planet out of its state of shock."

"Maybe. Or maybe it'll just get a lot of people hurt or killed and only make matters worse. That's what usually happens when the shooting starts. I would think you'd know that better than any of us."

"I do. But the low-risk approach means taking out the *Deragathon* from a distance. And getting rid of the good guys along with the bad. Unless you want to argue that we're not morally obligated to do whatever we can for them."

"I want to argue against taking out anything," Helen said. "But I'm not sure I can. Are you absolutely certain of what you're doing? Because if you're not, then you're taking a terrific gamble."

"I'm as sure as I can be," Mark said.

"Well I'm not," answered a third voice, which issued from the doctor on the table in front of Helen and sounded very much like Val Nordland.

"Val, have you been listening?" he asked.

"Of course I have," he said. "That's why they called you down here. I'm using one of our back channels to call you through the doctor. It's a secure link for now, and I don't think anyone aboard the *Cousteau* suspects it exists. You know, you were pretty good today. I'm wondering why you never became a consensus builder."

"I'm afraid it isn't a niche I'm prepared to fill – talking people into something I haven't checked out for myself," Mark said.

"I just wish I didn't feel like you're on the wrong track," Val replied. "You were very persuasive. I'm sure you're sincere. But I just don't see how you can pick sides like this and get involved with their battles."

"Are you speaking in an official capacity as a juror?"

"I could be. But mostly I'm speaking as the head of the cultural survey team and I'm talking about the kind of uncertainty that we both know goes into this kind of evaluation. When it comes to deciding what a culture is, we impose meaning, create significance, and produce artificial reflections of our own agendas, our own values, our own experiences. We lose our objectivity. We forget how much of our interpretation is part of ourselves and we end up losing sight of the other culture and begin describing only our own."

"I know that, Val. And I know how easy it is to get caught in that trap. But I am looking at it objectively. I know just how bad these creatures can be. I've been a target down here for days now. But bad as they are, maybe there's some redemption here. I mean, who's to say that the deficiencies of chamalian cultures aren't the products of frustrated genius? How do we know that liberating them from the chains of their irrational history won't allow them to bloom into something unique and marvelous and inspired?"

"Do you have any evidence that it will?"

"Suridash is the best example I can think of. Look at Zepp's tribe and its patriarch. Here you have a culture dedicated to knowledge and wisdom, that was born out of the liberation of slaves, and that practices an aggressively inclusive approach to socialization in a world of biologically exclusive social groups. Any good impulse that exists in the chamalian race can be found here in this city."

"And every bad impulse as well," Val said. "I don't doubt the moral evil of the creatures aboard the *Deragathon*, Mark. I just wonder if the long-term outlook is going to be good for a planet where Suridash is the site of the only good impulse on the planet."

"I don't know, Val. Remember your Bible. God promised Jeremiah that he wouldn't destroy Sodom if he could find ten honorable men out of the thousands in the city."

"I know the story, Mark," Val said. "But you should remember that in the end, Sodom was destroyed."

***

The sun had set and a couple of moons had come up by the time the crew of *Cousteau* had eaten its dinner and the jury reconvened. The difference in time was severe enough to scramble the internal clocks of everyone on Chamal – except Barrett and his troopers, who kept to the internal clock of the *Belle Marie*.

Mark ate with Helen in the archives and sat with them when the entire human company at Chamal had mustered in virtual assembly. He was ready to do some more arguing and convincing when they met, but it wasn't necessary. Barrett was more than happy to do something, anything, rather than sit around playing target for the next attack. Red and Oboke had been convinced earlier. The others were sufficiently dispassionate and flexible to support Mark's plan. And even Val Nordland fell into line before they were done.

"I do not personally subscribe to everything that Mr. Paradis has said," he told the panel. "But my criticisms are neither rigorous nor powerful enough to muster a veto."

And Captain Fletcher made it unanimous – once he knew how everyone was going to vote.

Helen sat around for as long as the law required, but the minute the jury was finished with its work, she left, muttering something about "genocidal idiots" and "overgrown adolescents" under her breath.

Mark left too, but headed upstairs to find Zepp. He told him the news and sent him off to get the pilgrims ready. Zepp seemed to understand perfectly what was going on. At least he never questioned the sudden decision to come to the aid of tribesmen aboard the *Deragathon* and their allies.

CHAPTER TWENTY-FOUR

Zepp felt the rough hilt of Sherbek's blade poking him in the back as they crowded around the viewscreen. The pain reminded him that he should not trust his cousin, no matter how sincere he may sound or how much support Tedrak had given him.

After all, Zepp knew the truth – that the work of Jobe had decayed over the centuries. The Seedkeepers had replaced the slave trade with their own commercial enterprise and the pilgrims had become a tool of statecraft. Tedrak had been the one who had employed blackmail and extortion to put Zepp into the position he now occupied, and he could just as easily have levered Sherbek into a similar position.

On the screen, the elaborate carved face of the riftwall fortress slid by, silent and majestic in its aging decay.

Up above, through the open hatch, he could hear Lieutenant Barrett, the angel warrior, muttering softly. The wise teacher translated: "I hate joint ops ... I hate joint ops."

When they found the gun emplacements, the ship slowed to a stop. Mark called down from the bridge to Zepp to tell him it was time to make his plea. Zepp found the spot in the panel where he'd been told to speak and chirped twice to clear his throat.

"Griddle, it's me, Zepp," he said. Speakers in the viewscreen sent the echos of his voice into the chamber, packed with angel troopers and the pilgrim company from Ring Po Do. "We've come to help you. Come out and we will lift your curse for you."

He repeated the words twice, and in the middle of the fourth time through, a small blue figure appeared at the edge of the great embrasure and waved.

"Meet us below," Zepp said.

Griddle waved again, then disappeared. The angels' vessel dropped down to the ground as gently as a leaf. They waited for a long time before Griddle emerged from the forest, then a longer time still while Helen talked to the reluctant hermit.

Zepp wasn't quite sure he understood the motivation of the different angels. Barrett was all behind the attack on the *Deragathon*, but did not believe in taking one side against another in the chamalian disputes. Mark was opposed to the attack in principal, but understood the need for it. Helen was opposed to it, saw no need for it, but insisted on coming along as a nurse to care for any of them who might be hurt. And as an added demand, she insisted that they stop to find Griddle, so she could treat the curse that left him here in the ruins of the Red Monkey fortress.

Zepp was willing to help her with that, since he was reluctant to return to the *Deragathon* without Griddle in tow. That was how he had survived his first passage through the warship, and he didn't want to take a chance with a new approach.

*****

Zepp was attentive when Helen explained how the potion she carried would work. His fears would be relieved, his sadness removed from his shoulders, and his fortitude returned to him. It sounded so inviting, Zepp was almost tempted to ask for a sample himself –

except that his single experience with potions had been frighteningly negative.

Griddle, on the other hand, didn't require much convincing at all. He had never been hard to direct, lacking any strong will of his own. The long years of exile from his own kind had broken any inner purpose, reducing what remained into a surly stubbornness that appeared when pushed only slightly, but which retreated under concerted effort.

But here the blue cat's will seemed to emerge without struggle. "If it will end my suffering, I will drink it," Griddle announced with rare certainty, "even if it turns out to be a poison."

Mark and Zepp sat on the blocks of black basalt that littered the base of the riftwall while Helen offered Griddle the tiny bottle of green liquid. He made a terrible face at the taste of the stuff, but swallowed it all.

Nothing happened for a long time. Helen inspected Griddle with several instruments and devices, but said nothing to indicate what she saw.

Then, after half an hour, Griddle began to laugh.

He started with a tiny chuckle, then a string of chitters, followed by a joyous cackling that bounced off the stone walls behind them, and finally a breathless, barely contained jiggering.

"What's so funny?" Zepp asked.

Griddle struggled to find his voice, then spat out: "I'm laughing at all the terrible things that ever happened to others around me. All the mayhem and misfortune and misery. And I'm laughing at all the poor miserable souls who blamed me for it and chased me on my way. Little lives led in darkness and ignorance, while I was set on a journey across the great wild world.

"I'm so sorry now that I never took the time to appreciate the irony. Or the journey. I've lived a life so cramped and crippled by fear and resentment that I've wasted the great opportunities my curse has given me."

He stood up, stretched his short legs and arms, then bounded to the top of a block of stone. He danced on the corner of the crystal, turning around once on each foot.

"Look at me! I am so free! No tribe makes a claim on me. No nation demands taxes. No empire treats me as subject. No cult demands my sacrifices. I go where I want and when I want, and when the time comes I am welcomed on my way. And all these years, I saw this as a burden and a curse, not as an adventure and a liberation."

Zepp felt his stomach churn with uncertainty as the incongruously wise words spilled from such a low source as Griddle.

"How silly I was," Griddle said as he leaped from stone to stone like a playful halfling. "This is what it really means to have wisdom. Zepp, that patriarch of yours knew it. Wisdom goes out into the world and sees it for what it is. There is no wisdom in binding yourself to place or family or time. True wisdom must be free to fulfill itself."

Breathless, the blue cat sank to the ground and rested against the bole of a tree. "I am sorry I have not done all I could to do that. I apologize to you, to the world, to great emptiness beyond the world, to the gods, who punish us for our great sin and to the angels who have come here to destroy us for that sin."

Zepp gasped in sudden fear at what the angels might think to hear these words translated. He had tried so hard to keep his own understanding of them concealed as much as possible – out of caution and fear. But now Griddle was throwing both into the rushing torrent.

"That is why they have come, Zepp. You know that, don't you. You can hear the guilt in their words, if you know how to listen. They have come to judge us and we cannot face that judgment. It'll be better once they've done it, though. The world will be cleansed of our sin, and then we can start over again with the frogs and see if better creatures can rise up from the swampy muds."

Griddle jumped up again, renewed, and grabbed Zepp by the hands. "Oh Zepp, you can't believe how good I feel. My, my. For the first time in my life I feel good, and happy, and alive, and unafraid. And all this from a little potion. The angels are truly wiser than we are, as we are wiser than the wild steplings and halflings. You should listen to them before the time comes for them to destroy us. They will tell you things you never imagined you could know."

"I have," Zepp said, wedging the words in forcibly as Griddle yammered on. "And you're right, they are wondrous things to know."

"But you are here for a reason," Griddle sighed at last. "And you want to bring me with you. Are you going back to our warship? Of course you are. Why else bring me along? Very well. It will be worth it to live life once more in the face of death. I'm ready, shall we go?"

Griddle nearly raced them to the entrance to the spacecraft, while Zepp hung back with Mark and Helen.

"Did you expect it to do that?" Mark asked.

Helen shrugged, which the wise teacher had said was a confession of ignorance, the same as tipping the head from side to side. "I didn't know what to expect. We tried it on the test animals back in the seed pens and there were no harmful effects. But this was the first time we've given it to a chamalian who could talk. I guess we should have expected something like this, though."

"How could you know what to expect? It's just that kind of a world," Mark said.

Zepp smiled at Mark's admission. They were both coming late to an understanding of that fact.

A moment later, Griddle was inside, making friends with the pilgrim company, and Mark was securing the door against the journey into space.

***

Ever since Mark had explained the truth about the angels and about the curses wisdom was prone to, Zepp had been wrestling with the ideas.

The struggle was not an easy one.

The ideas were structured like interlocking mirrors – one idea reflecting the other in an endless series that grew ever more complex. But at the same time, they offered a way out of the bouncing reflections. At least that was what the Wise Teacher of the Wise had promised. Zepp had spoken with him at length as well.

The wise teacher was not a simple translator, Zepp had learned, but a subtle expert on the way language shapes the knowledge of the wise. He showed how the split between the inner self and the outer world was embedded in the structure of language itself. Subjects and objects.

But there were some things that shouldn't have objects, the wise teacher said. "Faith, for example. If you put your faith in a powerful idol, it becomes the all-powerful object and you become the powerless subject. But if you have faith, without giving it to the object, you avoid the idolatry and preserve the original power of wisdom."

Zepp had played the word game over in his mind. Faith in the tribe, in the clan, in the rules of old, in the customs of the ancients, in the dictates of the rulers, in the cleverness of plans, in the arrogance of wealth, in the heart of a mate – all ran the risk of creating idols.

But what powered such idolatrous faith in the first place?

The wise teacher had an answer – the unresolved questions of life and wisdom itself. "They have made up rationalizations to explain the world in which they find themselves. Those rationalizations are partly true and partly false. The false part takes on the shape of the missing pieces of the truth and tries to explain them away or justify the part without the whole. But their very partiality makes them false, and rather than face an incomplete understanding, wisdom pretends completion. And demands absolute and unquestioning faith in the pretense."

"And is there any escape from this?"

"Of course. You must overthrow the idols. It happens on a regular basis. But revolutions are difficult, painful, and unrewarding. If they weren't unavoidable, the angels would not have had so many of them."

"How do you do that? How do you overthrow the idols?"

"Historically, through radical action at the precise moment and place that is necessary. Usually long after it is necessary. A small band of determined revolutionaries smashing down the rotten door of a corrupt establishment, says Crane Brinton."

"And how do you know when the right moment and right place are?"

"From the reports and analysis of the angels' history, the

participants seem to know when they get there, but seldom before."

"Isn't there some clue or sign? Can't you parse it out with numerology?"

"I am afraid the experts say you cannot. It is a sort of art, requiring the artist to work with the medium until the solution emerges on its own. Because after all, you are not a simple subject acting on an unknowing object."

"I suppose not," Zepp said slowly. "Especially not on this world, where everything alive is both an object and a subject."

The more Zepp reflected on Mark's idea, the more he came to appreciate it and, in a way that only a child of Jobe would understand, to adore it. The perversity of the theory was downright chamalian.

In the beginning, wisdom transcended nature, and became alienated, turning in on itself. But that was because wisdom was small and had not gone out into the world. As it grew, wisdom acquired the power to transcend the alienation – but at the same time, the alienation grew ever more powerful. Wisdom erected cities, nations, and empires in its face, and they became only greater tools for the forces that stole the soul from wisdom.

Until now, when wisdom from out of the world had come to restore the balance.

And the moment for the restoration was upon them.

***

For the past eighteen hours, Zepp had been unable to sleep, unable to eat, unable to think. He had instead encamped himself at the heart of the radio exchange where the messages came in from the

Pilgrimage Houses around the tight globe of Chamal. Each day at noon local time, each house would transmit its report on the status of the world. More than a hundred houses, sometimes a message every few minutes, sometimes none for an hour. And each of them told of the rising crisis that gripped the planet.

In Shipar, the stargazers had stopped burning hundreds of scrolls of astronomical records, but they were still tossing observatory staff off the high cliffs overlooking the caldera at the top of Parishaldemain. Zepp knew that the important records were still hidden in deep caverns, secure against anything but an eruption of the volcano itself. But it was a shame to think of all that work gone to waste – not to mention the workers themselves.

In the Rift Valley, the loyalist divisions of the Blue Monkey army had surrounded Ring Po Do. Rockets continued to land throughout the city – and in the Pilgrimage House compound – with casual abandon. The tree cats and the rift hounds were locked in a desperate battle to the death. And the spaceport had been overrun by masses of unallied city-dwellers who blamed their misfortunes on the alliance.

In Kwikorak, the wise old snow-bears had abandoned the cities for the high ground, there to await the coming of the end of chamalian history. They had left behind a treasure trove of electronic and cybernetic toys, but no one knew how to operate any of them.

In the tropical belt, the dozens of self-important kingdoms and empires were using the arrival of the angels to settle old scores, or to start new ones. Raids, assaults, and full-scale invasions were setting the forests afire.

On the steppes of Birhat, the great landholders were barricading their stations. They had gathered their herds together and were systematically eliminating any of them that showed the least bit of defiance. But they still could not shake the fear that the wisest sheep would know better than to look up into the eyes of the predator cats, and that the rebellion they had started would continue until the blood of the big cats ran through the gutters of the abattoirs.

In the great cities of Rikabar, political execution squads roamed the streets, seeking out rebels, labeling them as predators, and shooting them without further delay or due process. The party bosses, however, had long since fled. The highest of them were already aboard the *Deragathon*, but the mid-level functionaries had sought refuge in the highlands to the west.

In the southern hemisphere, the primitive tribes of the vast briar patch that wrapped around the planet knew of the struggles being waged elsewhere. But they continued to tend their campfires, hunt the steplings and halflings of the thicket, and sip from the wells of sweetwater, blissful in their lack of civilization.

In Arkaria, the great city of Arkar continued to burn from the fires set by the awful explosion that brought the sun to ground and swept thousands of fliers from the sky. Many reported blindness and burns from the mysterious blast. Others were beginning to suffer from a strange sickness that robbed them first of balance, then of wisdom, and finally of life.

In Meshkar, bank failures had started the great wheel of war turning once again, as trading house set upon trading house and warships filled the high equatorial sea.

In Suridash, the children of the dust who lived in the open spaces between the enclaves were beginning to doubt the wisdom of the tribe of Jobe as word of Zepp's return, his vision, and the attack of the dissenters spread through the streets and alleys of the city.

All over Chamal, the moment of decision was drawing nearer and nearer. Chaos was increasing. Madness was mounting for a final campaign, ready to sweep all wisdom before it.

And here again Mark's theory showed its perversity, that wild chamalian twist, of the abstraction tied suddenly and completely to the specific.

Until this very moment, the angels had always been unreachably alien in some frightening way. They were complete, whole, and self-contained creatures, not like the unfinished, raw beasts of Chamal, still slaves to their irrational passions. But Mark had at last presented him with an idea that could grow and take root in the dubious soil of Zepp's world.

He saw the idea in all its multidimensional glory now – the topology of change. Volumes of representational space, caught in momentary cross-sections as bounded areas of a plane. But as the spheres swelled and contracted, the bounded areas grew and shrank. And when the cross section of the moment reached the end of the sphere, its bounded circle shrank, tying him in an ever-tightening noose, until it collapsed upon him, turning him into a tiny point of light streaking through the spheres, across the lines and circles, as the outer edge of one became the center of the next. It was a descriptive geometry, not a predictive one, but it was marvelous nevertheless.

And it always brought him back, in ever-tightening spirals, to the current moment, where the fate of his world hung in the balance.

***

Mark's nerves were cranked as tight as a steel guitar as the *Belle Marie* made its approach to the *Deragathon*. All stealthed up with countermeasures the chamalians never dreamed of, the pinnace was invisible to their comparatively primitive sensors – radar and EMF detectors, from what Zepp had told them. But that didn't help Mark any. He knew that one malfunction was all it would take to leave them exposed to the murderous weapons of the alien warship.

And with Griddle aboard, the chances of a malfunction seemed so much higher.

The last few hundred meters he held his breath, the muscles in his chest finally burning with fire, as they came within plain sight. Anyone looking out a window or watching a viewscreen would be able to see them. And this was the slowest the *Belle Marie* would be moving relative to the *Deragathon*.

When the hulls touched with a gentle tap and a soft groan, he almost exploded. But the silence that followed was broken only by the harsh breathing of dozens of human and chamalian warriors and not the terrible pounding of hostile fire.

A few minutes later, a trooper from below called out to report his task complete and the warriors began to flow from one vessel into the other. Mark tightened a strap on his spacesuit, tilted the spherical glass helmet from side to side to remind himself of the limits on his motion, then took his place in line.

The compartment he entered was small, dark, and crammed full of warriors. The place had been swept clean of fittings by explosive decompression, but a few objects remained fastened to the walls – flat images of several chamalians, a document full of ornate writing, and a long, curved blade with a hand-carved wooden handle. This had been the admiral's cabin, before a mutineer had put a rocket through the bulkhead.

Mark felt the sweat pooling under his arms in zero-G. The chamber was dead silent unless he switched on his commlink, and he didn't want to do that just yet.

Then he felt a strange tugging on his spacesuit. And a moment later, he began to hear the sound of rustling bodies, creaking armor, the tapping of boots against bulkheads as troopers and chamalians held their weightless stations.

They were pressurizing the compartment. When the outside and inside pressures were equal, they would be able to break through the patch that the chamalian engineers had placed over the entrance to the cabin.

That moment came sooner than Mark was ready for. The troopers made a series of guttural sounds that seemed like commands or cheers, he couldn't tell which. Then the door burst open. Light spilled past dark shapes that shot through the open doorway.

Mark waited for the flare of automatic weapons fire and the thump of grenades, but it never came.

Instead, the troopers sprayed an aerosol containing a drug similar to that given to Griddle, but softer and more broadband. The chamalians who inhaled the vapors were freed of depression and anxiety, just like Griddle. But they were not filled with new energy. Just the opposite. They were taken into a dreamlike euphoria, with little interest in resisting.

By the time Mark pulled himself through to the bridge of the *Deragathon*, the pilgrim warriors were rounding up the crew, while the human troopers secured the entrances to the large spherical chamber that housed the warship's nerve center.

A brief round of fire echoed from the curved walls, pulling Mark's attention to the rear of the compartment. The troopers had encountered a trio of white-haired, yellow-fanged warhounds of some sort.

They seemed to lack what Zepp called wisdom, either through a fault in their genes or their upbringing. Probably the former, judging by the size of their skulls. Not enough room there for much besides a battle computer and a sex drive. Now they didn't even have that. Two troopers cleaned up the bodies and stowed them in a corner.

Lieutenant Barrett was at the heart of the deadly serious business, speaking into his commlink, waving troopers on with hand signals. This was his element. Forcible entry, by the numbers. You could tell that he was as eager for the fight as the now-defunct warhounds had been. Though Mark had to give him credit for having more wisdom. Even if he wouldn't understand what had brought them here.

CHAPTER TWENTY-FIVE

The once-humble and **once-great** acting Admiral Pym was once again humble, his eyes rolling under the influence of the angels' aerosol. Pym was a short, round creature with stiff, bristly fur. Zepp was glad for the spacesuit he wore, since it sealed out not only the spray, but Pym's obnoxious personal odor.

Pym had been an ensign when the *Deragathon* met the *Cousteau* in orbit above Chamal, and his father had been the admiral in command of the warship. But the destruction of his cabin and the shrine to his ancestors, the mutinies and rebellions that struck his command, and the ultimate betrayal of his mission by Zepp and Griddle had reduced the Meshkarian officer to a quivering wreck and placed his son in his stead.

Now Pym was quivering himself, though from spasms of laughter instead of despair.

Zepp had a hard time getting any information out of him. He was frustrated and angry at it, but knew there was nothing he could do about it. So he pulled himself through the weightlessness of the bridge to a communications station and started trying to contact someone who could provide him with the information he needed.

Before long, Griddle and Sherbek both drifted over to where he worked, Sherbek to look over his shoulder and Griddle to hang loosely in the air, one leg wrapped around a stanchion. Zepp had noticed that for a commander, Sherbek was giving very few commands. Frit was leading the pilgrims and doing it well. Sherbek's true mission remained a mystery to Zepp, though his speculations about it only made him feel more uneasy.

He chided himself now for bringing Griddle along. He had hoped that the blue cat would once again fulfill his role as a jinx – and as a secret protector against misfortune. But that idea had relied on bringing the Griddle who had been chained to him for those long, deadly, frightening hours while they were chased from one end of the *Deragathon* to the other. This creature was different in too many ways. Zepp didn't even recognize him anymore. Zepp was afraid that by relieving him of his cursed disposition, the angels had also relieved him of his hidden power to confound the devices and plans of wisdom. He wondered if it all had been nothing more than superstition in the first place.

Suddenly the communications panel in front of him squeaked, squawked, and sizzled, then emitted the sibilant voice of Whirlpitt himself.

"Is that you again, Pym?" he asked.

"No, it is I, Zepp, ambassador to the angels and spy for the tribe of Jobe," he replied.

Whirlpitt hissed in admiration. "So you have survived this turmoil after all. And returned to repay the favor I granted you, no doubt."

"What favor was that?"

"Continued life, what else?"

"That was part of my purpose," Zepp admitted. "Though I'm not sure if we are here in service of any purpose of our own."

"Probably not, if the angels are as powerful as we all believe. Nevertheless, you are in a position to do us all some good. Better than the position in which I find myself."

"And what position is that?" Zepp asked.

"Supine and dormant, at the moment. Much has changed since we sent you on your journey to dwell among the angels."

Whirlpitt described the current state of battle aboard the *Deragathon*. The warship was a long cylindrical structure built around a heavy thrust-bearing beam. The bridge sat at one end, while the hangars, flight deck, and engines sat at the other. In between, six separate containments arranged in two sets of three held the different groups of chamalian conspirators who had dared to raise themselves up in defiance of the heavens and challenge the angels. The containments rotated around the central shaft on great bearing rings to produce artificial gravity for their inhabitants.

Suridash possessed one of these, as did Kwikorak and the Blue Monkeys. Rikabar, Meshkar, and Birhat owned the other three.

When Zepp was dispatched to the angels' starship, Whirlpitt and his allies – the Arkarians from the Cult of the Lost Argument, the Kwikorak snow-bears, and the Meshkarians – held the bridge, the central shaft, the hangars and flight deck, the engines, and their respective containments.

But since then, the Birhat cats had quelled the rebellion of their herds, the Rikabarians had silenced the political dissenters in their midst, the Blue Monkeys had suppressed their mutineers, and all three had staged a combined attack that took back the central shaft.

Now the crews from Suridash, Meshkar, and Kwikorak were bottled up in their containments. The Arkarians still held the flight deck and the engine room, but the Blue Monkeys had taken back the hangars. And war parties had laid siege to the bridge.

Whirlpitt's estimate was that only a few days stood between them and defeat at the hands of their enemies.

"Then we seemed to have arrived at just the right moment," Zepp said.

"So it seems," Whirlpitt said. "Assuming you and your angel friends can make the most of it."

"That remains to be seen," Zepp said. "After all, this time, we do not have the advantage of surprise or subterfuge." He told them of the strange potion Helen had given Griddle and his doubts about Griddle's powers under its influence.

"It shouldn't matter," Whirlpitt said. "We never put much faith in him anyway."

"That was a mistake that shall be remedied," Griddle said unexpectedly from his inverted perch above the communications console.

"Griddle, is that you?"

"None other," Griddle said. "Though I do not think I am really myself today. I feel unlike anything I have ever felt before. And I see the world in a light unlike any I have ever seen before. Therefore we cannot judge this day by any we have ever lived before. The moment of change is upon us all and none of us shall escape."

"A very cheering thought," Whirlpitt said.

Zepp said nothing, but shook his hands nervously as his tail curled around one leg. He was about to ask for more details about Whirlpitt's condition, when the clatter of slugs smashing against the entrance to the bridge distracted him.

He looked up in time to see angels and pilgrims flying through the air to take up combat positions.

***

Mark had to admit that despite the limits of his character, Barrett was a good military commander.

At the first sign that they were being attacked, he had his troopers on the move. The speed of their actions impressed Mark. There was something reassuring in the confident precision of their moves. They seemed like a single organism with a number of component parts moving in unison.

The fire-teams seemed to instinctively leapfrog one another from position to position, flowing steadily and swiftly forward.

Only here and now, aboard the *Deragathon*, there was no place to maneuver towards. There was only the single entrance and the sound of bullets smacking against it was not reassuring. A muffled "crump" marked the end of the fusillade, but nothing more. The hatchway held and the warriors relaxed.

But not their leaders. A moment later, Barrett and Frit had their heads together. For all his disdain for the aliens and for joint ops, Barrett was quick to incorporate Frit and the pilgrims into his plans. When they were done, Barrett came straight to Mark.

"You stay here," he said quickly on a private channel. "I'm taking them outside for a flanking move. I figure we've got training at vacuum ops that the mutts don't. Once we've secured the hatch, you come out with them. I don't want to lose touch with anyone in the party. But I can't spare anyone to stay behind and guard you."

Mark nodded, but his heart wasn't in it. Without trying, Barrett had put the fear of death into him and his blood was running colder as every second passed.

The action seemed to take forever, but Mark knew it was just his nerves. He wished he could keep himself busy like Zepp and Griddle, but he didn't have anyone aboard the alien warship that he could phone up.

Then the pilgrim guarding the hatch came to the alert, signaled to Frit, and a moment later they opened it to reveal a human trooper waving them through.

Mark moved quickly to keep up, making sure that he wouldn't be the last one through into the central section of the *Deragathon*. But the pilgrims held him off anyway, sending him through only after both Zepp and Griddle had made the passage.

He found himself in a large plenum chamber separating the bridge from the rest of the ship – a massive beam of steel was anchored against the rear of the bridge and protruded back into the rest of the ship from there. On the near side, the bulkhead was scarred by smoke and flame and pitted by bullets. A half dozen weapons emplacements had been demolished – some only wrecked, others obliterated. Mark didn't want to think about how that had been accomplished.

On the far side, a large bulkhead was broken by a number of hatches, a couple of trapezoidal voids leading deeper into the vessel, and a large circular opening in the middle that was now surrounded by troopers. As he watched, the pilgrims launched themselves across the chamber, taking full advantage of the weightlessness of the environment aboard the *Deragathon*, and flew down the main shaft.

Troopers opened fire, ripping the air with their weapons. The echoes of more fire spilled out of the shaft.

Barrett waited until the rate of fire from all involved slowed to a trickle, only a matter of a few long seconds. Then he signaled Frit and took Mark's arm and launched the two of them towards the great round hole.

Darkness swallowed them up. Then, just as Mark's eyes were beginning to adapt, light splashed all around them from the handheld arcs carried by the troopers.

They reached another bulkhead a few dozen meters along the shaft. Now the place was getting crowded as the warriors from both races clumped up at the far end. A couple of engineers from each party were working on the next hatch. From what Mark overhead in reports to Barrett, this wasn't as critical as the exit from the bridge, since there were several passages through the surrounding compartments that would get them around it. But they waited a long time before the next flanking maneuver.

This time it was the pilgrims, working their way through alternate routes to the next major objective. Back here, the troopers made ready to go through the hatch on their own. Communications inside the vessel was strictly line-of-sight, so they had to rely entirely on timing. "I hope their watches work like ours," Barrett said.

"I don't know any reason they should," Mark replied, eliciting a scowl that was visible from across the plenum chamber.

"Here we go!" Barrett shouted when the moment arrived.

Mark was at the tail end of this bound as well – and glad for it. The next section of the ship consisted of a large cylinder with the thrust beam running down the center. The cylinder was broken by a metal ring that rotated quickly, about once every ten seconds. Mark realized that the deep thrumming he felt through the walls of the ship was the bearings on this rotating section of the hull.

Three wide openings stood at equal intervals around the ring. These were the entrances to the spinning containments that held the main body of the *Deragathon*'s crew. According to Zepp, each breed of chamalian had one of their own, which they had built and filled with their own equipment, crewmembers, and weapons.

Mark sized up the situation in a matter of a few seconds.

A number of motionless figures drifted in the air around them. He couldn't identify them immediately by breed, but he knew they weren't human troopers. Nevertheless, he was distressed by the sight of the casualties.

And the flash of small arms from one of the entrances only added to his woes.

***

Zepp was relieved to see the firing let up when the angels sprayed their aerosol at the entrance to the Birhat containment. The cats were good shots, but only when they felt like shooting. A few whiffs of the misty peacemaker and they lost any such will. The master was ready to lie down with the lamb when they were through.

Nevertheless, Frit insisted that everyone remain alert. He kept them in covered positions along the thrust beam as the angels advanced to get a closer look. The first squad spilled over the edge of the opening like tree-squirrels. A moment later, a figure came drifting out. Then another, lashed to the first by a piece of plastic line. And then more, in a long, well-punctuated sentence.

The other angels pulled them in and passed them back to the pilgrims, who secured them with a second strap of plastic around the wrists and fastened them to the bulkhead with a length of wire.

The cats from Birhat were purring loud enough to make the hull shake. One of them curled over in place and offered up a yellow-spotted belly to be scratched. Others shook their heads in drug-induced bliss.

Zepp allowed himself to breath more easily. But that pleasure was to last only a moment, as more small-arms fire erupted from the opening to the Blue Monkey containment a third of the way to spinward.

The pilgrims advanced quickly into the fire.

Zepp watched aghast as they flung themselves onto the rotating collar that linked the three containments, each of them in turn swept away by its motion. They surrounded the opening and hunkered down behind structural braces and fittings.

A slug found a home in one of the warriors, and Zepp's blood grew thin at the sight of him doubling up around the wound. He heard a buzzing sound and the snap of energy pulsing into a spot on the bulkhead a few hands away from him – a death ray!

He feared for the angels suddenly. He knew that their curious armor could stop bullets, but was it proof against death rays?

But the angels turned the spray on the Blue Monkeys, and they too stopped shooting and were transformed into passive prisoners.

The third party – the guards at the entrance to the Meshkarian containment – gave up without a fight. The angels sprayed their concoction into that opening before the shooting began, avoiding any further damage.

They had barely finished securing the area when Barrett hurried them on, through the hatchway that led aft. The angel's precision execution of the drill was a demonstration of the perfection of these visitors from the heavens – pure and precise. Two went through with weapons trained and ready to fire. Two more followed and went to ground – a difficult evolution in a weightless environment. Two more flew past the initial four and took up their posts. Then the six-parted creature moved on, its rear element moving on to the front, while a new fire-team repeated the moves.

When they were all gone, Frit gathered up the pilgrims remaining after a squad had been assigned to watch the prisoners and started throwing them down the passageway to the next set of containments.

The angels were cleaning out the guards who had bottled up the snow-bears from Kwikorak and Zepp's own contingent from Suridash when Zepp reached that section of the ship. He paused in the hatchway to watch. Mark floated just a few hands to his right, and Barrett issued orders from a place next to the thrust beam itself.

Zepp was about to pass through into this section of the ship when a dozen dark shapes exploded out of the entrance to the Rikabar containment and opened fire.

Metal slugs bounced off the metal bulkhead all around him. The crackle and snap of death rays ripped the air and patches of bulkhead blistered from near-hits. Angel troopers and pilgrim warriors clung to the thrust beam and tried to make themselves two-dimensional.

The angels with the aerosol filled the air with their chemicals. But the attackers plunged through the cloud and continued with their slashing attack. Zepp could see the helmets and air tanks strapped across their heads and shoulders. Spacesuits!

An angel warrior was hit by a death ray a few hands to Zepp's right – his armor bubbling and smoking across his back.

Zepp caught Mark's eye where he had anchored himself. He stepped back through the hatchway and huddled against the passageway wall. Mark burst through the opening, bounced off one wall and into the other.

"They're in spacesuits," he said. "The aerosol won't work."

Zepp shook his hands. The angels were the ones who had insisted on using their bloodless devices. They said there was no way they could separate the friendly chamalians from the hostile ones. But that was not the way of Chamal.

The pilgrims, on the other hand, were equipped with the weapons they needed to carry out the assault, and now they used them to proper effect. A moment later, the attackers from Rikabar were reduced to a single fire team.

Unfortunately that team found a secure position behind a hatch leading further aft. From there, they could keep their opponents pinned down. And the best marksmen among the pilgrims were hard pressed to do more than harass them back.

Zepp prepared himself for what was likely to be a long process of infiltrating warriors along the thrust beam to outflank them. Mark hunkered down and clutched a handhold in the wall.

"This isn't going so well," Mark said. "Where's Griddle?"

Zepp felt his blood pound at the thought that their attack might be jinxed. He looked around. Behind, along the passageway forward, was where Griddle should have been. Zepp had been ahead of both him and Sherbek.

But now they were gone. Once again he shook his hands in distress.

"They were back there," Zepp said.

"Maybe we should go look for them," Mark said. "We're no help here."

Mark spoke, but before the wise teacher could translate, slugs began ricocheting off the wall around them. One thudded into Mark's chest, spending its energy in his armor and eliciting a loud shout. They bounded away from the threat, pulling themselves forward amid a shower of bullets. Zepp realized he had seen a flutter of movement beyond the hatchway just before the firing began – more Rikabarian attackers.

They flew past a short side corridor. Zepp recognized it as leading into the communications center. He snagged a stanchion and pulled himself to a stop. Mark did the same a couple hands up the passageway, reversed direction, and flew into the hallway beside him.

"Come with me," Zepp said. "I have an idea."

***

Mark was happy to get in out of the shooting.

He didn't know which was more unnerving – being shot at, or the way he had calmly and dispassionately moved to dodge the bullets as the attack developed. Only afterwards, once he was safe from the battle, did he appreciate how close he had come to disaster.

He wondered still if he could blame any of it on Griddle. And in that doubt, he realized suddenly, lay the source of the superstition. It was an irrational doubt that could not be answered. And it fed an irrational faith in things like Griddle's jinx.

Zepp led him down a darkened corridor, twisting and turning as they went so that in a matter of seconds he had lost all sense of direction and couldn't possible find his own way back to the main passageway alone.

Then they burst into a large compartment where the lights still worked. The space was crammed with metal boxes, wires, dials, gauges, flashing displays, and vacuum tubes all mixed together in that mad, anarchic style that Mark had come to recognize as purely chamalian. The air was probably thick with ozone, he realized, though he had no desire at the moment to take off his helmet and expose himself to find out. The corners of the compartment were lined with frost-covered pipes with metal blades – a cooling system that was probably as effective as it was primitive if it allowed this equipment to continue operating.

They found Griddle and Sherbek in the middle of it. They were straddling the bars of a cage in the middle of the equipment, perched against sling seats mounted in the framework.

"Is this area secure?" Zepp asked.

Sherbek shook his hands, but Griddle piped up: "The pilgrims chased the regular crew out of here with the peacemaker spray. Sherbek asked to see the communications center, so I brought him down here. You remember the last time we were in here, don't you? Wires were burning, fuses snapping, electricity zapping everywhere. None of that this time, I'm afraid. And through it all I was so completely self-involved. That was a shame. The ultimate experience of a lifetime, the ultimate betrayal of our planet, and I barely paid attention. But the drama is much more powerful this time, don't you think?"

Mark wanted to find an antidote to Helen's happy drug – or at least a way to calm Griddle down. His nerves were tight enough without the running commentary. Then, on a sudden impulse, he said: "Professor, can you filter him out? Or at least lower the volume."

The AI complied with his request and the room became suddenly more tranquil – except for the chittering sound Griddle made when speaking.

"What have you got here?" Mark asked. "Is this all radio, or do you have microwave links? How about lasercomms?"

While the professor struggled a bit over the technical terminology, Zepp managed to describe a wide range of systems all running simultaneously. The communications center held a combination of equipment from all the members of the alliance. The Birhat shortwave voice radio sat next to a Kwikorak digital encoding microwave burst transmitter. Rikabar carried analog video and telemetry on its broad-band system, while Meshkar digitalized the signal. Suridash relied on a shortwave system of its own, though more sophisticated than the one the panther's used. The Arkarians relied on the Kwikorak system, but maintained monitors that eavesdropped on planetbound radio traffic – particularly in the equatorial forest belt nearest Arkaria.

Zepp knew all these things about the system, but that was the limit of his wisdom. "I couldn't operate a single one of them if my fate hung in the balance," he said.

Mark shook his head and marveled at the alien technology. The diverse collection of equipment, the mix and mismatch of capabilities, the riotous variety of the physical designs all integrated, apparently in some cases by pure force of will, into a single system – this was what Chamal was all about. The pattern even repeated into their instrumentality.

He turned towards Zepp to say so and suddenly froze where he was.

Two things were terribly out of place in the tableau before him.

First, Zepp hung in space with his eyes closed, his arms wrapped around himself while his tail whipped back and forth like an angry whip. Mark couldn't tell if he were ill or simply withdrawing from the world.

Second, Sherbek had drawn his blade and had maneuvered himself around the monkey-bars to a place where he could use it against Zepp – an act that was nearly imminent, given Sherbek's posture at the moment Mark encountered them.

Things seemed to move in terribly slow motion from that instant.

Mark was rooted to the spot, but his muscles bunched up as he prepared to spring across the short distance to Sherbek. At the same time, he realized he had little to use against a short piece of sharp metal being wielded by an alien of unknown physical strength.

Sherbek uncoiled from his perch, the arm with the blade swinging along a trajectory that appeared to intersect with Zepp's neck.

And from behind Sherbek, the shadowy blur of motion that Mark now noticed turned itself into the shape of Griddle. The blue cat had stopped talking. He now flew through the air on a course as precise as that of Sherbek's sword, but with a much higher velocity. His trajectory, however, intersected with Sherbek's midsection, and he hit his target first.

The impact sent random moment arms throughout the dynamic system that included Sherbek, Griddle, and Sherbek's blade. The blade went askew, missing Zepp's neck entirely – but the flat side of it smacked against the back of his head, sending a wave of adrenaline up Mark's back. The adrenaline was next to useless, though, since Mark still had nothing to use against Sherbek's blade. It occurred to him that Griddle was no better equipped than he was, but did not hesitate to act.

By now, Mark's muscles were ready to spring. The combination of taut nerves, a burst of hormonal energy, and a will to move sent him flying into the middle of the melee.

He felt the jarring collision with the two chamalians in his shoulders. Then he started grabbing for a handhold before he caromed off and into the monkey-bars. Apparently he found a purchase in Sherbek's spacesuit, which slowed him down as he reached back for a second swing.

Now Griddle grabbed for Sherbek's wrist. Sherbek reached out with his other hand to stop him, but Mark saw his chance and grabbed it with both hands. He wrapped his leg around a bar to anchor himself and the slowly spinning collection of creatures, feeling the momentum try to pull him away as he shifted its direction.

Sherbek struggled, but Griddle and Mark held fast. Then they all came up hard against the cage. Griddle pried the blade loose from Sherbek's hand. Mark's eyes, however, were fixed on the Sherbek's bared fangs. The only thing that kept them away from him was the heavy glass bowl of his spacesuit helmet – something Sherbek apparently forgot he was wearing, judging by the way he kept snapping and snarling at Mark.

Griddle continued to struggle with Sherbek now, even as Mark held tight where he gripped his arm. While Sherbek tried to get leverage of his own against the monkey-bars, Griddle worked on the back of his spacesuit.

Mark was puzzled at first, then realized with sudden horror what Griddle was trying to do – he was working on getting Sherbek's helmet off.

"No!" he yelled. "Don't do that!"

All Mark could see was Sherbek's fangs. All he could imagine was them sinking into the soft skin of his own suit and the soft meat of his own body.

But the clamps holding the helmet down sprang loose, and Griddle yanked the glass bowl forward. It spun off across the compartment and banged into a radio set. Sherbek snapped and snarled and twisted to get his teeth up close to Mark's arm. Griddle snatched at Sherbek's ears and pulled them hard before he could reach Mark.

Then Sherbek took in a deep, hard breath – and stopped

struggling.

He shook his head, breathed deeply once more, and relaxed entirely.

"Is he for real or is this just a trick?" Mark shouted. Griddle replied, but Mark heard no translation. Damn that AI! What should he do?

Then Griddle released his hold, sprung back, and flourished the blade. Mark followed suit quickly. Sherbek remained inert where he was, drifting softly against the bars.

Mark ordered the professor to resume translation of Griddle's remarks. Then he went after Zepp.

The green ape had been stunned by the blow from Sherbek's blade. But Mark looked him over quickly and he appeared to have suffered no other harm. He opened his eyes and blinked.

"Mark?" he said. "What hit me?"

"We had a disagreement with Sherbek," Mark replied. "He wanted to have your head for a trophy. We wanted you to keep it a while longer."

"I knew that was coming," Zepp said. "I just hoped it would be a little longer before he made his move."

"Are you all right? You looked like you were having another seizure. Or was it one of your night visions?"

"Neither," Zepp confessed. "But I have had an inspiration. I know what I have to do now. I'm just not sure how to do it. Maybe you can help me."

CHAPTER TWENTY-SIX

Zepp was glad that the angels had left the pilgrims to guard the prisoners and secure the cleared sections of the *Deragathon*. The angels would never have let him tinker with the communications gear. The pilgrims, however, were more inclined to let him have his way.

That half of them were obsessed with radio, electronics, and toys like these was only an added gift from fate.

"We have to get some power in here," one of of them called. An instant later, two of them were tracking down the cables, looking for broken connections.

"This one's going to take a few minutes to tune up," hollered another voice from deep within the thicket of tubes, wires, and rack upon rack of equipment.

"Watch the ground on this one," called another. "It's got a demon's own temper."

In the meantime, he prepared himself for what he knew he must do next. The words had filled his mind for days now. All the things he had seen and learned and come to know. And all the things he knew that he had to share with the wise creatures of Chamal.

As the pilgrims worked to establish a link with all the world beneath them, Zepp steeled himself and ordered his thoughts, as if anything borne of Chamal could be considered orderly.

After a while they were done. The equipment was powered up,

and the antennas energized. One of the pilgrims had contacted the navigation bridge and was coordinating each system with its targeted receivers on the ground. Everything was in readiness for Zepp to begin.

And no one felt more surprise than he when the words began to flow from his mouth.

"This is Zepp, Ambassador to the Angels, speaking to you from aboard the *Deragathon*," he announced.

"I have a message for all the children of wisdom on the surface of Chamal, for all the seed of the gods, for all who know the spark of knowing within themselves, for all the true breeds of the world, for all the clans and all the tribes and all the kingdoms and all the nations.

"The time has come to rise up as one race, one wisdom, one seed, one knowing and understanding, and meet the new day without fear, even though the universe has come to our door and found us in the midst of our sin. The time has come to stop, to end the fighting with one another, to put aside the gun, the sword, and the bow, and to turn our faces to the heavens.

"And let me tell you why."

The thought he had in his mind when he began was the way they started all the stories of Jobe: "Jobe walked in out of the desert one day and began to talk."

He started to talk.

He told them of his story. He explained how he was marked for death by the paranoid old general who was his master in the Hall of the Seedkeepers. He described the scene on the seacoast on their way back from the Rikabarian tradetown when Snomisch, the general's servant, tried to kill him. He told of how he arranged a death squad from the refugees of the general's homeland to eliminate the threat to his life. And he explained how that drew the attention of Tedrak and Whirlpitt, who ensnared him in their plotting.

He spoke about the dark blood extortion they used to bind him to their will – the night his sisters trapped him into mating with the potion Whirlpitt had described for them. And he told of smuggling Griddle aboard the *Deragathon* months later, after Tedrak had sent him to train for the mission to stop the angels.

He told of how he and Griddle had run afoul of a devil-cat master-at-arms when the plumbing backed up aboard the *Deragathon* and were thrown into the brig. In great detail, he described the chase through the ship when Whirlpitt released them from their cell, chained to one another at the wrists, and how he announced to the ship's company that Griddle was a jinx, loose aboard the vessel.

And he revealed how he had brought the mighty warship to a stop just as the angels arrived, thwarting its purpose and preventing a disaster more terrible than his world had ever known.

Then he told them of all that had happened since – the research aboard the *Cousteau*, the convoluted trek back to Suridash, the vision of time suspended, and the long, deep conversations he had held with Mark and with the wise teacher.

He explained Mark's theory of what wisdom did to itself in the course of growing up. "Wisdom holds onto the knowledge it has acquired until that knowledge becomes a weight holding it down. It holds onto a problem until it becomes a source of torture and despair. It waits until the last possible instant to admit the possibility of change – and then releases the old knowledge to fly up towards the new, releases the problem to enjoy the solution. Only when things are at their worst can we see most clearly the root cause of our suffering. And only then can we change what is necessary to go on."

And he explained his own understanding of what the world was about to face. "It's easy enough to understand," he said. "You just have to think differently. You just have to change. It's what we do best."

Zepp had been fascinated by the history of the angels' superstitious religions. So many of them were about the ideal, the changeless, the eternal. There was nothing chamalian about them and no purchase for his mind. And yet the things the religious organizations did within their world were marvelously perverse – and regarding things and in ways that his race would have dealt with much more straightforwardly.

Like this, for example. There was no need to dress up his story in the moralism of allegory and parable. Everything about it was clear to see and was just what it was.

"Jobe showed us the first face of wisdom," he said. "Wisdom goes out into the world and returns – and changes itself. My tribe, my city, and all that they have accomplished show the truth of that. But now we have arrived at the next phase. No one individual can accomplish this part. It will take all of us together.

"For in me, Zepp, wisdom has gone once again out into the world and returns to itself – but this time to change the world. To change all of you. To all become better than we are."

His spacesuit water bottle had gone dry long ago, his throat was raw and hoarse, his tongue raw from rubbing against his teeth. He must have been talking for an hour. His nerves were as full of energy as the collection of radio equipment before him. He felt like he had reached the end of a long journey and the time had come to stop walking. His words had exhausted themselves – and him.

"I have said enough," he sighed at last. "Everything change now."

***

Mark was amazed.

The professor maintained a careful and complete translation of Zepp's long monologue – and recorded every word of it in both English and Zepp's own tongue.

Even Griddle fell silent.

Mark had kept track of the time carefully. Zepp went on for an hour and twenty-five minutes.

One of the pilgrims approached him and, when he seemed to have recovered his wits, chattered softly to him. Zepp sagged as he spoke.

The professor was slow in translating, and asked a few questions of the pilgrim before providing the subtitles. "He says the orbital precession of the *Deragathon* was not favorable for good coverage of the planet," he said at last.

"The what?"

"Orbital precession. He said the *Deragathon* hasn't got much altitude and our radio signals don't cover much of the surface at any one time. The last two orbits have carried us over Birhat and Kwikorak. But as Chamal turns beneath us, Meshkar, Suridash, and Ring Po Do will come within range. Sometime in the next few hours or two orbits."

"What's the problem?" Mark asked.

The pilgrim stepped forward cautiously, then said: "He needs to repeat the message for them."

Mark laughed. No wonder Zepp looked so unhappy. He rescued the pilgrim quickly. "No need for that," he said. "It's all in the can. The professor recorded the whole thing. We'll just play it back for them."

Then he thought about it a minute and realized that the *Deragathon*'s communications rig was nothing compared to the one the *Cousteau* carried with it. A few minutes later, he was flying down the passageways, the pilgrim guiding his way to the bridge. He fumbled through the bars and stanchions that ringed the chamber and then zipped through the admiral's cabin and back to the *Belle Marie*.

The trooper on duty there let him patch through to the *Cousteau* and Val Nordland. He explained his idea, and within ten minutes, the signal-monitoring team was on-line. And a few minutes after that, they were in direct contact with the pilgrims down in the communications room of the *Deragathon*.

By the time Mark found his way back to the radio shack, the *Cousteau's* signal team had all the data they needed to mimic the entire suite of transmitters. And they didn't have to worry about orbital precession – they had the whole network of communications relay satellites the *Cousteau* had been sowing since its arrival.

If Zepp wanted his story to get out, Mark was going to make sure they didn't skip one receiver anywhere on the planet.

The pilgrims told him that they were even using the Arkarian monitoring system to pinpoint the signal regimes through the equatorial belt and send the message there. Although in places, they said, they were going to have to wait until the *Deragathon* was directly overhead to punch through with enough power to break into the local traffic.

And the pilgrimage houses along the Way of Jobe were translating the message into the local dialects and re-broadcasting it on their own equipment. Mark told them to explain that to the *Cousteau's* team so they could pick up the translations and start sending them out through their own net.

Before the end of the watch, there wouldn't be a single radio, video, or data receiver on the planet that wasn't being blanketed with Zepp's words. Within a few days, the message would be repeated by word of mouth, distributed in written and printed copies, and carried by runners to the far corners of Chamal. And with every repetition, its power would grow.

"Everything change now."

***

Before the end of the watch, a number of additional events intervened as well, though none of them prevented the broad distribution of Zepp's message.

First, Lieutenant Barrett found his way to the *Deragathon*'s radio shack. He wasn't pleased by what he found.

"A political statement with no specific military content," Mark said, when asked to describe the message. Barrett wasn't buying it. But when Nordland and Fletcher told him that they had monitored the transmission and approved of the content, he backed down without a complaint.

He looked terrible – his boyish features were marked with deep creases and his eyes twitched slightly. He relaxed briefly and talked about the battle farther aft, rambling on to no one in particular, but only to let the words spill out before they choked him.

"Those mutts are murder," he said, cranking up the oxygen bleed on his suit. "They were pretty bad at first, until we got everyone under cover. But then they'd concentrate their fire on the hatches and send a team through for a chase down the corridors. They knew all the places to hide and we'd have to go in after them. If you waited more than a few seconds to chase them, they'd get the lights off and you'd have to do it in the dark. We'd still be chasing them now, but your buddies sent out a platoon of little guys in O2-masks to outflank them. None of them was more than a meter high. But they chewed the other mutts up real good – kept coming no matter how bad their losses – and chased them back down their holes."

Barrett wiped his brow, then continued.

"So we got the hangars and the fighter deck and the engine room. I've never seen one of those mutts with wings before. That's something impressive when they open up and spread 'em. Like a vampire or something."

Barrett calmed down after a while, much to Mark's delight. He preferred Griddle's endless patter to Barrett's high-stress reel. But Griddle had never regained his tongue after falling silent before Zepp's monologue. In fact, he seemed to have drifted out of sight – something Mark noticed once Barrett went into a huddle with his troopers at the far end of the compartment.

He began to worry. He wasn't sure why he should, but with Griddle out of sight, almost anything could be happening. Zepp was still in his station in front of the main control consoles. Sherbek remained trussed up tightly against the jungle gym.

Barrett straightened out, stiffening his limbs against the natural curl of zero-G, and cranked up the volume on his channel. "Now hear this," he announced. "The hostiles still have control of their own containments. We've got teams on every bolthole, but it looks like we're going to have to go in after them. I want volunteers for the first squad. Sound off now -- "

The officer was interrupted by a sudden lurch in the ship around them. Mark felt a sudden wave of vertigo. Barrett started looking all around, signaling to his troopers. The pilgrims were at the ready without hesitation.

"We're moving," someone reported over the main channel on Mark's helmet.

There was another lurch, and Mark's vertigo faded quickly.

"We've stopped moving," came another report.

Then the hull shook with an explosive BLAM!!! The jungle gym rattled and the communications gear flickered on and off, sparks shooting out of one box.

"What was that?" Barrett shouted.

One of the pilgrims at the radio sets grew excited and began chattering loudly. "They blew the seals! They blew the seals! They're getting away! They're getting away!"

"What seals? Who's getting away?"

"The main seals connecting the containments to the *Deragathon*," hissed a new voice in translation by the professor.

"Whirlpitt," Zepp groaned.

"Everyone is getting away," said Whirlpitt, who slinked into the compartment in a long flexible movement. Mark looked the long-necked creature over carefully. So this was the mastermind behind all of the plotting that had brought Zepp and him together. "The containments are flying away from us already, gaining distance with every breath we take. The lurches you felt were the engines aligning the ship with the horizon. By waiting until we were into position, they have avoided sending themselves into doomed orbits. They are now free to do their will."

"Oh no they're not," Barrett shouted. "Troopers, on me." He

bounded for the door.

Mark thought he had better follow. He tagged along with the troopers, matching their best speed down the passageways, then fell behind as they crossed the gap at the entrance to the bridge. He was almost too late when he finally reached the admiral's cabin. Barrett was waiting for him when he got there, along with Helen Castain.

"No you don't, Paradis," he said, shaking his head. "You're not coming on this one. You stay here with her and take care of this."

He shoved a small blue shape at him from the entrance to the *Belle Marie*. It tumbled slowly as it flew across the compartment. It was Griddle.

"He got into the formula," Helen said. "I don't know how much he took, but I think it was a lot."

Mark looked closer and saw that Griddle's eyes were glazed over and his face slack. How many vials had Helen made? A dozen? More? And how many had Griddle taken? Half of them? More than that? The only thing Mark was sure of was that the poor alien had taken far too many than were good for him. Enough to turn him into a mindless lump of chamalian flesh and fur.

"You'd better get them out of this compartment, Paradis," Barrett warned as he started to shut the door. "In a moment, it's going to be full of hard vacuum and you're not going to be able to open the door."

Barrett never mentioned what it would do to Griddle, but Mark had enough imagination to move quickly out of the chamber, pressing Helen forward and passing Griddle's limp body ahead to her. He even took the precaution of closing the blast door before the *Belle Marie* broke seals herself and headed off hunting chamalians.

Mark wasn't sure what authority Barrett had for the mission he was undertaking, but he decided he didn't want to ask. Better let him make up for the failures of Tycho than try to repeat them here on Chamal.

In the meantime, he was stuck aboard the *Deragathon* for an undetermined period of time, surrounded by potentially hostile chamalians who were beginning to recover from the effects of Helen's peacemaker aerosol. He wondered if Barret was going to get his revenge for being maneuvered and manipulated after all.

***

The main advantage of the departure of the various antagonists to Zepp's tribe was that it left what remained of the *Deragathon* entirely in friendly hands. Though Zepp was never sure just how friendly they might be – not considering Sherbek's attack.

And Whirlpitt was never one to inspire trust.

None of that offset the concern that Zepp felt for Griddle. The poor thing was still slack-faced and stiff. His breathing was labored and difficult, and from time to time he would gasp, inhale deeply, and start to breath regularly once again. Nothing Mark could do changed that. "Helen said she could synthesize something to counteract the potion she gave him," the angel had told him. "But until she can get it to him, it won't do much good. She didn't say so, but I think she's expecting the worst."

Zepp couldn't figure out why that news saddened him.

Over the next several hours the reports came in from below. The *Cousteau's* relays picked up the daily signals from the pilgrimage Houses and sent them here. Tedrak had ordered unusual dawn reports in the wake of Zepp's message. And more were to be filed at nightfall as well.

The most important day in the history of Chamal dawned first in Ring Po Do. The news there was that the loyalist armies surrounding the city were going over to join the Assembly of Traitors, turning on their Blue Monkey masters, and delivering them up to crowds. They had stopped firing rockets into the city, and the Rift Hound Bund had declared a truce with the Tree Cat Guild.

The fires were out at the top of Parishaldemain. The astronomy students in the high observatory would sleep easier tonight knowing that no more of them were to be tossed into the dry, cold, caldera below. Some of them were even trying to track the movement of the spacecraft by calculating their orbits based on their observations.

Sunrise at Suridash found all peaceful and well. Tedrak had words of hollow praise for Whirlpitt, who had lost control of the *Deragathon* and allowed the attack that had nearly destroyed the center of the city – and Tedrak along with it.

On the broad, steaming sea of Meshkar, the lifting fog revealed that the Wheel of Struggle had turned once again, and the warring of the different factions paused. Some of the failed bankers appeared at the seashore to be weighted and tossed into the waves from high platforms, others piled precious metals into their trucks and headed down into the jungle. They declared a holiday for the stock casinos.

Rikabar saw the masses overwhelm the party police in the streets of the capital and in the provincial centers as well. The word was coming in from along the southern shore of the ocean that Rikabar's subject nations were throwing off the shackles of empire in the face of the collapse of the Royal Onion Party back home. Without the party bosses on site or in radio contact to maintain order, the organization dissolved into chaos, with every member running for their life like the scared prey of the hated carnivores.

And on the far side the steppes, the herds rose up as one and stampeded across the stations of their feline masters.

From Arkaria, however, came nothing but silence. No more word from the site of the great explosion. No more pictures of the flash, the wall of wind, and the fires. No more video of winged Arkarians dropping in flames from the sky.

As the hours wore on, the fires in the cities that had raged for days began to burn themselves out or were extinguished. Armies withdrew from the front lines and dug in. Rebels triumphed. Dictators, kings, emperors, overmasters, and warlords were beheaded, impaled, or imprisoned. Mutineers rallied around their new leaders. Rains began to cleanse the air of the smell of charred wood and fiber. The wounded and shell-shocked were collected and tended to. Walls were shored up and holes in roofs repaired. Water collected, bread ovens fired, gardens raided, and meals prepared in ways that almost reflected the normal life before the arrival of the angels.

And everywhere, chamalians were talking about Zepp's message. Repeating his stories, debating his arguments, recasting their own thoughts and biases, rearranging their mental furniture to accommodate the strange new events that had overtaken the world.

The ideas continued to spread. Down in the equatorial belt, where civilization penetrated little if at all, the word passed by drum, by messenger, by every alternate trail and byway to the depths of the rainforests. Out in the southern thicket, runners found their way through the briars to clearings and meadows in the vast webwork of that world to pass on Zepp's word.

And it was working.

By the end of the day, Zepp had allowed himself to believe that it would continue to work as long as the ideas spread. But as the night fell back on Suridash and Zepp grew tired, he began to worry that all was not as it seemed. Of course it wasn't, he told himself sternly. On Chamal, nothing ever was. The wild always produced unexpected wisdom – and wisdom was always unpredictably wild. Of one thing he could, however, be sure – if all was peaceful and harmonious now, in a short time it would not be.

He tried to share with Mark the fear he felt at the way things were turning, but the angel was preoccupied. He said little, but Zepp could tell that his thoughts were with the angel warriors who were chasing the Birhat cats, Rikabarian party bosses, and Blue Monkey renegades.

And with something else – Mark had a look of terrible weight on his shoulders that Zepp had learned to recognize in recent days. He didn't know what was bothering the angel, and he was afraid to ask.

CHAPTER TWENTY-SEVEN

Some time in the middle of the day, the *Cousteau* came within the horizon of the *Deragathon* and remained there for nearly an hour.

Mark knew this because the professor, without warning or announcement, suddenly turned into Val Nordland and began to argue with him about what he had done. This was only possible while the *Cousteau* was in direct line-of-sight, unless Nordland wanted to use conventional communications channels – something he was reluctant to do, since any messages sent that way would be kept on the record.

"Do you have any idea what you and Zepp have unleashed?" Nordland asked.

"None at all," Mark replied. "And please don't overstate my role in this. It was Zepp's idea to broadcast a plea to his race, not mine. I never suggested such a thing. It was pure inspiration on his part. And I think it was a good one."

"Do you have any evidence on which to base that opinion?" Nordland countered.

Mark stammered and bit his tongue. "No, not really. I got some of the reports from the pilgrims – but only second-hand. They say the fighting has died down."

"For now," Nordland said. "But you should see what our monitors say. Fighting has died down, but everyone is just digging in. Nothing has been resolved. The total amount of alienation in the system has not been reduced, simple accumulated, collected, and directed at us. And no one can predict what that will mean."

"I am aware of the theoretical dimensions of the situation," Mark said. "But I'm not afraid of what that may mean. I'm not afraid that something we didn't predict could happen."

"Then how about the things we can predict? What about the chamalians who don't agree with Zepp's point of view? The dissenters within his own tribe launched a violent assault on your apartments, as I recall. And the upshot of the dissent was a bloody purge, correct?"

"Again, you can't blame me for that. Another of Zepp's inspirations."

"I'm not trying to blame you, Mark. I just want to know what you expect to do when things come apart. The Arkarian problem still remains to be resolved – and I don't think Zepp is going to be able to talk them into dismantling their weapons or their weapons program."

Mark remained tight-lipped. He could see that there was no correct response to Nordland's questions. His purpose in the conversation was not to elicit information or transmit a warning – it was to chastise him for stepping too far out of line.

To an extent, it worked. Mark couldn't help but feel guilty for his role in this terrible adventure. There was no doubt in his mind that thinking, self-knowing creatures would die who would otherwise have lived if he hadn't interfered in the course of events. But there was almost no way to take action that didn't involve some kind of awful consequences.

He had nothing to rely on but faith – faith that things would work themselves out. The only history he had to back him up that of his own race. Humanity had managed to avoid destroying itself, and had even managed to grow up a little in the past century. Certainly Chamal was capable of a similar transformation. The chamalians would just have to figure out how for themselves.

Nordland finally faded away as the *Cousteau* slipped over the horizon and cut off his signal. But not before he left Mark with one more warning: "Don't trust anyone, Mark. Not even Zepp. None of them have any interests at heart but their own. Even him."

***

By midday, Mark and Helen had moved out of the radio shack and into a smaller compartment nearby. It was a wardroom or lounge by the look of it – zero-G frames and straps on the walls, a few vertical surfaces with a sticky, but dry, covering, softer lights, and not much else.

It was Whirlpitt's idea, Zepp had told them. The weaselly minister from Suridash was afraid that their presence would stir up the other chamalians, now that they had fully recovered from the effects of Helen's tranquilizer gas.

Griddle was brought to them a short while later, which didn't cheer Mark at all. Another of Helen's drugs was due to wear off – if it hadn't already. For now, Griddle was an unconscious lump of alien flesh tethered to the far wall, with only a period of snoring or occasional coughing to disturb his drug-induced stupor. When he woke up, who knew what effect he would have on things. Zepp showed no confidence on the subject at all and tried to keep the conversation away from it.

Mark was suspicious about Whirlpitt's desire to move them away from the radio shack. Which chamalians did he think they were going to upset? The only ones down there were Zepp's pilgrims, and they were dedicated to the service of humanity's only ally among their race. But under the circumstances, Mark didn't want to question the decision until the *Belle Marie* was back within range of the *Deragathon*.

Not long after they were moved, another transmission arrived over the professor's back-channel. This time, however, it was an official call. The jury was being re-convened.

A few minutes later, all of the members appeared to be squeezed into one end of the chamber. Although Mark knew it was just an artifact of the professor's holographics, he couldn't help but laugh at the distortions of their faces as the images jammed together.

"This is going to be short," Captain Fletcher said. "Lieutenant Barrett has come within range of the first alien vessel and has asked for a full release of batteries. For those of you who aren't familiar –"

He looked over at the Barrett's image, which float disembodied at the far left end of the group.

"It means that we don't have to keep our full level of technology under wraps," Barrett said. "It means that we can use all our capacities to intercept and interdict the target."

"But there is a drawback," Val Nordland said. His face was long and narrow, but ballooned outwards above the eyebrows – until he leaned forward and everything slipped down to his expanded jaw. "In the process of employing all your weapons, you reveal to the chamalians the full strength of our technology."

"That's only if there are any survivors," Barrett said.

"That was my point," Nordland replied.

Mark shook his head. He hadn't expected Nordland to be the one who balked at the full consequences of Barrett's request. But he realized that he probably should have.

"I don't know if that's really what we want to do," Nordland said. "It means no survivors."

"Mr. Nordland, that is the usual result in a battle in space with modern weapons. I just wanted to make sure that everyone is clear on that subject."

"And just who are the targets you plan to take out this way," Mark asked, pulling everyone's attention away from Barrett and Nordland.

"The Blue Monkeys are on my tracking screen right now. An hour after that, I can take out the Birhat cats, and before midnight I'll have three more scratched. The last one will be a few hours after that, since it's on a real eccentric orbit."

"You're going after all six," Mark asked.

"Have you got a problem with that?"

"One of them is from Suridash, one from Meshkar, and another from Kwikorak. They're supposed to be on our side."

"If they see what I do to the others, they'll be too much of a threat to be allowed to live."

Mark covered his eyes with one hand. "Mr. Barrett, I think you've lost sight of our original reason for coming aboard the *Cousteau*. In spite of what you seem to think, it was not to provide you with an excuse to kill chamalians indiscriminately."

"I know that," Barrett said. "As I understood it, the original reason was to provide you with an excuse to kill them. You're just mad because I'm ready to take out your buddies along with their enemies. What you don't seem to realize is that we can't afford to take sides. Not once the killing starts."

Mark said nothing, but shook his head. He couldn't begin to respond to Barrett's harsh words. Luckily, he didn't have to.

"Lieutenant Barrett, I think that's more than enough," Captain Fletcher said suddenly. "I don't like killing any more than Mr. Nordland or Mr. Paradis do. We've got reason enough to protect ourselves and Chamal from the villains on the *Deragathon*. But there's no reason for us to engage in wanton butchery. Unless you have a personal motive."

Barrett looked sheepish, but not ashamed. Mark could tell that he was only sorry that he had been caught expressing himself too candidly – and not for the content of his words.

Nevertheless, the captain had settled it. The vote by the jury was five against and one abstention – Barrett – on pursuing all six containments.

A second round of voting – on releasing all the *Belle Marie*'s weapons for use against the three main targets – was unanimous. All six agreed that the time had come to eliminate them from the equation.

Barrett mumbled something under his breath and scowled at Mark, then he declared: "Aye, aye, sir. Your orders will be carried out."

When the images all faded away and Mark was alone once more with Helen and Griddle, he found himself wondering how far he could trust Barrett.

***

Chamalian night had fallen and the lighting grown dim when Griddle finally roused from his stupor. This was accompanied by a fit of coughing and a weak effort at escaping from the restraints of the harness that held him in place.

Helen was at his side in an instant, half-swimming, half-flying across the compartment to him. She had been monitoring his vital signs as well as she could. She was using the first aid equipment from the *Belle Marie* and the records from earlier observations to indicate normal patterns. When Mark asked her how he was doing, all he got was a dark, angry look from her and stony silence.

Damn it, it wasn't his fault that they had to get involved in violence. This was a violent world and they'd known from the beginning that sooner or later they would have to shoot back.

But he wasn't about to get into an argument with someone with strong emotions to guide her and fifteen years experience to give her leverage. So he kept his mouth shut and watched from a distance as Helen nursed Griddle along.

The coughing spasm left him still unconscious, but Helen said that the crisis seemed to have passed with his breathing and circulatory systems. "They don't have a heart as such, but a series of pumping chambers throughout their circulatory system," she said. "But breathing and blood pressure are closely linked to the pumps, and the drug overdose had the effect of increasing the blood pressure and interfering with the breathing. He was beginning to suffer the equivalent of congestive heart failure."

"But now he's not?"

"I don't think so. The blood level of the anti-depressant has dropped significantly. He's sleeping, not comatose. A few hours and he may wake up naturally. But it was awfully close."

"He was awfully happy for a while, though," Mark said wistfully.

"We need to find some chemistry that is easier to fine-tune. I thought we'd given him a much smaller dose. I never expected the kind of character change that we got."

"In some cultures that's considered quite normal," Mark said. "The Appalachian Church of Hallucinogenics is a good example. And it seemed to cure him of his curse."

"Are you sure? Were you looking for evidence? Or just ignoring it because you don't believe he's a jinx anymore?"

"That's a good question. And I don't have an answer. But I was surprised with how smoothly things went. Maybe his curse becomes a blessing when you've got him full of anti-D's. I can just imagine what he's been doing for the planet – orbiting overhead for hours, blissed out on too many pills, radiating positive vibrations from the heavens. Do you think that might be the real reason things have calmed down on the ground?"

"I think you've been awake too many hours," Helen said.

"Well you can believe what you want to, and I'll believe what I want to, and the world will go on its way regardless."

***

He was no longer alone. That was the first thing that Zepp noticed when he awoke. The room was black as grave, but he could tell. Something wild within him knew. The second thing he noticed was the metallic scent of blood. Again something wild within him recognized the smell and set his blood to pulsing.

Those two points of data suggested a small range of equally unpleasant possibilities. There was someone in the compartment with him who was bleeding. Or there was someone in the compartment with him who had acquired the scent of blood elsewhere. Or –

A light came on, small and dim, just enough to reveal the face of

Whirlpitt. And enough to reveal the motionless mass of a lifeless pilgrim bodyguard floating near one wall.

It was all starting again, Zepp realized with a start.

The last time he had come to Zepp in the dark, Whirlpitt had launched him and Griddle on their death-run through the length of the *Deragathon*, chained together, spared their fate only by Griddle's strange power. One of Whirlpitt's messengers had sent them to a machine shop within the core of the ship that had been sealed off inadvertently. Then Whirlpitt himself had sent the crew of the ship to cut through a bulkhead to get them out.

In that moment, Zepp had faced his demons and turned about to chase them back. No slow, cold death for him. The time had come again for that. But he was afraid that this time he didn't have it in him.

Whirlpitt revealed a small hand-sized weapon, pointed it at Zepp, and hissed: "Come with me."

Zepp obeyed in silence. This was not the time for the bravado he had shown once before in defiance of the dark minister. There was more going on here than he could see all at once. So he glided along and bided his time.

Whirlpitt strapped a tether on Zepp's unfortunate pilgrim bodyguard and tugged him along after them as they left the compartment where Zepp had been napping. They slid down a dimly-lighted passageway until they came to a door. Whirlpitt ordered him to open it, then motioned him through the doorway with his weapon.

He found himself in a large wardroom, reunited with Mark, Helen, and Griddle. His eyes fell on the smashed bits of what had once been the Wise Teacher of the Wise.

Then he saw a fourth figure on the other side of the compartment – Sherbek, his cousin, armed with a weapon identical to Whirlpitt's.

"So, little cousin," Whirlpitt said, his eyes narrowing into long slits, "do you think changing the world is as easy as you make it out to be?"

Zepp felt his blood pound in his veins. For a moment, he was too stunned to talk. What did he mean? But Zepp couldn't ask him that aloud. Then the words spilled from his lips. "Do you think stopping it from changing is going to be any easier?"

Whirlpitt laughed, a rapid chittering sound in the back of his long throat.

"You have been corrupted by the angels," he said. "There is no other way to explain your foolish belief that overnight every creature of wisdom will stop fighting because you have told them that everything has changed now."

"I only told them what was true. There's no power in a lie."

"But there's where you're wrong, my little cousin. There is so much power in a lie that it would make your head spin. For example, the lie I am about to tell. About how the angels betrayed you, how they attacked you, how you fought back bravely, and how you managed to kill them before succumbing to your own wounds."

Zepp felt a stiff chillness in his bones. He looked for an opening to escape, but there was no place to run. Not with both Sherbek and Whirlpitt carrying weapons. And that would leave the others behind. He couldn't do that. His loyalties were what they were now – to the angels and not his tribe. Not even to his own race.

Whirlpitt knew that too. That was the logic behind his plan.

For most of his life, Zepp had been afraid of death – until the wild escapade aboard the *Deragathon* cured him of that fear. But since then, he had imagined many times the manner in which death could come. He had seen enough of it in these past days, Jobe knew. And now that it was here, he realized that there had never been much to fear. If he managed it right, it would come quickly. And if he had half a chance, it might even yield a reward in the bargain.

"You just don't understand power, Zepp. That was something Tedrak didn't recognize. You have your Uncle Tapp's wits, but you don't have his taste for real power. That's why we had to get rid of him, of course. Oh, and you thought it was the Blue Plague. That was what we intended."

Zepp's soul was white-hot. He couldn't believe what Whirlpitt had just revealed. It couldn't be true. It had to be some twisted way Whirlpitt had devised of inflicting a last bit of emotional pain on his victim.

But he held his anger within himself. Now he saw that his death could be a way of avenging his uncle. Then he drew in his breath and saw that this was his own tie to the past – and that it was as wrong for him to pray for revenge as any other member of his poor benighted species.

"The world is in chaos now, thanks to the angels – and to you. What it needs is a strong hand. This was the plan from the beginning, you understand. Once we had eliminated the other members of the alliance as a threat, and you had neutralized the power of the angels, it would be time for us to step in and take control. You have prepared the way for us much more thoroughly than we had envisioned, but the time has come just the same."

Whirlpitt hissed and swiveled his head around to study the two angels. He twisted in the air and drifted to Griddle's side, where he poked him with his weapon. "Your companion seems to have made himself ill. Too much of their potions, correct? You shouldn't have trusted them, Zepp. See where it got you?"

He motioned with the weapon and Sherbek worked his way around the bars and stanchions of the room to close on Mark and Helen.

Zepp knew that the time for action had come at last. He wished there had been some way to thank the angels for all they had tried to do, but the wise teacher was broken and there was no more time.

He tensed his muscles and prepared to lunge, aiming straight at Whirlpitt's neck. His teeth were sharp enough and his jaws strong enough to carry out his plan.

Suddenly a blue shape erupted from the lattice next to Whirlpitt. It was Griddle. He flew a few hands across the chamber and smashed into Sherbek. Griddle bounced one way, Sherbek another. But Griddle whipped around in mid-air, snared Sherbek's foot with one hand, and pulled the two of them together.

Sherbek struggled, but Griddle was determined. An instant later, he had sunk his teeth into Sherbek's arm. Sherbek howled. He twisted, and jerked, and snapped – and let go of his weapon. Which went flying across the chamber towards Zepp.

Before it reached him, Whirlpitt was in motion.

The weasel's sleek black arm swung with unnatural slowness in a long arc, the weapon in his hand exaggerating the moment arm, until hard metal and cool flesh pointed straight at Griddle.

The weapon erupted with fire and smoke. The report stabbed Zepp's ears. The blunt end of Sherbek's weapon hit him in the chest. He scrambled desperately to get a hold on it as Whirlpitt's long arm swung again, seeking a new target.

Helen screamed. Mark shouted.

Zepp got a grip on the weapon with both hands. One digit found its way to the trigger-lever. He swung it in a much shorter arc than Whirlpitt's. And he jerked on the lever with more frantic energy.

BLAM! BLAM! BLAM!

The third shot was followed instantly by a quieter echo from across the chamber. Whirlpitt's body was spinning backwards from the momentum of the bullets. His weapon had discharged before the weasel could bring it to bear on Zepp, and now it floated loose, turning slowly as it traversed the room.

Whirlpitt did much the same, trailing a stream of blood as he went, until he bumped into the bars and stanchions that lined the far wall.

Zepp launched himself at Griddle immediately. But when he reached his companion, it was too late. A large hole in his chest had put an end to his curse and his suffering forever – and much more effectively and completely than any potion the angels could cook up.

He looked at Helen and Mark again. Water poured from Helen's eyes. Mark was baring his teeth, something that had a variety of meanings, according to the wise teacher. He wished he could ask him what it meant now.

Sherbek clung to a stanchion nearby, clutching his arm, which bled slowly, and cursing. Zepp felt pity for him, but no anger. He knew that Sherbek was not alone. There would be a great many dissenters, and many of them would be as dangerous as his cousin. He would have to figure out what to do with them.

Maybe the angels would know.

He could ask them in the morning. Right now, he was terribly tired and he wanted to sleep. So he closed his eyes and let the darkness swallow him up.

CHAPTER TWENTY-EIGHT

The desert streamed by beneath the *Belle Marie* at a stomach-churning pace. A salt marsh flew by, then a wadi, a hilltop crowned with yellowish vegetation, and a herd of grazers. The ship had to be doing a thousand klicks an hour and it wasn't more than a hundred meters off the surface.

Every time they dipped to follow a depression or popped up over a ridge line, it left Mark's insides behind.

The breakneck pace added to the air of urgent danger already thick aboard the pinnace. The troopers were all below, battle ready the instant they landed, all but one stout fellow who manned the weapons systems while Barrett concentrated on flying. Mark had been shanghaied onto the mission only hours ago. His billet was in intelligence, interpreting ground-sensing data and evaluating images. It was a natural adjunct to his main duty of determining technological culture from orbital sensor data. And it meant that when they wanted someone to make sure they attacked the right target, he was the man for the job.

They passed over a final rise before the city came into view – a blur of blue shapes rising above the horizon still dozens of kilometers away. But Barrett cursed when the pinnace announced that they were being scanned by microwave radiation.

"This thing was supposed to be stealthy," he said. "They'd have to be doing some fancy tuning to get us."

Najib, the trooper at the battle board, nodded. "They're running their radar up and down the freaks, just the thing to pick us up. Funny thing is, though, I don't know if they're doing it on purpose or if their rig just runs that way."

A moment later, clouds of gray smoke appeared in front of them, with little orange hearts at their centers. They passed through the first bank of them without notice. But then the clouds appeared much closer and all around them. The *Belle Marie* shook from the power of explosions. Shrapnel clattered against her shields.

"Anti-aircraft artillery," Barrett said.

"They're tenacious," Najib replied.

Mark gripped the arms of his seat and clenched his teeth.

The flak grew more intense as they got closer to the city, reaching a crescendo as they passed over the walls that marked its outer limits. Now missiles reached up at them from below, streaming long ragged tails of white smoke as they fell harmlessly behind.

Now Mark focused on the two screens before him. One projected the holographic model of the Arkarian city he had generated from orbital data and input from drones near the surface. One was the real-time display of the *Belle Marie*'s position.

The first screen included color-coded images of the building they wanted, the second a scale image of the pinnace above the city.

Identifying the building by radiation and chemical analysis was simple enough, they still had to pick it out of a labyrinth of streets and blocks and buildings of alien purpose and design. Making things worse was the way the city was laid out. Arkarians were fliers, which meant strong vertical integration, and lousy groundwork. There were no broad boulevards or great squares, no meticulous grid of straight streets and avenues.

Towers of stone and metal rose from a squalid sea of lower blocks of apartments, factories, mills, and low commercial tenants. Barrett flew in a tight circle around a smaller tower, close enough for Mark to see its winged residents cowering on balconies and porches.

The slaves who maintained the lower parts of the economy had their paths, of course, along with the needs of trade. But the urban organization wasn't centered on them.

The buildings they were searching for were part of this groundling morass. But the only way to locate them was in relation to the loftier towers. Dodging the pyrotechnics thrown at them by the city's inhabitants did not make the task any easier.

Three explosions to the right rocked the pinnace. Mark looked over in time to see a triangular piece of metal bounce off the window-screen.

He turned back to his model and called out to Barrett: "Target bears oh-seven-five true, seven klicks."

"Seven at oh-seven-five, aye," Barrett echoed. The deck tilted as he swung the *Belle Marie* in a tight pivot, then steadied up on course. They dropped closer to the surface, almost at rooftop level.

Mark could see figures running in the streets from here as they zeroed in on the Arkarkian labs. Missiles and anti-aircraft fire had lost track of them in the ground clutter, making the last few seconds a more peaceful ride.

Then Mark's gut wrenched one more time as they pulled up abruptly almost directly above the buildings. Mark studied the streets below, comparing them to the data-model. This was the important part – making sure that they were in the right place and entering the right building.

"That's the one," he declared. "The long one with the red doors."

Barrett dropped the pinnace to the ground. The landing was hard, but not destructive. Barrett slapped the release on his seat harness, then did the same to Mark's as he hurried towards the ladder. They were down it and through the door in a minute, surrounded by a dozen troopers.

Two of them were twisting the controls on a small box with treads – a ground probe. Mark carried a small data-display slate that showed the probe's video output.

"Move fast," Barrett said. "We've only got a couple of minutes before they come after us."

Mark noticed the absurd quiet in the neighborhood around them. Everyone must have run from the smoke and flame of the pinnace's landing. But Arkarian warriors would be on them quickly.

A loud BOOM! echoed across the street from the red doors of the lab entrance, followed by a cloud of brown smoke and dust. Then the troopers rushed forward with the ground probe. Mark followed along as its handler moved it forward.

The probe wheeled through a couple more sets of doors, each requiring a rapid attack and demolition by the troopers. But Mark could tell when it finally reached the main part of the building – a high vaulted ceiling covered a huge expanse of work area. And filling the floor below were the rows of gas centrifuges used to purify the nuclear materials used in the Arkarian weapon.

"This is it!" he called out.

"Go, go, go," Barrett ordered.

Ka-BOOM!!!

The street shook with the sound of a powerful explosion. Smoke and fire rose up from behind Mark, on the far side of the *Belle Marie*. The troopers ignored it and rushed through into the building carrying large packs – the demolition charges.

As Barrett explained it, there was no way they could be sure of destroying the equipment from space or from the air. The only way they could purchase the certainty they wanted was to make a ground assault and take them out by hand.

Mark waited nervously at the doorway with the rear guard – two heavily armed troopers – while Barrett took the rest of the party in. Three more explosions – rockets, the troopers said – shattered the air around them.

Then Barrett and his troopers came rushing out the door. A few seconds later, the ground shook with the first of a growing barrage of shock waves and overpressures – the demolition charges inside the lab.

At the climax of the orgy of fire, an Arkarian rocket exploded almost directly overhead. By now, Najib had maneuvered the *Belle Marie* into position to pick up the strike force. The pinnace's screens protected them from the force of the blast, though not from all of the side-effects.

The heat of the explosion scorched Mark's face. And the terrible metallic tearing of air and sky left his ears ringing in almost unbearable pain.

Barrett waved his arms like windmills as the troopers rushed in to the *Belle Marie*'s landing site. Mark shook his head, then joined the rush.

And just in time. A he stepped through the door, he saw squadrons of Arkarian warriors filling the narrow sky overhead, spilling air as they descended.

The door slammed shut behind him. He winced painfully at the noise, then his knees sagged as the pinnace lifted skyward.

He cursed Barrett, he cursed the termination assessment jury for allowing the mission, and he cursed the Arkarians for making it necessary. If there had been any way around it, he would have vetoed the assault on Arkaria. But there wasn't.

Zepp had done wonders in the last few days.

When word spread of how he had killed Whirlpitt, his stature grew immensely. The Masters of the Pilgrimage had sworn obedience to him in their noon orders to the Pilgrimage Houses. The houses, in turn, had repeated that oath in their noon reports. In Ring Po Do, the Assembly of Traitors had recognized his authority over them and authorized him to speak to the angels on their behalf. Tedrak hadn't needed much more than this breeze to judge the direction of the political wind – he had Zepp named to the Council of the Elders immediately, suspending the rules requiring him to actually be an elder. Meshkar's trading states asked Zepp to assume the role of supreme judge, with authority to mediate and arbitrate their disputes. And Kwikorak's spiritual leaders had certified his vision as authentic.

Holdouts in Birhat and Rikabar and up and down the Rift Valley still remained. But the balance of the conflict had shifted. The forces of the old order were on the run everywhere, and those working for change were becoming more and more confident every day.

Mark was amazed at the speed with which political developments were proceeding. At this rate, everything that they had learned since arriving in orbit would no longer be valid by the end of the month.

He didn't envy Zepp his fate at all. It was going to be hard and frustrating, and it was going to be risky and unrewarding. But Zepp seemed ready to accept it.

Mark, on the other hand, was anything but happy to accept his own fate. There was no joy in this work. The lab with its gas centrifuges was only the first target of the mission. Now came the crucial part.

They flew away from the city, away from the anti-aircraft fire, the missiles, and the rockets. Across the desert, past black mountains sculpted by wind and sand, past salt flats and murky, green lakes.

Then they came upon the main target. Anti-aircraft batteries opened up, but to no great effect. A few rockets rose up from the desert floor, but Barrett flicked them away with tractor beams. Then Mark saw it.

The complex sat in the midst of a sea of white sand, a set of small and unimposing buildings. The rooftop of one was marked by a roosting pad and entry. Another was marked by great open doors.

Barrett asked Mark to confirm the target. Mark carried out his duty. This was indeed the place. Current radiation sensors verified it. Inside the building below were at least a dozen devices in various stages of completion. The probes and drones had learned that much. Somewhere to the west of here were the launch bases for missiles that could carry the warheads around the planet – or into orbit.

Several drones were in place around the site already. Images of the *Belle Marie* as it approached were visible on datascreens over Barrett's seat. They were documenting this for all Chamal to see – and to use as proof of their dedication to protocol when they returned home.

"Ready for action," Barrett said.

"Ready, aye," Najib replied.

"All ready," Mark said.

"Ready below," came a voice on the intercom.

Barrett swept low over the buildings, then slowed to a stop a few hundred meters away, close enough to the ground for them to see the buildings from the bridge of the pinnace. Mark saw figures lurking in the shadows of the open building.

"Activating field generator," Barrett said.

The *Belle Marie* began to hum with power as the equipment built up strength. The equipment was similar to that in the main drive of the *Cousteau*. But while the starship's engines were capable of ripping a hole in the fabric of space, this equipment was powerful only to alter some of the basic constants of physics within its range.

They had programmed the equipment to do nothing too dangerous to the pinnace or its crew. But they had focused in on one particular constant – the one that determine the probability of decay within the nucleus of heavy elements like uranium and plutonium.

They were altering that constant to make such decay more likely.

It would be just as easy – or difficult – for them to do just the opposite. That would make the nuclear material in the Arkarian warheads useless, incapable of exploding.

This made the nuclear reaction much easier. It also reduced the critical mass required for a nuclear explosion. That was what made this a very risky operation.

But if all worked as planned, it would not come to that. As the field generator built up strength, the nuclear material in the warheads would begin to react. The trick in building a nuclear device was to bring the material together at precisely the same instant and in precisely the same place, resulting in the terrible blast of a nuclear explosion. Anything less produced a much less spectacular "squib" explosion – something that could range from a chemical blast down to a sort of meltdown.

Before any of the nuclear material would reach critical mass, it would blow itself up in one of these squib blasts. Or that was the expectation.

No one spoke as the *Belle Marie* tested the theory in real time.

When the first device went off, Mark almost felt his heart stop. The flash of light came from within the open building, followed by clouds of smoke. Mark wondered how dangerous that smoke was, filled with radioactive oxides. Dozens of figures rushed out the open doors into the desert sun.

A second blast tore the doors and windows out of another building – and produced another wave of evacuees.

There were more, some less powerful, one that blew the roof off a building on the edge of the complex.

And then it was over.

Mark breathed a sigh of relief. The pictures would be broadcast around the planet within a day. And then every creature of wisdom on Chamal would know two things.

First, that the angels were indeed all-knowing and all-powerful, at least in comparative terms.

And second, that the angels would use their knowledge and power to prevent any creatures on Chamal from building weapons that the angels did not want them to have.

Mark just hoped it would be enough to keep them safe – at least for the years they planned to spend at Chamal.

EPILOG

Several years passed before Mark heard the beating wings of an Arkarian flier and saw the shadow pass over the ground.

It was just outside the entrance to the Red Monkey enclave in Suridash. He was walking alone, without the escort of pilgrim guards that once accompanied him while he explored the streets of this city. The broad avenue narrowed considerably as it approached the ornately carved and decorated wall that marked the domain of the Wisest of the Wise, the True Survivors of the One True Race.

The broad golden sun that warmed the stones of this planet stood high above him, leaving a small puddle of shade around his feet, the only relief in sight.

The shadow passed over first. The flier was almost as silent, but not quite. In the still air, Mark could hear the whistle of his pinfeathers as he glided on the pillars of hot air welling up from the street.

Then came the steady thumping of the air as he cupped his wings and beat them hard to drop to the ground.

Mark turned quickly, searching for the shadow first before turning his head up into the sun. He found it, and oriented himself to greet the winged chamalian face-to-face. He felt suddenly alone and exposed. He should have taken along a pilgrim – if only for a guide and a companion.

But Zepp had told him to come alone, and these days his orders were best taken quite literally.

Mark put a hand to the butt of his pistol, pressing the gunbelt down against his hips. He was still dressed for the rainforest, complete with the requisite armament for that environment. There were times, he recalled, that it was equally suitable for the streets of Suridash.

A cloud of dust and sand rose up from the paving stones as the Arkarian touched down. He was a frail and bony beast, a thin and muscular body covered with long feathery strands of fur. He struggled to remove a leather helmet and dark goggles, standing on one foot while using the other on the headgear.

A strong human could take the creature down with a single well-placed stroke, Mark noticed. He recoiled briefly at the violent thought, but remained ready for anything the Arkarian might do. After all, they had long memories. The Cult of the Lost Argument was only one example of that.

When this Arkarian drew a long, thin blade from its sheath, Mark's heart became a lump in his craw. His fingers scrambled clumsily to unsnap the holster.

But by the time he had his weapon out, the Arkarian had already turned his back on him and was clacking and whistling into the sky. The professor made translation for him, doing its best to capture the true tone and character of the Arkarian pattern of speech.

"Unwield that weaponlette, Man-Thing-Who-Claims-To-Be-An-Angel," he said. "I am Upright Sky-in-Morning, an adept in the Lost Argument, and I have no desire to inflict random and sadistic pains upon you prior to dismemberment. Like you, I am summoned by He-Who-Must-Be-Listened-To – the one you call Zepp."

"You're a long way from home, Upright," Mark said. "Which

reminds me of an old joke I learned as a kid. I'll bet your arms are tired."

Upright didn't know the reference, and Mark wasn't sure he would recognize a joke if he lost an argument over it. "My arms ache no more than my heart to be so far from Arkaria. Though I must admit the weather here is acceptable, even if the air is a bit thin."

Zepp had told Upright no more than he had told Mark about the purpose of the meeting. Or else the Arkarian was unwilling to divulge what he knew. Probably more of the former than the latter, Mark decided.

They continued on to the gate, where a halfling in a wooden cage began squawking to announce their arrival.

"I have a question for you, Thing-That-Calls-And-So-On," Upright asked while they waited for the gatekeeper. "Is it true or a foul and subversive lie that your own self-imagined angels (Creatures-Who-Bring-Messages-From-God) are winged, much like the One True Wise Race ourselves?"

When Mark finished chuckling, he replied: "Truth, I'm afraid. God's messengers travel on heavenly wings, just like you."

Upright Sky-in-Morning doubled over in what looked like a sneezing fit, then recovered. "Then I snicker the snicker of snide discovery of unintended irony."

Mark's jaw dropped at the brazenness of the Arkarian, but he quickly recovered. "Maybe I should describe some of the creatures of human imagination who also travel on wings." He ran through vampires, valkyries, and harpies before Upright begged relief.

"And the other thing you might consider is that on my planet, there is an entire race of creatures that lives in the air and the trees and the rocky heights. They're like chamalians in their variety and diversity."

"And do any of them bear the seed of wisdom?"

"Only a small amount – what all creatures need."

"My breast is torn in two with grief for them," Upright lamented.

"This is probably not a good time to mention fried chicken," Mark said softly to himself.

"Do you really want me to translate that remark?" The professor asked. "It could have serious repercussions."

"Do I really want to? At the moment I do. But you're right. Let's just keep that one to ourselves."

The gatekeeper arrived – a chamalian with a striped face and pointed ears who wore a robe of shining blue cloth. The robe caught Mark's eye with its shimmer. He wondered if it could be the equivalent of silk or of Lycra. Either was possible on this planet – especially where the Red Monkeys were concerned.

He welcomed them through the doorway with a stiff formality, then led them inside.

***

Mark recognized the architectural motifs of the Red Monkey enclave from their roots in the Rift Valley. The elaborate design work that suggested dozens of manic woodcarvers and stonemasons working around the clock with no pattern but the unseen image in their own twisted minds, the brightly colored ideographs painted on broad walls, the labyrinthine complications of walls and paths, all were much the same as those he'd seen in Ring Po Do.

The complex centered on a broad plaza ringed by statues of Rift Valley demons in various poses of intimidation and attack. The plaza's gray paving stones had been cut haphazardly, but arranged in almost airtight patterns.

Mark, Upright Sky-in-Morning, and the Red Monkey escort were halfway across the wide empty prospect when the attack came.

The howling of the warhounds tossed echoed off the walls surrounding the plaza, making it hard to locate their source. But only for a moment. Then their shapes became visible on the far side, the hot sun painting them with blobs of white light.

The escort gulped loudly, then began to shake. Upright turned to Mark and scowled. Mark tracked the movement of the hounds with some detached part of the brain, plotting their trajectory forwards and back. At their source, he saw the tall figure of a Rift Valley overmaster, identifiable by his impossibly long arms. He was striding purposefully after the warhounds, who were on an interception course with Mark and his party.

Mark continued on. The escort found it difficult to keep up the pace with his legs shaking as badly as they now were. Upright was skittish, his wings open and cupping the hot air.

The warhounds drew closer. Mark could count three of them, tightly packed. They were practically flying, their hind legs overtaking their forelegs to maintain momentum, while their tongues flew back from their mouths like red pennants.

When they were within thirty meters, the Red Monkey escort fell to the ground and huddled into a ball, face down, with his hands over his head. This was enough to send Upright aloft in one great sheet-flapping move.

Mark stood alone against the attacking force.

His gun was already in his right hand, targeting the lead hound. As they neared, that detached part of his brain that had begun tracking them set his left hand scrambling for his knife, sheathed on the wrong side of his belt.

The blade was out before the first hound was upon him. He made his plan quickly – shoot the leader, try for the second one, and then use the knife on the third if there wasn't time to shoot him too.

But then the hounds split apart, separating widely enough to make it almost impossible to aim at more than one in the few seconds remaining.

The overmaster was loping across the plaza now, moving nearly as fast at the hounds. Mark began to realize just how tall the creature was – nearly three meters – with long shaggy fur that hung from his overlong arms and grew thick around his short neck.

A couple years in the rainforest had put Mark's reflexes in fine tune, but he was afraid that there was nothing he could do about this situation. He gritted his teeth in anticipation of pain.

Suddenly the shadow of Upright's wings fell across the first of the warhounds as the Arkarian swooped down from the sky and snatched at its back.

Mark tried to remember what Barrett had told him about shooting at a pack of charging animals. Did you try to take them down quick and clean? Or did you want to cripple the first one so that his cries of pain would demoralize the others?

He had decided on the former and was about to carry out his plan when the plaza was split by the sound of a loud whistle.

The warhounds slowed abruptly to a canter, then a trot. When they were only a few meters from Mark, they stopped and sat down. All but the one being attacked by Upright, which snarled and snapped, but refused to be baited into a fight.

The overmaster continued towards them. Mark could see the

nasty club he carried in his left hand – all spikes and sharp edges – and his guts recoiled at the thought of it in action.

The hounds kept their places even as the overmaster passed them. Now Mark could see the tiny pink eyes beneath the creature's thick brow. Ordinarily, overmasters were ridden by Red Monkeys who would perch on their backs and whisper orders in their ears. But this one was on his own.

Still Mark held his fire. He wasn't sure what the hounds would do if he shot the overmaster. And he still wasn't sure quite was happening. He trained his gun on the overmaster's forehead as soon as it came close enough, right between the tiny pink eyes.

He raised the club over his head, putting it a good five meters into the sky. Mark feared for Upright now, as well as himself. With a reach like that, both would be in danger. But not until the overmaster came close enough. A few more steps, though, and that would be it. Mark wouldn't like it, but he'd have no choice but to fire.

Then the whistle cut across the plaza once again – this time with a more complex tune.

The overmaster stumbled to a halt, and to Mark it looked as if he began to sulk.

Then a party of a dozen Red Monkeys emerged into the sunlight from a nearby building – Zepp at the head of them.

***

It was a long time before Mark got a chance to talk to Zepp about the attack. First he had to sit through a long meeting in the Red Monkey Hall of the Ancestors. The simultaneous translation from the professor gave him a headache and involved nuances of the relationship between the Red Monkeys and the city of Suridash that Mark no longer cared about. Eventually, though, even the chamalians tired of the endless pursuit of dispute, and Zepp made a brief ceremony before sending everyone away.

Everyone but Mark.

Even Upright Sky-in-Morning was surprised at that. But Zepp told him they would meet later, and the Arkarian was gone as well. That made Mark a bit more relaxed. After he and Zepp inspected the room with Kwikorak and terrestrial equipment to satisfy that no one was eavesdropping on them, he felt even more relaxed.

"I want to apologize again for the display out in the plaza," Zepp said. "It must have been uncomfortable for you."

"That's not the word for it," Mark said.

"Should I search for a better one?" the professor asked.

"No," Mark answered. "Let's not try to parse the variations of fear."

"Nevertheless, it was necessary," Zepp said. "It demonstrated a number of things to the Red Monkeys. It showed that I have power with the angels. It showed that the angels have power over the Arkarians. And it showed that they cannot intimidate you or the other angels with their ordinary tools of violence."

"I'm glad I didn't disappoint you," Mark said. "What would it have shown if I'd shot the overmaster between the eyes?"

"That you are as ruthless as we are."

"And if I'd let it tap me with that love-stick a few times?"

"That you are unafraid of pain and suffering."

Mark shook his head. "Not quite," he said. "And by not shooting him, what did I show?"

"What much of Chamal already knows – that you are hesitant to destroy life even when necessary."

"I'm glad I could be of service to you," Mark said. "But next time, how about inviting Lieutenant Barrett to the party? He's much better at this sort of thing than I am."

"I thought of that," Zepp said. "But there are things I need to discuss with you."

"That's what the message said. Things that can't be handled by regular channels?"

"Things that cannot be translated," Zepp said.

"I am very concerned about the direction of this conversation," the professor interjected.

"Then don't be," Mark snapped. "No one is going to discuss things that you cannot translate. I'm sure that Zepp here has a few legitimate questions and I'm sure we're going to do our best to answer them for him."

"Exactly," Zepp said. "And my first question is, what are you doing out in District 195?"

Mark smiled broadly and winked. "Breeding frogs," he said.

For more than a year now, he had been living in the rainforest far to the east of Meshkar and north of Arkaria. He was surprised it taken this long for Zepp to ask him what he was up to. At least he could be truthful in his answer. They were conducting a broad-range genetic test using amphibian populations in the distant reaches of Chamal's equatorial belt. As for what he did in his spare time, they could discuss that later. Mark quickly turned the conversation about.

"And how about you?" he asked. "How are you doing with Operation Apple Tree?"

"The tree of knowledge is quick to take root in chamalian soil," Zepp said. "Sometimes too quick. Electoral politics is sweeping the

Rift like a spring flood, with new political parties springing up in every ward and borough and village. The trade unions we established in Meshkar have invented socialism and split into bickering factions. And the snowmen of Kwikorak are nearly finished with their world-wide computer network. Sometimes I am not sure what to do next, but then a vision comes and I struggle on."

"I know what you mean. About the struggle, I mean, if not the vision."

"Now tell me, and this time don't avoid the point. What are you doing out there in District 195?"

"I told you – breeding frogs."

"And what else?"

"Do you have spies to warn you of things like this?"

"Not things like this. For that, I rely on my friends. And to correct you, I ask the question only because I know you. You would not sit idle out there, and you would tell me what you were doing if you did not. You haven't done either, so I ask the question."

"I guess you do know me."

"In the past few years, I have come to know all the angels much better than I did at first. You are so complicated and so difficult to fathom sometimes. Tentative where chamalians are bold. Reluctant where we are reckless. And yet you are different. You are trying to learn how to be a chamalian."

"Just like you have learned how to be human, Zepp."

There was a moment of silence from the chamalian. "I know you are correct in this, because it is an observation I have made many times myself. And now I ask for a third time. What are you doing out in District 195?"

"Preparing the way for the coming of that which cannot be

mentioned," Mark said. "Some day the world you are creating will be swept away. Everything is transient and transitory – especially in the face of the great unmentionable."

"I know this better than you do," Zepp said.

"Well remember this, when that day comes, you will need help. So I'm out there running my own little anthropology shop, my own little laboratory. I'm turning out cultures just as fast as I can, planting them with the locals, and sorting out which ones work. When the time comes, we'll all be ready."

Zepp sighed deeply. "My mind already races with the potentialities in your vision," he said. "This is no small undertaking you have attempted."

"You're telling me. Playing god is not something I recommend as a hobby. The hours suck and it takes a long time before your projects come to maturity. At least the frogs breed quickly, I've learned."

"I will follow your progress with great interest."

"I will find a way to communicate with you that doesn't involve going through our friend, the Wise Teacher of the Wise. That's something I should have done a long time ago, but just never had the time."

"This is good to know."

"And one more thing. Please don't call our little spread District 195. We've given it a name of its own, after me. We call it Paradise."

***